THE HOLLAND SAGA
PART FIVE

GHOST TOWN
BY
CLEVER BLACK

The Holland Family Saga Part Five

All rights reserved. No part of this book may be reproduced in any form, or by any means without the prior consent of the Author and publisher. Except for brief quotes used in reviews.

ISBN:978-0-9853509-9-4

This is strictly a work of fiction. Any references to actual events, real people, living or dead, or actual localities, is to enhance the realism of the story. Events within the novel that coincide with actual events id purely coincidental.

All material copy-written and filed on site at The Library of Congress.

The Holland Family Saga Part Five

DECEMBER 20, 2012

8:24 P.M.

Sagas are usually regarded as reconstructions of the past, imaginative in varying degrees and created according to aesthetic principles. Important ideals in sagas are heroism and loyalty; revenge often plays a part. Action is preferred to reflection, and description of the inner motives and point of view of protagonists is minimized. (Webster's Online Dictionary)

I so hope to reflect the above statement and deliver another quality read for all to enjoy, only I hope to maximize the characters motives throughout this read. Because here, the story gets deeper. Here, the essence of what it means to be a Holland is divulged. Here, lies the truth behind the tragedy.

I can't express how grateful I am for the enthusiasm surrounding The Holland Family Saga. I remember a while back when folks were uncertain about the Saga and where it was headed; but many have found each installment surprisingly refreshing. I hope to continue on with that tradition.

In the beginning, few were on board and the list was short, now the train is nearing full capacity. Not quite there yet, but there are far too many names to list. With that said, I must send love to Black Faithful Sister and Brothers, My Urban Books, Just Read Book Club, Let's Talk Relationship and Books, Building Relationships Around Books, Fun(4) daMental, Urban Ink, and every other Book Club that has supported the project.

I also want to send love and a heartfelt thanks to Readers from the great states of Connecticut, New York, Maryland, Florida, Wisconsin, Illinois, Colorado, Georgia, California, Virginia, the Providence of DC, Alabama, Mississippi, Oklahoma, Kansas, and Michigan just to name a few. I laugh now because I can never forget my home state of Louisiana, baby! One!

It is my intention to make you all think. To make you all feel. To have you all take a look at real life through these fictional stories and characters and have you all appreciate familial love in this troubled world we live in. The importance of friendships, and never forgetting the past can never be understated and I try to convey that through a fictional format while taking you on an adventure that can be compared to real life. Enjoy this story for what it is worth, and may you all be blessed, and be entertained as we delve further into The Holland Family Saga,

Clever Black.

CHAPTER 1
HOLLAND HISTORY

"Holland girls come into the world as twins. That comes from great mama Nashotah. And we sometimes have a small dot right here," seven year-old Naomi Holland said as she pointed to a birth mark that was just beneath her left eye. "We get the hair from momma and the dimple in the chin comes from our father. That's what grandma told me just today. She said we look like everybody in our family."

It was a warm spring morning in April of 1962 in Sylacauga, Alabama, a small town about sixty miles southeast of Birmingham, and Naomi Holland, a somewhat plump, tan-skinned, dark-eyed, pony-tail wearing little girl of Negro and Creek Indian descent, was on her parents' front porch talking to her younger brother, five year-old Samson Holland. The little girl sat Indian style in front of her brother on the porch of the Holland family's two story log home and talked to him, as her two youngest siblings, three year-old identical female twins Mary and Martha Holland, slept quietly.

"Where's momma and daddy?" Sam, a shy little boy, asked in a near whisper.

"They went to town. They should be back any minute now." Naomi answered just as her twin ran out the front door and jumped down the stairs and ran out into the open field.

"Where're you going, Ruth?" Naomi asked.

"Grandma said for me to get some onions from the garden for the deer pie she's making. Wanna race me over there?" Ruth asked as she skipped backwards.

"I have to watch our brother and sisters."

"Naomi, go ahead if you want to. I'm done hanging the clothes out back so I'll watch the babies and Sam," sixty-three year old Eileen said as she stood in the door way of the large two-story home.

"Okay! Ruth you got a head start, but I'm gonna catch you!" Naomi said as she ran from the porch and began chasing her sister, who was laughing loudly.

"You'll never catch me! I'm too fast, Naomi!" Ruth said as she ran at full speed across the family's sprawling farm.

"And don't feed any paper to the goats while you are down there you two!" Eileen yelled aloud as she stepped onto the front porch and eyed Mary and Martha as she was certain the loud talking had awakened them. "The babies are still asleep. Sam, can you say your ABC's?"

"Yes, ma'am."

"Come on, let me hear you." Eileen said as she sat beside Sam, who began to recite his ABC's as he climbed into his grandmother's lap.

Naomi Holland and her siblings resided on a 55 acre farm with their father, thirty-eight year-old Rutherford Holland, their mother, thirty-seven year-old Nituna, and Rutherford's mother, sixty-three year-old Eileen Holland-Devon.

The farm was a fun place for Naomi and Ruth, who often ran around on the acreage and explored its many interesting features. Standing out on the porch looking across the land, to one's right, a bit of ways down the hill from which the home sat, lay a thick forest of oak and pine, over three dozen acres of seasoned, tall, mature timber. To the left uphill sat the family's red barn and its stock of cattle, hogs, sheep and horses. Straight ahead was the farm land, fertile soil that produced some of the best produce in Alabama. Off to the right at the foot of the farm was the goat pen, which sat opposite a small onion patch on the other side of the road leading onto the farm. The family grew their own food there, and also slaughtered livestock for consumption in a slaughterhouse that sat a distance away from the onion patch nearby a slow-moving shallow stream. Days spent inside were rare on the Holland farm, especially for Naomi and Ruth, who'd always found something to get into on the farm, even during winter months. Their mother and father would often have to search for them as they loved to play hide and seek all over the place and there was no telling where Naomi and Ruth would be hiding whenever Rutherford and Nituna searched for the two adventurous and sometimes mischievous twins.

Rutherford met Nituna in 1942 when he and Eileen went into to town to make a withdrawal at the local bank. Mother and son were there to withdraw funds in order to bury two family members after they had perished in a tragic accident.

Eileen's husband, Freeman Devon and her identical twin sister, named Elizabeth, were returning home from Illinois via railway. The well-to-do family often did business on the Chicago Mercantile Exchange, a major agriculture hub where the family sometimes bartered produce in return for livestock. During the return trip from the Midwest, Freeman and Elizabeth's train derailed and fell into the Ohio River during a powerful winter storm that had swept it off its rails on the Kentucky-Indiana border.

Rutherford and Eileen often made the trip, but the two of them had stayed behind to harvest the onions and tend to the trees that the Holland family leased to the nearby lumber yard, otherwise, they too would have died and the Holland family would have been void of any living survivors.

Eileen and Rutherford were taking the loss of their family members hard, but the two of them now had the responsibility of running the family's business and keeping the Holland family namesake alive. They went into town to make the withdrawal and it was there that eighteen year-old Rutherford saw seventeen year-old Nituna exiting the local post office on a cold autumn day in October of 1942 with a package in her hand that seemed too heavy for her and Eileen quickly took notice.

Eileen, at age forty-three, was a strikingly beautiful woman with such style and class. A woman of Caucasian, Negro and Creek Indian descent, she had these dark, dazzling eyes that were radiant and alluring. Her coal black hair, which she wore pinned up with curls hanging down on either side of her tan-skinned face, coupled with the many ankle-length dresses she wore that flared out at the bottom gave her a royal appearance. Eileen was a woman sought after, even before the death of her husband. She played around with men often in her early years, dating two or more men simultaneously, but she'd remained faithful to Freeman and her marriage after giving birth to Rutherford and was now beyond birthing kids. She had a son to carry on the family name and each time an opportunity presented itself, Eileen would encourage Rutherford to talk to the opposite sex with the hopes that her son would began a courtship that would lead to marriage and children. This cold day in October of 1942 would be no different.

Eileen noticed the look on her son's face as they approached the bank and followed his eyes over to the full-figured, tan-skinned, long dark-haired young woman with beautiful brown eyes. She smiled and said, "She's peeking at you out the corner of her eye, Rutherford. I think she has a thing for you, son."

"Excuse me, momma." Rutherford said before walking over and giving the woman a hand by loading the package into a horse drawn cart. She thanked Rutherford and he merely watched with longing eyes as the woman rode away with her horse pulling the cart before he walked back over to his mother.

"What was that?" Eileen asked in dismay with her arms stretched out.

"What was what?" Rutherford questioned with a smile.

"Son, you need a lesson in romance. Your father would have a thing to say about you being shy if he were alive. Ohhh my God, he was such a man." Eileen sighed as she fanned herself.

"Don't know the meaning of the word shy, momma. Just

don't wanna be too aggressive at the start."

"Aggressive is what works these days. She's a beautiful woman, Rutherford and she may not be on the market for long. Opportunity missed," Eileen said as she and her son entered the bank.

Rutherford never forgot the beautiful brown-eyed woman with the cute dot under her left eye, though; he went into town everyday thereafter for almost a month with his mother's words planted firmly on his mind. The muscular brown-skinned, 6'4" 225 pound young man walked around town looking into shops and stores, and standing by idly on sidewalks, hoping to hear the familiar sounds of horse hooves traversing the streets of downtown Sylacauga that would be transporting that lovely woman he'd come to adore after one chance meeting.

Finally, after a month of searching and waiting, the young woman rode into town on her horse pulling a medium-sized cart behind her. She, too, had hoped to see the young man who'd helped her with her package the month before in town again as she'd been thinking about him ever since the day she'd met him briefly. She smiled when she saw him standing in front of the post office and enthusiastically guided her horse-drawn wagon towards the white wooden structure and brought it to a halt in front of the young man.

"Mornin', miss. Mind if I help ya' off ya' horse?" Rutherford asked politely on a cold morning in November of 1942.

"Thank you. My name is Nituna. It's a Creek Indian name—it means daughter. My last name is Grunion and it's a French name." Nituna said excitedly from the top of her horse.

"I'm Rutherford Holland."

"Nice to meet you, Rutherford," Nituna said whilst smiling as she tightened a tan scarf around her neck before extending her hand.

Nituna was dressed in native Creek Indian apparel. She wore a pair of tan deer skin boots, a pair of brown, tight-fitting suede pants and a brown suede vest with a thick tan wool coat that was slightly open. She looked very appealing in her native attire, her hair hanging freely, flowing gently from beneath the brown beaver fur hat she wore, eyes teeming with joy. She stretched forth her hand to take hold of Rutherford's hand and when the two touched, there was an immediate spark. They smiled at one another shyly as Rutherford helped Nituna from her horse and walked into the post office and waited for her to retrieve her packages.

Nituna had more packages than she had the time before and she shyly turned to Rutherford and chuckled before she said, "So, you're gonna wait until I'm nearer my cart again to take these packages, Mister Holland?"

Rutherford walked over and assisted Nituna and followed her out the door where the two talked beside her cart. He asked was she full blooded Creek Indian, and if so, how did she remain in Alabama when all the Indians were driven out in 1836?

"I'm glad to know you know of our history somewhat, Rutherford," Nituna replied as she tied a rope around her packages. "But that's not the whole story. Yes. I am a full-bloodied Creek Indian. My parents, grandparents and great grandparents grew up on a farm about ten miles north of here. They are nice people, the Grunion family. They are French. The French settled this part of Alabama in 1540 and the Grunion's have been here since 1543. My people were here long before that though. When the Europeans took over and sent the Natives away, the Grunions, who were friendly to my people, they hid many of us Creek Indians. Because of our light complexion, we were able to pass as the French people's nieces, uncles, cousins and so forth. With the promise of their own land in Oklahoma, my parents went west after my grandparents passed away. I chose to stay with the Grunions. My father, Apollo is his name, he believed I was in love with the Grunions' son—but the truth is Rutherford, I just love Alabama. My mother, Sapphire, she said if I wanted to remain here, she would give her blessing. She got my father Apollo to agree and I was able to stay. The Grunions allow me to stay on their land and I farm for them along with seven other Creek tribe members. And you?"

Rutherford told Nituna about his father and aunt's death and how he now assists his mother on the farm.

"I'm sorry you lost part of your family. But no one knows what the future bears. My parents are up in age now. I'm their only daughter and they spoil me with Creek artifacts. Every month they send hand-woven cloth and crafts from Oklahoma. It's their way of reminding me of my Native American heritage, but it's something that I'll never forget ever. I love the gifts more than anything."

"It must be really nice having both your parents still alive. I miss my family. We shared a lot. My father was an excellent carpenter. Taught me everything I know. And my aunt Elizabeth was an excellent cook and always kept the family entertained. She could play a guitar superbly and had a wonderful singing voice. With them all gone, and with just me and ma left, it gets lonely on the farm for the both of us."

"Are you always there alone? Just you and your mother?"

"Yes. Just the two of us. At sunset we usually fix dinner, listen to the radio and before you know it, another day has passed and another is on the horizon."

"I get lonely too. Many men, especially white men, ask for my hand in marriage and they often offer me gifts."

"Do you accept those gifts?"

"No. I want something more out of life than just token gifts that are meant as way to get me into bed."

"What is that you seek, Nituna?"

"My own farm, and a good, strong man with family values. That's what Apollo said I deserve and I believe that. Most men only want to take me to bed. I'm not an easy girl. I may appear so, don't know why, because I'm often aloof while they're talking. I value family and relationships and most of the men I talk to have no intention on starting a family." Nituna responded as she looked Rutherford in the eyes and then looked away towards the ground in shy silence.

There was a long awkward pause between the two before Nituna raised her eyes once more and saw Rutherford staring at her with a bright smile. They blushed at one another before Rutherford asked, "Can you leave the Grunions' farm?"

"Anytime. I am a free woman, Rutherford." Nituna said as she smiled.

"I do a real good beef stew, Nituna. On a cold day like today? A good bowl of stew can warm the heart and soul."

"I like stew, Rutherford. Are you asking me to dinner?" Nituna said as she smiled.

"Not dinner—lunch. Right now if you're able. I stay maybe three miles east of here. Follow me and I'll show you our little operation. We sell produce to town's people and ship some to Birmingham on the train."

"I know. The Grunions talk of Holland produce all the time. I finally get to meet the man behind the myth."

"It's no myth, ma'am. Holland produce can't be beat." Rutherford stated as he took control of the reigns of his horse. "Let's be on our way."

"I didn't accept your offer Rutherford."

Rutherford stopped his horse and looked over to Nituna, "Oh. Well, I just—"

"You assumed I was going to say yes. I told you I'm not easy."

"I did."

"Assume I was easy?" Nituna asked as she sulked slightly.

"By no means, Miss Grunion. I was referring to you accompanying me for lunch. Was I wrong about that, ma'am?"

"I'm sorry," Nituna said sadly, noticing the disappointed look on Rutherford's face, but at that moment, she couldn't help herself. "I'm sorry again," she then said through laughter. "I can't pretend any longer! But I couldn't resist teasing you at first. The look on your face was worth a million bucks! I'd be honored to have lunch with you, Mister Holland."

"Funny lady you are," Rutherford said as he smiled. "Come on. Let's go have lunch."

The Holland Family Saga Part Five

The two rode to the Holland farm where Rutherford began unpacking fresh beef he had secured in an ice box on side the family's log cabin. As he did so, he watched as Nituna left the front porch of the two story three bedroom log home and walked through the field with Eileen. The two began picking up onions and tomatoes that were left behind after the harvest as they talked, placing them in a hand-woven basket. The young woman knew her way around a farm, Rutherford noticed as he carried the meat into the kitchen.

As the stew brewed, Nituna and Rutherford became better acquainted once she returned from her walk through the field with Eileen. They talked for almost two hours getting to know one another while preparing the stew and Nituna then ate lunch with Rutherford and Eileen. The lunch was pleasant and the conversation was very friendly. Nituna had a sense of humor, was very knowledgeable of her culture and was a genuine naturalist. She loved farming, animals, and even designed her own clothing. Her entrepreneurial spirit fit right in with Eileen and Rutherford, who'd owned their own business for years.

Eileen told stories of her father and how he kept the land in the family and taught her how to become a cultivator of land. Fond memories of Freeman and Elizabeth's lives was told as well. It was a pleasant lunch, and by its end, it was fair to say that Eileen and Rutherford both had grown fond of their guest.

Nituna thanked Eileen and Rutherford when they'd all finished as she got up to wash the dishes and Eileen was all smiles. She could clearly see that this young Indian girl was surely trying to capture her son's heart just as much as he was trying to seize hers and she was glad they were getting along. "I'll leave you two be," Eileen, not wanting to be a third wheel, said as she got up from the table. "I'm going upstairs to listen to the radio. Nituna, it was really nice to meet you and I hope to see you again."

"Same here, Miss Holland."

"Call me Eileen. There's no need for formalities around here, Nituna." Eileen replied before she grabbed her sterling silver tray that held her cup of tea and ascended the stairs of the log home.

"Rutherford, the meal was delightful. How'd you learn to cook so well?" Nituna asked as the two convened before the fireplace once the dishes were done.

"Practice. Nobody else eats but me and ma, so if I mess it up no one knows but us. Guess I got lucky with the stew." Rutherford responded, bringing about a chuckle to Nituna.

Silence ensued as the two stared at one another and drew nearer to one another's faces, taking in each other's features. Nituna's heart pounded fiercely, she wanted this man, and Rutherford, in complete harmony with Nituna's emotions, believed she was the most beautiful woman he had ever seen. The two sat side-by-side beside and leaned into one another for a kiss that was all so sensual, and affectionate at the same time.

"I've never done that before." Nituna said as she back away and stared at Rutherford.

"First time for the both of us, Miss Grunion."

"I like that, especially coming from you, Mister Holland."

"Wanna take a walk?"

"Sure."

The two walked across the fertile plain of the Holland farm hand in hand talking further about their lives. Nituna told Rutherford she visited her parents in Oklahoma at least twice a year, but hadn't been in a while because she'd been real busy doing the harvest. She liked to make wool sweaters and blankets and loved to sing. Rutherford mentioned his grandparents passing away some ten years earlier and talked about his expertise as a carpenter. He and his father, shortly before his passing, had built the family's home from the ground up, along with the buggies he and his mother used to transport their produce. By day's end, it was fair to say Rutherford and Nituna had a thing for one another.

"I, I like your family's farm. I feel a part of this land and I like being here. Can I come back tomorrow?" Nituna asked just as she and Rutherford arrived back at her horse and cart.

"Come by anytime you like. My door is always open to you, Miss Grunion."

"Okay. I'll see you tomorrow. For lunch?" Nituna asked just to confirm.

"I'll try to delight your taste buds again—but don't be mad if I mess things up."

Nituna laughed and said, "You'll do fine Mister Holland. You're an excellent cook. See you tomorrow."

"Tomorrow." Rutherford ended as he watched the Indian woman tighten the reins on the horse and roll forward, exiting his farm and disappearing into the afternoon sun.

When Rutherford entered the home, Eileen was at the foot of the stairs with her hands on her hips and side-eying her son. "You two like each other," she said with a wide smile. "I knew it! Ever since the day you saw Nituna you had to go to town for something. We have everything here on the farm, but you made it a point to go there. You're not fooling anyone."

Rutherford removed his coat, hung it up on the hand-crafted oak wood coat rack and said, "I still need lessons in romance, momma?"

"Not bad, son. Not bad. You know how to pick 'em I give you that. So, are you two courting for marriage?"

"Slow down, momma," Rutherford said as he and his mother entered the kitchen and fired up the wood burning stove. "I do like her. And marriage? I would really like that, momma. And we can have something to pass on to our kids. I think it'll work out between us if I pursue it."

"Pursue it, son. You deserve a good wife. And by all accounts, Nituna would make an excellent wife and mother. Freeman, and Elizabeth should be here to see this happen. Our family is growing once again. Rutherford," Eileen then said as she leaned against the sink and laughed, "we're getting ahead of ourselves! Look at us! You two have had lunch only once and already we're talking about you two getting married and having children. Such dreamers were are. You and I."

"It's a good dream, momma. A dream worth chasing. She's coming back tomorrow too by the way."

"You two are courting for marriage! Yes! I'm not getting

ahead of myself! Rutherford she is wonderful! I love her already!"

"I think I do too, momma. She is a special person. I can't wait to see her again."

Nituna had a gift for Eileen and Rutherford when she returned the next day. She gave them hand-woven wool blankets to keep them warm on those cold winter nights in Alabama during the winter of 1942. She and Rutherford then walked the land once more, holding hands as they walked over to the goat pen where they fed the animals and then milked the cows. The couple then ate lunch with Eileen, and Nituna and Rutherford did some light harvesting before returning home for dinner.

Nituna's visits were becoming longer and longer as time passed by and slowly, over time, she and Rutherford's courtship had developed into a full-blown love affair. The two courted one another throughout the winter of 1942 and became engaged on New Year's Day. The loving couple then married in the spring of 1943 on their own land. Nituna took up residence on the Holland farm where she divulged herself fully into the family business and helped them earn a decent, honest living farming onions and tomatoes, along with a few other vegetables. The family also earned income by allowing the lumber yard to forest their trees, which sat on over 40 acres of their property. After building a sizable nest egg for the family, Rutherford and Nituna decided to bring forth children—much to Eileen's delight and relief because it had taken eleven years for Nituna to conceive and the want-to-be grandmother was worried that the couple was infertile and the family would not have any survivors to carry on the namesake and uphold the family business. Eileen was surprised, however, because when the birthing began, it happened in rapid succession and the family had increased in numbers beautifully.

In 1954, Nituna give birth to female twins, Ruth and Naomi Holland. Three years later, she gave birth to Samson Holland, who was named after the biblical figure Samson, the strongest man to ever live according to the bible Nituna often read. In 1959, another set of female twins were brought forth; their names were Mary and Martha. Rutherford and Nituna had named all of their children after fabled bible characters.

Shortly after Mary and Martha were born, in April of 1962, however, the Holland family began having problems with the local government officials in Sylacauga. Eileen and Rutherford were second and third generation free slaves and had a storied history behind them and they weren't going down without a fight because it wasn't in their nature to give up so easily.

Bob Holland Junior, a freed slave of white and black descent, inherited the land from his white slave owner and father, Robert 'Bob' Holland Senior, when he died in 1874. Bob Junior was only seventeen at the time and was a little wet behind the ears when it came to farming, but he soon met a young Native American woman named Nashotah, whose name in her Native Creek language meant twin, because she herself was a twin, having lost her sister to illness during the climax of the Civil War. Bob Holland Junior and Nashotah rebuilt the business over the years and gave birth to twin daughters in 1899, Eileen and Elizabeth Holland.

Eileen met Freeman Devon, a farmhand, in 1922 inside a local juke joint on the outskirts of town. Freeman had a good work ethic, was strong and very handsome. His dark, smooth skin is what attracted Eileen to the man. The two became a very loving couple, bringing forth one son, Rutherford Holland in 1924, a year before they married. When she gave birth to Rutherford, Eileen was more than overjoyed because she now had son with the last name of Holland to keep the family namesake going. And even after she'd married, Eileen never stopped using her given last name. The last name Holland would remain for all times.

Bob Junior was the only living relative to Bob Senior and rather than sell the land, Bob Senior had passed it down to his illegitimate son. The land had been passed down from generation to generation and the business Bob Holland Senior had started back in 1821 had been kept alive and was thriving with all credit given to Bob Junior and Nashotah.

Bob Holland Senior was very influential in Sylacauga. A county commissioner with ties to men who'd fought for the Union during the Civil War, he often spoke out against racial prejudice, in spite of being a former slave owner himself. His way of not being hypocritical to the Cause was to pass his land down to his son, whose mother was a former slave that had died during birth. Because of Bob Holland Senior's wealth and influence, the peace between the local government officials in Sylacauga and the Holland family had remained intact even after his death; but Bob Holland Senior had been dead now for nearly ninety years and new players were arriving on the scene, people who could care less about Bob Holland Senior and his kindness towards those outside of his race, and the legacy his name carried.

Bob Junior and Nashotah had ridden the Holland name to profitability and did good business with people of all races until their deaths came about in 1930 and 1932 respectively. Freeman, Rutherford, Elizabeth and Eileen had picked up where their predecessors had left off; but when Freeman and Elizabeth died in the accident, the Holland family had entered into a weakened state. On top of that, the people who often did business with the Holland family, namely the white people who knew of Bob Senior's reputation, were dying off.

This new breed of government officials in Sylacauga, who'd always believed the freed Holland family members had no right to the land since it had been owned by a white man, now saw an opportunity and sought to swindle the property away from the Holland family. They were taking their time at the out-set, but with the birth of five siblings by 1962, town officials knew the Holland family would grow strong once again. If they were going to make a move, they had to act and act soon if they wanted to overtake such pristine land with a profitable operation.

The Holland Farm had the best of everything when it came to running a farm: stud horses, healthy lamb, chicken and sheep, goats, cattle and hogs. The land was plowed routinely and was always kept fertile and properly watered. Eileen was a masterful business woman also; despite her Creek and Negro heritage, two of the most hated races of people in the south, she churned out the best produce in the entire region and had customers far and wide. Ripe, overly large and sweet onions and tomatoes were her specialty, although she also produced

The Holland Family Saga Part Five

and sold cucumbers, snap beans and red beans. Eileen would load up her red and white hand-made wooden cart and attach two of her most prized jet black mustang horses to the front and she and Rutherford would ride into town and sell every item. The Holland family, at the height of its inception, was a well-to-do farming family that had their own land and a thriving business, but behind the smiles of many of the town folk lay a seething hatred that was close to boiling over.

The first thing the town officials did once they'd decided to enact their plan was to place a false lien on the Holland estate in April of 1961. The local bank had sent a telegram through Western Union claiming Eileen owed back taxes. The amount she was asked to pay, nearly $10,000 had taken the family by surprise, but they were able to foot the bill.

Rutherford saw right away that town officials were trying to steal the family's land, a common occurrence throughout the south as many former slaves who owned land had had their land swindled right from under them, or outright taken by force, and he wanted to fight the allegation immediately. Eileen was going to take a more diplomatic approach. She'd convinced Rutherford to pay that first year, at least until she could use the law to regain control and remove what she knew to be a false tax lien.

In April of 1962, Rutherford went down to the local bank to withdraw all of his family's money at Eileen's request because her plan was nearing completion. When Rutherford was told his mother now owed more than she had saved and the government had frozen the family's account, he grew angry. He drove home and grabbed his shot gun and went back to the bank on this fateful day in April of 1962 with Nituna, who had become aware of the situation, and had gotten into the car to plead with her husband to try and convince him to not go through with his act.

This entire scenario had gone unbeknownst to Eileen, who was out back of the home with Ruth hanging clothes out to dry. Eileen knew Rutherford hated the town officials, and she herself had come to despise the men because of their incorrigible behavior and disdainfulness towards her family.

The Holland Family Saga Part Five

The sixty-three year-old woman had a plan working, however; she was in talks with a young congressman the next town over named Raymond Eufaula Senior, who had a Creek Indian heritage and a son working on the Sylacauga police force.

Eileen was preparing to move the family's money to a bank in New York, fight the tax lien and seek protection for her family at the same time because she knew once the town officials caught wind that she was fighting for her land, the racial threats would soon follow. Eileen was a shrewd woman with calm patience and knew how to work the system to her benefit. Had she known what her son was about to do, she would have stopped him; instead, a routine day on the Holland farm would unfold into a living nightmare and would forever change the course of the family's history.

"Naomi! Look after your brother and sisters! Me and you all's father will be back shortly!" Nituna yelled from the passenger seat as Rutherford backed away from the family's log home. "Rutherford, please don't do this! Let's, let's let them have this land! My mother and father have a large estate in Oklahoma and no one's there now. We can farm there and pay the back taxes we owe here. Let's take momma and the kids and go to Oklahoma!" Nituna pleaded as Rutherford drove towards town.

"These white folk been stealing from us for over a year! Nituna I'm a man! And the Holland family been landowners since before the turn of the century and they just gone try and take it from us? I rather die before I see that happen!"

"That's what they'll do! That's what they want you to do Rutherford! They will kill us all and take our land! Rutherford let them have it!" Nituna said as she pleaded with her husband.

"They are not going to run us away from Alabama, Nituna! That's my land! *Our* land! Our *home*!" Rutherford said just as his car entered into downtown Sylacauga.

The pristine 1961 black Cadillac pulled up in front of the bank and Rutherford, wearing a dark grey trench coat, black slacks, black shoes and a grey fedora, exited the car and walked up the sidewalk towards the bank.

"No!" Nituna hollered as she got out the car and grabbed her husband, trying desperately to pull him away from the bank's entrance. "This is not right! You are going to get us all killed! Think about your mother! Our kids! Our family!"

"I am thinking about family! We did nothing wrong to these people! Been playing by the rules ever since we married and now they turn on us just because of our Native American and Negro heritage? This is what this is all about, Nituna! This isn't about taxes and you know it just as well as I do! They will not rip us off again! They will not steal one more red cent of the Holland family's money!" Rutherford remarked as he broke away from his wife's grip and entered the bank.

Rutherford walked into the bank manager's office, who was in on the scheme to swindle the Holland Farm from its rightful owners, with the gun hidden beneath his trench coat as Nituna followed quietly with her head bowed.

"Mister Holland, nice to see you," the bank manager said with a pretentious smile on his face as he stood up from his seat. "I've come up with another payment plan on the taxes owed in order to save your farm. I was just about to send you a message via courier."

"What message? What kind of plan?"

"You can pay one hundred dollars a month, and still stay on the land until you've paid back the back taxes."

"I've got over fifteen thousand dollars here in this bank. We've paid what you've asked already. Ten thousand dollars has been paid. Now what do we owe now?"

"Well," the bank manager, a slender pale white-skinned thin man of fifty-two stated as he smiled at Rutherford and Nituna, "the government as of now has seized your funds because of unpaid interest. The lien placed upon you entitles us to the land —but I'm willing to work with you people to get this matter resolved. In ten or fifteen years, the land will be returned to you, providing you pay the interest on the taxes."

The bank manager had just outright lied to Rutherford and he knew it all-too-well. If the government had placed a lien on his property, he knew he would have received written notice and several warnings in advance. Not to mention the so-called taxes had been paid.

"Fifteen years? Interest on taxes? This is nonsense! You didn't think my momma was going to be able to pay the ten thousand dollars! Now that she has, you, you come with *this* sham?" Rutherford asked as he stood before the bank manager.

"Rutherford, let's go!" Nituna asked as she stood beside her husband. The woman knew her husband was growing furious and knew not how to calm him down. She regretted not calling for Eileen when Rutherford returned home because the situation had now spiraled beyond her control. Her husband was standing inside a bank with a loaded shot gun, an angered temper, and was being lied to by a white racist—a deadly mix of emotions and power.

"No, Nituna! I'm not leaving until this man confesses! He knows we own the land and he's only trying to get us to concede! Nonsense!"

"There's no need for you to yell, Mister Holland! I've been nothing but nice to you people—"

"We are not you people! We are the Holland family! Rightful landowners of the Holland Farm that you are trying to steal! A thief! Thief!"

"The bank owns that farm now and you people will comply or otherwise I'll have *your* nigger ass, and your savage wife as well as your half-breed mother and kids kicked the hell off those premises!" the manager yelled angrily.

Rutherford knew even if he did comply on this day, another situation would arise that would ultimately force him and his family from the land. He felt as if his back was against the wall and he had no choice; his land was being swindled right from under he and his family and he would not allow that to happen. He quickly drew his weapon and demanded his money. "Give me my money white man!" he yelled as he aimed his shot gun at the bank manager.

The bank manager fell back into his chair in fright, tripping the alarm as he did so and causing the alarm to ring loudly throughout downtown Sylacauga. Nituna, now worried about her mother-in-law and kids, and knowing Rutherford was on a path to destruction, ran out of the office. She ran through the empty bank just as she heard the bank manager scream aloud. Nituna turned briefly to see the bank manager stagger from his office as he held his hands over his bloody mouth and fall onto the bank floor.

Rutherford exited the office and aimed his weapon at the two white female bank tellers. "Open the damn safe!" would be the last thing Nituna would hear her husband speak before she turned and exited the bank doors.

The terrified woman could hear police sirens far off in the distance as she ran through the streets of downtown Sylacauga back towards her kids and mother-in-law. She had to get them off the farm. They were all she had left. She ran through a field under the bright spring sun, crossed a hill and cut through a thick forest. She then crossed a low-lying creek and continued running at a hurried pace. She fell down mid-way to her home; her two thick plats splayed across the ground as she lay on her back looking up at the sky and crying silently, all-the-while wishing her husband had not done what he had done on this day and regretting the fact that Eileen hadn't gotten the chance to talk to Rutherford before he left. A couple of minutes later, after she had gathered herself, Nituna jumped up and raised her ankle length skirt to prevent herself from tripping again and continued her run. Her vision was blurry from the incessant tears that rolled down her face.

Nituna's plan was for her to gather her kids and Eileen, concede the farm and somehow raise money to relocate to her parents' land in Oklahoma because Sylacauga was quickly becoming a nightmare for the family. The humble woman never really wanted to go to the bank with Rutherford, but she had to try and talk sense into her husband. Nituna now understood that Eileen should have been told, but she never figured Rutherford would go so far as to rob the bank. The damage he'd done was immense, possibly unforgivable, but Nituna was ever hopeful. Hopeful that she could make it home in time and save her mother-in-law and kids, who were of the utmost importance at this point and time because the farm no longer mattered.

Seven year-olds Ruth and Naomi were returning from the onion patch near the front of the farm when they heard their mother yelling out loud from a distance across the field. The twins turned around and saw their mother emerge from behind the barn running towards them; at the same time, Rutherford was speeding up the dirt road leading to the family home.

Naomi saw her father speed by in his car and she began to cry aloud for her mother as she stepped out into the road, believing something was wrong. Ruth, however, was focused on the remaining cars headed their way. The police were tailing Rutherford at a fast past—four car loads of white men who called themselves cops, but were really out for blood.

Naomi had her back to the road, standing amidst the trail of dust her father had left behind as the police cars approached and Ruth saw the danger. "Naomi!" Ruth called out aloud. "Naomi get out of the road!"

Ruth ran and pushed Naomi aside, forcing her back into the onion patch and was preparing to dodge the cars herself, but she'd slipped. When Ruth got up to try and run, the lead police car purposely swerved in her direction and mowed her down. The child's body slammed into the ground and she was run over completely. Naomi was lying on her back when she witnessed her sister get run over by a speeding police car and she began screaming horribly. Ruth was still alive, however; she was crawling towards the side of the road, calling out to her twin. "Naomi! Naomi help me!" she screamed aloud just before the second police car ran over her mid-section.

Naomi could not believe what she'd just seen. She lay motionless and watched in horror as the third police car ran over Ruth, dragging her body several feet underneath the car. Her bloody, mangled body lay in the middle of the road only to be run over by the last police car as it, too, sped towards the Holland home. Seven year-old Ruth Holland, an innocent seven year-old child, had just been murdered on her own homeland while trying to save her twin sister's life. She'd become the first murdered member within the Holland family, and the terror had only just begun.

Nituna had seen her daughter get run over. She was yelling aloud as she ran at a furious pace towards Naomi and Ruth. Eileen, meanwhile, upon hearing the police sirens, emerged from the rear of the house just as Rutherford was pulling up in front of the home.

"Momma," Rutherford yelled aloud. "They come for our land! They come for our land!"

"What did you do, son?" Eileen asked as she eyed the police cars speeding towards the home.

"I have our fifteen thousand dollars! All of our savings! That's all I took, momma!" Rutherford answered as the four police cars pulled up and eight officers quickly jumped out.

"You robbed the bank? Why did you do that?" Eileen cried out in disbelief as the officers surrounded her and Rutherford. "This is not right, son."

"I didn't hurt nobody, momma! And this is *ours*!" Rutherford said as he held two satchels full of money before his mother.

Eileen slapped Rutherford in the face and said, "You were wrong! You're becoming more and more like Freeman! The two of you can be hot-headed and stubborn to the point of stupidity at times!" she yelled as she took the money and stepped in front of her son and eyed the officers as she held the satchels of money out before her. "Here's the money! Take it and leave! Even though it is ours rightfully ours, you can have it—for now!"

One officer snatched the bags of money from Eileen and shoved her back towards Rutherford and said, "You think this will make things right, Indian? You still owe the town! This is Sylacauga property now according to the bank!"

"Thieves! All of you! What have we done to deserve such treatment?" Eileen asked aloud as she stepped towards the officers.

"Get your half-breed ass back over there!" an officer yelled as he shoved Eileen back towards Rutherford and pointed a shot gun at her.

"To hell with you!" Eileen screamed aloud.

"No. To hell with you, Indian," the officer yelled in return as he and his comrades opened fire on Eileen with twelve gauges, shooting her a half dozen times.

Rutherford was stunned. He dropped his shot gun and knelt down before the bloodied corpse of his mother and gently scooped her head up into his arms, "Momma," he said lowly. "What the hell is wrong with you people? We are Hol—"

"You're a dead nigger is what you are!"

Rutherford was hit by a barrage of bullets from the officers and fell dead beside his mother.

Naomi, meanwhile, was kneeling beside Ruth crying over her broken, bloodied and mangled flesh when she heard the gunshots. The seven year-old was frozen with fear and confused as to what was transpiring on this day and was crying hysterically when her mother approached her. Nituna had witnessed the murders of her husband and mother-in-law along with the death of oldest daughter as she ran across the field towards Naomi and Ruth. She paused and grabbed her heart when she saw her daughter Ruth lying dead on the side of the road and ran and knelt beside her. "Look what they did to my baby. Ruth!" she screamed aloud. "Ruth!"

Out the corner of her eye, Nituna saw officers running her way. She grabbed Naomi and said, "This is not our home anymore, Naomi! We're going away to Oklahoma," before she kissed her eldest daughter's forehead as the police were descending upon them.

Nituna wanted to run away with Naomi, but she knew her three remaining kids were still up to the home and she couldn't find it within herself to leave them behind, no matter how terrifying the tragedy unfolding. She walked towards the officers waving her hands in surrenderance and said, "You can have it! Take the land! You've murdered my husband and mother and there are no more men here! Only a woman and her kids! I don't care! Take the land! We're leaving for Oklahoma!"

"Who gives a fuck about Oklahoma? Your savage ass should've left when we ran your kind off over a hundred years ago!" an officer said, amidst the sniggles of his comrades, all of whom were holding shot guns and smiling wickedly at Nituna.

"Why are you doing this? Haven't you heard anything I said? Take the land!" Nituna said as she placed Naomi behind her back. Naomi held onto her mother with a death grip with her eyes planted firmly on Ruth and still unable to believe what she'd witnessed moments ago. To Naomi, nothing made sense. She didn't know what was going on. All she knew was that her sister had been run over by cars, gunshots were ringing out across the land, and her mother was speaking something about Oklahoma. The seven year-old only wanted whatever it was that was happening to come to an end so somebody could help Ruth.

"We'll take this land, savage. But you will not be going to Oklahoma." the officer replied.

"Please," Nituna pleaded. "We mean you no harm. I didn't, I didn't do nothing! And I'm not going to fight you!"

The officers pulled Nituna from Naomi's grip and she screamed for mercy as she was dragged across the road into the onion patch.

"My kids are all I have! Please! I'm begging you not to do this to us! Let us go!" Nituna screamed as she was thrown to the ground. She scurried about and crawled over to an officer and grabbed his legs and looked up with pleading eyes. "Sir, please, my kids only have me. I tried to stop him," she said lowly referring, to her husband. "I tried to stop him."

The officers knew Nituna had nothing to do with what happened in downtown Sylacauga. And although the bank manager was relatively unharmed, receiving only a punch in the mouth by an angered Rutherford, what Rutherford had done had given the swindlers a segue into what they'd always wanted to do, which was to take the Holland family's land away from them. The officers could care less about Nituna's pleas because as far as they were concerned, a 'nigger' and a 'savage' had robbed the city bank and had attacked a white man and that is the story they were going to sell to the public if ever their treacherous act was uncovered.

The lead officer walked up to Nituna and punched her in the face and she fell onto her back and spewed blood from her mouth along with several of her teeth. Naomi watched her mother roll around on the ground helpless as the officers all joined forces and kicked and spat on her.

"I mean you no harm! I mean you no harm!" Nituna said repeatedly through a bloody mouth as she was beaten mercilessly.

Nituna now lay on her stomach as the officers kicked her in the sides. She was grimacing in pain, all the while pleading to be left alone as she suffered a brutal beating. "Take me to jail," she pleaded. "I'm a thief! Take me to jail!" Nituna knew if she went to jail, she could still fight for her kids. The officers knew, however, that leaving her alive would cause problems because she was a witness to everything taking place on this day and would undoubtedly tell what she knew. Nituna's pleas were falling on nothing but deaf ears.

Gathering courage, and wanting to help her mother, Naomi ran towards the police, but she was frozen with fear when an officer fired his shotgun into the ground, the buckshot landing mere inches away from her feet. She stopped in her tracks and yelled aloud for the officers to stop hurting her mother, who was crawling away, facing away from them all.

"Don't hurt her! Please! Don't—hurt—my child!" Nituna screamed through a bloody mouth as she lay on her back looking up at her attackers.

"Momma, why they doing this? What's going on? Why they hurt Ruth?" Naomi asked through terrified tears as she was being held by two officers.

"Shut that nigger bitch up, now!" the lead officer yelled as he racked his shot gun and aimed it at Nituna.

Nituna saw the man point his gun at her and she turned over in an attempt to crawl away. She was staring her daughter directly in the eyes when she screamed aloud, "Naomi, I'm sorry!"

"Momma!" Naomi screamed.

"Naomi!" Nituna screamed.

Her mother calling her name would be last word seven year-old Naomi Holland would ever hear her mother speak, because while she was being held, she witnessed her mother take two shotgun blasts in her back as she crawled away from the officers, trying desperately to reach her. Nituna Holland had died instantly and Naomi had fainted upon witnessing the horrible sight.

The officers then took Naomi and dragged her back to the home where officers were ransacking the place. The police were emerging from the Holland family home with jewelry and Indian artifacts, handmade clocks and wooden artifacts along with pristine fur and leather coats. Every item worth stealing was taken from the Holland home.

"Here's the others, Eastman," an officer said as he emerged from the front of the home with Sam, Martha and Mary, the twins still lying in their basket, only this time, they were crying to top of their lungs. Sam was quiet and unawares. All he knew was that some men had pulled him from inside a dark place and now had him stand on the porch in silence. "That Indian lying dead beside her nigger son tried to hide them in a floor cellar, but I heard them."

"You should have left them there to die."

"Why?" the officer asked with a slight reluctance.

"Why? Because we're going to burn this place to the ground." Eastman, the officer who had killed Nituna, said before he shoved Sam and Naomi back into the house and grabbed the basket with the twins. Eastman entered the home, guided Sam and Naomi into the living room and had them stand in the center of the room. He then placed the basket containing Mary and Martha in front of Sam and aimed his weapon at Naomi.

Another officer, realizing what was about to take place, quickly walked into the home and said, "They're just kids, sir. Let them be."

"They're half-breeds. Half nigger, half savage. They ain't no better than their thieving ass parents!" Eastman replied as he pointed the gun at the top of Naomi's head.

The angered, terrified and bewildered seven year-old eyed Eastman coldly as she cried, taking note of his name on his badge. Eastman would be firmly planted in her psyche and would never be forgotten. Eastman was her mother's killer. Eastman was the leader. Eastman, if ever the day comes, will have to pay for what he'd done to her family.

"I have kids. You have kids. We won. Don't do this sir, please." the officer pleaded with Eastman.

"What do you care about these bastards?"

"Sir," the officer said, "you mean to tell me that we are going to kill these four children in their own home? And then burn the place down with the bodies inside? The parents I can see, but, but we talking about kids, sir. This is as black-hearted as it gets! And if people working for civil rights ever caught wind of *this*? We'd never live it down! Killing innocent children? We'd be ostracized by our own kind! No matter how many of us hate *their* kind! Killing kids, sir," the officer asked as he shook his head in shame and disbelief. "No."

"What do you suggest we do with them all?" Eastman asked.

"We can send them away and split them up so they won't tell. I don't care about their parents, and by the time these kids are grown, they won't even remember what took place today." the officer speaking on the children's behalf stated.

"Okay, okay," Eastman remarked lowly as he lowered his rifle and walked away whilst shaking his head. "You do that. You make sure these kids are separated. Make up a lie, about those two," he then said as he walked out of the house and looked over towards Eileen and Rutherford's lifeless corpses. "No go on the kids, gentleman," he then said aloud. "We got a good Samaritan amongst us! Guy makes sense though as much as I hate to admit. For all we need is that son-of-a-bitch King bringing his nigger ass down here with the NAACP kicking up dust."

"What about the little girl and the lady at the front of the road?" an officer asked as he and another officer went through Eileen's jewelry box sitting atop their patrol car and removing precious gems, a diamond watch and pairs of gold and diamond earrings by the karat.

"Bring the bodies inside. We'll burn them inside the house." Eastman replied nonchalantly.

"What shall we say concerning the parents, sir?" the officer who'd stop the kids' slaying asked.

"I don't care. Most niggers are on smack now-a-days. Tell everybody, tell the papers if they ask that their parents were junkies. The mayor and the sheriff will cover things back in town—this is all their idea anyway. Just make sure these kids never speak about what took place here today when you cast them off." Eastman ended as he walked away.

Naomi and her surviving siblings were spared, but this event, this tragedy, would forever change the course of the Holland family. A once prosperous and peaceful, law-abiding existence had been shattered at the hands of pure racists who were bent on reaping a profit off of ill-gotten gains.

An hour later, Naomi, now sitting in the back of a patrol car with her siblings, grabbed hold of Sam and sat quietly beside Mary and Martha and closed her eyes as she cried over the crackling sound and the smell of smoke coupled with a stench, a horrible stench that began filling the air. Soon, the Holland siblings were driven off of their property. Naomi had not a clue where she and her siblings were being taken, but she told herself that if ever she were able, she would repay the officers for what they'd done. She would never forget the face, or the name of the man who had taken her mother's life before her very eyes. What happened in Sylacauga had changed Naomi's demeanor entirely, and at the age of seven, she had unwittingly become the family's oldest living member. The Holland family, in the year of 1962, was truly in a weakened state and was facing a very uncertain future—possibly even—that of eradication.

The Holland Family Saga Part Five

CHAPTER 2

SURVIVE

"Okay, what do we have here?" Kevin Langley, the assistant manager of The Orphanage Home in Selma, Alabama, asked the deputy sheriff of Sylacauga.

It was a month after the massacre on the Holland estate. Seven year-old Naomi, five year-old Sam, and three year-old twins Mary and Martha were taken to the local church in Sylacauga and later moved by nuns to an orphanage in Birmingham before being transferred to Selma, Alabama. Sam, Mary, and Martha were too young to understand what was going on; but Naomi, who had witnessed the murder of her mother, and overheard the many conversations Eileen had with Nituna and Rutherford about the problems the family was having with Sylacauga politicians and lumber yard big-wigs, knew exactly what happened—the 'white man' had murdered her parents, grandmother and sister, and had taken their land.

"What we have here," the deputy replied as he stood behind the four children, "what we have ourselves here is a bunch of half-breeds. Half nigger, half savage. Their parents were junkies. Stupid husband tried ta' rob the local bank. The mother, a junky herself, tried ta' attack several officers and was shot and killed. With no surviving family, we got no choice but to make these bastards wardens of the state."

"Niggers and savages are not terms we use here at The Orphanage Home, sir. Neither is the word bastard." Kevin stated angrily.

"Whatever nigger lover! It's outta Sylacauga's hands now! They are all yours." the deputy said as he shoved Naomi forward, and literally pushed Sam and the twins to the floor.

"You killed my momma and daddy!" Naomi screamed as she ran and attempted to hit the deputy. The deputy only laughed and walked off as Naomi pounded her fist against his backside.

Kevin pulled Naomi back and ordered his staff to take the children to their rooms and he began looking over their files. He sat down at his desk, perplexed as to how such beautiful children could be reared by drug addicts. To him it didn't make sense, but taking care of the children was his main priority. Naomi was an angry child, Kevin quickly discerned. Sam was mild-mannered, a shy little boy, and the twins were oblivious and appeared hungry. As Kevin studied the children's' files, one of his staff rushed into his office and said, "The oldest child? She won't release her siblings, Mister Langley! She's lying on top of the three of them!"

Kevin quickly walked down the long hall and rounded the corner and saw Naomi lying on her back on the floor, covering her brother and sisters and crying loudly in the threshold of the door leading to a room in which Mary and Martha were attempted to be placed inside by the staff member. "They killed our momma and daddy! Now they trying to split us apart! Why can't somebody help us?" Naomi asked Kevin as she cried.

Kevin's heart immediately went out to these children. "Take them all and place them in room 302," he said calmly.

"But Kevin, we place them by age. The state law says—"

"Forget the damn state law! While I'm on duty here I determine what's best for these children! Room 302! The four of them shall remain together for the time being!" Kevin yelled before walking off.

Naomi spent the first night in the home with her siblings crying her heart over the things she had seen and what was happening to her family now. The next morning she was awaken by Kevin who said, "You have a story to tell. What happened in Sylacauga?"

Naomi said nothing right away. She looked out the window at the morning sun in wonderment and disbelief, remembering her family as silent tears rolled down her face. She then turned to Kevin, her lip trembling and said lowly, "They killed them! My mother's name is Nituna Holland, and my father is Rutherford Holland. The white people back there killed them both and took our land, and then they sent us here." Naomi had more to tell, but she didn't trust Kevin fully. Still, she let go of a few details in hopes that he would be able to bring the people responsible to justice.

"I'm sorry. I'm so sorry Naomi."

"You the first white person ever called me by my name. Why they call us niggers? What's a half-breed?" Naomi asked inquisitively.

Kevin looked away in shame. He was shame of his race, and ashamed of America. Children were gifts from God and America was supposed to be God's country. *"What hypocrites we are!"* Kevin said to himself as he turned back to Naomi. "What school did you attend back in Sylacauga?"

"My mother taught me at home. My brother too! He knows his ABC's!" Naomi said proudly as she looked at a sleeping Sam. Naomi then lowered the covers and showed Kevin Mary and Martha, who were nuzzled together right beside her sleeping soundly. "These two are my sisters. This one's Mary. That's Martha. This is my brother Samson. I'm Naomi. We are all Hollands." Naomi ended as she smiled briefly at Kevin.

Kevin then smiled back at Naomi. The man knew this little seven year-old girl had seen her parents murdered before her very eyes, which was her story, and if she was correct, then that meant that she had been stripped from her own land; but through it all, this little girl still found reason to smile. "You will be a great woman someday, Naomi. The word 'nigger' is a hateful term, anyone that calls you that is not your friend. There's no such thing as a half-breed for we are all *human*. Remember that, we are only *human*, all of us." Kevin said lovingly.

"What's gonna happen to us?"

Kevin had not the heart to tell Naomi that she may someday be separated from her siblings. Not wanting to upset her, he told the child the she and her siblings would remain together for all time. He'd just lied and it hurt him to do so, but unbeknownst to Kevin, the words he spoke to Naomi on this day would stay with her forever.

Things were normal at the orphanage for over two years and Naomi had grown real close to her surviving siblings during that period of time. She also began a journal six months into her stay at the orphanage, creating a chronicled detail of her family's history based on what she knew and remembered. She wrote in it often and told her sisters and her brother exactly who they were and where they came from three times or more each and every day. Naomi was really beginning to trust the people at the orphanage, but her trust in the staff would be shattered in February of 1965.

Naomi awoke from her bed and saw Sam being dressed neatly by a member of The Orphanage's staff. She wasn't worried at first because the staff always dressed Samson first before dressing Mary and Martha to take them all to breakfast; but when a coat was placed onto Sam, Naomi ran and grabbed her coat. She also grabbed Mary and Martha's coat. When the administrators stopped her and told her Samson was to leave the room by himself this morning, ten year-old Naomi, who never went anywhere without her siblings, knew something was astir.

Sam was quickly ushered from the room and the door was locked. Naomi cried as she tried in vain to unlock the door. With a face full of tears, she ran to the window and saw Sam being loaded into a van and all his belongings were with him. Naomi grew more agitated as she watched staff members place Sam's trunk into the van and she began to pound on the window and cry loudly, her cries arousing the twins and causing them to cry aloud as well. Naomi had just lost one of her siblings—her seven year-old brother, Samson Holland.

The Holland Family Saga Part Five

Samson Holland would live out his life in New Orleans. His adopter, a lady by the name of Ms. Newsome, was told by the orphanage's general manager, who was being paid by politicians from Sylacauga, that Sam's parents were junkies and that he was the only child. Sam Holland would grow up believing he was the only child of two drug addicted parents who were deceased. The Holland family was being taken apart systematically and methodically.

Six months later, Naomi awoke early one morning to find the twins missing. She ran to the door, and to her relief, it had been left unlocked. She hurried back to her bed and grabbed her journal, but she dropped it on the floor when she saw Mary and Martha being loaded into a station wagon just outside of her bedroom window. Naomi ran out the room without the journal, but she quickly thought that Mary and Martha would not remember what she was planning to say to them, so she ran back into the room and scooped up some of the pages, and took off running towards her sisters once more.

Naomi was an emotional wreck. She was facing the inevitable fact that she would possibly lose Mary and Martha in the same fashion that she had lost Sam and at the same time trying desperately to make sure she had information that Mary and Martha could use. Information to allow them to not forget that they were Hollands. The ten year-old was doing all within her power to not allow Mary and Martha to leave without knowing who they were.

Naomi only had a small portion of her journal in non-sequential order in her hands as she ran from the orphanage towards the car that was taking her sisters away. She wasn't able to tell Sam, but she was determined to let the twins know their history. She ran from the orphanage as the twins, who were riding in the backseat of the station wagon waved good-bye.

"No, this is not the end! This ain't good-bye!" Naomi yelled through tears as she ran alongside of the car.

Administrators rushed to grab hold of Naomi as she ran to catch up with the car as it rolled slowly down the road leading away from the orphanage. The ten year-old was holding onto the side of the car, pleading for the driver of the car to stop, but he never even acknowledged her. Naomi's eyes were full of tears as she called out to the black man that was riding off with her sisters. She had a sad pleading look on her face as if to say to the man, *"why are you taking my family away from me?"*

As Naomi ran alongside the car, she eyed the staff quickly approaching. Six year-old Mary, who was short enough to stand on the floor board, was hanging onto the window of the car staring back at Naomi and waving happily as the car rolled forward at a slow pace. Martha was kneeling on the backseat and she only stared at Naomi from the rear of the car as she held onto a baby doll.

Naomi quickly stuffed the disheveled pages of her journal into Mary's hand and began to speak quickly. "I told you who we were everyday! Remember who we are! This is who we are! Don't let anyone but you and Martha read it! You hear me, Mary? This is about our family! You have a brother named Sam Holland! They took him! Your brother is Samson Holland! I'm Naomi," Naomi yelled as she looked back at the staff as the three white women grew nearer. Naomi then looked back at Mary, and nearly out of breath from keeping pace with the car, she continued to yell aloud, "My name is Naomi Holland! I'm your big sister and I'll find you someday! We family! You hear? We fam—"

Mary held onto the papers as she watched the girl fall from the side of the car. Naomi lay on her stomach screaming loudly as she watched Mary and Martha ride away. Martha looked over the backseat at Naomi and waved good-bye as Naomi cried her heart out; her arms extended as if she were pleading for Martha to come back. "I love you!" Naomi yelled.

Neither Mary nor Martha could hear Naomi's screams any longer, however; they both believed she was sad to see them go, but they didn't fully understand the reasons why. Six year-olds Mary and Martha Holland were simply too young to fully comprehend the magnitude of the tragedy that had befallen the Holland Family during the early sixties. Two staff members from the orphanage finally caught up to Naomi and grabbed hold of her and pulled her up from the ground. "Why?" she screamed as she was dragged by both arms back towards the orphanage kicking and screaming. "Momma! Mommmaaa!" Naomi called out aloud as she threw her head back and fainted.

Naomi's heart was torn apart on this day. She had lost her entire family and had been thrust deeper into her nightmarish experience; only this was a nightmare she could not wake up from. Naomi knew her family's history, and she knew in order for the Holland Family to survive and be reunited, she would have to survive. The day Mary and Martha were taken, another deep change overcame Naomi, she now had only one goal in life—survive.

Meanwhile, inside the station wagon, Mary held on to the folder and neither the man nor the woman sitting in the front seat of the car tried to take it away. Mary and Martha liked the girl named Naomi; she was nice. They would miss the girl named Naomi; and they knew not how greatly their lives would be changed over the years to come, but they, like Naomi, would do whatever it took for them to simply put, survive.

The Holland Family Saga Part Five

CHAPTER 3
DON'T LOOK FOR US!

"After you're done with the bathrooms I need you to help Mary outside with the yard Martha!" Donna Jacobs yelled aloud from the bottom of the stairs.

Donna Jacobs and her husband were foster parents residing in a large two-story home in Tuscaloosa, Alabama about thirty miles south of Birmingham, in the year 1976. The 45 year-old full-figured black woman was married to Johnny Jacobs, an assistant head coach for the University of Alabama's football team. The Jacobs had a son named Reynard who resided in the home with identical twins Mary and Martha Holland who were now seventeen, and eleven years removed from the orphanage in Selma, Alabama.

The twins had been residing with the Jacobs since 1965, and ever since they could remember, it seemed as if they were outcasts inside the Jacobs' home, at least in the eyes of one of the twins, who only saw the Jacobs as using her and her twin sister as their own personal servants. For so long the twins had been tending to the needs of the three people inside the sprawling five bedroom home. They had to wash everyone's clothes and hang them out to dry, they had to clean the entire home, and fix breakfast and dinner everyday of the week except Saturdays. On top of that, they had to keep over an acre and half of lush green lawn neatly kept with only a push lawn mower.

Mary and Martha were in good shape because of the constant labor. Both were 5' 9" and a fit 140 pounds with brown eyes that featured a beauty mark, which was a small dot under their left eye, in the exact same spot on their faces. They had long sideburns with thick, dark eye brows, full, curly, sexy lips that produced a wide smile that revealed snow white teeth. They had coal black, long, thick, coarse hair that they often wore in two plats braided to the back. The plats flowed gently down to the tops of the twins' shoulders. They were both tan-skinned, and somewhat hairy with a thin layer of dark brown hair covering their arms, and legs, and a light layer that flowed down the nape of their neck all the way to their lower back. There was a slight darkness on their upper lips although no hair had ever grown on either twin's face; and although the twins were hairy females, they didn't have to shave their body hair; it was a natural form of beauty the females possessed. It was a well-known fact to many of the young males at Tuscaloosa High School that Mary and Martha were two of the sexiest females that ever graced the school grounds. Many knew of their Creek Indian heritage, and they attributed their hairy bodies to their native tribe, but still, when you looked at the twins, you could tell they had Negro blood flowing through their veins.

Martha and Mary received very little attention from the Jacobs in the home, but the girls were often paraded about town with the Jacobs as if the five of them were a happy and loving family. The Jacobs family, behind closed doors, however, secretly viewed the twins as their own personal servants. Martha wanted to run away, but she was having a hard time convincing Mary to do so and she wasn't leaving without Mary. Mary, on the other hand, felt blessed to be raised in a home where she was being taught responsibility.

Martha, however, felt as if she and Mary were being used as servants ever since she could remember and she had a hard time convincing Mary to see what she saw. Mary was easy-going, humble and optimistic whereas Martha was outspoken, daring and suspicious. Martha believed everyone was out to get her and Mary, especially the Jacobs family.

The twins were excellent students, Mary more than Martha.

Mary was always in the top percentile of her class. Martha made good grades, but she only did what was required at the appropriate time. Whenever Martha had a test that she wasn't prepared for, Mary would take her place in class. No one could tell the twins apart, except by their demeanor, but when they were silent, no one could tell, not even the Jacobs. If Martha said she was Mary and vice-versa, people had no choice but to accept what was said. It was a clever form of deceit that both twins were using to their advantage with great success during this period of time.

The Jacobs' estate was situated on a large, hilly patch of land just outside the small town of Tuscaloosa. The twins loved to explore the wilderness that surrounded the area. They mainly hung out by a brook that flowed lazily behind the Jacobs home at the far south eastern edge of the property. They would run across the yard hand in hand and head down the hill through the thick grove of trees and sit atop a huge rock that overlooked the brook. There, they would read the journal given to them by Naomi over eleven years ago. The girls couldn't remember neither Sam nor Naomi that well, but the journal said that Naomi was their older sister and they had an older brother named Samson. Naomi's twin Ruth, according to Naomi's journal, had died and they were the youngest of the remaining four. They learned that their parents had died and they were sent to an orphanage.

The papers describing what actually happened in Sylacauga was dropped the day Naomi handed the girls the journal. Mary and Martha only believed they were orphaned after their parents died. They never knew that Nituna and Rutherford were actually murdered along with their grandmother, Eileen. Martha and Mary cherished the journal. On hot summer days, Mary would read aloud, and as she read, Martha would recite the journal word for word as she swam in the brook. They would then switch. By the time they were sixteen, the twins had memorized nearly every last word of the eighty plus pages that Naomi had managed to give to them that day back in 1965. Martha and Mary wanted to know who Naomi and Samson were; only neither twin knew how to go about beginning their search. Sylacauga was over a hundred miles away; besides, the last portion of the journal had the girls and Sam in an orphanage in Selma. No Holland family members were residing in Sylacauga any longer according to Naomi's journal.

Martha dreamt of knowing what happened to her siblings someday, but Mary was simply going along with life with the Jacobs. She believed the Jacobs cared, besides, her real parents weren't around. The truth was distorted about Rutherford and Nituna and the events that had transpired on the Holland Farm. The family's history had become a somewhat twisted and confusing story to both Martha and Mary, and they were now residing with people who Martha resented, and Mary had taken a liking to.

Martha only wanted to be left alone. She believed she and Mary would be fine on their own if given the opportunity. Mary didn't want to leave, however; she believed in her heart that the Jacobs cared for her and her sister. Mary, however, would receive a wake-up call during the fall of 1976.

"How come y'all don't have Reynard clean up behind his self? I shouldn't have ta' pick up his dirty drawers from the bathroom floor!" Martha yelled aloud from the bathroom on the second floor of the Jacobs home.

"Don't talk back to me! You do as I say and get your behind out there and help your sister when you're done! And then come and prepare dinner! I took out some chicken for you and Mary to bake tonight!" Donna ended as she headed out the door with her son on a warm Saturday afternoon.

Alabama University was playing Ole Miss this day and Donna and her son Reynard were headed to the game. The twins would have to stay behind and tend to the house. Mr. Jacobs, an assistant coach on Alabama's football team, was steadily gaining favor with Bear Bryant, head coach of Alabama football. He was hoping to become offensive coordinator, and maybe work his way into the NFL and become one of the first Black assistant coaches. The twins were merely a prop; an attempt to show Mr. Jacobs' humanitarian side. Martha knew they were merely pawns in the Jacobs' game, but Mary liked the Jacobs household. The twins would get into a debate on a regular basis as to why they should stay and why they should leave.

When Martha saw the Jacobs 1976 Buick Skylark rolling down the long winding driveway and disappear from sight, she flushed the toilet, quickly wiped the counters and ran into her sister's room and grabbed Naomi's journal and ran from the second floor, down the stairs, through the kitchen and burst from the back door of the home.

"Mary! Mary!" Martha screamed in delight as she ran towards her twin who was pushing the lawn mower. "Mary! They gone! You can stop working now! Let's go to the brook and sit on the rock." she said excitedly.

"What? I was enjoying pushin' the mower. Look at my legs, Martha! I got muscles in my calves!"

"You need a muscle in your brain!" Martha replied as she turned off the mower and pulled her sister from behind the machine.

"Martha! Wait girl! We gotta finish our chores!"

"Mary, the game is on for over two and a half hours! Take a break sister!" Martha exclaimed as she pulled Mary away from the lawn mower and the two sisters erupted into laughter as they ran hand in hand towards the brook; their flower sundresses blowing into the warm fall air.

"Momma name is Nituna! Rutherford is our daddy! Naomi is our sister and Sam is our brother!" seventeen year-old Martha screamed as she took off her sundress and jumped into the brook wearing a pair of tight blue jean shorts and a black tank top. When she emerged from the murky depths, she began to tread water and yelled back to Mary, "Where we from?"

"Sylacauga, Alabama!" Mary yelled in response.

"What are we?" Martha then asked as she turned and swam to the opposite side of the fifteen foot wide nine foot deep brook.

"Creek Indian and Negro!" Mary yelled proudly as she watched her sister swim to the opposite side.

Martha reached the opposite side of the brook and Mary watched as she ran into the thick brush and reemerged a few minutes later with both of her hands full of small green plants. Mary watched as Martha pulled out a plastic garbage bag and stuffed the plants inside and tied a tight knot. Martha then reentered the water, and swam back towards Jacobs' side of the property where she exited the water and opened the bag and stared down at the green leafy plants.

"What's that?" Mary asked with an inquisitive look in her eyes.

"Mary Jane."

"That plant got my first name?"

"Yes it does Mary, yes it does." Martha replied as she closed the bag, grabbed her clothes and began walking towards the Jacobs home with Mary following close behind.

Martha had gotten marijuana seeds from a member of the high school football team. He told her how to cultivate the plants and reap them for profit. Martha's plan was to raise enough money so that when she and Mary graduated high school in 1977; they could leave the Jacob home and start their life anew somewhere else.

In October of 1976, Reynard, who attended a private Catholic school, happened into Martha's room, something he did on a regular basis unbeknownst to Martha. He was searching for some of Martha's panties to masturbate to, but he happened upon Martha's stash of marijuana whilst searching her dresser drawers and took a portion for himself. He waited until the following day and rushed home early from school and baked the marijuana into brownies. He had a plan for which ever twin he could corner first, namely Mary as she was the most easy going and somewhat naive.

When the twins came home from school, Reynard began plotting. Mary wore a navy blue dress and navy blue shoes. Martha had on a pair of blue jeans, a white blouse and white sneakers. Reynard didn't see the girls dressed up before he left and they weren't speaking. When they began their chores, he carefully studied the two and discerned which one was Mary and who was Martha when Martha called out to Mary for a rag to wipe the counters. Martha had to tidy up the bathrooms and wash clothes. Mary had to tend to the yard, and it would be with Mary that Reynard would seize his opportunity.

He approached the seventeen year-old with the brownies and offered her one and Mary kindly took one of the brownies and ate. She ate another and before long she was feeling light-headed and she began to giggle uncontrollably. Reynard escorted Mary away from the home and into the woods and began to strip off her garments with Mary giggling the whole time. "You taking my dress off, Reynard!" she giggled as she moved his hands away.

"Mary, look at this here." Reynard said as he unzipped his pants and revealed his erection.

"Reynard, you got your penis out!"

"Lay down, Mary." Reynard whispered as he gently pushed Mary into the soft grass hidden beneath and behind the thick woods. She fell gently onto her back and felt a jolt of pleasure when Reynard pressed his body to hers and gently kissed her lips.

"Reynard, what are you doing to me?" Mary asked in between kisses.

Reynard said nothing, he backed away from Mary as if he were about to leave, but Mary inched her head forward in an attempt to kiss him again. Mary was slowly being seduced and taken advantage of; she was being deceived, but the feelings emanating from within her most private parts had her body in an intense state of arousal. It was wrong indeed for Reynard to deceive Mary Holland, but Mary, who was under the influence of marijuana, wanted the pleasure to continue because she liked the way Reynard was making her feel this day.

Reynard raised Mary's skirt and tugged her panties down, and she moaned as she rose from the ground and allowed him to slide her panties off completely. When the cool air blew across Mary's labia, her body trembled and she felt a wetness seep from between her inner folds. Reynard ran his hands across Mary's outer lips and she quickly spread her legs wider and placed her hand over Reynard's and moved his hand, guiding it to the exact spot that produced the most pleasure. A trickle of sweat ran down the right side of Mary's temple and she stopped moaning and was now panting, gasping for air and had a sudden rush of anticipation and want as she ground her hips against Reynard's hand.

The rotation of her hips produced feelings within Mary that she didn't want to ever stop. Reynard slowly slipped a finger into her tight opening and she grimaced at the intrusion, having been penetrated for the first time in her life. Soon, however, Mary had her legs raised and Reynard had placed two fingers inside of her dipping wet pussy. Mary, her legs raised and spread wide, bucked and ground herself against Reynard's fingers until she felt a tingling sensation from deep within her inner being. She placed fingers in her mouth and gently bit them as her body quivered and she cried out, "Reynard! Reynard! What are you, what you doing to me?"

"You want me to stop?" Reynard whispered.

"No, it feels good to me." Mary answered softly as she stared Reynard in the eyes.

Reynard then got in between Mary's legs and placed his member at her entrance and began to penetrate her virgin pussy. When she grimaced, Reynard pulled back and eased forward slowly. Mary was panting and staring up at the tree tops with her eyes wide. What Reynard did to her hurt, but it felt good at the same time. She eased up off the ground and tried to capture Reynard's member with her vagina, and Reynard, sensing Mary's want, slowly eased forward and his stiff member slipped inside of Mary fully and the two moaned in unison.

"Ohh, that, that feels good! What you doing to me?" Mary asked again as she stared up at the Reynard.

"You want me to stop?"

"Nnn, noo, don't, don't stop. Do it fast. It feel good when you go fast." Mary moaned as she wrapped her arms around Reynard's back and pulled him close as he began to steadily and rapidly piston in and out of her vagina. Reynard had to cover Mary's mouth with his hand to conceal her incessantly loud moans.

Mary lay on her back, her dress raised above her waist and her panties off to the side. Reynard's pants were down around his ankles his shoes still on as he humped her at a rapid, steady pace. Mary rubbed her cheek against Reynard's and she was now nearing his lips. She was making love, but Reynard was only out for a quick fuck. He had been lusting after the twins since he struck puberty at age twelve, and his fantasy was now coming to fruition. Mary had never experienced the sensations emanating from her body. She wanted the pleasure on this day, to last forever.

The combination of the hashish and the sensations her body was producing caused Mary to grab hold of Reynard's face and drive her tongue deep into his mouth. That kiss drove the two seventeen year-olds over the top. Reynard pounded Mary for all he was worth until he felt a tingling sensation rising within his loins. His body quivered and he and Mary both moaned aloud. Fluid erupted from Reynard's penis and Mary felt the depths of her vaginal walls being coated with a hot boiling liquid that made her eyes water. She stared up at the tree tops with her mouth agape, in awe over the pleasure that was bestowed upon her delicate body.

Reynard, in turn, pressed his full body weight upon Mary as she wrapped her legs around his back, trying to pull him deep within her inner folds. She raised her head to kiss his lips, but Reynard quickly pulled away and climbed up off her body, leaving Mary wanting more.

"Do it again." Mary pleaded. "Please, make love to me again, please," she pleaded as she lay on her back heaving heavily, desperate for Reynard to lay on top of her again.

"I, I gotta go!" Reynard said in a panicked tone as he pulled his pants up and dashed from the woods.

Mary lay on her back staring at Reynard as he scurried away. She wanted him to hold her, to love her, at least say he loved her as she was beginning to love him. She dozed off in the woods and awoke an hour later feeling heavy-headed and groggy as she looked around, wondering how she had gotten out into the woods and why was she lying on her back with her dress up around her waist. She wobbled back to the house with her panties in hand and went and took a bath. From that point forth, Reynard acted as if what happened between he and Mary had never even taken place. Mary somewhat remembered what happened, although the memories were vague, real vague; but it wouldn't be long before the truth would come out.

****

Two months later during Christmas break, Mary and Martha were sitting in Mary's room reading Naomi's journal. As Martha read, Mary stood in front of her mirror with her hands on her hips. She then turned to the side and said, "Martha, come stand beside me."

Martha sat the journal down and stood facing Mary, both twins then turned towards the mirror and Martha could see for the first time that Mary was bigger than she.

"What the hell you been eatin', Mary?"

"The same thing you been eatin'! I'm gettin' fat, Martha!"

"You better slow down your eating. People gone tell us apart now! And I need you to take my exam next month in Science." Martha quipped as she returned to reading the journal silently.

Mary stayed in front the mirror and continued talking. "Martha I can't stop eating. I'm always hungry! And I got these crazy cravings like, like hotdogs and peanut butter, or a big bowl of ice cream covered in syrup. And you know the good part? I don't even have a period no more!"

Martha's eyes widened, "Mary!" she exclaimed as she scrambled from the bed and ran and locked the bedroom door. "You might be pregnant!"

"A baby? Me?" Mary asked somewhat dismayed.

"Yea! Who you been having sex with?"

"Who you been having sex with?" Mary asked in return.

"Never mind me! I'm not the one that's pregnant."

"I sort of remember me and Reynard in the woods kissing, but my head was so light. He gave me some sweet brownies and then we went in the woods. He laid on top of me, we were kissing, I remember that part. I also remember how good I was feeling when he was on top of me."

"Mary? Reynard your baby daddy?"

"I guess. He the only one I been with. I know that for sure, if that's what happened."

"This ain't gone sit well with the Jacobs. And I should bash Reynard face in for taking advantage of you like that!" Martha snapped as she pounded her right fist into the palm of her left hand.

"Reynard didn't take advantage of me, Martha. He made me feel good and I wanted it."

"He tricked you Mary! If it wasn't for you being high you would have never done that!"

"I wasn't high, Martha!"

"Yes you was! He put weed in the brownies! I know Reynard went and took some of my weed! I can tell when somebody go in my drawer, because I leave it certain way. All that day I was thinking about that! That happened about two months ago. I remember! Reynard took some of my weed and used it in them brownies he gave you that day."

"Well, it's done now. And when Reynard finds out he got me pregnant we'll be okay."

"He act like he don't even know you, Mary! Y'all ain't gone be all right!"

"I know Reynard ignores me. I think he's just scared of me."

"Mary get real! That boy ain't scared of you! He don't wanna be affiliated with you after what he done because he know he was wrong! Besides that, he might already know you pregnant! And the Jacobs family ain't the average family. They keep up images around here. If word got out that Reynard got you pregnant out of wed-lock, the Jacobs would never forgive us— even if their son *was* in the wrong! And believe me, they would hide the fact that you got pregnant by Reynard, maybe even take your baby! Naomi said we should never split up. We might be able to make this work in our favor if you really want to leave this place, Mary."

"Why leave? I mean they treat us good here."

"Treat us good? Mary! They only take us out to take pictures for the paper! Take us to charity events! We do *everything* around here! We like *slaves* in this place!"

"That's not true! We in school and we can go to Alabama University."

"Look at that raggedly school we go to! If they care, how come we not in private school like Reynard? They buy us cheap clothes and Reynard get all the good stuff! And Donna already said if we don't earn a scholarship we going to community college! I'm tellin' ya' they don't love us!"

"They do! And I'm gone tell Reynard I'm pregnant, and he gone tell his parents and we gone get married! That way I'll be in the family. We both can be in the family."

"Mary wake up! Even if they did care, that's your stepbrother, you can't marry him anyway."

Mary fell back onto the bed and looked up at the ceiling in disgust, not believing a word of Martha had said. Her heart told her that the Jacobs family would welcome her into their family and she expressed that thought to Martha, who then decided to let the whole scenario play out. She knew Mary was only setting herself up for rejection, but by allowing it to happen, Martha hoped Mary's eyes would be opened and she would be willing to leave the Jacobs home for good.

****

On Christmas Day, the Jacobs were opening their gifts when Mary and Martha came down the stairs fully dressed and greeted the family nicely. They only got mere nods and mumbles and neither of the Jacobs' made eye contact with the twins because they were too enthralled in opening their gifts. Mary and Martha had made cards in their art class for the Jacobs family and they handed the cards to each family member, who merely sat the cards aside without reading them. The twins then walked towards the tree and noticed they each had a small box with their name on it. They opened their respective gift and each discovered they had gotten aprons with their names engraved. Martha was insulted. She then looked around at the gifts the Jacobs had given each other—an expensive watch for Reynard, along with a new color TV. Mrs. Jacobs had gotten a white mink coat and matching mink hat. Mr. Jacobs had gotten a pair of leather boots and a wool trench coat. Martha tossed the apron back under the tree and got up and ran back upstairs. She was pissed. The Jacobs had belittled her for the last time.

Mary placed the apron in front of her and smiled down at the item. She was grateful. She then turned to Donna and said, "Misses Jacobs, I think I'm pregnant."

Reynard immediately grew worried as he stared at his mother and father.

"Did you have intercourse with one of those boys at school Martha?" Donna asked sternly.

"I'm Mary. And no, I had sex with Reynard."

"What the hell did you say?" Mr. Jacobs asked as he got up from his chair and approached Mary, who was sitting on her knees beside the Christmas tree.

"I said, Reynard got me pregnant."

"Is this true son? Did you have sex with this girl?" Donna asked her son.

Mary took offense at being called 'this girl'; but she just knew Reynard would admit to what he had done.

"Daddy? Mary is a liar! Somebody at her school must have done it to her because I never touched her."

Mary's heart dropped. She stared at Reynard in disbelief as she got up from the floor. "Yes you did have sex with me," she said matter-of-factly. "We had sex in the woods two months ago right after I came home from school!"

"Stop lying, Mary! I never touched you!"

"Yes you did! This your baby I'm carrying and you know it!" Mary said as she ran towards Reynard.

Mr. Jacobs got between the two. "You heard my son! It never happened. Now, take your gift and go upstairs with Mary!"

"I am Mary! Reynard got me pregnant! Nobody else!"

Donna stepped in and slapped Mary hard across the face and Martha, who was upstairs in her bedroom laying across the bed, grabbed her jaw and sat up and wondered where the sharp, sudden stinging sensation on her right cheek had emanated before she shrugged it off and lay back in her bed.

Mary, meanwhile, had stumbled back, grabbed her jaw and stared at the Jacobs, who were sneering at her as if she were an alien. They had a sickened look on their faces, as if they were appalled by the mere sight of her. Mary turned, bowed her head and walked up the stairs and ran to her room and fell down on the bed and cried softly. *"Martha was right, they don't love us,"* she said to herself.

The next two months were pure hell for both twins. Mary was pulled from school as the Jacobs would not let her attend classes for fear the family secret would be revealed. Mary wanted her child, but the Jacobs were hoping that she would lose the baby. Martha was keeping Mary fed, but she wasn't receiving the proper medical care.

In the middle part of February of '77, Martha came home from school to find Mary in the kitchen crying. Donna had called and ordered her to prepare dinner. Mary wasn't feeling well and she alerted Donna of that fact, but the woman only cursed Mary and called her a 'slut'. Those words hurt her heart, but still she was doing as Donna ordered.

"What's wrong, Mary?" Martha asked in a concerned manner.

"I, I told Donna I wasn't feeling well, but she still making me cook dinner. She called me a slut, said I, said I was only trying to get money from her son. I never, I never asked Reynard for nothing! Donna hurt me today." Mary said as she moved about the kitchen whilst crying.

"Put that shit down!" Martha yelled as she grabbed a pot full of collard greens from Mary's hands and pulled her upstairs.

The twins stayed in Martha's room until Donna and Reynard

came home and Martha ran out her room, down the stairs and told Donna that Mary needed to go to the hospital.

"I don't smell any greens in here! Did she fix dinner?" Donna asked, ignoring Martha's statement.

"Fuck dinner! My sister need a doctor!"

"Take her yourself!" Donna snapped as she walked into the kitchen, hoping and praying that Mary was having a miscarriage on this day so her family could continue their charade with the twins.

"Alright!" Martha said matter-of-factly as she backed away whilst staring at Donna and Reynard.

Mary and Martha came back down the stairs a few minutes later with their coats on and Martha politely walked into the kitchen where Donna was beginning to prepare dinner and grabbed the keys to the family Skylark.

"What the hell are you two doing?"

"I'm taking my sister to the hospital!"

"Reynard get my keys from those two!" Donna said nonchalantly as she began to stir her greens.

"Don't fuckin' touch us!" Martha yelled as she pulled out a black .38 snub nose.

Reynard ran and hid behind his mother. Donna, however, turned to face Martha and said, "Martha, if you don't drop that gun, I'll kick your ass all the way back to Sylacauga!"

"It's better than this dungeon!"

Donna walked over to Martha in an attempt to take the gun and she hit her in the face with the pistol's wooden butt. Donna fell against the kitchen table and grabbed her face in shock, understanding fully that Martha meant business. "Sit the fuck down!" Martha commanded Reynard.

Martha took duct tape and rope and tied Reynard and Donna up tightly in their chairs. The two sat pleading with Mary to help them, to make Martha stop. "Why," Mary asked. "After you deny the fact that your son got me pregnant? Took me out of school and kept me hid from sight? You deserve whatever happens to you! Both of you!" she yelled as she stood and stared at Reynard and Donna as Martha ran upstairs.

A few minutes later, Martha came back downstairs wearing Donna's mink coat and matching hat. She handed a leather coat to Mary, along with a knit hat and a pair of leather gloves. Mary took off her old tan wool coat and put on the lavish leather coat, hat and gloves and looked herself over. "Not bad," she said.

"Now," Martha then said as she waved the gun at Reynard and Donna, "we leaving forever! Don't look for us! And if you even find us, we gonna tell everybody what happened here. See how y'all gone look when Tuscaloosa find out Reynard had a child out of wed-lock! We gone tell 'em y'all sent us away after he took advantage of Mary in order to hide her pregnancy!" Martha ended as she stuffed socks into Reynard and Donna's mouths, took the keys to the Skylark and she and Mary drove away from the home.

Martha had never driven a car before, but she figured it couldn't be that hard. She steered the car slowly towards the bus station and hit a parked car in the parking lot, but she didn't care, the car wasn't hers anyway. The twins went into the bus station and quickly walked to the counter as people eyed them admiringly, believing that they were entertainers from up north, singers from Motown Records or some other booming recording company that had numerous singers aspiring to be stars in the music industry. Martha knew exactly what she was doing. She believed by wearing the fancy coats, she and Mary would be treated with respect and not looked down upon; and Mary could also hide the fact that she was five months pregnant.

"Hello," Martha said politely towards the ticket agent, "what time does the next bus leave and where's it headed?" she asked with a smile.

The white man behind the counter smiled at the lovely teen and said, "We have a bus boarding in twenty minutes going to Jackson, Mississippi ma'am."

The Holland Family Saga Part Five

Martha looked back at Mary and both twins stared at one another with a serious look. Martha was thinking. She knew Jackson, Mississippi was a city, and neither she nor Mary had ever been to a city; but Martha didn't care where the bus was headed, just so long as it was headed out of Tuscaloosa. Mary knew after what she and Martha had done, they could never return to the Jacobs' home. She also knew Martha was eager to leave. When Mary nodded her head slowly to say yes, Martha turned around to the cashier, smiled, and said happily, "Two tickets to Jackson, Mississippi please," as she pulled out a wad of cash.

While Martha and Mary were preparing to leave town, Mr. Jacobs returned home and found his wife and son tied up. He freed them and they immediately told him what happened. The twins had the Jacobs family dead right so they did not call the police. The Jacobs then took a tally on their belongings and it was discovered that besides the coats and hats, Martha and Mary had taken $1000 dollars in cash and a valuable diamond necklace. The twins could have seriously bribed the Jacobs had they been wiser; their young age hindered them, but Martha's boldness had freed them at the same time. The Jacobs would have gladly paid the twins much more than what Martha had stolen to keep them quiet, but they didn't have to worry, they knew the twins were gone for good, and the Jacobs would have no further ties to the twins by telling their friends that they were off to a private school.

Martha and Mary rode inside the bus down the highway towards Jackson, Mississippi with two new coats, one worth a couple of thousand dollars, $1700 dollars in cash, when coupled with Martha's earnings from selling marijuana at school, a fully-loaded .38 snub nose and an expensive diamond necklace that could only be priced through appraisal. They had enough to get started, but getting Mary to a doctor for proper care was top priority for Martha. They still had a lot of work to do, but so long as they had one another, the twins believed that they would do just fine in Jackson, Mississippi, their soon-to-be new home town.

The Holland Family Saga Part Five

CHAPTER 4

WELCOME TO GHOST TOWN

"Trailways number 2646 will be arriving in Jackson, Mississippi in approximately ten minutes. We wanna thank everybody for traveling with us and we hope that you enjoy your stay in the beautiful southern city of Jackson, Mississippi," the driver of the bus spoke aloud over the intercom aboard the bus.

"Mary! Mary wake up! We in Jackson!" seventeen year-old Martha said excitedly to her twin sister.

Mary stirred from her slumber and immediately grabbed her stomach. She was feeling real bad at that moment and she expressed those feelings to Martha. As the bus cruised into downtown Jackson, Martha spotted a hospital. She stared at the building until she saw the name, Jackson Memorial. She would take Mary there once they exited the bus.

The twins walked slowly through the bus station and people eyed them in their nice coats, admiring the fact that they were identical twins. They looked so attractive, people couldn't help but to wonder who they were.

"Why they staring at us, Martha?"

"Maybe they want this mink coat! I don't want to, but if anybody touch us wrong, I'm gone shoot 'em!" Martha replied as she eyed the people in the bus station cautiously.

Martha was ever protective of her sister. Mary was the oldest by a few minutes, but it was Martha who was the most protective. She made it a point to look after Mary always, even more so now that she was pregnant. The twins made their way to the taxi stand and Martha requested that the two be taken to Jackson Memorial. Once there, Mary received the proper medical care she needed. She was somewhat under-nourished and dehydrated, but other than that, she would be just fine. The doctors ran an ultra-sound and Mary was informed of the fact that she was to have twin daughters.

"Twins? Man, we can barely afford to take care of ourselves!" Martha told the doctor as the three sat in his office.

"Well, your sister can consider adoption, or maybe an abortion," the doctor replied calmly.

"No, sir. I want my kids. Are there programs?" Mary inquired.

"Yes there are programs available. But you have to meet certain criteria to qualify which I believe you will. Do you girls have a place to stay? You'll need an address so you can receive all your information and packets."

Mary was about to speak the truth, but Martha interrupted and said, "Yes! Yes we do have an address! Can we come back next month and apply for benefits?"

"You most certainly can," the bald-headed elderly doctor remarked as he grabbed a note pad and began scribbling. "Come back on this date and I'll have a counselor on hand that will be glad to help walk your sister through the process. I think Mary here is a perfect candidate for the new programs that are available through the government. Now, this service you received today, Mary, will be paid for by the state and next month when you come back we'll complete the paperwork to get you all set up with some health care, food stamps, and possibly even cash from the government. I implore you girls, especially you Mary, to use the government's heath care and welfare programs to your benefit until things get better for you." he ended with a smile as he handed Mary a prescription.

Martha and Mary left the hospital and filled a prescription for prenatal vitamins. Mary was also ordered to drink plenty of liquids so two gallons of orange juice were purchased. The two sisters walked down the streets of downtown Jackson during the early morning hours looking up in amazement at the tall buildings. They were pointing to the sky and bumping into people who were trying to make their way to work. Martha knew she had to get shelter for Mary. It had been a long night and morning and they both needed a bath, food, and rest.

Martha found a Howard Johnson's hotel and rented a room and was given a complimentary newspaper and she and Mary settled into their suite. Martha ran a bath for Mary and ordered a huge breakfast consisting of steak and eggs, grits, hash browns, biscuits and gravy, cereal and oatmeal. When Mary came out of the bath, her hair hanging down and wrapped in only a towel, she eyed the buffet style breakfast her sister had ordered.

"Come on, Mary. Eat up, girl! My nieces starving!" Martha said as she pulled out a chair.

"They not the only ones." Mary said as she sat down in front of the items on the small table.

Martha watched as Mary scanned the food with a smile on her face and then said grace before she began fixing a plate. She smiled to herself as she stripped to prepare for a bath, thinking about Mary's attributes. To Martha, Mary was never one to complain, she rarely raised her voice, and was always appreciative and optimistic no matter how dark or bleak the situation. Martha knew she had to look out for her sister because Mary was an easy going spirit. In Martha's eyes, the world was full of cruel-intentioned people, people like the Jacobs family that would eat a sweet, innocent person like Mary alive. She was not going to let anything happen to her sister if she had anything to do with it. As she sat in the warm water running into the tub, seventeen year-old Martha began formulating the next move for her and Mary. They needed a place to stay in order to receive the benefits the doctor spoke of and that was to be her first goal to accomplish. She leaned back in the tub, closed her eyes and thought about what she and Mary were doing. They had just run away from a somewhat stable home and now had to fend for themselves. *"We can make it,"* Martha said to herself as she sat back in the warm, soothing water.

When Martha exited the tub thirty minutes later, her hair hanging down and wrapped in a towel, she saw that Mary had eaten over half the items and was still going at it. "I saved you a steak, some grits and eggs too." Mary said as she handed Martha a plate.

Martha fixed her plate, sat down and opened the newspaper to the classified section and began searching for a home for her and Mary. As she eyed the rental section, Martha began calculating the amount of money she now had, which was just over sixteen hundred dollars—more than enough to rent a home, activate the lights, and buy clothes and food to hold them over until their eighteenth birthday, which was a month and a half away.

"Hey Mary, they got this three bedroom house on Casper Drive—where ever that is—and it's only two hundred and fifty dollars a month. So that's like five hundred for first and last month rent. That's the cheapest I can find. We need lights and food, clothes, and gas too, so I think," Martha said as she counted out the money she took from the Jacobs and added it to the profit she had made from selling marijuana for a short period of time, "I think we gone be all right sister." she said proudly as Mary smiled at her as she held a biscuit in her left hand.

The two twins sat across the table from one another and stared at each other for a minute or so and smiled. "I look like you, sister." Mary said lowly with a smile, breaking the silence.

"Thank you Mary. That means I'm beautiful. Just like you, sister." Martha replied lovingly as Mary grabbed a bowl and poured her sister some grits.

"Come on, you gotta eat too." Mary stated.

Later that day, after a long, peaceful slumber, the twins sat out to find a department store. They stumbled upon a Sears and Roebuck's and went in to purchase new dresses and shoes and jeans. Martha's plan was to buy sophisticated jeans and dresses and new shoes, along with make-up for her and Mary in order to make themselves look older than what they were in order to rent the home Martha had come across in the paper. The twins had no identification at the time, but their good looks, and Martha's shrewdness was getting them by just fine.

The next day, Martha and Mary, neatly dressed and their hair styled into a single ponytail, set out to meet the landlord in front of the house on Casper Drive. They caught a cab over to the place and waited out in front of the home for the landlord to appear. As they did so, Martha scanned the area on this cool February morning in '77. The house she and Mary were planning to rent sat on the corner of a street called Casper Drive and another side street. Martha now stood facing the home and scanned the neighborhood. She saw that the side street that intersected with Casper Drive was named Friendly Lane, which was on her right. Friendly Lane had a row of houses on the left and right, but the houses on the right side of the street ended halfway down the block where a thick mini forest started. Friendly Lane then t-boned into a canal and curved left led back to the main street. Martha then turned to her right and looked straight down Casper Drive and could see that the street dead ended into another street about a half-mile down and curved left.

The home the twins were interested in sat on a small hill. A small, two-foot brick wall ran in front the home and down its side on Friendly Lane. The brick wall grew taller and taller, almost four feet as it trailed downhill on Friendly Lane; it ended at the rear of the house just before the driveway. The houses in this particular neighborhood, some brick, some wood, were somewhat close together. There was little room on side of the houses in the middle of the block; but the front yards were all spacious. All of the houses in the neighborhood had a two foot high light blue brick wall out front with a fence sitting on top of the brick wall. An opening in the middle of the fence and the brick allowed for entry onto the property.

Martha then eyed Mary, who was eying the house with delight as she walked around in the front yard. She then took stock of the house herself and could clearly see that the house on the corner of Casper Drive and Friendly Lane was a little different because of the wall running beside the house; and unlike the rest of the homes in the middle of the block, this house not only had a nice-sized front yard, but it had a back yard twice as big as the houses in the middle of the block. Mary's twins would have plenty of room to run around and play. The house behind the house on Casper Drive sat facing Friendly Lane; its yard was directly behind the home Martha and Mary were planning on renting and was separated by a driveway and a fence.

Martha then looked to her left towards the main street. On the right corner at the intersection of Casper and the main street, which she knew to be Hanging Moss Drive, was a Dairy Queen, on the left was a large convenience store. Martha saw on her way into the neighborhood that the store sold milk, meat, can goods and the like, it was more like a small grocery store. And even though it didn't have shopping carts like the big grocery stores, it had the necessities of life. A bus line also ran directly in front of the store and that was an extra added convenience. Martha liked the area, she and Mary wouldn't have to go far for food and if they needed to get downtown, the bus line was close by and the neighborhood seemed quiet.

As Martha contemplated those thoughts, a young black man in his mid-twenties approached riding a bicycle. Mary and Martha stared at the man, who was around 6' 5" and real skinny. "Y'all interested in my house?" the young man asked.

Martha laughed lowly. She thought the man was joking; after all, he'd ridden up on a bicycle. She was really expecting to see an old white man pull up in a Cadillac or something, not a young black man riding up on bicycle. "This your house, slim?" Martha asked as she smiled at the young man.

"How you know me by that name?"

"I'm looking for Mister Coleman." Martha then said, ignoring his question.

"That's me. My name Santana Coleman. They call me Slim back here in The G," the man answered in a slow deep-pitched voice as he rode pass Martha and let the kick stand down on his bike and entered the house's front yard. "Y'all want the house, right?" he stopped and asked seriously as he pulled out a set of keys.

"Man, you ain't that much older than me. How you get a house like this?" Martha asked.

"This how Folk do it back here in The G. Anyway, how the hell you get that pretty fur coat while ya' asking me about my house?"

"This your house for true? Because I don't wanna get ripped off, man." Martha stated, ignoring Slim's question again. Martha had her .38 special on her and she was not going to let no one take advantage of her and Mary. If Slim came at her wrong or was trying to run game, she was going to deal with him.

Slim pulled out the deed to the house and handed it to Martha. "I get this all the time," he said as he curled his lips and shook his head. "'Cause I'm young and black I get doubted a lot, especially by white folk. I had one white potential tenant? And when they found out I was black, they sped off quicker than a rabbit dodging a pick-up. Now, I take care of my property, and I'm fare with the price. If you don't wanna see it just say so." Slim said as he started walking towards the front door.

Martha then thought, if Slim was telling the truth, they would have a black landlord close to their age in a seemingly nice neighborhood. He may understand if they ever had difficulties paying the rent. She and Mary talked amongst themselves and decided to look inside the house and they were pleased with what they saw. The home was a carpeted three bedroom home with a furnished kitchen, medium-sized living room, and immaculate bathroom. When you walked into the home, the living room was first straight ahead; to the right was a threshold that led to the kitchen. To the left was a hall that led to the bedrooms and bathroom. A bedroom was first on the right and the second bedroom was down the hall on the same side. The third bedroom was on the left opposite the second bedroom at the end of the hall and the bathroom was at the end of the hall separating the last two bedrooms. The home had plenty of closet space as well. It wasn't overly large, but it wasn't' small either. Mary liked the home, and Martha, sensing the vibes coming from her sister, agreed to rent the place.

Slim told the sisters the home would be ready at the first of the month. Martha didn't flinch, but she knew the first was over two weeks away. The hotel was costing $35 a night so that would eat up over $400 of the $1300 she would have left, not to mention food and toiletries; but because Slim seemed pretty cool and the house was in such a good locale, Martha accepted.

The next two weeks were tense; Martha counted her stack daily, worrying that the money would run out before she and Mary moved into their new home. The lights were on, so was the gas, but by March 1, Martha had only a few dollars left for food. She knew she had the diamond necklace from the Jacobs home, but she felt that the necklace would be more valuable later on down the road. As she and Mary sat in their empty home inside the living room a week after they had moved in, Martha looked over to her sister in a depressed manner, having just spent her last three dollars on a pack of luncheon meat and a loaf of bread that barely suppressed her hunger. She and Mary were also drinking water from the faucet with their hands because they had no dishware whatsoever.

Mary, meanwhile, was sitting in the corner reading a magazine she had taken from the hotel. She smiled as she bit into her sandwich and read the article from the Ebony magazine. Martha again marveled at her sister's appreciativeness, but she wanted more than just a sandwich. She and Mary had been eating luncheon meat for the last three days and Martha was fed up, on top of that, she had to do something for Mary to keep her from getting malnourished. Mary deserved better and Martha believed that in her heart. Determined to make things better, she got up from the floor that night and headed for the door.

"Where you going, Martha?"

"I'm going take a walk. I'll be right back." Martha replied as she headed out the door.

It was almost mid-night and the neighborhood was void of people and quiet out. The weather was cool also, so Martha had worn her pristine, white fur coat. She tore the sleeves off the blouse she wore underneath before she left home and as she walked on the side of the corner store, she tied one of the torn sleeves around her mouth and walked into the store and pointed her gun at the cashier. The female cashier froze when the gun was stuck in her face. When she was ordered to empty the register, she did as she was told and handed a wad of bills to the assailant. Martha fled the store with almost one hundred dollars and ran home believing she had gotten away with her crime that night; but unbeknownst to Martha, she had been seen.

****

The next day, Martha and Mary were planning to ride the city bus to another store and buy food. They were exiting the front gate when they were greeted by Slim and a young woman who was displaying a gun in her waist band.

"The fuck you doin' robbin' on 'G' turf?" the young woman asked angrily under her breath through clasped teeth as she stared at Martha and Mary coldly.

"I ain't rob nothing on G turf!" Martha stated as Mary stood beside her.

"Ya' lyin', mutherfucka," the woman hissed. "I watched you walk down there last night, rob the store and run back down here in that fuckin' white ass coat! You lucky we didn't kill your ass last night," the young woman stated lowly as she stepped closer to Martha.

"We just tryna eat! Look at us! We ain't got shit!"

"You gotta big white fur coat! Sell that mutherfucka! Don't rob *nothing* back here in Ghost Town! *Period*!" the young woman snapped back, this time loudly at Martha as she placed her hand on top of her gun.

Mary was scared. Martha, however, didn't appreciate a female she didn't know trying to tell her what to do, even if she did have a gun on her. She stood in front of Mary and eyed the woman with a cold dead stare. "Slim," she said, "who this is you got in front our door tryna check me on some bullshit?"

The young woman standing beside Slim was named Irene Charles. She was an eighteen year-old slender woman standing about 5' 10" weighing around 140 pounds. She was brown-skinned with thick, coarse hair that she wore platted to the back. She had big, dark round eyes and small lips with a round, smooth, creamy face.

Santana 'Slim' Coleman and Irene Charles, A.K.A. 'Twiggy', were ranking members of the Folk Gang. Folk, as they were called, originated in Chicago, their colors were blue, and their insignia was the six point Star of David and a pitch fork that lay across the star. Twiggy had told Slim over the phone the night before that she knew Martha was the one who had robbed the store because she had watched her go down the block and run back home. The police arrived on the scene shortly thereafter and the cashier told them that a light-skinned black female in a white fur coat had robbed the store.

Slim knew Twiggy had a hot temper, so he told her the two of them would talk with Martha the next day. Lucky for Martha, Twiggy decided to call Slim the night before and inform him of his new tenants, otherwise, Martha and Mary both may have been killed by Folk gang members who would have gladly kicked down their door and shot them on the spot. Twiggy had been secretly watching the twins the whole week, and from what she'd observed, they rarely if ever came outside. When they did, they sat on the front porch for a while and went back in; they stayed to themselves and things were cool until Martha robbed the corner store. Martha didn't know it, but Folk members like Twiggy protected their neighborhood at all times.

"We don't do that back here in The G, Martha. Everybody family back here. And by right? Y'all two shouldn't even be in this place because y'all only seventeen—but I over-looked that because y'all seem cool and y'all birthday later this month. But if y'all gone be with all this robbin' and shit? I'm a have ta' renege on the lease." Slim said, and then added, "This here my girl Twiggy. She stay right there cross the street three houses down. She might can help y'all get on y'all feet."

"Look," Martha said to Twiggy, "you right. I shouldna robbed the store, but my sister was starving, me too. I had no choice. My back was against the wall—literally speaking."

"You hungry just ask somebody, Martha. We family 'round here."

"So you had plans on shooting us?" Martha asked, believing Twiggy was no longer the threat she posed at the out-set.

"Nahh, not your sister," Twiggy replied as she pulled her t-shirt over her gun. "She pregnant. But you? You had it comin' because you a scrappy somebody. You get a pass this time—Martha! That was some real gangster shit last night. You did what you had to do without fail, but despite that, we gotta go back and pay Chug-a-lug."

"Who's Chug-a-lug?" Martha asked.

"He own the store up there." Twiggy answered as she handed her .357 magnum to Slim. "Go put your piece inside Martha, ain't nobody gone fuck with you back here in The G."

"How you know I gotta gun?"

"Umm, you robbed the store last night, remember? I bet you don't go nowhere without your piece. You bold Martha, but you kind of forgetful." Twiggy said as she cracked a sly smile at the two sisters. "Come on, y'all need to get in tune about how things go back here in The G. We gone walk around for a little bit."

"We need to make some groceries." Mary sated.

"I'll take y'all later in my brother car, but come on, so y'all can know what's going on." Twiggy stated as she watched Martha run back into the house and stash her weapon. "And hey," she called out to Martha, "take that fancy ass coat off! This ain't Hollywood, this the 'hood!" she said as she and Slim burst into laughter. "Mary, keep your coat on, you fine, you gotta cover that belly! When you due?"

"Early June. I'm having twins."

"Damn! I see why Martha went all out! You eatin' for three sister!"

Martha came out of the house with only the torn blouse from

the night before on her arms so Twiggy ran and got her a blue hooded sweater and the two headed towards the corner store named *Tom Thumb's*, although everybody called the store Chug-a-lug's.

"Now," said Twiggy as she walked with Martha and Mary up Casper Drive, "back here in The G, we organized. No robbing, no stealing, no killing, unless they snitches or hooks."

"What's a hook? And The G?" Martha asked as Mary trailed the two, looking off in all directions.

Mary was looking at the different houses as she listened to Martha and Twiggy. She noticed some houses were low to the ground with a low porch and others were raised with a high porch. Some had nice flowers planted; some had trees in the front yard and all of the homes and yards were tidy. Mary liked the neighborhood. She imagined that she would plant herself a garden during the latter part of spring to beautify the landscape as she listened to Twiggy and Martha's conversation.

"The G is short for Ghost Town," Twiggy told Martha. "We call it that 'cause of the street names. This Casper Drive we on right now. Right beside y'all house is Friendly Lane. Casper runs all the way to White Street, and White Street curves to the left and runs dead into the canal back there. It's a big circle back there, a cul-de-sac what they call it. Another street shoots out to the right. That's Ghost Drive. Ghost Drive run right beside the woods into this white neighborhood. So you got Casper Drive, Friendly Lane, White Street and Ghost Street. You know Casper the friendly white ghost? All the streets back here are named after that ghost and that's how we come up with the name Ghost Town," Twiggy stated proudly. "Now," she continued, "a hook is our enemy and they wear red. They wear their hats to the left too. Folk wear our hats to the right and we wear blue. The word hook is a diss to Vice-Lords, our enemy; in turn they call us doughnuts. They have a five point star with an umbrella for their insignia. We got a six point star with a pitchfork." Twiggy stated as she used her thumb and first two fingers to form an E and then flipped it upside down to produce what looked like a pitchfork. "Hooks do this here," Twiggy then said as she held out her hand with all extremities held tightly together in the form of a five. She then stretched her fingers wide to 'blow up the five', which was another diss to Vice-Lords.

The three females walked into the empty corner store and eyed an over-weight black man sitting on a stool behind the counter. He was about 6' 7" tall and weighed well over three hundred pounds and was around twenty-five years of age, with a baby-like face and bald-headed.

"Chug-a-lug!" Twiggy yelled aloud. "I caught the robber from last night!"

Martha grew nervous and began to believe that she was being set up. She grabbed Mary and headed for the door quickly.

"Hold up y'all!" Twiggy said as she laughed at the twins.

Martha and Mary stood by the door. "What's this all about?" Martha asked.

"It's cool," Twiggy said. "Remember, if wanted to do something to ya', Martha, I coulda done it last night. It's cool for true. Come on, man. I'm serious, Folk." Twiggy beckoned. "Mary, we not gone hurt your sister. I promise."

Martha had Mary stand by the door and she walked over to the counter and stood before Chug-a-lug, who was already clued in on who had robbed his store because Twiggy had went up to the store after the police left and confirmed with the female cashier what she saw and believed—that a light-skinned female in white fur coat had robbed the store. Twiggy then called Chug-a-lug that same night after she had talked to Slim and told him who robbed him and that she would straighten things out. Twiggy knew Martha ran the serious risk of having a hit put out on her if Chug-a-lug had found out on his own who had robbed his store so she intervened on the twins' behalf. The two calls she'd made to Slim and Chug-a-lug had defused the tension that was arising in Ghost Town the night before, compliments of Martha.

Chug-a-lug was a top member of the Folk Gang also; although he ran a different part of Jackson known as The Queens. He supplied all of Ghost Town and The Queens with guns and drugs that were brought in from San Antonio, Texas. Chug-a-lug was the 'go to guy'. He sold pounds of marijuana and various types of fire arms right out of his store to gang members in Ghost Town during the day, so it was crucial that the heat get kept down as much as possible. Martha's robbery the night before had created a stir in Ghost Town, but it was slowly being defused in an organized manner.

Twiggy could have killed Martha the night before, but she had been watching both girls; she knew they had no furniture, because she had asked Slim just to confirm and he did. Twiggy figured the girls had no money; besides that, they were new to Ghost Town and weren't hip to the rules. When Martha didn't back down from Twiggy and explained why she had done what she had done, without apologizing for it, Twiggy made up her mind right then and there that Martha was all right and she had heart. Twiggy immediately took a liking to Martha and Mary at that moment because to her, Martha was bold and outspoken, like she, and she liked that about her. Twiggy couldn't help but to like Mary because she was just so sweet and humble.

Twiggy knew Chug-a-lug had lost almost a hundred dollars the night before and she had gotten her brother to agree to pay him back on this day. She then introduced Martha and Mary and told Chug-a-lug the twins were new to Ghost Town. "This one here kinda shy," Twiggy said as she pointed to Mary, who was still standing in the doorway with her hand on the handle, "how she got pregnant I don't know. Her name is Mary. Now, ole Martha here is the stick-up kid. She just didn't know. Can she get a pass?"

Chug-a-lug stared angrily at Martha as he sized her up. He was pissed she had robbed his store because nobody had ever fucked with his shit in that manner and got away with it. This young chick had heart, he had to admit, but she obviously didn't know what the deal was. And deep down, Chug-a-lug liked Martha; he also saw, like Twiggy, that she had heart. That, along with the fact that Twiggy was vouching for her, had earned Martha a reprieve. "This time," Chug-a-lug said as he stood up from his bar stool, his figure now towering over both Twiggy and Martha, "this time on the strength of your word, Twiggy? She get a pass. But I want my fuckin' money *today*—or I'm gone be pissed off all over again! I don't play that shit! And you know Folk don't do that back here in The G!" Chug-a-lug ended matter-of-factly as he stared angrily at Martha.

Twiggy agreed and had made the peace between Chug-a-lug, Martha and Mary. The three females then left the store and walked to Twiggy's house. When they got there, they saw Slim sitting on the porch of the tan-colored home talking to another black male named Albert Lee.

Albert Lee Charles was Twiggy's older brother. He was twenty years-old and stood an even 6' and weighed 170 pounds. He wore a huge Afro and had a neatly trimmed goatee and sported numerous Folk tattoos—six point stars on both arms, a pitchfork on the forearm and a huge three point crown on his back. He often wore a pair of sunshades over his eyes; although underneath the glasses were big round eyes identical to his younger sister Twiggy's eyes. Albert Lee nearly always sported a blue bandanna around his head just under his Afro and had six gold teeth in the top portion of his mouth, gold teeth he'd purchased from *First and Claiborne* dentistry down in New Orleans a year earlier.

Slim lit a joint and passed it to Albert Lee as the two men eyed the three females approaching the front porch. *Voo-Doo Child* by guitarist Jimi Hendrix could be heard blaring from the inside of Albert Lee's home as the females stepped into the yard.

"So y'all got that shit straight with Chug-a-lug?" Albert Lee asked Twiggy in his deep pitched-voice as he eyed the twins.

"Yeah. They was 'bouta run at first, but we all cool now. They all squared away with Chug-a-lug."

"You gotta lotta nerve, Martha. I respect what you did, tryna feed ya' sister and all, but I guess the two of y'all now know that The G don't operate like that. Right?"

"Yeah we know now," Martha replied, "but when ya' hungry —"

"You do what you gotta do." Albert Lee said as he finished

Martha's sentence.

"Right." Martha replied.

"Uncle Albert! Peter Paul won't let me watch Sesame Street!" a four year-old little boy yelled from behind the screen door.

"What the fuck I told you 'bout rattin' on mutherfuckas?" Albert Lee snapped as he held the weed in his hand and stared back at the little boy.

"He fuckin' me over up in here, man!" the little boy replied.

"Well you kick his ass and make him stop!" Albert Lee replied.

"He bigger than me!"

"You got a fuckin' problem nef!" Albert Lee said as coughed from the weed he inhaled and passed the joint back to Slim as the two men burst into laughter. The little boy ran back inside the house.

Mary and Martha looked at one another in surprise over the language used by Albert Lee and the little boy as they'd never heard such foul language coming from a child, let alone an adult speaking towards a child in the manner in which Albert Lee was speaking.

"Albert Lee! Albert Lee!" another voice then called from the house a few seconds later.

"See these li'l mutherfuckas here? They gone make me beat the fuck out 'em today! Shoulda sent they asses to school like I started to!" Albert Lee said angrily as he got up from his seat and walked into the house. He emerged a minute or two later with the little boy, and the older child in either hand, but he was now laughing.

"What happened?" Slim asked.

"Simon was 'bouta cut that mutherfucka! That's how ya' do nef! Size ain't shit!" Albert Lee said as he laughed aloud.

"Man, I woulda took that fuckin' knife! I ain't won't hurt that li'l nigga!" the older child stated as Albert Lee dragged both kids into the front yard.

The Holland Family Saga Part Five

"Fight!" Albert Lee yelled at the two kids as he knelt down at the foot of the stairs and grabbed the joint from slim.

The two kids looked at one another, both with their jaws clinched tight and their fists balled up. "Simon, swing on that mutherfucka! And Peter Paul don't let 'em do like he did last time! Watch for the upper cut!" Albert Lee said as everyone watched the kids size one another up in the front yard. "Y'all gone learn ta' get along or we gone do this shit everyday out here!"

The two boys stood toe to toe before nine year-old Peter Paul looked down at his nephew and said, "Go watch your fuckin' TV show," as he stepped aside and let Simon walk up the stairs.

Peter Paul knew he had the advantage over four year-old Simon and he didn't want to hurt his nephew. Albert Lee made the two dap each other off and they both went back into the house.

Twenty year-old Albert Lee was the top dog in Ghost Town. He and his brother Nolan started the Folk faction in Jackson, Mississippi three years ago, in 1974 when they came down from Chicago with their sister Irene 'Twiggy' Charles, who was fifteen at the time. Nolan was killed two years later, in 1976 and that left Albert Lee in charge of Ghost Town. Albert Lee also had to take over the caring of his nephew, four year-old Simon Charles, and his younger brother, nine year-old Peter Paul after Nolan was killed.

Albert Lee's parents were Folk members as well, but they were both serving life sentences in Illinois state prison for a quadruple homicide on four rival gang members back in Chicago. The Charles family had a violent reputation back home in Chicago and they brought those traits with them down south to Jackson, Mississippi. When Albert Lee turned seventeen, he and his then twenty-seven year-old older brother headed down to Jackson on orders of top leaders in Chicago and started the Folk Gang in Jackson, Mississippi. The Vice Lords soon followed and a gang war broke out that left Nolan, who was twenty-nine at the time, dead, and the top Vice Lord dead as well. Now, in 1977, the Folk Gang was under a newer, younger reign, 20 year-old Albert Lee Charles. Slim was second in command, and Twiggy controlled all the female gang members in Ghost Town.

Albert Lee earned money from selling weed in Ghost Town. That's why the situation with Martha had to be resolved quickly. Drug-selling was the only hustle permitted in Ghost Town, and whoever sold drugs, had to be a member of the Folk Gang.

Slim used his drug profits to buy the home Martha and Mary were residing in; money from marijuana was plentiful in the late seventies and Slim was smart enough to invest his earnings. Albert Lee was purely a gang-banger. He made enough money to buy his home and two cars, and support his family, and also had money stashed away, but money didn't matter to Albert Lee, the twenty year-old just loved being a part of the Folk Gang.

Albert Lee eyed Martha as he sucked down the weed he and Slim were smoking. She was sexy to him with her two thick plats she wore with her gleaming brown eyes and slim, curvy legs coupled with pert titties and a round bubble butt, and smooth, light-tan skin. Martha had been eying Albert Lee as well. She liked his neat Afro, the way he wore the bandanna, his muscle-toned tattooed physique and captivating smile along with his deep voice. She bit her bottom lip like a shy little girl, her hands tucked behind her back and standing in a prefect stance as she and Albert Lee smiled at one another, both shaking their heads up and down seductively.

"You still taking us to the food store?" Mary asked Twiggy, snapping the silence.

"Yeah, yeah. Albert Lee, let us use the Caprice to go make groceries."

Albert Lee went into his pocket and handed Twiggy the keys and watched as the three females walked towards the car, his eyes focused on Martha's delectable-looking ass.

"You got your eyes on Martha, huh, Folk?" Slim asked Albert Lee.

"Umm hmm! That's sexy right there, Slim." Albert Lee said as Martha stared back, smiling at him before she hopped into the car. "Welcome to Ghost Town, Martha and Mary." Albert Lee said aloud as Mary waved at him and Martha smiled sexily. "Welcome to Ghost Town."

The Holland Family Saga Part Five

CHAPTER 5

SETTLED IN

"Hey, Martha! Martha!" Twiggy yelled through the screen door into the twins' home the following day.

Martha came to the door and greeted Twiggy and invited her in and she looked around at the empty home for the first time and really felt for her new friends. They only had two milk crates in the living room and some blankets Slim had given them when they first moved into the place. "Martha," Twiggy said lowly, "y'all need furniture, sister."

"No shit, Twiggy!" Martha said as the two laughed.

"Serious shit though, my brother paid Chug-a-lug back yesterday and he said he don't want the money back. Albert Lee like you Martha, that's the only reason he did that shit for you. But a good move would be to at least show him the money and offer it to him, that way, you earn some street credibility around here."

"We spent the money on groceries yesterday, Twiggy. I ain't got nothing to give him right now."

"Yea, but that fur coat! Sell that coat in Ambush Alley for like $2000 and you can earn points with Albert Lee and have money for furniture. Anyway, the police looking for a female in a white fur coat back here. You don't really wanna be caught wearing that thing now—do you?"

Martha thought for a minute, she had hidden the diamond

bracelet in a secret spot inside the home. No one knew about that bracelet, and the coat, according to Twiggy was hot. The sisters did need money, so selling the coat wasn't a bad idea, and Martha saw right away that she could still hold on to the diamond necklace. She agreed with Twiggy's suggestion and went into her room and grabbed the coat off the shelf and came back and went into the kitchen where she eyed Mary making a sandwich. Besides not having furniture, the sisters had no cooking utensils; they couldn't even produce a meal, although the fridge was well stocked.

"Mary, me and Twiggy going take a walk right quick. You gone be okay?" Martha asked.

"Yeah. I'm just so *bored*! I wish I had a radio to listen to." Mary said as she spread mayonnaise onto her sandwich with her fingertips.

Once again, Martha eyed the appreciativeness within her sister. Mary didn't ask for a bed, a TV, or a sofa, she only wanted a radio so she could listen to music. Martha was further moved to earn money to furnish their home. She and Twiggy walked out the back door of the home on this cool afternoon and walked towards the back of Ghost Town which was White Street. As they headed towards White Street, Twiggy spoke to various people in the neighborhood, some sneered because they knew and believed Twiggy was trouble; others were friendly. The ones that sneered wanted no affiliation with the Charles family because they knew the family was populating the neighborhood with drugs, guns and gang activity.

"A lot of people back here act stuck-up, Martha—but fuck them! They really got some cool ass people back here in Ghost Town. Like this lady right here." Twiggy remarked as she waved at a young woman walking out of her yard holding a baby about one years-old. "Hey, Miss Green!"

"Twiggy, twig! What's up, Folk?" the woman said.

"Coolin'! This my friend Martha right here. Jesse! What's up li'l one?" Twiggy replied as she reached out and tugged one year-old Jesse's hand.

"Hello, Martha." Jesse's mother responded, then added, "I'll talk to you girls later! I gotta catch this bus downtown to the clinic to get Jesse his shots."

"That baby right there is named Jesse Green. I like that baby name, Martha. That's a gangster name. Jesse Green. They gotta lotta kids back here that's gone grow up with Mary twins." Twiggy said as she and Martha turned left onto White Street. "Like this one here. This my baby right here. Clark Junior!" Twiggy yelled as she and Martha stared at a baby boy sitting in a high chair at the foot of the stairs of the raised porch leading to the home that sat at least four feet off the ground.

Martha then eyed a young man cutting hair on the home's porch, that was somewhat hidden by two oak trees, and looked over to the little boy who was sitting in the high-chair smiling at Twiggy. Clark Junior was two years-old. The high-yellow-skinned baby had a head full of curly hair and a wide pretty smile.

"Gimmie that pacifier, boy! You know you too big for that shit!" Twiggy stated as she stopped in front the house's gate and threw up a pitchfork at the gang members, both male and female, that were hanging out on the on the porch. "What up Folk?" she yelled aloud.

"Twiggyyyy! Six in the house! Ghost Town! Blow that five up G-Queen," various gang members yelled aloud at random as they, too, produced pitchforks.

Just then, Clark Junior took the pacifier from his mouth and threw it at Twiggy.

"See there, Big C? He finish with that nook!" Twiggy said through laughter as she and Martha moved on down the block.

'Big C', or Clark Milton Senior was CJ's father. He was the neighborhood barber and also a ranking Folk gang member.

Martha had watched Twiggy speak to many people as they walked through the neighborhood, but she noticed Twiggy was especially nice to people who were receptive to Folk, or Folk Gang members themselves. Martha was beginning to see the big picture—Folk ran Ghost Town—and her new friend Twiggy was heavy into the gang lifestyle.

Twiggy and Martha continued on down the block to the end of White Street until it began to descend downhill, before long Martha found that she and Twiggy were walking on a sidewalk atop a six foot concrete wall that had subtly created a small valley where the street lay. Martha noticed that the wall beneath the side walk on the other side of the street was spray painted with much graffiti—blue six point stars, blue pitchforks, blue R.I.P. tags and exploding five point stars with names crossed out in red.

"This here the set!" Twiggy told Martha. "This right here is the ass end of Ghost Town. This our hustle spot."

The two females walked on the side walk atop the six foot wall with a blue painted railing and descended a pair of stairs and stepped onto White Street. There was a huge circular section to White Street at that point, a cul-de-sac. If you were staring at the cul-de-sac at the end of White Street, you could see where the canal running from Friendly Lane banked left and disappeared back into the woods. Where the concrete circle ended, over to one's right, a gravel road began. That road was Ghost Street.

Ghost Street was once the main entrance to Ghost Town, but as the neighborhood behind Ghost Town grew in size, the entrance became obsolete. The city had never bothered to repave the road, and Casper Drive became the main entrance into Ghost Town. That change worked in Folk's favor because the only people that used the dirt road now was people looking to score drugs. Twiggy and Martha then came upon four more Folk gang members to their left that were sitting underneath a huge oak tree in front of the thick mini forest that stretched from Friendly Lane to White Street. The four men were staring out at Ghost Street, which was a narrow gravel road bordered on the left by woods, and to the right by the last two houses in Ghost Town.

"They call this here Ambush Alley." Twiggy said lowly to Martha as she gave handshakes to the four gang members.

"Why they call this Ambush Alley?"

"My brother Nolan got killed right down that road." Twiggy

answered as she pointed to Ghost Street. "Nolan, he umm, he was, he and his girlfriend Wanda Charles, my brother was married to Wanda. Wanda is Simon momma, *was* Simon's momma, I mean. Anyway, Wanda and my brother was coming home one night last year in August. Nobody don't gang bang in that other neighborhood down there, it's mostly white people. So when it was late, Nolan used to ride in through the back way just in case some hooks was waiting for 'em up there by Dairy Queen. He rode through here, and some hooks was waiting on him. They jumped out from them woods on the left and shot Nolan car up and killed my brother and Wanda. Wanda and Nolan went out like Bonnie and Clyde. They got ambushed. Ever since then, this spot right here been called Ambush Alley, or just Ambush." Twiggy ended sadly.

"I'm sorry about your brother, Irene." Martha said lowly.

"Nahhh, fuck it! The hooks won the battle—but Folk won the war! It's been quiet ever since. And ain't nobody gone catch Folk slippin' like that again. That's why we always hang down here. You can see everything from here. 'Big C' on the block, and my brother got up front. This here is where we hustle. Anybody come up Ghost Street know they better be scoring, otherwise, they get murdered. You know them hooks had the nerve to try and pull that shit off again? We killed their leader right here in the same spot. We own this cut right here. The fuckin' police don't even ride up Ghost Street! If you ain't Folk, you gone get killed fucking around back here, understand?" Twiggy said as her voice hit an angry crescendo and she started to give the Folk Gang handshake to the each of the male gang members that were listening to her speak.

Martha nodded as Twiggy grabbed the white fur coat from her arms and began talking to the gang members, telling them that Martha wanted to sell the coat for $3000 dollars. The gang members told Twiggy and Martha to just sit and chill. Pimps often came through Ambush to score weed and they would be the top candidates to purchase the coat.

Twiggy and Martha waited for almost two hours for a pimp to show up and when a pimp did arrive on the scene, the two showed the man the coat. The man got out of his Jaguar, brushed his black mink coat free of lint with a mini-brush, grabbed hold of Martha's coat and said, "They should have a hat with this mutherfucka, right? My main bitch can't wear this shit if it ain't complete. It's slick, but I need the hat. My bitch like to dress to the fullest extent possible," the short, muscular pimp said as he stared at Twiggy and Martha.

"I got the hat at home. Let me go get it!" Martha said as she took off running towards Casper Drive.

"I'm a go get it!" Twiggy yelled, causing Martha to stop in her tracks.

Martha watched as Twiggy handed the coat to the pimp, eyed her for a few seconds and then went over to the gang bangers and spoke a few whispered words. She then took off running through the woods back towards Friendly Lane. "This a short cut, Martha! You don't know about this yet but I'm a show you when I get back!" she yelled as she disappeared from sight.

Martha saw the whole play and she now figured she was being set-up for robbing Chug-a-lug two days earlier and she was not about to be taken advantage of in Ambush. If anybody tried something stupid, she was prepared to fight for what was hers. She stood beside the pimp's Jaguar, waiting cautiously, expecting the worse, having to shoot somebody.

When Twiggy disappeared from sight, Martha watched and listened as one of the gang members asked to see the coat that the pimp held onto. When he handed the coat over, the Folk members began to mishandle Martha's pristine fur. The gang members were holding the coat out in the open admiring the luxurious artifact and Martha saw that her coat was getting closer to the ground. She walked over and stood amongst the men with her hands tucked inside her hooded sweater and watched the young men for a minute until she realized that they were going to ruin her coat and prevent her from making the sale. She got upset and snatched the coat from the gang members.

"The fuck is your problem?" a gang member asked as he eyed Martha coldly.

"You 'bouta get my coat dirty! If he gone buy it, it shouldn't be dirty!"

All four gang members then walked towards Martha, but she didn't flinch. The young man holding the coat at the out-set snatched it back from Martha and then trotted over to the canal and waved the coat over the canal's water. The pimp was getting ready to leave until Martha said,. "Hold up, man! That's my shit and he ain't gone fuck over my shit! Gimmie my fuckin' coat mutherfucka!"

"The fuck you gone do bitch?"

"This right here, mutherfucka!" Martha snapped as she pulled out her .38 snub-nose and pointed it at the young man. "Now hand me my shit!"

The young man laughed just as Twiggy burst back down from the trail she had just run up holding the hat to Martha's coat. "Eh, Twiggy! Martha got *plenty* heart!" the foot soldier said as he handed Martha her coat. "Don't point that fuckin' gun at me again though, twin!" he then stated seriously as he sat back down beside his comrades.

Martha then realized she had been tested—and she'd passed.

"Don't worry 'bout it, Martha! Y'all don't fuck with my friend like that no more! She in with me now, Folk!" Twiggy said to the gang members as she grabbed the coat and she and Martha walked over and stood beside the pimp's 1977 white-on-white Jaguar where they sold the coat for $2500 dollars.

Martha, getting in tune with the way things went in Ghost Town, gave Twiggy $500 dollars right away. "Thanks, Martha. Look, let me show you this trail right here. It's a short cut back to Friendly Lane and y'all house." Twiggy stated as she and Martha walked towards the trail.

The girls exited the woods on Friendly Lane and went over to see Albert Lee where Martha repeatedly demanded that he take the $100 dollars she owed him until Albert Lee reluctantly accepted. Twiggy and Martha then took Albert's Cadillac and headed downtown to Sears. Mary was sitting on the porch reading over her social benefits packet when she looked up and saw Twiggy and Martha riding off in Albert Lee's Cadillac with *I Wanna Be Free*, by the Ohio Players blaring across the eight track player.

"We be right back, Mary! Stay right there!" Martha yelled over the music as Twiggy drove the car up Casper Drive passed the twins' home towards the main drag.

Mary wondered what Martha and Twiggy were up to this day. The two had been running around the neighborhood for a while and now they were riding off somewhere. Hoping the two weren't getting into trouble, she got up and went back inside to wipe down walls and counters, the only thing she had to do around the house really besides staring at the walls. She was wiping the windows a couple of hours later when she saw Martha and Twiggy pull up in front the house with huge cardboard boxes strapped down to the slightly opened trunk. She could also see large boxes on the back seat. Albert Lee and Slim walked over and helped Twiggy and Martha unload the items, and when Mary saw the Panasonic name on side one of the boxes, she screamed with delight. Martha had gotten her a component set complete with double cassette player, two fifteen inch house speakers, a turntable, a set of pots and pans, dinnerware and silverware.

Mary, Twiggy and Martha washed and placed the cooking and eating utensils into the cabinets while Albert Lee and Slim hooked up the sound system. Albert Lee then went and got Mary some albums from his collection so she could have something to jam to. Mary, who loved music, hugged Albert Lee's neck and thanked him. She cried as she hugged Twiggy and repeatedly hugged and thanked Martha for what she had done. "You the best sister in the world. This is all I ever wanted Martha. Thank you. Now I can cook for us and sing to Rene and Regina."

"Mary, you named the babies?" Twiggy asked excitedly.

"Yes. I been had their names picked. Y'all like those names?" Mary responded as she picked up an album, pulled it out of its cover and placed it onto the turntable.

"Yeah. Who will be Regina and who will be Rene?" Martha asked.

The Holland Family Saga Part Five

"Good question. I thought about that too, Martha! Whoever arrives first shall be Regina, her sister is Rene." Mary said proudly. "Let's see how the stereo sounds." she then said excitedly as she put the needle on *The Wind Cries Mary* by Jimi Hendrix.

It was a good day for the Holland twins. Mary had used her cooking utensils later on in the night and prepared fried pork chops, gravy and rice and sweet peas and she, Martha, Twiggy, Albert Lee and Slim sat on the front porch and ate. Neither Twiggy, Albert Lee, nor Slim had ever tasted such flavored pork chops and thick, dark gravy. The meal was fantastic, even the sweet peas were sugared to perfection. They all complimented Mary on her cooking as they enjoyed the sweet sounds coming from the new component set as they drank cold beer from Chug-a-lug's.

Things around the house in Ghost Town got even better the next day when Martha and Twiggy took Mary furniture shopping. She was given full control over the decoration of she and her twin's home and she delivered. Within two days of Martha selling the white fur coat, the twins' home had a color TV, a black velvet sofa and love seat in the living room with an ebony-wood coffee table that matched the component set and a gold-trimmed three piece mirror set on the wall. The kitchen now had eating utensils, pots and pans and plates to eat off, along with a four-chair wooden dinette set. Two of the bedrooms had full sized beds, and the other had a bunk bed set and two cribs that was paid for by Twiggy, Albert Lee and Slim. The bathroom was neatly done in cream and white and had two fresh ivory plants hanging from the ceiling. Mary had also qualified for food stamps and welfare the day after she and Martha turned eighteen and some of that money was used to help furnish the house. In a month's time, thanks to Twiggy's help, the twins, at age eighteen had finally settled into Ghost Town.

The Holland Family Saga Part Five

CHAPTER 6

THE DAY THE TWINS WERE BORN

"Chug-a-lug! Push the mutherfucka up over the sill!" Albert Lee yelled through a strained voice as he held a tight grip on a huge A/C unit inside Mary and Martha's living room. Albert Lee and Chug-a-lug were installing an air conditioner for eighteen year-olds Martha and Mary on this warm sunny morning in late June of '77.

"I'm pushing, Folk!" Chug-a-lug strained as Martha stepped into the living room and assisted Albert Lee.

"Put some more ass in it, Chug! What you big for?" Albert Lee remarked as Chug-a-lug grunted and pushed the unit over the sill. "There ya' go, big man. Move back Martha and let me screw it in," Albert Lee then said, a phrase that made Martha blush as she stepped aside.

Twiggy came out of her home at that moment and eyed Chug-a-lug outside the twins' living room window on side the house. She then spotted Mary in the front yard wearing her leather coat planting flower seeds. "Hey," she yelled out. "Take that hot ass coat off, sister! It's June, Mary! Everybody know you pregnant so stop tryna hide that shit!"

Mary smiled and waved, and Twiggy went over to greet her. "What the hell you doing in that hot ass cow skin?"

"I don't know! I just like this coat, Twiggy."

"You like heat strokes too? You gone damn die out here."

Mary laughed as Twiggy removed the coat and complimented her on how beautiful she looked as a mother-to-be while assisting Mary with the planting of her seeds. Mary was planting four 'o' clocks. She told Twiggy that when the flowers bloom, they would open their petals in the evening, around four 'o' clock. Twiggy didn't believe Mary so they made a bet. Twiggy wanted Mary's leather coat, Mary wanted some of Twiggy's Beatles' albums as she was a huge rock and roll fan. The two were shaking hands on the bet when they heard Martha scream Mary's name.

Twiggy thought something was wrong so she quickly ran up the stairs and entered the house. Mary sat her bucket of seeds down and followed. *"Thanks for making sure I was okay, Irene,"* she said to herself with a slight chuckle as she slowly walked up the stairs. When Mary entered the living room, she saw Martha standing in front of the TV beside Chug-a-lug.

"Mary? Naomi still alive!" Martha said as she stared at a burning saw mill.

Mary looked at the TV and saw the burning building and said, "How you know Naomi did that?"

"Mary? That fire is in Sylacauga, Alabama. Naomi told us if she could, she would burn down that whole city. Sylacauga? I remember that! It's in the journal remember?" Martha said as she ran to the hall closet and grabbed the journal and flipped through the pages and read aloud, "For what they did to us, if I could, I would burn that whole town. But I'm only eight and I can't do it all by myself. Not now anyhow. Someday, I will make them pay." Martha ended.

"That could just be an accident, Martha." Mary said. "Fires are common. And it's a saw mill, wood burns easily. Naomi said nothing about a saw mill in the journal."

"I don't know. I just got a feeling, Mary. Our sister done that right there. She still out there." Martha said as her eyes welled up. "I wish ta' God I knew where she was y'all."

"Let me see those papers." Chug-a-lug said as he reached for the pages Martha held.

The Holland Family Saga Part Five

"No!" Mary and Martha yelled out in unison.

"Naomi said not to let nobody read it but us. We gone obey that request." Martha said as she wiped tears.

Twiggy rubbed her friend's back to console her and said, "Okay, Mar. We cool on that. Mary, go put that up for your sister, please?"

"Who's Naomi?" Chug-a-lug asked.

"Weren't you listenin'? Naomi is our big sister, Chug." Martha stated proudly.

"Big sister? Y'all ain't got no big sister!"

Martha turned to Chug-a-lug and yelled in a loud angry voice, "We do got a sister! Her name Naomi! You don't know our whole story, boy! We got a fuckin' sister! A big sister named Naomi! And a li'l brother named Sam! And even if Naomi didn't start the fire, we still got a big sister and younger brother! You don't know all what we been through! That's what Naomi said! She said we gotta younger brother named Sam and if she could she would burn Sylacauga down for what they did to us! I believe what my sister said! And I believe she burned that saw mill, or whatever the fuck it is! You don't know us," Martha said as she cried and stared at Chug-a-lug. "You don't know all that happened to us," she said lowly. "Fuck!" she yelled. "We don't even know what the fuck happened to us! Why the fuck we here and not with our family? I hate this shit!"

Martha then took off running through the kitchen and out the back door and sat on the stairs and placed her head in her lap and cried aloud. Twiggy immediately came out and sat beside her and said nothing at first. She'd heard the story about how the twins were adopted and ran away from the Jacobs family from Martha, but that was about all she knew. Just like Martha and Mary, Twiggy had not a clue what happened early on the twins' life that had landed them in a foster home. All she knew was that they were now a part of Ghost Town, but through it all, she believed Martha to the fullest. "Hey, fuck what Chug say, Martha," Twiggy finally said. "You know how that boy be trippin' and shit. He think everything funny. But you know, and I believe it too, that you got a sister and a brother. But Martha, we family right now. I swear on everything I love, I really hope you find your brother and sister someday. I'll, I'll even help you find her if that's what you wanna do, but for now we right here, and you and Mary? Y'all gotta survive right now sister." Twiggy said as Martha fell onto her shoulder and sobbed.

"We got people out there and they don't even *know* us! They don't know us Irene! That shit hurt, but I love them—even if they don't know me, that's my folk, just like everybody back here, y'all my folk." Martha ended as Albert Lee's voice rang out from inside the house.

Martha wiped her face and entered the home and Twiggy followed close behind. When they entered the living room, they saw Mary stretched out on the sofa holding her stomach. Seeing Martha get upset had caused Mary to become distressed and she was now going into labor. Mary was panting as she stretched her hands out to Martha. Twiggy grabbed the phone and dialed the operator as Martha grabbed her sister's hands and sat beside her. The operator became unfriendly when Twiggy gave Martha and Mary's address. Twiggy, in turn, cursed the woman out and slammed the phone down. "They ain't comin' back here! We gotta take Mary to the hospital!" she said before she ran out the house.

Everyone else was puzzled as to what to do. Mary was still panting, she was sweating even though the air was on; she then grimaced in pain as her water bag burst. Martha ran into the bathroom and wet a towel and placed it on Mary's head just as she heard a car horn blowing furiously—it was Twiggy. She exited her brother's car and ran onto the porch and said, "Come on, man! She 'bouta have the twins! Albert Lee! Chug! Pick Mary up and put her in the car!" she yelled as Martha ran and grabbed Mary's overnight bag and rushed back to the car.

By then, Albert Lee and Chug-a-lug had carried Mary outside and placed her on the back seat. Albert Lee was about to get behind the wheel, but Twiggy shoved him aside and said, "This girls only, Albert Lee! When Martha have your baby then you can come!"

The Holland Family Saga Part Five

The baby twins came into the world on June 22, 1977. The first born was Regina, the second child was named Rene, just as Mary had requested. These two were not only identical, they were exact replicas of one another. In the beginning, only Mary could distinguish the two, but Martha would pick up on their identity over the months spent with the babies, and she taught Twiggy how to discern the difference. Everyone else would have to be told which was which. A new generation within the Holland family had come into existence in June of 1977, bringing much joy to Martha, and Mary Holland, who now found herself a mother of two daughters at age eighteen.

The Holland Family Saga Part Five

CHAPTER 7

THE DAY MARTHA GOT MADE

"He wear no shoeshine—he got toe-jam football...he got monkey finger—he shoot Coca-Cola...he say I know you—you know me...one thing I can tell you is you got to be free...come together right now—over me..."

The Beatles' song *Come Together* blared across Mary's component set on a warm spring day in late June of '78. The newborn twins were now a year old. Regina and Rene, or Dimples and Ne`Ne` as they were now called, were beautiful babies. Caramel skinned with thick, jet black coarse hair, beauty marks under their left eye, pouty lips and slender, dark eyes. Even at an early age, Mary could tell that her kids were going to be hairy just like she and Martha.

Regina and Rene Holland had slight hair on their arms in their young age and their black hair contrasted with their caramel skin. Martha and Twiggy had nicknamed the babies a few months after they were born. Regina Holland, known as Dimples, earned that name from Martha because she smiled a lot and produced the cutest dimples that were more profound than Rene's dimples. That was the secret to telling the twins apart—their dimples.

Rene Holland, or Ne`Ne` (Nay-Nay) got her nick-name from Twiggy; it was merely a repeat of the last syllable of her name. Dimples and Ne`Ne` were adored throughout Ghost Town. Mary, Martha and Twiggy would always take them out in their strollers during the warm months and everyone would run up and greet the two adorable baby girls. Mary and Martha were unique to Ghost Town as they were the only twins back there; they were doubly unique throughout the whole community since Mary had borne identical twins herself. People just simply liked Martha, Mary, Dimples and Ne'Ne'.

"Hey, Mary? How long we gone have ta' listen to the Beatles? You won the bet! Let it go, sister," nineteen year-old Twiggy said as she shook Regina and Rene's hands as the twins sat inside their rockers in the living room of nineteen year-olds Martha and Mary's home.

"Don't get upset, Twiggy. You didn't believe me when I told you about the flowers and this is the price you have to pay whenever you come over here."

"I like the Beatles too, but you making it hard for me. At least give me some time to miss their songs before you play 'em again. I shoulda known by the name of them flowers that you was telling the truth. That's what I get for dropping out of high school." Twiggy said. "You babies ain't be gone be stupid like your auntie Twiggy now is ya'?" she then referenced herself as she continued playing with Regina and Rene.

"You not stupid, Twiggy." Mary responded. "Hey, me and Martha enrolling in this G.E.D. program in August, and in three months we can have our high school diploma. You should join us."

"That might work for y'all, but believe me, I quit school 'cause I hated it! Just hated it! Nahh, you and Martha do that. I'll baby sit the twins."

"Thank you, Twiggy. You want a sandwich or something?"

Twiggy accepted and the two continued chatting as they sat in the living room and ate their ham and cheese sandwiches.

Martha, meanwhile, was in her room getting dressed, having just taken a shower. During this period of time, Martha had come to realize that she and Mary were getting into a bind. With the twins coming into existence the bills were adding up. Mary had gotten an increase in food stamps, and welfare as well, but the sisters were barely scraping by. Martha had used all her money to furnish the house, now she was broke to the point that she had to get money from Albert Lee and Twiggy to give her nieces and Mary a Christmas back in '77.

Now, in June of '78, after many restless nights trying to decide what to do, Martha had resorted back to an old skill—she began selling marijuana—in Ambush. Mary's welfare check was getting the sisters by, and the food stamps kept their bellies full, but the family wasn't making progress. If her babies needed clothing, Mary would have to skip a bill. Whenever Martha needed something, Mary would purchase it for her. Mary would do anything she could for Martha; she would give her whatever money she had, even if it was her last. The two sisters were just that close. Mary cared deeply for Martha and she never forgot how she had taken care of her and protected her when they were at the Jacobs home and how she led the way when they got to Ghost Town. Now, Mary was the one looking out for the entire household, and she never once viewed Martha as a burden.

Martha on the other hand, wanted to help out around the house; she never said a word to anyone about her feelings, but the truth was, Martha was beginning to view *herself* as a burden on Mary. Having made her decision, she borrowed money from Twiggy the week before her nieces turned one and purchased an ounce of marijuana and sold it in three days. She had to wait another week to buy another one, but in the meantime, she had helped finance her nieces' first birthday party. Mary never asked where Martha got the money, but she didn't have to, she knew Martha was selling marijuana in Ambush, everybody did; but unbeknownst to Martha, she was treading dangerous grounds.

It was during the attendance of Dimples and Ne'Ne's birthday party that a decision was made about Martha's weed venture. Twiggy and Albert Lee knew what she had been up to over the past week, just as well as everyone else. Twiggy was all right with what Martha was doing, and as lead G-Queen, she could prevent other G-Queens from harming Martha; but Albert Lee was over the whole neighborhood and he knew he had to put a stop to Martha's actions. She had done a lot of violating of the rules in Ghost Town, but because Albert Lee and Twiggy more than liked her, she often got a pass; but selling marijuana was the last straw for Albert Lee. He ordered a 'jump in' on Martha, and that meant that Twiggy would have to fight her before she could be acknowledged as a bona fide Folk member.

Albert Lee felt he had no choice because Martha was operating all on her own, violating one of the major rules that Nolan had instituted in Ghost Town at its inception—only Folk members could sell drugs in Ghost Town. Martha was breaking one of the highest laws in Ghost Town and was in danger and didn't know it. Albert Lee was trying to resolve the situation before it got out of hand. He didn't want to have to argue with Martha and be thrust onto an opposing side and the young man believed he was making the right decision for everyone involved when he ordered the 'jump in'.

Twiggy liked Martha as well. She didn't want to fight her friend and she pleaded with Albert Lee not to go through with what he was asking. "Just let me tell her to stop selling in Ambush, Albert Lee." Twiggy requested as she and her brother conversed in the backyard of Martha and Mary's home as they attended the twins' first birthday party.

"Look here Irene, Martha trying' ta' survive. She don't wanna hear about no rules. I know that girl, and I know she not gone obey orders—unless she a Folk." Albert Lee remarked.

Albert Lee and Martha got along well, he liked her, and Martha liked Albert Lee, but taking care of her family came first for Martha. Albert Lee knew of that fact. Martha had no time for rules; neither twin did. And Martha was only trying to survive; she didn't want to have to sleep around to earn money because that wasn't her style. She had no diploma, so a job opportunity was scarce, and she saw no wrong in selling a little weed to get on her feet. Mary was busy raising her kids. Frequent trips to the doctor, meetings with her social worker and attending various workshops for welfare recipients kept her busy as well; survival was of the essence. Albert Lee reflected on those things and spoke again, "Martha ain't got time, neither them sisters got time to be tryin' ta' listen to Folk rules Irene, but if she get made, Martha can hustle. It's the best way and the only way."

Twiggy then reflected on the past events that had transpired with Martha. She had robbed Chug-a-lug and got a pass from her. She drew down on foot soldiers in Ambush over her coat and she got off for that, and now she was selling weed in Ambush without permission and the worst Albert Lee was willing to do was 'jump her in'. Anybody else would have been dead, no matter who they were. "Look man, we both love Martha. She like family Albert Lee and she really like you and you like her as well. You should just tell her to stop then. Martha cool, she might listen to you."

"If Martha don't stop, I gotta order a hit on her, Irene. And you gone be the one to have to do it. I been knowing Martha for over a year and I like her, understand? I don't wanna kill her, but I can't risk my reputation by letting her get away with this shit, Twiggy, and you know that."

"Do you like her for true?"

"I do. But rules is rules. You gotta move on Martha next time she step off in Ambush. That's an order."

"Albert Lee," Twiggy said lowly as she and her brother continued to discuss the situation, "that's my fuckin girl, man. And you askin' me to do this shit here?"

"You jump all the females in you know that."

"Yea, but Albert Lee? I was never close to the other girls like that. Martha like the sister I never had. She get involved with this gang shit man, and, I don't know Albert, this shit with Martha different."

"You right, it is different. Martha should be dead and you know it. You almost killed her yourself. What you think the rest of Ghost Town gone do, Irene? So before the gangsters back here decide to hurt her bad, this is the answer, 'cause Martha ain't gone stop. She just like you, she do whatever the fuck she want to *when* she want to. She can't keep breaking the rules. If another Folk wanna earn stripes, Martha would be the first to get took out for the simple fact she not Folk. Making her a member gone keep all that from happening. Now do you understand why I'm asking you to do this shit here, Irene? If she like a sister, help me rectify this shit with Martha and keep her ass around." Albert Lee said seriously as he stared down at his sister.

Twiggy was loyal to Folk Gang. She knew the rules as well, but jumping Martha in was not something she really wanted to do because she knew the consequences; but hearing Albert Lee speak on it put things under a different light. The last thing Twiggy wanted to see was Martha get hurt, because if anybody, Folk member or not, hurt Martha, she would retaliate. Albert Lee was right, to prevent "all that from happening", Twiggy knew she would have to jump Martha in.

Twiggy knew Martha had heart, and if she passed this final test, she would rapidly excel in the ranks. Somewhat apprehensive, but hopeful, Twiggy agreed to 'jump in' Martha. "Next time she out there, me and the other G-Queens got her Albert Lee." Twiggy stated lowly as she shook Albert Lee's hand in Folk tradition which was the sliding of the fingers together to form one pitchfork with both members right hands entwined.

Twiggy thought back to that day as she sat and listened to the Beatles as she played with Regina and Rene. She bit into her sandwich and watched as 5' 9" 140 pound, nineteen year-old Martha, with her thick black hair braided to the back, dressed in a pair of black jeans, white tank top, and a pair of black clods, walked through the living room and entered the kitchen, kissed Mary good-bye and walked out the back door.

Twiggy knew where Martha was headed this day. She had been watching her ever since the birthday party the week before. Martha had scored a half pound of weed from Chug-a-lug the night before so Twiggy knew she was headed straight to Ambush. Albert Lee had given the order, and Twiggy now had to fulfill it. She smiled down at Dimples and Ne`Ne`, knowing she was about to inflict bodily injury upon their aunt, and then announced to Mary that she had to go, knowing Mary's twin, and the fate of the Holland family's survival in Ghost Town all hinged upon what Mary's sister would do when confronted with a form of animosity neither twin had ever encountered.

Martha made her way through the wooded trail on Friendly Lane and exited on White Street and posted up in Ambush. Folk members were around, but word had already spread that Martha was to get 'moved on' the next time she stepped off into Ambush. Before word got around about Martha, Folk members were always friendly, but on this day, she noticed the cold shoulder she was receiving. She brushed it off as she began making a few weed sales from customers that knew her and liked the weed she sold.

An hour later as Martha stood alone just in front the wooded trail leading back to Friendly Lane scoping the scene, she looked to her right and eyed Twiggy and five other females descending the stairs from the side walk on White Street walking her way. Twiggy was dressed in a pair of blue Lee jeans, black tank top, and black boots with her hair done in Afro puffs. She also wore a blue bandanna around her neck and blue lipstick and black eye-liner. Both her wrists were clad with gold cuff-link bracelets, signifying that she was lead G Queen in Ghost Town. The other females, in their late teens and early twenties, were dressed the same as Twiggy minus the gold cuff-link bracelets. A few had large Afros with blue bandannas tied around their foreheads. Twiggy and the other female Folk members, or 'G Queens' as they were called, were in their war gear. They shook hands with the other male gang members as everyone, even Twiggy, stared coldly at Martha.

Martha stared back at Twiggy. She knew not to smile as the look on her face told her this wasn't a social call.

"What's up, Twiggy?" Martha asked as she eyed the six females approaching her.

"You violating! That's what's up!"

"Violating? Violating what?"

"The rules in Ghost Town!"

"And what that mean?"

Twiggy didn't answer Martha. She just walked up to her and

pushed her hard, forcing her back into the brush at the foot of the trail. Martha quickly jumped up and said, "Twiggy, what you doing? I thought we was friends!"

"Just fight, Martha!" Twiggy said, her fists balled tightly as she stared at her friend with watery eyes.

"I don't wanna fight you, Twiggy." Martha stated lowly.

"It's the only way! Fight me, Martha!"

"No! You supposed to be my friend! What's all this shit?"

"I'm sorry." Twiggy stated lowly as she went and hugged Martha.

Martha hugged Twiggy back and she closed her eyes and cried softly because she knew if Martha didn't fight her on this day, the next time Martha sold weed in Ambush, this scenario would play out again, only the next time, she would have to kill Martha. Twiggy didn't have a gun on her this day, and she did not want the day to come when she would have to pay Martha a final visit. Twiggy knew she had to force Martha to fight her so she pushed her away from her and swung and hit Martha in the face.

Martha fell down again and quickly got up and charged at Twiggy. No one could see it, but Twiggy began smiling on the inside at that moment because Martha was actually fighting her back. She would not lose her friend, but now, it was really time to get down to business. The two females squared off and Martha landed a blow to Twiggy's right eye and it caused her to stumble a little bit. With one eye closed, Twiggy and Martha squared off again. This time, Twiggy hit Martha in her face in the same spot as before and it quickly swelled. The fight was a wild furious one, with Martha landing blows to Twiggy's face and Twiggy striking Martha in the face and upper torso. Martha stepped back a little and grabbed Twiggy by the hair and hit her in the back of the head and Twiggy fell to one knee. Martha stopped swinging and asked was Twiggy okay through heavy gasps of breath, but before Twiggy answered, the other five females jumped on Martha.

Once again Martha began to swing. She'd dished out a black

eye and a bloody mouth, but she was heavily outnumbered this go around. A blow to her left jaw gave her weak legs and she started to back-peddle towards the center of the cul-de-sac as she continued to fight with the five females. The G Queens surrounded Martha and took turns pounding her all over her body, jumping in and out of the mix at random until Martha could fight no more. The blows she received had weakened and bruised her badly and she was now feeling the pain. She fell to her knees and the G Queens began punching and kicking her, forcing her down on the concrete. They were steadily kneeling down to punch her in the body and kicking her at random until Twiggy, who stood by watching for several minutes, jumped in and began shoving the five females away from Martha.

"That's enough! That's it! She in! She in!" Twiggy yelled as she shoved the females away and quickly grabbed Martha and stood her up and hugged her friend tightly. "I'm sorry, sister. I'm sorry, Martha." she said lowly as she hugged her tightly.

Martha asked through tears, "Why you doing this to me? What did I *do*?"

"You got made, Martha. You just got made. You may not understand, but I had ta' do this." Twiggy responded.

The other five females surrounded Twiggy and Martha as the two friends embraced, five male Folk members came nearer the scene as well and everybody were awaiting Twiggy's signal. As Martha gripped Twiggy's body for support and cried on her shoulder, Twiggy gripped Martha's back tightly with her left arm and slowly raised her right arm and made a pitchfork with her fingers. She placed her cheek tightly against Martha's, closed her eyes, and with her back turned to most of the gang members she said aloud, "This Martha Holland, Folk Nation member, G-Queen foot soldier, factioned to Ghost Town."

The other gang members began to slowly clap and walk up and hug Martha and show her much love, for showing much heart on this day. Twiggy then took the battle weary Martha home. As they walked through the wooded trail towards the house, Twiggy explained why she had one what she done on this day and Martha quickly understood. She was now a gang member, but she would rather that, than running the risk of being killed by gang members in Ghost Town, who were now her allies. When the two entered Martha's home, Mary could see that they were both bruised. She ran over to her sister and sat her on the couch and said, "What happened? What happened to my sister, Irene?"

Twiggy knew not what to say, but Martha spoke up. "I'm all right, Mary. I got jumped and Twiggy helped me."

Mary covered the lower part of her face. She knew what went on in Ghost Town when people got jumped. "You with Albert Lee 'nem? You a gang member?" she asked in surprise. "Twiggy why you do that my sister?"

"I wanted in, Mary. You know I sell weed back here. I just got made to sell weed and earn a little money that's all."

"That's gone lead to other things, Martha. I'm worried about you."

"I'll be fine. I just sell a little weed that's all. I promise."

"That's all you gone do? You not gone kill people?"

"I promise. Unless somebody try and kill me."

"Them hooks might try anyway, just because." Mary stated worriedly.

Martha and Twiggy then laughed. To hear Mary use street terminology tickled the two.

"I'm serious y'all."

"Girl, hooks don't come in Ghost Town no more. I'm gone be fine, Mary. I promise nothing ain't gone happen." Martha ended as she got up to take a shower.

Twiggy went home to clean up as well and told Albert Lee Martha had got made that day. Albert Lee was overjoyed. Now, he would take Martha and make her his woman. The two became intimate in the winter of '78 after she and Mary received their G.E. D.'s and they were going strong as the summer of '79 got underway.

CHAPTER 8

A WALK ON THE WILD SIDE

Albert Lee was throwing a huge block party for his 22nd birthday on this hot summer's day in July of '79. House parties were common place in Ghost Town. Martha and Mary had a large 20th birthday party a few months back in March, and Dimples and Ne`Ne` had their 2nd year party a month earlier. The people in Ghost Town knew how to celebrate. On this hot sunny day in July of '79, the sun was out and there wasn't a cloud in the sky. The weather was hot and the neighborhood was filled with the sounds of children playing. Mary's component set, blaring *Strawberry Letter 22* by the Brothers Johnson, and laughter from young adults that hung out by each other's house smoking weed and cigarettes and drinking cold beer and *Thunder Bird* wine, could be heard throughout the area surrounding the twins' home. The whole day was filled with music, bar-b-cue, and football games held on Friendly Lane beside Martha and Mary's house as very few cars traveled that street.

Kids were running up and down Casper Drive in front of twins' home. Eleven year-old Peter Paul and six year-old Simon wore boxing gloves and were sparring in Albert Lee's front yard with other kids in the neighborhood and Mary had prepared a pot of chicken dumplings that had everyone talking. Two year-olds Dimples and Ne`Ne` were in their yard beside their house playing with their ABC squares as four year-old

Clark Junior, and three year-old Jesse Green ran around the twins' yard chasing a football that bounced about. Mary, dressed in a tight pair of white jean shorts, white and black striped blouse and a black pair of sandals with a two inch heel, played with her daughters, Clark, and Jesse, throwing the football and watching as the two kids chased the ball around in the yard.

People were out in front Albert Lee's home as well, but most were on side and in front of the twins' home as word had gotten around about the tasty chicken and dumplings Mary had cooked. The young males in the neighborhood, although they wanted the dumplings, had other reasons for asking Mary to fix them a plate of food. Mary was looking gorgeous this day. She was turning heads and raising eye brows. Her hair was braided to the back neatly and she wore black lip and eye-liner. Martha was credited with Mary's transformation and the young males in Ghost Town were quickly taking notice.

Martha had been selling weed for over a year and whenever she went shopping, she took Mary and her nieces with her. Martha was careful not to buy Mary attire that may be mistaken for gang apparel. In the past, Martha and Mary always wanted to be indistinguishable, but now that Martha was a member of Folk Nation, she knew it would be best if people could easily distinguish the two. Mary wanted to live a little as well. Dimples and Ne`Ne` were now at the point to where they could sleep through the whole night and Mary now had time to explore her sexual side.

After almost three years of celibacy, having had intercourse only one time, twenty year-old Mary's body craved attention. There were quite a few young men in Ghost Town, but to Mary, most were too rugged, too immature or insincere in their endeavors. A select few of the young men did peak her curiosity, however; one in particular was twenty-three year-old Clark Senior. Clark and Mary talked and formed a rapport during Dimples and Ne`Ne`s second birthday a month ago where Mary learned that Clark was single, and raising his child on his own and taking care of his mother, who was stricken with diabetes and had gotten hurt on her job. Those responsibilities gave Clark a level of maturity that was above most of the males in Ghost Town in Mary's eyes.

To Mary, Clark was strong, handsome and honest. She knew he didn't want a steady woman in his life, and she wasn't ready for a steady relationship either; but Clark had stated to her that he didn't mind keeping her company, if that is what she wanted. Clark put the ball in Mary's court and left the decision up to her and it was a good move on his part because Mary had now chosen a lover for herself. Clark was a little taller than Mary; brown-skinned with nice muscle tone and a neatly trimmed goatee, and to Mary, he had the most sexiest pair of lips she had ever seen on any man. The two had been talking off and on all month long and the day of Albert Lee's party found the two laughing and gently tapping one another's arms and shoulders, their eyes both saying to one another, "*if only we were alone*".

Twiggy noticed the two and she thought it was funny. Clark was a lover boy type, Twiggy knew that to be a fact and she told Mary so as she stood beside her watching her throw the football. Mary told Twiggy she already had the info on Clark and she was fine with it because she didn't want any attachments either; she just wanted passionate love-making and she believed Clark could deliver.

"I haven't been with the opposite sex since October of '76. It's July of '79, Twiggy. Anyway, this isn't an audition for marriage. I just want to be touched by a man."

"I hear you sister, nothing wrong with a little walk on the wild side. Hey, Mary, how you learn all these recipes? Them dumplings was real good." Twiggy inquired as she and Mary stood beside Mary's home and began watching Albert Lee and a group of other males play football.

"The Jacobs family had me and Martha doing everything in their house since we could remember, including preparing dinner. I learned fast. Martha can cook too, but Twiggy, my sister hated those people with all her heart. She always said they didn't love us, but my foolish behind couldn't see the forest for the trees. When their son got me pregnant I received a big eye-opener."

"You ever think about your babies' daddy?" Twiggy asked.

"Not really. I mean, I wonder what ever became of him, but I'll raise my daughters on my own because I believe if the Jacobs and their son really cared about the matter they would have never did what they did to me and Martha. They let us go our way and I've come to terms with that fact. When the twins are older and they ask me about their father I'll tell them their daddy backed down and that's the truth. He didn't step up when he had the chance so I say to hell with him. We doing just fine without him anyway so it's no big deal."

"You stronger than most, Mary. You and Martha? Y'all some real survivors, baby," Twiggy replied as she squeezed Mary's shoulder and patted her back and the two young women continued to talk whilst watching the game.

As Twiggy and Mary talked, Martha emerged from the wooded trail having just come from Ambush with her pockets stuffed with five, ten and twenty dollar bills. She had sold the last of the two pounds of weed she had purchased early in the month. Martha simply loved to hustle. She wasn't greedy though; she purchased two pounds of weed a month and was earning about five hundred a week whenever she had her product. Jealousy did not exist in Ghost Town; if you hustled you had better had a plan or else you got out done. Martha was a smart, disciplined hustler; she was doing the out-doing so to speak.

As a result, in less than two years, twenty year-old Martha Holland was appointed Treasurer of Ghost Town. She kept an accurate count of the funds that were raised to purchase guns for Folk members and also paid the bail of Ghost Town members that went to jail and had a reasonable bond and she did her job well. Whenever a gang member went to jail and got a low bond, which was anything under $10,000, they felt at ease because they knew no matter the time of day, Martha would be down there to bail them out. Martha was well liked and respected in Ghost Town and through her actions, the entire household on the corner of Casper Drive and Friendly Lane got much love and respect.

Martha walked along the sidewalk watching the game as she

slowly approached Mary and Twiggy. She was dressed in a tight pair of blue shorts, blue blouse, and a black pair of sandals with a one inch heel. Her hair was braided to the back neatly and she wore blue lipstick, and black lip and eye-liner.

Martha looked gorgeous, and as she walked up the sidewalk, Albert Lee began eying his woman while defending his opponent. He tried to show off for Martha when he jumped to defend a pass, but he over extended himself and came down awkwardly and twisted his knee, and everyone, including Martha, rushed to his aide. A few gang members helped Albert Lee to his porch and Twiggy and Martha tended to him. The rest of the day went well and as night fell, things had quieted down in the neighborhood. Everyone was now sitting on Martha and Mary's porch listening to *Sparkle* by Cameo when Albert Lee asked Martha to help him home and re-wrap his knee. As the two left, Twiggy, Chug-a-lug, and Slim all snickered. They knew what was about to happen between those two. Clark and Mary, meanwhile, were eying each other seductively; they wanted one another and Twiggy knew it all too well.

"Hey, Slim, Chug, let's go get some rolling papers from the store and go back in Ambush and smoke this here weed Martha gave me." Twiggy remarked.

"Y'all two go get the papers. And us three gone be *right here!*" Slim joked, knowing full well that Mary and Clark wanted to be alone.

"Come on, Folk!" Chug-a-lug stated through laughter.

"Mary? I got a four person limit on my house! Another little person in my house gone put you and Martha over the limit. Clark be careful, she drop 'em in twos!" Slim stated through laughter as he, Twiggy and Chug-a-lug headed out of Mary's gate and walked towards the store.

"Well, we alone now, twin."

"Yes we are. My kids are asleep, everyone is gone about their business and it's just you and I, Clark."

Clark got up from the porch, grabbed Mary's hand and the

two walked inside. Cameo's song still played and Mary turned the volume down and locked her front door and turned and faced Clark. She didn't tell him, but this would actually be like a first time for her. Reynard had taken advantage of her early on, but she *wanted* this to happen with Clark on this night. Mary wasn't the least bit shy or nervous about sex and she never forgot how good Reynard had made her feel, even though she was tricked into having sex. She knew if it felt good then, how much more so it would feel when she actually craved it? Clark appealed to her and she wanted to give of herself, willingly.

The two embraced into a passionate kiss and before long, their tongues would be exploring one another's most intimate parts. "Let's shower together," Mary requested as she giggled and broke free of Clark's embrace and headed towards the bathroom.

Clark went over to the stereo and placed Teddy Pendergrass' album *Life is a Song Worth Singing* onto the turntable and placed the needle on *Close the Door,* and as the song began to play, Mary paused in the hallway and snapped her fingers and rocked her hips, *"He's a romantic,"* she thought to herself as she continued down the hall and checked on the twins to make sure they were still asleep. After putting fresh towels in the bathroom, Mary walked back into the living room and Clark pulled her into his body and the two slow-danced to Teddy Pendergrass' song, Clark singing into Mary's ear as he held her tight..."*I've waited all day long...just to hold you in my arms...and it's exactly how I thought it would be...me loving you...and you loving me...close the door baby..."*

Mary was up in the clouds. This sensual, romantic specimen of a man was indeed pushing all the right buttons and making her moist between the legs. The two danced until the song ended and walked hand in hand towards the bathroom and stripped slowly. Clark stared at the perfect specimen of flesh standing before him. Mary, all 5' 9" 145 pounds of tan-skinned feminine delight, stared back at the 5' 10" 175 pounds of chocolate man flesh that looked wickedly delectable in her eyes. Clark stared at Mary's flesh, she was a hairy woman, but her body hair made her sexy to the eye. Clark had seen the light hair on her arms and legs, but seeing Mary naked showed just how sexily hairy the woman was. She had hair down the nape of her neck that flowed gingerly down her back and a thick bush covering her pussy, a thick patch of hair that did little to hide her glistening outer lips.

The two embraced again and shared another kiss before stepping into the shower and washing each other's flesh clean. They then adjoined themselves to the bedroom where Clark lay Mary down gently and then lay on top of her as she wrapped her arms around his body and pulled him tight against her flesh and their tongues began assaulting one another at a furious pace. Clark slid gently down Mary's body and nuzzled his nose into her sex. She smelled good down there and her entire body was soft and sweet-smelling to him.

Mary was trembling with anticipation. She had heard of pussy-licking before, but she never thought it would happen to her so soon. She moaned aloud when Clark parted her silky, soft pubic hairs and spread her outer lips and flicked his tongue over her clitoris. Before long she was holding the back of Clark's head and thrusting her ass off the bed, grinding and humping his face. Clark was enjoying the sweet sounds, the groans, the moans and the repeatedly calling of his name aloud by Mary and he dove in face first, engulfing her pussy and sucking for all he was worth.

"Clark! Clark! That's enough! That's enough, baby! I can't take no more. No more! Please!" Mary begged after her second orgasm.

Clark sat up and crawled to the head of the bed, his hardened member throbbing viciously and dangling directly in front of Mary's face. "You want me to do this?" Mary asked as she kissed the head of Clark's dick.

"Umm, hmm." Clark moaned as Mary licked the head of his dick, swirling her tongue over Clark's engorged angry purple phallus. "All this like my first time Clark, feels good to me," Mary said sexily as her mouth slid over his thick shaft. Clark couldn't wait no more, he loved the warmth and softness of Mary's lips, but he didn't want her mouth around his dick, he wanted the warmth and snugness of Mary's pussy engulfing his stiff dick. He quickly rolled on a condom as Mary rested on her elbows and watched as his body hovered above hers. Mary grabbed Clark's penis and guided it to the entrance of her dripping wet vagina and held it there, and while looking into Clark's eyes, she bit her bottom lip and let out a low, sexy grunt as Clark pushed forth into her wanting vagina. The two then moaned in unison as Clark filled Mary to the hilt and slowly began to piston in and out of her pussy. She wrapped her legs around Clark to keep him inside her and the two began a long, sweet, rhythmic love-making session as the Teddy Pendergass album played on.

Meanwhile, as Mary and Clark made sweet love, another form of love-making was taking place over to Albert Lee's house. Peter Paul and Simon sat in the living room watching *Saturday Night Live* as they listened to the loud, angry, animalistic statements coming from Albert Lee's bedroom.

"Come on! Fuck this pussy! Fuck it!" Martha yelled aloud as she sat astride Albert Lee, bouncing up and down on his long, slender pole.

Martha was in the throes of a serious orgasm at this moment in her life. She leaned forward, resting on Albert Lee's chest as he dug off in her pussy, the two of them going at it like wanton sex-fiends. Albert Lee was on his second condom and as he and Martha fucked, she held another in her hand, ready for the next round.

"Ohh, you good pussy mutherfucka! Yea, bounce that ass on this dick!"

"Albert! Give it to me, baby! Oooh oui! Fuck the shit outta me! Fuck me! Fuck me!"

"Martha! Damn, baby! Damn! Damn! Damn! Ride—this—muther—fuckin—dick!" Albert Lee yelled aloud as he ejaculated into the condom just as Martha's body shuddered and she threw her head back.

"Aww, fffffucckkkk! Damn, Albert! Shit! Shit! Shit!" Martha cried as she pressed her face to Albert Lee and the two laughed aloud in between ruggedly rough kisses and heavy gasps of breaths. The two rested for a few minutes before Martha, still somewhat panting, rolled over and asked Albert Lee, "You think Peter Paul and Simon heard us?"

"So what if they did? They know what go on between me and you up in here."

"I know. I just wonder if they be listening." Martha said as she grabbed Albert Lee's t-shirt and threw it over her body to hide her naked flesh as she opened the bedroom door and entered the hall where she immediately spotted Peter Paul and Simon staring back at her from the living room.

"Yea, bounce that ass on this dick," six year-old Simon said through laughter as he slapped his forehead and pointed at Martha.

"Ride—this—muther—fuckin—dick!" eleven year-old Peter Paul then said as he thrust his hips back and forth towards Martha.

Martha stared at the two with her mouth wide open. "Sit y'all bad asses down! Nasty behinds!" she snapped as she scurried into the bathroom and slammed the door.

When Martha closed the door, Peter Paul and Simon burst into Albert Lee's room. "Aww, man! It smell like pussy up in here!" Peter Paul said as he and Simon held their noses.

Albert Lee lit a marijuana joint and laughed. "Yea? When y'all get old enough y'all gone be craving to have this smell in your own fuckin' room."

"I got pussy before!" Peter Paul stated to Albert Lee.

"From who?"

"This girl named Gina Cradle that stay on White Street. She let me roll on her everyday."

Albert Lee laughed. "What about you Simon? You fuckin'," he asked his nephew.

"Yea. This big girl named Kenyatta Branch be lettin' me touch her titties by Clark house when I get a haircut sometimes."

"See," Peter Paul stated with a smile, "we got some hoes

too!"

"Look here li'l ones, now, I don't mind fuckin' around with y'all, but Martha not just another hoe. I like her understand?"

"You like all the girls you sleep with, Albert Lee." Peter Paul stated.

"Just remember, Martha not a hoe. She not my hoe alright?"

"Whatever, man! I ain't gone never have feelings for none of these hoes back here in Ghost Town!" Peter Paul stated as he walked out the room.

Albert Lee jumped from the bed and grabbed Peter Paul by the back of his neck and drove him to the carpet. "All women ain't hoes! It's a big fuckin' difference! I'm tryna teach your li'l ass something but you too stupid to understand! Watch how you treat women in your life li'l brother because you never know when you gone need a woman to help you out!"

"I ain't gone never need a bitch except for one thing!" Peter Paul stated angrily, the left side of his face meshed into the carpet.

"With that attitude you won't be gettin' much pussy, boy! And the hoes who do fuck with you only gone end up hurtin' your li'l ass!"

"All they gone get from me is dick!"

"You gone learn the hard way, Peter Paul! Simon, don't ever listen to this mutherfucka 'cause he don't know shit but how ta' be ignorant!" Albert Lee said angrily as he let go of Peter Paul and returned to his room.

Martha then came out of the bathroom, having heard the conversation in the hall. She sat beside Albert Lee on the bed and merely shook her head. "Peter Paul gone be wild as hell when he get older."

"That li'l boy in there got a lot to learn about women—about life in general. Simon gone grow up cool, but that damn Peter Paul? He gone be wild and ignorant." Albert Lee remarked.

"Sometimes they have to learn the hard way." Martha stated as she nuzzled up against her man.

"Right, but for some lessons you don't get a second chance." Albert Lee ended as he took a toke off the weed and passed it to Martha.

An hour later, Martha got dressed and headed home. "We'll use this one next time." she said through a pleasant smile as she sat the unused condom on the dresser and kissed Albert Lee good-bye for the night.

As she crossed Casper Drive, Martha saw Clark exiting the back door of her house. The two eyed one another and laughed as they grew nearer and talked for a minute before going their separate ways. Martha entered her home and saw Mary in a night gown sitting on the sofa listening to Teddy Pendergrass with a smile of contentment displayed upon her face.

"Hey, I see you and Clark lovers now, huh?" Martha asked.

"Umm hmm. That's about all. I know Clark a li'l player, but I just knew he could make me feel good. I never knew how right I was. He can love me down anytime. I don't wanna be tied down with a man, but a walk on the wild side from to time ain't gone hurt nobody." Mary said as the sisters laughed.

Over the next year or so, Mary and Clark shared one another's company just as much as Martha and Albert Lee. And as 1980 got underway, Martha was still prospering in her profession and Mary had gotten a job as an assistant manager at the Dairy Queen on the corner of Casper Drive through the on job training program she had been enrolled in. Things were going well for the Holland household as their lives move forward into the eighties.

****

Mary and Martha, now age twenty-one, were talking inside their living room one mosquito-ridden night in the summer month of August in 1980 when they heard a rumbling sound coming from behind their house. Martha got up from the sofa and peeked out the back window inside the kitchen and saw a U-Haul truck backing into the driveway of the house behind theirs; she then saw a white lady exit the truck and enter the home.

"Well, well, well. Look like we got a neighbor back there, Mary. That house been empty ever since we got here." Martha said as she grabbed an eight ounce bottle of Miller beer from the refrigerator. "I wonder if they cool or not." she added as she returned to the living room.

"A neighbor? That's great! We'll go meet her tomorrow and welcome her to Ghost Town." Mary replied. "Ohh God, I'm messing this foot up!" she then remarked as she looked down at the ruined finish on her left foot. Martha took the nail brush from Mary's hands as the two sang along with the Spinners' song *I'll Be There*. The sisters looked into one another's eyes and sung the song's chorus as the song reflected the love they had for one another. perfectly.."*Whenever you call me...I'll be there...whenever you want me...I'll be there...whenever you need me...I'll be there...I'll be around...*"

"We gone always be there for each other, Mary I love you, sister! Martha shouted before she began polishing Mary's toe nails, as the two began discussing what their new neighbor may be like.

CHAPTER 9

ALRIGHT THEN, I'LL HOLLAR

"Hello, my name is Mary Holland and I just came over to welcome you to the neighborhood," twenty-one year-old Mary said with a wide smile as she stood on her new neighbor's porch day after the the woman had moved in.

Martha, Twiggy, Albert Lee, Slim, and Chug-a-lug were standing in the twins' back yard watching Mary talk to the woman. They were laughing as they did so because they had seen a side of the lady that neither of them liked. The lady's name was Pauline Washington. She was a fifty-eight year-old white woman from Atlanta, Georgia. Her son, a real estate agent, had bought the home when he married and moved to Portland, Oregon. Mrs. Washington's son hated his mother; he thought by buying her a home he could keep her from interfering in he and his wife's affairs. Pauline's son had married a black woman and that was fine with Mrs. Washington, really, but the woman came of age during the Jim Crow Era and she still held onto to some of her old ways. Plainly put, Mrs. Washington had black people stereotyped, and Martha and company knew it all-too-well.

Mrs. Washington's son never came and looked at the home he purchased for his mother, the previous owner was white, so Mr. Washington figured everything was fine in the neighborhood. Just like his mother, Mr. Washington still held stereotypes himself, even though he married a black woman. The man thought that because the previous owner was white, the entire neighborhood was white, but he had thrust his mother into a predominately black neighborhood filled with gang members. Mrs. Washington didn't mean no harm in the way she spoke, really, but the people in Ghost Town didn't see things the way Mrs. Washington saw them; she offended them often, but she wasn't doing it on purpose, really.

Albert Lee, Slim and Chug-a-lug caught wind of the woman's stereotypes when they offered to help her unload her furniture earlier in the morning. The young men in Ghost Town were always helpful. Whenever someone moved in or out, the males, if they were around, always pitched in. Albert Lee and his friends thought this day would be no different until they heard Mrs. Washington speak.

"You need help, Miss?" Albert Lee asked from the sidewalk.

"Ohh, thank you! Just what I need some nice strong Mandingoes to lift this furniture." Twiggy and Martha were in the woman's yard and they snickered as they looked at the shocked expression on the young men's faces.

"We ain't no damn Mandingoes!" Albert Lee stated angrily.

The two black workers from the U-Haul company, who'd driven the lady down to Mississippi, only shook their heads at Albert Lee and company as they began unloading furniture. The whole trip they had to listen to Mrs. Washington views on race, politics and religion, subjects that could easily offend a person with different views if tact wasn't used, and tact was something this lady lacked severely, that, right along with awareness. Mrs. Washington often offended people so much so that one wondered if she was doing it on purpose, or was just that much unaware of the fact that what she was saying actually offended the people she was talking to.

"Oh, no, I'm referring to your muscles. You are some strong-looking colored folk." she told Albert Lee.

"We Black! Black *men*!" Chug-a-lug answered.

"Yes. Yes you are. I'm sorry if I offended you boys, really. I have twenty dollars for each of you if you would be so kind," she remarked as she gestured towards the rear of the truck.

The Holland Family Saga Part Five

Albert Lee and his friends unloaded the lady's furniture, but the whole two hours, they listened to her rambling on about how her son 'ran-off' with a 'colored' woman. By the time they were done, Albert Lee and his friends were furious with the woman. Mrs. Washington paid them twenty dollars each, but she then insulted the young men when she came out with a watermelon. It was cool at first, really, until the woman said, "Just what you people like, a nice cold watermelon."

"What do you mean by 'you people'?" Albert Lee asked angrily.

"Ohh, it's nothing. I just know all colored folk love a good watermelon. Nothing wrong with a little seed spitting, right?"

Albert Lee, Slim, and Chug-a-lug immediately got up and walked off the woman's porch.

"Hey! Don't you want to finish your melon?" Mrs. Washington asked aloud as Twiggy and Martha, who were now standing in Martha's backyard, fell to the ground laughing as Albert Lee and his two friends made their way back over to the yard.

"Nahh, don't worry 'bout it! We gone hollar!" Slim said as the men quickly left Mrs. Washington's yard and entered Martha's yard.

"She Klan. She gotta be fuckin' Klan," Albert Lee said as he looked back over to the woman, who was entering her home with the melon.

"You right about that, Folk. She tryna be nice, but she don't know nothin' 'bout black people." Chug-a-lug stated.

"Hey! Mandingo! You, you wanna slice of good cold melon? How 'bout some fried chicken thighs?" Twiggy stated as she and Martha mocked the young men.

Just then Mary came out the back door holding a fresh baked pecan pie. She was planning on welcoming the new neighbor. "Good, she's all settled in." Mary said.

"She a bigot Mary. Don't go over there." Martha remarked.

"Martha this 1980. We passed that!"

"In America? In the south no less? No racism in the south? Mary, please! Go 'head over there. Pauline gone show you a whole new side of life watch." Martha stated as everybody laughed and watched the scene unfold from the backyard.

Mary walked over and rung Mrs. Washington's doorbell and greeted her and offered her the pie.

"Well thank you, child! You know, there's a colored girl look just like you around here."

"That's my sister. We're identical twins. And we're not 'colored' as you say, we're Black and Creek Indian."

"Ohh, okay. Well that explains the nappy hair."

"Excuse me?"

"Your hair. It's real thick like a nappy bush or something."

"Umm, miss, I wear my hair like this 'cause it's just the way my hair is *textured*. There are black people with long straight hair as well, you know?"

Mrs. Washington laughed and said, "All niggers have nappy hair! Don't try and fool me with that Indian blood-line story missy!"

Mary shoved the pie into Mrs. Washington's bosom and walked off her porch as Martha, Twiggy, Albert Lee, Slim and Chug-a-lug erupted into loud laughter. When Mary got to the bottom of the stairs she turned and stared angrily at Mrs. Washington and said, "What the hell is your problem? This is 1980! Nobody talks like that no damn more!"

"What did I say that was so wrong?" Mrs. Washington asked as she wiped pie from her clothing.

"We don't call each other 'niggers' back here! Wake up old lady!" Mary yelled as she walked back into her yard. She then ran inside, furious over what had transpired. Everybody else was all over the ground laughing at the event.

****

A month later, Mary was out tending her gardens in the front and back yards of her home. Three year-olds Dimples and

Ne'Ne' were following close behind helping their mother. "Momma, I got you a flower," Ne'Ne' said as she handed her mother a sweet smelling four 'o' clock.

Mary knelt down and reached for the flower just as Martha, with Twiggy at her side, ran up and snapped a picture of her taking the flower from Ne'Ne's hand. Mary heard the snapshot so she turned and watched curiously as a picture slid from the front of the camera and Martha began fanning the photo. She got up and wiped her hands on her apron and walked over and watched the picture develop. "How did it do that? What kind of camera is that, Martha?" she asked curiously.

Martha kept fanning the picture and said, "It's a Polaroid camera. The pictures come right out when ya take them."

Martha was doing real good with her marijuana hustle, so well in fact, that she had brought Twiggy in with her and the two of them now had the biggest supply of marijuana in Ghost Town. Martha had purchased the camera because this day was a special day. She had just purchased a 1979 two door Cadillac convertible. The car was powder blue, had chrome, custom Cadillac rims, white interior and a personalized *G-TOWN* license plate.

Albert Lee and Slim had gone to pick the car up because Martha wanted to snap pictures of her car as it rode down Casper Drive. When Albert Lee and Slim pulled up in front of the twins' home, Martha and Twiggy both took pictures of the car. Mary and her kids took pictures, and people that were out had to admit that Martha now had the freshest car in Ghost Town. The medium-sized group of people was listening to the car's custom stereo system when Mrs. Washington rode down Casper Drive in her 1977 Chevy station wagon and turned on Friendly Lane and headed home. A German Sheppard began barking loudly at the group of black folk on the corner in front of the twins' home and they all just shook their heads in disgust.

"Lord! She done went and got a prejudice dog." Martha stated as everyone laughed.

Mrs. Washington was the odd-ball in Ghost Town. She liked

her home, but she just couldn't connect with the people in the neighborhood. She thought that by purchasing a dog, she could get the kids in the neighborhood to come and play in her yard. Mrs. Washington could have done better with a Labrador, or maybe a Chow-Chow. Instead, she chose a Sheppard, a very protective beast that would only agitate the situation further.

Many young people in Ghost Town were beginning to hang out on Friendly Lane during this time. The street was shaded by trees, and had very few cars traversing the block, and Martha and Twiggy, who were fast becoming idols in Ghost Town, often hung out on Friendly Lane. Not to mention Mary always had a pot of something going morning, noon and/or night on her off days. Mrs. Washington's dog, however, was fast becoming a nuisance and the kids that hung out on the street came to resent the dog, whom Mrs. Washington named Blackie, which only further insulted people in Ghost Town.

The dog barked at the kids constantly. He barked all day, and all night, and it was beginning to annoy Martha to high heaven. Before Mrs. Washington moved in and bought that dog, Dimples and Ne'Ne' slept soundly through the night. Martha watched the twins during the morning while Mary went to work. The twins were always up and about before Blackie showed up, but ever since he'd come on the scene, they'd become cranky, and were tired all day. From Martha's point of view, Blackie had disrupted her daily routine. The twins usually napped during *The Young and the Restless* and were up and about when Mary got home. Now, because of their lack of sleep, the twins slept late and would be up into the wee hours of the night; and that began to interfere with Mary getting adequate rest in order to perform her duties at Dairy Queen the following day. This went on well into 1981. Mary, and even Martha had pleaded with Mrs. Washington to calm Blackie down. Mrs. Washington always said she would, but that had never come to fruition.

The Holland females slept soundly some nights, but most nights, 'that damned dog' as Martha was often heard yelling, was up barking—barking—barking. Martha would lay in her bed and just listen to the nonstop incessant yelps, howls, and ferocious barking coming from Blackie. Finally, just before

Martha and Mary's 22nd birthday in March of 1981, Martha had had all she could take. She lay in her bed just after midnight listening to Blackie bark for several minutes and suddenly jumped from her bed angrily and walked to the back door and stepped out into the cool air. She went over to the fence and approached the dog and said in a low and calm voice, "This my first and last time telling you to shut your mouth."

The dog stopped barking and walked around in a circle sniffing the grass, but when Martha turned around to head back inside, he starting barking furiously, as if he wanted to kill her. Martha ran back to the fence and yelled, "Be the fuck quiet! Shut it up!"

Blackie, however, only continued to bark as he charged at Martha through the gate.

"This some bullshit!" Martha yelled as she backed away from the gate.

Twiggy was sitting on her porch smoking weed and she heard Martha yelling. She ran over to see what was wrong and Martha said, "This mutherfucka keeping me and my people woke all night!"

"Shit ain't that bad, Mar."

"Listen to this mutherfucka, Twiggy! All night! All—dam—night!" Martha yelled aloud as she stomped the ground while looking to the sky.

Twiggy laughed at her friend as she rolled another joint. "That nigga drivin' your ass to death." she said through laughter.

"Damn right he is. And then he sleep all day," Martha replied. "My nieces all fucked up. Mary be late for work sometimes! I'm tellin' you, Twiggy—Blackie ain't gone be 'round much longer!"

"Martha? You gone kill Pauline dog?"

"Who gone stop me?"

"Nobody. Maybe that bitch'll move the fuck from back here

with her prejudice ass."

"I don't give a fuck if Pauline move or not! But Blackie? Blackie gotta go!" Martha stated as Twiggy fired up the joint and the two sat in the backyard and just stared at the barking dog. "I'm a kill that li'l mutherfucka." Martha said lowly as she took a toke off the joint while staring at Blackie, who was steadily barking.

****

A month later, in April of '81, Martha, now twenty-two, was in her room counting the money from her marijuana sales. It was after 11 'o' clock when three year-old Ne`Ne` walked into her aunt's room and said softly, "Auntie I can't sleep with that dog making that noise."

Martha hid her nickel-plated .357 magnum and sat her niece on her lap and rocked her to sleep despite the dog's barking. The next night, the barking started even earlier, just after nine 'o' clock. Ne`Ne` and Dimples were up, but they should've been sleep by now. Mary was in the living room playing *Go Fish* with her daughters, but they were agitated and were ready for bed; only Blackie was steadily barking.

"That's it! That's—fuckin'—it!" Martha yelled aloud from her bedroom as she grabbed her .357 magnum and marched out of her room.

Martha stomped through the living room, knocking over one of Mary's ceramic lamps in the process. Mary watched her sister walk through the living room with the gun in her right hand. Ne`Ne` and Dimples watched as well. Martha stomped into the kitchen, unlocked the back door and pulled it open. She then pushed the screen door open and fired three thundering gunshots into the darkness. Silence then ensued.

"I said be quiet!" Martha yelled before she quickly closed the screen door, slammed the back door shut and locked it and returned to her room and slammed that door shut. Not only did Blackie stop barking after the gunshots rang out, but the crickets and frogs went silent as well, stray cats scattered for cover and bats took flight. A calm, tranquil, serenity took over the corner of Casper Drive and Friendly Lane at that moment.

Mary ushered her kids to their room, but Ne`Ne` wanted to sleep with Martha. Mary allowed her daughter to sleep with Martha and Dimples slept in her own twin bed. The next morning, Martha awoke feeling reinvigorated. She looked over to Ne`Ne` and saw that her niece was already woke.

"How ya' slept, Ne`Ne`?"

"Good, auntie!" Ne`Ne` said as she jumped from Martha's bed and ran out into the hall and was met by Dimples. The two twins ran through the house chasing one another happily. This was the same routine they used to do before Blackie arrived.

Martha got up from the bed smiling and stretching. "Yes indeed! Some good ass sleep last night," she said aloud as she caught the smell of bacon in the air.

Martha walked out of her room and went into the kitchen and saw her sister preparing breakfast. Mary looked up from the stove and said with a smile, "Girl, I hate to think what you did last night, but I gotta say, I haven't slept that good in weeks!"

Things were back to normal in the Holland household. Martha thought Mary had to work, but she was off this day. She was planning on going to the grocery store and since Martha had no plans, the entire family would spend the day together running errands and just hanging out about town riding in the convertible, but before they did anything, the family sat and ate breakfast on this bright, sunny, bird-chirping morning. There was much laughter, joke telling and storytelling at the table as Mary had prepared biscuits from scratch, scrambled eggs, crispy bacon and grits with cheese. The family then dressed and headed out the door. As they began to enter Martha's car, Martha noticed Mrs. Washington standing beside the fence bordering hers and Martha and Mary's yard staring down at the ground and shaking her head in disbelief as she sobbed lightly.

"How ya' doing, Misses Washington?" Martha asked in a friendly tone.

"He's dead!"

"What?" Martha asked.

"He's dead! Blackie's *dead*!"

"Ohhh nooo!" Martha said in all sincerity.

Mary said nothing as she got into the passenger seat of the car.

"What happened to Blackie?" Martha asked in a false voice of concern as she opened the driver's side door to her car.

"Somebody killed Blackie! What kind of an *animal* would do su—"

"Alright then, I'll hollar!" Martha said as she cut Mrs. Washington off and got behind the steering wheel and peeled out of the driveway, leaving Mrs. Washington alone with her dead pet.

Mrs. Washington would eventually move away from Ghost Town within two weeks after the tragic death of Blackie. She owned another home in Atlanta, Georgia, so she moved back to there in early June and rented the home to a white lady from Kentucky.

****

In late July of 1981, an overly-excessive speeding light-blue pick-up truck sped down Casper drive and swerved onto Friendly Lane blaring *Master Blaster* by Stevie Wonder. The truck came to a screeching halt in front of Mrs. Washington's old home, its tires leaving a trail of burnt rubber and smoke as it quickly backed into the yard.

Martha watched from the kitchen window as a white lady and white little girl got out of the truck. "Mary, we got some new neighbors! Them mutherfuckas is white!" she yelled aloud.

"Oh no," Mary sighed as she folded clothes on the couch. "They don't have a dog do they?" she asked as Martha laughed aloud.

CHAPTER 10

NOT YOUR AVERAGE WHITE FOLK

"Hey! What the hell y'all standing over there for? Segregation ended in 1964! Come on over here and put ya' hands on somethin'! Come on! Come on! I won't bite!" the woman yelled aloud to Albert Lee, Clark Sr., Twiggy, Martha, and Mary as she smiled at the five young adults who were now standing in Mary and Martha's backyard.

"Hey, you think this lady like Pauline was?" Twiggy asked the group.

"I don't believe so y'all. I actually think this lady here kinda of cool." Martha stated as the group walked over and began to help the woman.

As they walked into the yard, the woman introduced herself. Her name was Loretta Duncan and her daughter was named Sandy. The group was greeting one another when three chickens suddenly ran out the back of her truck. "Sandy! Grab them li'l mutherfuckas! Grab the fuckin' chickens! That's dinner running away!" Loretta yelled aloud to her eight year-old daughter.

"That's probably why they running momma," eight year-old Sandy replied as she chased the chickens around the yard.

Sandy couldn't catch all the chickens so Albert Lee joined in and he and Sandy collared the three birds.

"That's right! Hold them li'l mutherfuckas! When we done

we gone eat! Hey, quiet girl!" Loretta said to Mary, "take this twenty dollar bill and go get us some cold beer! These young mens gonna be thirsty when we get done!"

Mary took the money and she and her daughters walked to Chug-a-lug's.

Albert Lee and Clark Senior bucked up when they heard the woman speaking. She seemed to be a down to earth individual, and before long, the fact that the woman was white had escaped everyone's mind as they listened to the jovial outspoken woman.

"Alright now! Alright! On three we gonna pick this here couch up!"

Albert Lee and Clark Senior were on one side, and Loretta and Martha was on the other end. "Three!" Loretta said as she lifted the couch, leaving behind Martha, Albert Lee, and Clark. Loretta sat the couch back down and placed her hands on her hips. "What the hell wrong, people? I said three!"

"We thought you was gone go like one, two, and then three." Albert Lee stated as he laughed at the hyper woman.

"Aww hell naw! Just three! Look, I drove all night and I wanna drink some cold beer and eat some got damned fried chicken! On three, okay? Y'all ready this time?"

"Go 'head!" Albert Lee replied.

"Three!"

The four picked up the couch and walked it into Loretta's home and sat it in its designated place. An hour later, Loretta's truck was unloaded and while Mary and her kids played with Loretta's daughter, Sandy, Martha, Albert Lee, Twiggy, and Clark, sat on Loretta's porch drinking cold beer with the woman.

Loretta Duncan told the group all about herself. She told them she was from Paducah, Kentucky and was a twenty-four year-old woman with an eight year-old little girl. She was a thick, bow-legged Caucasian woman, with short, brown hair and crystal blue eyes. She had light brown freckles in her face and a K.S.P. tattoo on her left arm, and a black raven on her right

The Holland Family Saga Part Five

arm. Her daughter Sandy was a slender little girl with long brown hair and crystal blue eyes; she had light brown freckles on her arms, cheeks and the back of her shoulders as well. The group made fun of Sandy's name, stating that she was named after an actress.

"I know! How the hell I do that dumb shit?" Loretta asked herself. "I do like the Sandy Duncan Show, but that ain't it! I know I ain't name my daughter after that mutherfucka! Maybe, maybe Sandy just popped in my head from that show! Anyway, she cute just like her momma and she ain't nothing like that white hooker in Hollywood!" Loretta ended as the group laughed.

When asked about the tattoos she had, Loretta told the group that she had served six years in Kentucky State Prison for armed robbery. She said she was arrested when she was pregnant with Sandy. The state had taken Sandy and when Loretta was released she fought and won her daughter back. Loretta was then shunned by her family, who were prominent members of the Kentucky horse racing scene up in Lexington. She was the black sheep of her family. Martha and Mary knew how it felt to be shunned and it wouldn't take long for the three of them to start bonding.

"Yea, them mutherfuckas is goody-two-shoe back home in Paducah. Look, we was at the races in Lexington, right? Churchill Downs, you know where Secretariat, Man-'O'-War and the resta them walking leather coat mutherfuckas run? Well, I showed up with my daughter and you know my family wouldn't let me and my daughter take a fuckin' picture with the rest of the family?"

"Why?" Mary asked.

"Because I had a child out-of-wedlock! My family had my life mapped out, but when I got pregnant they didn't know me. And when I went to jail? When I went ta' jail? Them sons-of-bitches cut me off! I said fuck everybody in Kentucky and made my way down here! I still ain't far enough from them sons-of-bitches."

Loretta then got up from her porch and had everybody follow

her to the side of her home. "Let's eat y'all!" she said as she grabbed a chicken from the coop Sandy had set up.

Everyone watched as Loretta took the chicken in her right hand and twisted its neck. The chicken's head popped off and its body fluttered around on the ground as Loretta held its head in her hand. Dimples and Ne'Ne' screamed and ran behind their mother as Albert Lee, Martha, Twiggy, and Clark looked on in shock.

"Grab that fuckin' cock! Sandy! Grab that damn cock!" Loretta yelled out to Sandy as everybody burst into laughter while watching eight-year-old Sandy chase the headless chicken around the yard.

"This not your average white folk here!" Martha stated as she laughed along with her friends.

Sandy finally chased the bird down and before long it was in a hot pot of water and had all its feathers plucked. The group looked on as they drank beer and watched Loretta prepare fresh chicken. Blood and guts were all over the small metal table she had set up. It was a gory scene. Dimples and Ne'Ne' were scared to go near the table; they hid behind their mother the whole time peeking shyly as Loretta rinsed and seasoned the pieces of chicken with various seasonings and then floured and dropped the pieces into a huge deep fryer. When Loretta began to deep fry the chicken, the group couldn't help but savor the smell, but still they weren't sure about the taste.

Mary, who was a good cook herself, decided to go first when Loretta began pulling the fried chicken from the fryer. She gave Mary a thigh and she tentatively bit into the chicken. Everyone stared at Mary as she bit into the deep-fried bird, watching as her eyes widened. Martha felt sorry for her sister, and Albert Lee was glad he didn't go first. To their surprise, however, Mary said, "Ohh sweet Jesus! I, I gotta go make some gravy and rice for this! Martha! Taste that! That is good chicken!"

Everybody knew Mary could cook, and when she said it was okay, they all reached for a piece of the chicken. Moans and groans of delight spewed from their mouths as the group tasted the chicken Loretta had prepared. Mary added her home made gravy and a pot of steamed rice and the group ate until their bellies were tight.

"This is Kentucky fried chicken right there! The real Kentucky fried! The Colonel stole his recipe from Loretta Duncan!" Loretta stated as she ate right beside the group.

As the night wore on, the group had drunk two cases of Miller beer and by then everybody was full as they all went to their respective homes. It was just another day in the 'hood, and the people in the house on Friendly Lane had become a fixture in Ghost Town by the end of the day.

****

Martha was awakened by a sharp knock on the back door of her home in the early part of August. She peeped out and saw eight year-old Sandy smiling brightly. Sandy and Loretta were always up early and today was no different. Martha opened the door and Sandy darted into the house. Dimples and Ne'Ne' were already up and the three kids fell onto the living room floor laughing, Sandy tickling the two girls wildly. Sandy Duncan had become good friends with the twins the first day she had arrived in Ghost Town and the three now played together just about everyday.

Martha played cards with the three little girls that morning until Mary had awakened from her slumber. She was off this day so when Mary got up to watch the kids, Martha met up with Twiggy and the two headed to Ambush to make some sales. They walked through the trail from Friendly Lane to Ambush and posted up on the set. They were out there for over two hours making sales and things were going along smoothly. G-Queens were on the corner watching out for the narcs who, were beginning to ride through Ghost Town on a daily basis.

"Heads up!" a G-Queen suddenly yelled from the corner of Casper Drive and White Street. "Heads up!"

Martha and Twiggy had never lost a package, but on this day, they noticed the G-Queens that were standing guard were all running away from Ambush yelling that a raid was underway. Martha and Twiggy had just re-upped, but they had to toss their package, a tightly wrapped pound of weed that was separated into ten dollar plastic sacks, into the canal. The two then ran back through the trail headed towards Martha's house, but they were both greeted by four Hinds County Deputies just as they emerged from the wooded trail onto Friendly Lane.

"Freeze, mutherfuckas! Don't you fuckin' move! Get down! Get down! Get down! Get down!" the deputies shouted at random as Martha and Twiggy dropped to their knees.

The deputies handcuffed the two young women and walked them back through the trail out into Ambush where other deputies had four other G Queens and six male Folk members on their knees in the middle of the cul-de-sac at the end of White Street. They searched and searched and searched but no drugs were found. Two male members had warrants out for their arrest and they were taken to jail, everybody else was let go, including Martha and Twiggy, who'd dodged a bullet so to speak, but they had lost their package. On top of that, Chug-a-lug immediately sent word that he was seizing his supplies to Ghost Town because it had suddenly become hot. Martha and Twiggy were now out of their connect; their only option for the time being was to retrieve the package they had tossed in the canal, but neither dared to enter the twelve foot wide canal for fear of snakes and alligators.

Word quickly spread that Martha and Twiggy were offering a hundred dollars to anybody that retrieved the package in good shape, but no one wanted to enter the canal waters. Not even to take the product without Twiggy and Martha knowing. The water was just too eerie for anyone in Ghost Town. Eight year-old Sandy Duncan soon caught wind of the deal, however, and she went down to the canal with eight year-old Simon Charles shortly after the raid. Simon followed Sandy through the trail leading to Ambush, all the while pleading with her not to enter the water. Sandy told Simon he had no heart, and that silenced him just as the two kids emerged onto Ambush.

Folk members were out that evening and they laughed when Sandy told them she was about to get Martha and Twiggy's package. The gang members all knew Sandy and they didn't believe she was about to enter the murky waters; but as they watched, they saw she was headed directly down the hill at the foot of the cul-de-sac leading to the canal. Growing curious, they followed Sandy down the embankment to the foot of the canal and dared her to enter the water.

Martha, Twiggy, and Albert Lee were sitting on Albert Lee's porch when they got the word. They liked Sandy and they didn't want to see the little girl drown. No one dared entered the murky waters of the canal in Ambush, but Sandy was there stripping out of her shoes and socks preparing to enter the water. The three went and notified Loretta and they all ran through the woods to try and stop Sandy, but when they got there, Sandy was already beneath the surface of the water.

Loretta looked at the canal and sighed, "Aww, shit! I thought y'all had some real fuckin' water back here the way y'all was carrying on," she said unnerved as Sandy popped up from beneath the surface of the water. "You found the fuckin' weed?" Loretta asked her daughter as she placed her hands on her knees.

"Not yet, momma!" Sandy replied as she tread the ten foot deep canal. "Hey, they got guns down there too!"

"Fuck the guns! Just get the weed! Hey, my daughter pull that stash up we get ta' smoke some of that shit right?" Loretta asked Twiggy and Martha just as Sandy went back beneath the surface of the water.

"She ain't gone find that shit! A hundred more dollars say she ain't gone find it!" Twiggy said just as Mary, Ne`Ne` and Dimples emerged from the trail to see what had Ghost Town captivated.

"Alright! Alright! You gotta bet, Folk!" Loretta stated as Sandy resurfaced empty handed.

"See!" Twiggy yelled as she laughed.

"She can't hold her breath that long sometimes, but she gone find it! Sandy, we each get a hundred dollars if you find the stash!"

"Alright momma!" Sandy replied before she took a deep breath and sunk back beneath the surface.

Everybody waited as the water's surface went still.

"She been down too long! She been down too long!" Martha stated as she took off her shoes and was preparing to enter the water.

Sandy had been under for almost two minutes and the two dozen or so people watching were now beginning to get worried. Some were yelling for Martha to jump in and save Sandy as Mary grabbed her daughters and ran back up the hill onto the concrete.

"She fuckin' drowning! Aww, shit! Fuck the bet!" Twiggy yelled as she, too, took off her shoes and prepared to enter the water.

Loretta laughed at the two young women and shook her head. "Look over there," she said calmly just as Sandy emerged from beneath the water in between the thick woods that lined the canal about fifty feet away from the cul-de-sac.

"Give me and my momma our fuckin' money, Folk!" Sandy yelled aloud as she swam down the middle of the canal back to the cul-de-sac and tossed Martha the package.

The weed was soggy, but it was still wrapped in the plastic. Martha and Twiggy knew they could dry it out under heat lamps within a day or so, so they would not lose their product.

Loretta grabbed her daughter from the water and hugged her tightly, telling her how proud she was. "You all is gonna learn to respect these here Kentucky folk before it's all said and done!" she said as Martha and Twiggy each handed over a hundred dollars.

Martha and Twiggy stared at Sandy, and Sandy stared back at them as Loretta ushered her back through the trail towards Friendly Lane. Sandy showed heart this day, and the people in Ghost Town, namely Martha and Twiggy, would never forget what she had done. At the young age of eight, Sandy Duncan was already earning stripes.

The following day, Twiggy and Martha went over to Loretta's house and made the woman an offer. They wanted her to watch the corner on Friendly Lane right in front the trail leading to

Ambush and they also wanted to stash their marijuana over to her house.

"Well, I ain't got no fuckin' job right now, and my daughter do need clothes for school. Look," Loretta said seriously as the three sat at her kitchen table, "don't think I'm just a stupid-assed white woman from a hick town. You keep your stash here, you pay my rent and supply me with a gun and a smoke stash each and every month—plus $200 dollars cash. My rent is three-hundred, so y'all looking at a little over five hundred dollars altogether. I guarantee nobody won't touch your product! And whenever you back there in Ambush you'll get a heads up call if ever I see the law."

Martha and Twiggy were each pulling down over five hundred a week so what Loretta was asking was no big problem. Friendly Lane was the weak spot in Ghost Town. The cops were beginning to frequent the area and Martha and Twiggy wanted a full 'heads up' call whenever Hinds County Deputies were in the area. If they had kept their stash with them when they ran through the trail three days ago, they would have been busted with a pound of weed. The deal forged between Martha, Twiggy and Loretta solidified the only weak spot in Ghost Town, and the three were earning good money well into 1982.

Martha and Twiggy liked Loretta outright. She was a real person, not someone pretending to like black people just to keep peace. She was really down and talked shit with the best of 'em; but Martha and Twiggy wondered how Loretta Duncan would react when confronted with adversity. With the approval of Albert Lee, the two of them decided to put Loretta to the test in June of 1982. They wanted to know if Loretta Duncan was all talk, or could she back up the words she spoke so valiantly.

The Holland Family Saga Part Five

CHAPTER 11

WE AIN'T NO PUNKS OVER HERE

"Alright, I don't won't no mutherfuckin' name-calling. I don't wanna hear 'white bitch', 'ku-klux-klan mutherfucka', or 'redneck'. No racial slurs. Loretta been real since she got here, so treat her with respect while you whipping that ass." Twiggy commanded as she and Martha walked side by side, being followed by four other G-Queens.

Twiggy was wearing her gold bracelets, once again signifying her lead status in Ghost Town as the young women, all wearing black jeans, black tank-tops, blue Converse and blue bandannas and blue lipstick, prepared to do battle. The group walked past Martha's house as Albert Lee watched from his porch with his younger brother Peter Paul and his nephew Simon. Mary was tending her garden with her daughters and they all paused and watched the gang walking down the sidewalk headed towards Loretta's yard.

Loretta and Sandy were cleaning their chicken coop when she noticed the women preparing to enter her yard. Right away Loretta knew what was about to happen, she'd seen people get jumped in a time or two around Ghost Town and she was actually wondering when this day would arrive, if ever at all. "Sandy," Loretta, who was wearing a pair of cutoff jeans, a blue t-shirt and flip flops, said to her daughter, "momma got a little business to take care of today. How about you go over to Mary's house and play with Ne`Ne` and Dimples?"

"Okay, momma." Sandy said lowly.

Sandy knew what was about to happen as well. The nine year-old knew her mother was about to fight Twiggy and the rest of the females, including Martha. Sandy had seen this scenario play out just like her mother; she wasn't too worried, she just hoped her mother would be able to walk when Twiggy was done because the last two girls she saw get jumped in were sore for nearly a week afterwards. Sandy exited the yard, and spoke softly to Twiggy, who looked intimidating in the blue and black attire, heavy lipstick, and gold bracelets she wore. She smiled down at Sandy and rubbed her hair softly as Sandy waved at Martha and walked, then ran to Mary's yard where she, Mary, Ne`Ne` and Dimples looked on as the six young females entered Loretta's yard. Albert Lee looked on, as Slim and a few other Folk members in the neighborhood gathered on Friendly Lane to see what would become of Loretta.

Loretta wasn't new to gang warfare; she'd run with a gang while in prison and they jumped her in as well. Twiggy heard Loretta tell that story so she knew Loretta knew what was coming. Twiggy and the gang entered the yard one by one and spread out across the yard as they approached Loretta with their fists balled up. Loretta was deciding who she would take on first. A couple of the girls, including Twiggy, looked as if they would pose a problem. The youngest, around age fifteen, didn't even faze Loretta; in her mind, she would take on the leader, Twiggy herself, and deal with the others as they came. Twiggy looked off to the left and coughed as she grew close to Loretta, but instead of just striking out at her, Loretta decided to let Twiggy speak first. Twiggy said nothing, however; she merely walked up to Loretta and jabbed her in the face, stunning her and knocking her back a step. She was then hit by Martha in the jaw and the four other females quickly rushed her. Loretta broke and ran from the group to give herself some space and reset herself. She was now closer to Mary's fence as she turned and began to fight back. Mary backed her daughters and Sandy away from the melee, but Sandy ran back towards the gate and cheered for her mother. *"Don't fall! Don't fall, momma!"* she said to herself.

Loretta was taking a pounding this day, more fierce than the one she received in prison. She was landing blows herself, a punch in the mouth, a gut shot, and a few skull pounds. The licks Loretta was landing was of small consolation, however, because she was really intent on landing one good blow on Twiggy, who was in and out of the melee being a constant nuisance with jabbing stings to her face and body. Loretta wanted to hit Twiggy one good time to at least be able to lay claim to the fact that she did so. One G-Queen rushed her and tried to put Loretta in the mix once more, but she moved to the side and caught the girl with an upper cut that knocked her back. Loretta was about to go in on the female, but Martha had come up from behind and grabbed her hair and pulled her forward. Loretta broke free, turned around and swung wildly and hit Martha in the eye and she fell back and took a knee, which was the next best thing to getting a shot in on Twiggy in her eyes, but Loretta had unknowingly set off a fuse because Twiggy had taken what happened to Martha personal. She ran up and began to pound the top of Loretta's head until she was forced to take a knee. Twiggy then grabbed a hand full of Loretta's hair and punched her square in the face, knocking her onto her back. Before any of the other G-Queens began to kick Loretta, Twiggy backed them away. That last blow was all it took because she had damn near knocked Loretta out cold and had bloodied her nose.

"Get the fuck up!" Twiggy yelled aloud as she pulled Loretta up from the ground.

Twiggy really wanted to help Martha first, but that would have let everybody that was watching know that she had taken what had happened to Martha personally. Jump-ins weren't meant to become personal; they were procedures that had to be performed before one could become a Folk member; but when it came to Martha, Twiggy would bend the rules whenever she could because she loved her just that much. Twiggy stood before Loretta, bloody nose and all, and hugged the battle weary woman tightly and slowly raised her right hand and said, "This Loretta Duncan, G-Queen, Folk member. Foot-soldier factioned to Ghost Town."

Martha and the rest of the girls in Loretta's yard then walked up and hugged her and welcomed her into the ranks of the Folk

Gang.

After everything settled back down, things returned to normal in Ghost Town. Mary and her daughters returned to working the garden, Sandy went home to finish cleaning the chicken coop and Slim went and sat by Albert Lee's house as the G-Queens disbursed and returned to their previous duties. Jump-ins had become all so common in Ghost Town. People only watched because the jump-ins separated the real from the fake. If you pleaded for mercy during a jump-in you could never be considered a gangster, a hustler, a player, or whatever; you would have no right to speak on, or engage in any form of street activity again. In effect, a person who begged for a jump-in to stop would become an outcast, and there were a few of those roaming through Ghost Town, although most would eventually move away because they couldn't handle the pressure on the streets of this rough and tumble Folk Gang dominated set.

Loretta took her beating and was accepted into Folk Gang as the first white member in Ghost Town. After she cleaned herself up, the twenty-five year-old walked to Chug-a-lug's with her daughter, proudly wearing the blue bandanna given to her by Twiggy. Loretta approached Chug-a-lug's and turned the corner to the front side of the store and saw three young men wearing black jeans and red t-shirts run to a white Trans-Am and speed off from the parking lot. She jumped and quickly shielded Sandy just as Chug-a-lug burst from the store blasting a .44 magnum as the car sped off.

"Fuck!" Chug-a-lug yelled once he'd emptied his gun. When he saw Loretta kneeling down beside the pay phone, Chug trotted over and knelt down and said lowly, "Go back there and tell Albert Lee them Vernon District boys done hit the stash for me."

"Alright. Come on Sandy."

"Damn, momma! I wanted my vanilla cookies!" Sandy said disgustedly.

Loretta ignored her daughter's remark as she walked at a steady pace down the sidewalk and delivered the message to

The Holland Family Saga Part Five

Albert Lee, who was getting into his car with Slim, both of whom were already wondering about the faint gunshots they'd heard coming from the front of Ghost Town and were preparing to ride up there and investigate. When he got word, Albert Lee stepped out of the car with two shot guns. He handed one to Slim, lit a joint and nodded his head.

Slim went and stood in the middle of Casper Drive with his twelve gauge on display, whistled aloud and then yelled, "Folk! War Chief calling! Folk! War Chief calling!"

The message spread down Casper Drive, being repeated by different ranking gang members until it traveled down to White Street and made its way into Ambush. Before long, over seventy gang members were headed up to Albert Lee's house.

Mary, who was tending to Martha's black eye, looked out her living room window and saw the gang members gathering in front of Albert Lee's home and wondered what was going down. Martha knew what was going on, however; Twiggy had told her about the War Chief call a while back. She knew that call meant that Folk were about to plan a move on the Vice Lords. Things had been calm since Martha and Mary had moved to Ghost Town in '77. Five years later, the streets were suddenly about to heat up.

Martha left her home and joined the gathering in Albert Lee's back yard. Loretta had sent Sandy over to Mary's home as she, too, joined the meeting. Young kids in the neighborhood stared from the streets, some admiring the gangsters and eagerly awaiting their day to come of age. The gang members, mostly dressed in black and blue, shook hands and hugged one another in true Folk Gang tradition as they awaited orders and discussed whatever hustle they had going.

Chug-a-lug informed Albert Lee about the Vice Lords that robbed his store as he stood with Slim inside the Charles' kitchen. He said he knew their faces. They were foot soldiers from Vernon District that had a reputation for pulling off jack plays. They had taken ten pounds of weed from Chug-a-lug. Ghost Town's supply stash had been taken and retribution had to be exacted.

When word spread out into the backyard through Peter Paul, who was listening in with Simon, the foot soldiers wanted revenge right away. Albert Lee was a smart young man, however; and before he entered a war, he first wanted to find out if the Vice Lords that robbed Chug-a-lug were acting on orders, or merely acting on their own initiative. He put together three car loads of Folk members that were to ride into Vernon District and pay the Vice-Lords a visit.

Mary and her daughters, along with Sandy, and the rest of the spectators watched as Loretta got behind the steering wheel of the car containing Chug-a-lug and three other members. Martha drove for Albert Lee and his three soldiers, and Twiggy drove another car containing Slim and his three soldiers. Mary stared with worried eyes as her sister and two friends rode out of Ghost Town and headed towards Vernon District with fifteen gang members.

****

The group made the drive over to Vernon District and slowly entered the neighborhood, cruising slowly as they eyed various groups of foot soldiers, some known, others remaining in anonymity, but affiliated none-the-less. Vernon District was much like Ghost Town as far as the design. A large white-bricked convenience store was on the corner leading to the heart of the neighborhood, but as you entered Vernon District, you would pass under a railroad trestle on the main street. There, under the trestle, you would begin to see the red spray painted concrete, pyramids, umbrellas, five point stars and upside down pitchforks were tagged underneath the trestle. Woods were to your right, and the convenience store was on the immediate left just before Vernon Avenue.

The gang followed Martha and Albert Lee in the lead car as Martha turned left onto Vernon Avenue and entered the heart of the neighborhood. "Hey, what if they just start shooting at us?" Martha, asked lowly.

Albert Lee turned down the radio and said, "As long as we don't blow up the five, or raise pitchforks we cool. Everybody know the routine, so we'll be all right."

The Holland Family Saga Part Five

Albert Lee guided Martha to the neighborhood's YMCA Center, which was the main hang out of the leader in Vernon District. Vice Lords watched cautiously and pointed at the three cars as they traveled deeper and deeper into their territory. The three cars pulled up in front of the YMCA and Albert Lee quickly eyed Errol Boykins, leader of the Vernon District faction of the Vice Lords. Errol, or, 'E-Boy' as he was called, was a twenty-six year-old, twelve year veteran to Vice Lords. He, like Albert Lee, had traveled down from Chicago with older gang members and helped establish the Vice Lords. Albert Lee and 'E-Boy' had crossed paths a time or two and had known of one another back in Chicago, although they never warred with one another. 'E-Boy' was from Cabrini Green, a notorious project on Chicago's south side. Albert Lee and his family were from the Mitchell Projects on the brutally violent west side of Chicago near a town called Cicero.

Vernon District was the biggest gang set out of all the gang sets in Jackson, Mississippi, both Folk and Vice Lords. Whereas the Vice Lords in Jackson had more gang members, Folk Gang therein town had more money and resources. They didn't need large numbers to accomplish their goals because whenever they went to war, they came without remorse or fear and laid to rest everything in sight.

Nolan Charles, who was a student of ancient war tactics, studied Genghis Kahn and had learned through his studies that powerful raids and massacres during a seemingly peaceful period of time could greatly decrease one's will to fight. And that's how Folk under Albert Lee fought. Now was not the time to strike because the Vice Lords in Vernon District were undoubtedly on alert at this point and time, but just his riding through Vernon District under such animosity showed how much heart Albert Lee had and that kept his reign as Folk Leader intact. Nolan instituted those ideas and tactics before he was killed and Albert Lee carried on in the tradition. Folk Gang often struck when one felt they were under the least bit probability that they would be harmed. Today was not the day for such action.

Albert Lee, fully aware of the tactic Nolan had put down, also knew that the Vice Lords in Vernon District were alerted to the robbery that took place in Ghost Town, so their riding through wasn't a surprise. The deeper they rode into Vernon District, the more Albert Lee began to think that the Vice Lords weren't out for war. They'd had plenty time to open fire on the cars, but they hadn't as of yet. Martha slowed the car as 'E-Boy' leapt from the stoop and three of his henchmen stood beside him and watched the Folk members' cars come to halt in front of the YMCA. Albert Lee, Slim and Chug-a-lug emerged from their respective vehicles and walked up the stairs and stood before 'E-Boy'.

'E-Boy', the 5' 7" 160 pound stocky, dark-skinned bald-headed twenty-six year-old, threw up a five, and twenty-five year-old Albert Lee, who now wore his hair braided to the back with a neatly trimmed goatee, produced a pitchfork.

'E-Boy' eyed Albert Lee and said, "I gave no orders on Ghost Town. Now, I'm reprimanding my soldiers, but the product is being shipped to Brook Haven, Mississippi. Them young boys sold it to some white people right after they stole it."

Albert Lee removed his sunshades, placed one hand on his outstretched knee, leaned forward and said, "E, we outta ten pounds of marijuana. Unless somebody produces some cash, or ten pounds of weed, we gotta serious problem."

'E-Boy' placed his hand across his heart and said, "Albert Lee, if I could, I would pay you *myself* brother. But I ain't got that kind of money."

"Look here Folk, we gone work this out like this. You, and *you* only, until we settle this shit here? I'm asking that you buy the next ten pounds of marijuana from Ghost Town."

'E-Boy' and his soldiers laughed. Vice Lords and Folks didn't do business together ever.

"If word got back to the brothers up north? You and I would be kicked out of this gang shit."

"You say that like it's a bad thing, E. The last time a war kicked off I lost my brother. And the other Vice-Lord territory, Washington District? They took a serious hit during that period of time. It's only ten pounds. You and me don't have no beef as of now. And just by E-Boy scoring from Folk, it'll be like we even, at least I know I got the great E-boy to bow down one time."

"I don't bow. I may nod," 'E-Boy' said as he nodded his head up and down, letting Albert Lee know he had agreed to the arrangement. "But I don't bow. I'll be on Casper Drive in two days. Be ready. And I'll be by myself to show you it ain't no tricks—that's on the strength."

The two shook hands and Albert Lee, and thirty year-olds Slim and Chug-a-lug walked off and got back into their cars.

"We still won." 'E-Boy' said lowly as he watched Albert Lee drive away, his boys sniggling right along with him.

When Folk got back to Ghost Town, Chug-a-lug questioned Albert Lee about the deal he forged. "Even if he do score the ten pounds, what about the ten pounds we lost?"

"You got more weed, right?" Albert Lee asked Chug-a-lug as the gang members all dispersed and the two men talked as Twiggy and Martha sat and listened.

"Yea, I got plenty more. But it's the fact that—"

"I know. It's the fact that ten pounds was stolen. But see, we not punks over here in Ghost Town. They got some Vice Lords selling weed up in Yazoo City I know about. We gone hit them mutherfuckas and sell your ten to E-Boy and we still gone have more pounds than what we sold, understand me?"

Chug-a-lug smiled at the plan Albert Lee forged and said, "I shoulda known you wasn't gone let them hooks get off that easy," as he gave Albert Lee the Folk handshake.

"You shoulda known from jump street that I wasn't gone let them hooks get off that easy, Chug! They hit us, we hit 'em back harder. Fuck V.L. and the shit they stand for! It's all about Ghost Town and Folk Nation!"

****

It was a week after Chug-a-lug had gotten robbed. 'E-Boy' had purchased two pounds of marijuana from him inside his store and Albert Lee was now ready to execute his plan. All week he had been talking to Slim and Twiggy about the job in Yazoo City. The three Vice Lord members they were planning to rob were residing in a trailer park. Albert Lee had sent Loretta and Martha up to Yazoo City, which was a forty minute drive north of Jackson straight up Highway 49. The two were able to scope the trailer park out and report back to Albert Lee, telling him that everything looked okay, but he should go see for himself just to be sure.

Albert Lee and Twiggy dressed up as Jehovah's Witnesses and drove to Yazoo City early one Saturday morning and knocked on the door of the trailer home. One young man answered the door very sleepily and Albert Lee pulled out a bible and he and Twiggy got the young man to allow them to enter the home under the guise of being a religious couple. As Albert Lee talked, Twiggy was taking a mental picture of the place. The smell of marijuana lingered in the air and the place was neatly kept. Twiggy also noticed an Uzi lying on the coffee table. The young men were somewhat ready for a hit, but the job could be done easily if they were caught off guard, which was Folk Gang's main method of operation. After a brief conversation, Albert Lee left a bible with the young man and promised to return the following weekend.

Albert Lee would return, but not for a bible meeting. It was two 'o' clock Saturday morning when he, Twiggy, Slim, and Martha piled into a navy blue cargo van and headed back to Yazoo City. They all wore black jeans and black t-shirts and had black ski-masks handy. Albert Lee drove and Twiggy was at his side. The ride was calm and quiet. Martha sat in the back of the van clutching her .357 magnum as she and Slim shared a joint. Martha was feeling a little anxious about this episode. She was surprised Albert Lee asked her to go, but she didn't want to let her man down; on top of that, Martha believed in Albert Lee and never doubted his judgment.

The van crept slowly into the small trailer park, just on the outskirts of Yazoo City right off Highway 49 and came to a slow roll and stopped several yards away. Hearts were pounding, and the sounds of pistols being cocked could be heard inside the van. Albert Lee lowered his mask as did the others and the four exited the van and crept through the

The Holland Family Saga Part Five

darkness right up to the trailer home's door where Albert Lee kicked the door open and ran straight to the last bedroom and cornered a man and a woman. The female jumped from the bed completely naked and Albert Lee knocked her unconscious with the butt of his .357 magnum.

At the same time, Twiggy and Slim entered the second bedroom and cornered two young men, ordering them onto their knees. Back inside the other bedroom, Albert Lee had placed the barrel to one of his captive's head and asked for the Mary Jane. The man complied and went into the closet and handed over two large garbage bags filled with marijuana. Albert Lee then called for Martha and she grabbed the product and toted it back to the van and got behind the wheel of the vehicle. As she waited, she heard four rapid gunshots and then complete silence. About a half minute later, Martha heard a loud blast and then another. A few seconds later there was another loud blast.

Seconds later, Albert Lee, Twiggy, and Slim emerged from the home quietly and jumped into the van. Twiggy sat next to Martha holding her shotgun with wide eyes and was breathing hard as she stared straight ahead at the trailer as Martha backed out of the drive. Twiggy had a blank look on her face for a good while as Martha drove away from the trailer park. She finally looked over to Martha as Martha drove south on Highway 49 and it was then that Martha could see the blood and bits of matter on Twiggy's shirt. Martha said nothing as she drove back to Ghost Town.

****

After Twiggy showered, she and Martha sat and talked in Martha's backyard. Twiggy told her that Albert Lee had killed the young man and woman and then ordered her to kill the other two men. Twiggy said she hesitated, but once she squeezed the trigger the first time, it got easier.

"I saw the first hook head just bust open like a tomato. The second one, I shot in the chest. He was jumping around like a fish out of water so I shot 'em again."

"How you feel about that?"

Twiggy shrugged her shoulders, lit a joint and said, "Shit I don't care. That was my first time killing somebody. I shot people before, but to actually watch somebody die was a new one. I never seen no shit like that, Mar—but hey, if it was me, the hooks would do the same so fuck it!"

Albert Lee and the gang had stolen four lives and thirty pounds of marijuana. To top it off, 'E-Boy' was still purchasing pounds from Chug-a-lug and the Yazoo City faction of Vice Lords nor the police department never connected Ghost Town to the quadruple murders that had taken place. Albert Lee had avoided a war and still exacted revenge on the Vice Lords without ever being fingered. Only the four people that went to Yazoo City, along with Chug-a-lug and Loretta Duncan ever knew about the murders and they weren't about to tell anyone what happened. Over the next month and a half the entire stash of marijuana was sold off and Ghost Town now had more money, and new, stronger recruits. Ghost Town was riding high throughout 1982 and well into 1983.

CHAPTER 12

GHETTO DIPLOMACY

"Hey, Sandy? You watched Sanford and Son last night?" ten year-old Simon asked ten year-old Sandy Duncan.

"No I missed that. My momma had me watching the Sandy Duncan Show. Ain't that a bitch? I mean, the irony of it all!" Sandy replied.

"You know you named after an actress, Sandy?" eight year-old Clark Junior asked.

"No shit, Sherlock! How long it took you to figure that out?"

"You ain't rich or famous. So how you get that name?" fourteen year-old Peter Paul asked.

"I don't know. My last name Duncan and my first name is Sandy? Maybe that's it!" Sandy replied sarcastically.

"You a smart mouth li'l bitch!" Peter Paul snapped.

Sandy pushed Peter Paul and the fourteen year-old grabbed her hair and pulled it hard, causing her to scream aloud.

"Let her hair go, Peter Paul!" Martha yelled aloud as she stepped onto the front porch.

It was late September in 1983 and the school year was underway. Martha had just dressed her nieces and was preparing to take them to the corner in front their home and wait with them for the school bus as Mary had to work that morning.

Six year-olds Ne`Ne` and Dimples were dressed alike in blue jeans, a blue and white shirt and white Nike tennis and had matching Casper the Friendly Ghost lunch boxes. The twins were loved by all the kids in Ghost Town; they looked like little Black Barbie dolls.

Things were quiet in Ghost Town since the clandestine episode that had taken place in Yazoo City over a year ago and the focus of the gang had now shifted towards the younger generation coming up under Albert Lee, Twiggy and Martha, bona fide members and neighborhood idols to many of the young kids growing up in Ghost Town.

Martha kissed her nieces good-bye as the school bus pulled up and the kids all boarded. The twins waved happily at their aunt from their seats as the bus headed out of Ghost Town. Just then, Twiggy emerged from her house and walked over and greeted Martha.

"Hey, Martha, help me out with this li'l problem right quick."

"What's up, chick?"

"Alright look, this li'l G-Queen Gina Cradle who stay on White Street? She told me she had sex with her teacher in the high school gym office right? She said he told her he was gone buy her some tennis shoes but he never did. So Gina wanted me to handle that for her. We set a li'l something up this morning where Gina can take half his fuckin' check for the next two months."

"How?"

"Go get your camera and we gone take Albert Lee car up to Calloway High School. I'll fill you in on the way up there."

Martha grabbed her camera and she and Twiggy drove up to the high School and Twiggy shared her plan, which was for her and Martha to take a photo of Gina having sex with her teacher and then bribe the man. Martha and Twiggy entered through the rear of the school and met up with Gina, who had cut class that morning.

Gina Cradle was a petite, slender, red-boned 17 year-old with short black hair. Her mother was a powder cocaine addict so

Gina was just trying to get by the best she could. She told Martha and Twiggy that she was about to meet her teacher in the gym's office in ten minutes. "His office upstairs. Nobody that be in the gym ever go up there so I'm a just go up and leave the door unlock." Gina said before she walked towards the gym.

Martha and Twiggy waited in one of the school's rest rooms in the meantime, and while they were waiting, a female came in and asked did they have any weed.

"Look like I sell weed in this mutherfuckin' school?" Twiggy asked angrily.

"Oh I'm sorry, but they be in here selling weed all the time."

"Who be selling weed?" Twiggy inquired.

"These two girls from Ghost Town. I know y'all from there so I just thought—"

"What two girls?" Martha asked as she cut the girl off.

"Don't tell them I told, but Kenyatta Branch, and her home girl Wendy be selling weed."

Martha and Twiggy knew the two girls because they had jumped them in a while back. Fifteen year-old Kenyatta Branch was earning stripes in Ghost Town. She often held small caliber hand guns for Twiggy that had no 'jacks' or 'bodies' on them, meaning they weren't used in an armed robbery or homicide. Wendy was more of a follower, she followed Kenyatta wherever she went and did whatever she said.

The two fifteen year-olds were violating one of Folk Gang's most serious laws for the youngsters, however—no drugs in school. The student, who was afraid of Twiggy and Martha, left, but she begged the two not to tell the two girls, especially Kenyatta, that she had told on them because she knew Kenyatta would kick her ass if she ever caught wind of it.

"Go 'head. You cool, young sister." Twiggy said as the teen thanked her and walked out the bathroom.

After twenty minutes Martha and Twiggy walked through the

silent school halls unabated and entered the crowded gym. Some of the students recognized the two and they grew scared as they thought Martha and Twiggy were coming to start trouble. They were relieved when the two walked to the opposite end of the gym and headed towards the upstairs office. They crept slowly up the stairs and walked to the end of the hall and before long, they could hear Gina moaning.

Martha readied her camera as Twiggy slowly and quietly turned the knob and pushed the door slightly to make sure it was unlocked. She saw that it was and looked back at Martha and nodded. The man was standing behind Gina with his eyes closed driving in and out of the petite seventeen year-old at a slow and steady pace. Gina was slumped over his desk resting on her elbows, her tennis skirt raised above her waist as the man moved slowly behind her. Martha aimed her camera and focused and Gina, who had caught sight of Martha with the camera, turned slightly to the side and raised her body to reveal her bare breast and Martha snapped the camera. The noise caused the fifty year-old man to jump back. He quickly grabbed his pants and pulled them up as he tried to explain what he was doing.

"We know what you was doing ya' old pervert!" Twiggy snapped as Martha fanned the picture. "Now," she continued as she sat down and plopped her feet up on the man's desk, "my girl over here say you owe her a pair of tennis. And on toppa' that, you owe her some more money to keep this here photograph from reaching the school principal."

"I wasn't doing nothing."

"Wasn't doing nothing?" Twiggy asked in mocked shock. "Man, my girl got her titties out, she naked from the waist down, pussy leaking like a mutherfucka? Not to mention we got a nice snapshot, see?" Twiggy stated as Martha smiled and raised the picture.

"What do you low-lives want from me?"

"Hmm, ain't that the pot calling the kettle black?" Twiggy asked as she looked at Martha and Gina. "This is what we want, pervert. For starters, my girl need her tennis shoes—

today! And for the next two months she gets half your paycheck. Only then will you get this picture back ya' low-life mutherfucka!"

The man knew he was busted so he reluctantly agreed in order to, at the very least, save his job and his marriage. He handed over forty dollars and Twiggy and Martha took Gina to get her tennis shoes. She thanked them repeatedly as they rode back into Ghost Town. Twiggy and Martha dropped Gina off at home and now had to deal with Kenyatta Branch and Wendy.

Fifteen year-old Kenyatta Branch was a 5' 2", 135 pound brown-skinned thick-thighed female with short, curly hair and bowed-legs. Her friend Wendy was slightly taller, a little lighter with a small Afro and slender eyes. Martha and Twiggy waited until school ended and when the school buses started rolling through, they stood on the corner of Casper Drive and White Street waiting for the two girls. When people saw the two waiting on the corners of Casper Drive and White Street in their war time apparel, they wondered what was about to go down.

As Kenyatta and Wendy's bus pulled up to the corner, the two girls got off the bus knowing they were in trouble. "Twiggy", Wendy yelled aloud, "that was Kenyatta idea! She said you was cool with that shit!"

"Shut up, bitch! You scary mutherfucka!" Kenyatta yelled aloud to Wendy as Martha began to swing on the short and sassy fifteen year-old.

Twiggy swung at fifteen year-old Wendy, but she ducked the swing and broke and ran. She was run down by Twiggy a few yards away, grabbed by the collar from behind and Twiggy quickly turned her around and hit her three times in the face and knocked her to the ground, forcing her to take a knee, which was a sign of one's surrendering.

Kenyatta was little bit tougher. She fought toe to toe with Martha, but Martha was stronger and bigger than she. Martha took two blows to the face from Kenyatta, but she barley flinched. She shook off the jabs, shoved Kenyatta backwards

The Holland Family Saga Part Five

and then charged her, landing a series of punches to Kenyatta's body that caused the fifteen year-old to grab her sides. Martha then landed a solid punch to her face and Kenyatta was finally forced to take a knee.

Twiggy shoved Wendy back to the corner and sat her beside Kenyatta and told the girls to never sell drugs on school grounds again, scolding the two fifteen year-olds as if she were their mother. She and Martha then walked the girls down to Ambush and allowed them to sell their product down there as they stood guard. Twiggy and Martha had settled two problems this day, one was for a troubled seventeen year-old, and the other kept two wayward G-Queens from violating Ghost Town rules.

Twiggy and Martha were doing a good job at keeping order amongst the G-Queens in Ghost Town and their diplomatic street skills was never questioned by any of the female gang members. Being a part of Folk Gang gave the females in Ghost Town guidance and discipline, something many of them weren't receiving from their parents. Martha and Twiggy gave many of the young females love and support, such as in Gina's case, and guidance and discipline, such as in Kenyatta and Wendy's case. As wrong as it was, in Ghost Town at the time, Folk Gang was family to many of the younger males and especially the females.

Albert Lee, meanwhile, had a problem with Peter Paul this day. Peter Paul and Sandy had fought on the bus ride home after he'd called her a bitch for the second time. Sandy didn't tell her mother, however; she told Albert Lee instead. As Peter Paul entered his yard, he saw his brother standing with six young Folk members. The young males, dressed in blue jeans, white t-shirts, and wearing blue bandannas, stared at Peter Paul and Peter Paul, fully aware of what was about to happen, dropped his book bag and charged the young men, who began to wail on him furiously. The fourteen year-old fought bravely, but he was outnumbered. Six blows to his jaw forced him to the ground where he took a knee. Albert Lee picked his younger brother up and stood in the middle of the front yard and hugged him tightly, congratulating him.

The Holland Family Saga Part Five

Ghost Town was rapidly increasing in numbers and over the next four years they enjoyed a quiet peaceful reign under Albert Lee, Twiggy, and Martha.

The Holland Family Saga Part Five

CHAPTER 13

THE G-QUEEN WAR

It was now August of 1987 and twenty-eight year-old Mary had taken her now ten year-old twins to the skating rink. Mary spent a lot of time with her daughters; she took them to the movies and took them shopping often as she was earning more money now that she was a manager at the Dairy Queen in Ghost Town. Ten year-olds Ne`Ne` and Dimples were running through the rink towards the video games, each of them holding onto a stack of quarters given to them by Martha, who had joined her sister in the rink this day along with Twiggy, Loretta, and Sandy.

As the twins ran towards the game room, Dimples accidentally bumped into a young woman standing in the aisle. The woman turned quickly and slapped Dimples in the face and knocked her down. Ne`Ne` saw her sister fall to the floor and she rushed back to help. She pushed the young woman and turned to help Dimples up from the floor when the twenty-one year-old woman, named, Keisha, yelled aloud, "Somebody better come get they bad ass mutherfuckin' kids," just as she slapped Ne`Ne` in the face.

Mary was at the snack bar buying nachos and sodas and preparing to join her daughters. She stepped out of the snack area with her tray of food and drinks and saw people gathering outside the game room down the aisle to her left and rushed to the area where she saw Ne`Ne` holding her face crying as she helped her sister up from the floor. Keisha then punched

Ne`Ne` in the back and she gasped for air as she dropped to her knees once more. Mary went into a rage. She dropped the tray and screamed aloud, "What the hell is wrong with you," as she ran towards the woman and began lashing at her.

Keisha and Mary squared off beside the rink just outside of the game room. Mary was a humble woman—but when it came to her kids, she was very protective. What Mary didn't know was that Keisha's three best friends were on hand. They jumped on Mary and began to beat her, but Mary wasn't going to stop. She took their blows and dished out some herself, taking on all four women. A punch to Mary's face sent her back into the wall beside the rink and the four females rushed her again and began pounding her back and skull. Ne`Ne` and Dimples cried aloud, calling out to their mother and begging the women not to hurt her. Mary, who was battling furiously with the women beside the rink, righted herself and scrambled back to the middle of the aisle. "Dimples, move out the way!" she screamed as she fought back with the women, who'd now encircled her as a crowd began to form.

Martha and Twiggy had circled around the rink and Martha saw the ruckus and recognized Mary and heard Dimples and Ne`Ne` screaming. She quickly reversed her direction and skated off the floor with Twiggy following close behind as both females quickly came up out of their skates. They rushed to Mary's aid and no soon as they got to the fight, Martha, who was holding a skate in her right hand, hit Keisha in face with it and knocked her out cold. With the fight now even, Mary grabbed her daughters and pulled them from the scene just as Keisha's friends began to throw up gang signs.

The females all threw up fives and began shouting, "Washington District! V.L. mutherfuckas!"

Martha and Twiggy quickly threw up pitchforks and shouted aloud, "Ghost Town!"

"This ain't over, bitch!" one of Keisha's friends yelled aloud as she helped her up from the floor.

"Fuck all y'all hook bitches! Go get your homegirl some fuckin' stitches!" Martha yelled aloud as she went and checked on Mary and the twins, who were being consoled by Loretta and Sandy.

Mary had scratches on her arms and a bruised cheek, other than that she was okay. The twins were a little shook up, but they weren't hurt at all. The group then left the rink and headed home where Twiggy informed Albert Lee of what had transpired that night. Albert Lee knew the Vice Lords in Washington District wouldn't declare war on Folk male members, but Twiggy and her girls were now on alert.

A month later, Martha and Mary along with Ne`Ne` and Dimples were grocery shopping at a Kroger's grocery store not too far from Ghost Town. As they walked through the store they chatted about Mary's job as the twins threw *Froot Loops* and *Cocoa Puffs* into the basket along with packs of *Kool-aid* and Vanilla Wafer cookies.

"What's up now, bitches," a female voice suddenly asked aloud, her voice suddenly disturbing the family's peaceful outing. Ne`Ne` and Dimples immediately recognized the figure standing in the aisle and they ran and hid behind their mother and aunt.

"Keisha, this ain't the time or the place." Martha said calmly.

Keisha wasn't hearing Martha. She remembered the day she was knocked out and on this day she wanted her revenge. Keisha worked at a *Rally's* hamburger joint near Ghost Town and she was in the store cashing her pay check when she secretly saw Martha and her family enter the store. She now stood in the aisle staring Martha down.

"I ain't forgot what you did to me, bitch. You had to sneak me to get me." she told Martha.

"Whatever, Keisha. You see I'm with my people, so let that shit rest for now."

"Fuck you and your people," Keisha said as she went for a .38 Dillinger in her uniform pants pocket.

Martha saw the gun and the play that was about to unfold and charged, but Keisha was still able to pull the gun out. "Mary, run! Y'all run out the way!" Martha yelled as she began wrestling with Keisha inside the grocery store's cereal aisle.

Just as Mary grabbed her kids from amidst the scuffle, the gun went off. The bullets landed exactly where Dimples was standing a few seconds earlier, shattering a row of cereal boxes and lodging into the metal shelf as people scrambled for the exit.

"You trying to hurt my people, bitch?" Martha asked angrily as she began to get the best of Keisha.

Martha knew a .38 Dillinger pistol could only fire two bullets simultaneously before it had to be reloaded so she let go of Keisha's arms and grabbed a bottle of apple juice out another shopper's basket, which had been abandoned, and cracked it across her head. Keisha fell to the floor amidst the broken glass and spilled juice; again, she was knocked unconscious by Martha. She lay motionless as blood gushed from her head and mixed with the liquid that covered the middle portion of the long aisle. Martha, Mary, and the twins ran from the store leaving other shoppers looking on in shock as they piled into Martha's Cadillac and sped away.

Later in the day, Hinds County Deputies paid Martha and Mary a visit. Although Martha was defending herself, her sister and her nieces, she told the deputies that the fight was between her and Keisha, leaving Mary out of the situation completely. Martha feared Mary would be arrested this day, and she knew her sister didn't deserve to be placed in handcuffs and taken to jail. She was a working woman and had never been a part of the streets. Martha took the blame and was charged with aggravated battery. Twiggy bailed her out the day of her arrest and Martha went to court a month later only to learn the charges against her were dropped by Keisha and not picked up by the state.

In turn, Martha dropped the charges against Keisha. Keisha had been taken to jail the same day of the fight and was charged with attempted murder and illegally discharging a firearm in public. When Martha dropped the charges against Keisha in court, Keisha was free of the attempted murder charge. The state, however, charged her with illegally discharging a firearm in public. She got credit for time served and received one year's unsupervised probation, which was a slap on the wrist for a young woman like Keisha, who still wasn't through with Martha and the G-Queens in Ghost Town.

Martha and Keisha were playing the game raw. Keisha knew she could have been hit with an attempted murder charge and possibly have been facing a forty year sentence so she dropped the charges against Martha hoping Martha would read the play and do the same. When she learned Martha didn't press charges, she began planning her next move against the Ghost Town G-Queens. At the same time, however, Keisha, as she sat in her cell the day she learned Martha dropped the charges, couldn't help but give Martha respect for keeping it gangster. Both young women would hold court on the streets. When Keisha was released, Martha was notified by other G-Queens from Ghost Town who were doing time. Martha knew the battle still wasn't over between she and Keisha; she knew she and the rest of the V-Queens from Washington District had to respond. And respond they would.

****

It was now two months after the fight at Kroger's, late December of 1987, and it was a cold, rain and sleet type of day. Twenty-eight year-old Twiggy, twenty-one year-old Gina Cradle, and nineteen year-old Kenyatta Branch were Christmas shopping inside Jackson's *Galleria Mall*, a three story complex that held many clothing stores and gift shops. Twiggy and her two girls were walking on the third floor having just exited *The Gap* clothing store.

Martha, meanwhile, had taken a trip with her family to *North Park Mall* to do some Christmas shopping. Over the past four years, Kenyatta and Gina had both earned stripes. They both had heart and would fight side by side with the foot soldiers and often went on robberies with the older G-Queens, including Martha and Twiggy. Both women liked Gina and Kenyatta, and over the four year period of time, they had advanced to next the level—the dope game.

Gina and Kenyatta were now working under Martha and Twiggy selling weed in Ambush. Kenyatta's friend Wendy had moved away to Birmingham, Alabama in 1984, so Kenyatta had hooked up with Gina Cradle and the two of them had been tight for over three years and had excelled through the ranks of Folk Gang.

Gina and Kenyatta's hands were loaded down with shopping bags this day. The allure of easy money from selling drugs and the fact that they were in constant favor with Twiggy and Martha had the girls on an emotional high. They were bouncing in and out of clothing and shoe stores buying items at random, never even looking at the price because during this time of their lives, money wasn't a problem, they had plenty to spend.

Twiggy, dressed in a pair of black leather pants and a white silk shirt, black knee-length boots and a plush black and white chinchilla trench coat, stopped in front of a candle shop and was deciding on whether or not to purchase a sterling silver candle set for Mary. She already had a pair of solid gold bamboo earrings for Martha and identical outfits and sneakers for Ne'Ne' and Dimples.

"We goin' to the food court," Gina Cradle remarked as she and Kenyatta stood behind Twiggy.

"Alright. Order me a grilled chicken sandwich. I'm a meet y'all down there in a few minutes. Let me, umm, let me look at these candles and shit up in here," Twiggy replied before she entered the candle shop and began browsing around.

A few minutes later, Twiggy heard a loud commotion unfold, followed by terrifying screams that emanated from out in the mall's walkway. She ran outside the store and eyed a screaming Gina, who was looking down over the side of the railing. Three females were running away from the scene—and all were wearing black jean outfits and red bandannas. Twiggy ran over to where Gina was standing and looked over the railing only to see Kenyatta lying face down on the concrete tiles that were three stories below. Blood was spreading from underneath her face as her body convulsed rapidly and the nineteen year-old's shopping bags and merchandise was spread out all around her body.

Twiggy fell back against the wall and sunk to the floor. Her dark, round eyes filled with tears as she watched Gina scream aloud. She grabbed her stacked hair and wept openly as her body rocked back and forth. Kenyatta had just turned nineteen a month ago; but she was deeply mixed up in gang warfare and it had cost her her life. Twiggy had much love for Kenyatta. She had been excelling through the ranks of Folk Gang and was about to be appointed a Lieutenant and given more responsibility, but V-Queens from Washington District had retaliated this day. They rushed Gina and Kenyatta when they noticed the two and purposely threw Kenyatta over the railing. She died on the floor before paramedics even made it to the mall.

  Two days after Kenyatta's funeral, which was held on Christmas Day, Twiggy and Martha gathered up six G-Queens in order to exact revenge. "Kenyatta Branch got fucked over big time last week," Twiggy yelled as she gave her War Speech in Albert Lee's back yard. "Now, we been fuckin' around with Keisha and the resta them bitches in Washington District for almost four months and now they done killed one of Ghost Town's own! We the fuckin' best and the strongest! Kenyatta earned her fuckin' stripes! She was a fuckin' soldier out here on these streets! And her death has to be revenged! Tonight we get our revenge on them bitches in Washington District!" Twiggy ended as the women erupted into cheers before they all piled into two cars. Twiggy drove one car with three other G-Queens inside a stolen four door Cadillac Brougham; and Martha drove an old junked-out four door Chevy Impala with three other G-Queens inside.

  Washington District was located in an area near Jackson State University. It mainly consisted of apartment complexes that were scattered throughout the small neighborhood along with numerous shotgun houses. Washington Avenue was the main street leading into the neighborhood, and Twiggy drove straight into the heart of Vice Lord territory, headed towards the Palisades Apartments, a large complex at the intersection of Washington and Shirley Avenues, that had an easy way in and a quick way out. The Palisades were advertised as an off campus apartment complex for students attending Jackson State, but Twiggy knew V-Queens often hung out in the complex and used it as a drug spot. The gang rode into the red brick and white wood three story complex apartments and cruised slowly. Twiggy rounded a corner inside the complex and four V-Queens came into view.

"Right there! Hit them bitches right there!" Twiggy told Gina.

Gina quickly stuck her twelve gauge out the passenger side window and the G-Queen in the back seat rolled down her window and aimed a .38 revolver. The G-Queen sitting behind Twiggy sat up on the driver's side rear door and aimed a Colt . 9 millimeter semi-automatic hand gun over the top of the car's roof at the group as the car continued rolling at a slow pace.

Martha saw the play and she ordered the two girls on the passenger side of the Impala to open fire with their Tec-.9 semi-automatics just as Gina and the two other G-Queens opened fire. The four V-Queens ran from the scene, but Martha saw two of the girls go down. She was preparing to speed away, but Twiggy stopped her car in front of Martha, got out and ran up to the fallen V-Queens and saw that they were still alive. The girls pleaded for their lives as they clutched their wounds, but Twiggy merely ignored their pleas and kicked one of the girls silent and then released six bullets from a .44 revolver that penetrated both girls' skulls. They both died on the scene, having received three bullets each to the cranium, courtesy of Irene 'Twiggy' Charles. She jogged back to the car, the heavy hand cannon draping her left side; then and only then did the two car loads of gang members speed away.

****

New Year's came and went without much fanfare. It was found out that the two girls that Twiggy killed in Washington District were both lead members of the V-Queens in Washington District. The V-Queens were dealt a serious blow that night and for a while peace ensued.

As spring of 1988 came in, Martha and Twiggy were still enjoying supreme reign over the G-Queens in Ghost Town. It was the weekend of Martha and Mary's 29th birthday in the month of March and Martha had just purchased a four-wheeler —a birthday present to herself. All day, as Mary prepared dinner for her and her sister and other guests that were to attend the party, Martha and Twiggy could be seen and heard riding up and down Casper Drive taking turns driving. During her time to drive, Twiggy rode the four-wheeler into Ambush and she and Martha sat and talked with Gina for a while. Gina told the two women she was about to run out of marijuana and she needed more as sales were good this day.

"Martha, let's go by Loretta and re-up for Gina." Twiggy stated before she and Martha jumped onto the four-wheeler and slowly rode through the trail leading back to Friendly Lane.

As Twiggy drove the four-wheeler through the wooded trail, a Ford station wagon was turning onto Casper Drive with a lone woman behind the wheel. No one paid any attention to the car as the woman, who was wearing a flower dress and straw hat, drove down Casper Drive and turned onto Friendly Lane. Mary was inside with her kids and Loretta was in the yard with Sandy cleaning chicken for the party. The car slowed and the woman smiled and waved at Loretta, who politely waved back. The woman then drove on, headed towards the curb in Friendly Lane. As the station wagon neared the entrance to the trail, Twiggy and Martha emerged from the woods riding the four-wheeler.

The two were having the time of their lives, but of all that quickly changed when a female rose up from the back seat of the station wagon and opened fire with a .38 revolver. Twiggy hit the brakes just as she was flipped from the four-wheeler and Martha fell to the ground and quickly got up blasting her .357 magnum. Martha moved from right to left as she emptied all six rounds from her gun. The woman in the back seat of the station wagon fired back and emptied her gun as well. After the rapid exchange of gunfire, the station wagon sped off and drove out of Ghost Town.

Martha looked around for Twiggy and saw her friend lying in the grass just outside the trail's entrance gasping for air as she clutched her chest, blood trickling through her fingers. Martha took a step towards Twiggy and it was at that moment she felt a sharp pain in her left side. At the exact same time, Mary was in the kitchen preparing to place a pot of cold water onto the stove for boiling. When Martha clutched her left side and grimaced in pain, Mary, who was down the block inside her home, dropped the pot of water and clutched her left side and screamed Martha's name. She quickly righted herself and ran out the back door screaming Martha's name with Ne'Ne' and Dimples following close behind.

Mary was running towards the trail as Martha looked down and saw that she was hit. She dropped her gun and touched her wound. Mary screamed when she saw her sister standing motionless staring at her bloody hands. "Martha! Martha!" she yelled aloud as she ran towards her sister.

Martha stared back at Mary with a shocked expression on her face, dropped to her knees and fell over onto her right side, entering a state of shock. Mary ran up and grabbed her sister and held her close, shaking Martha out of her trance. She screamed aloud in agony as her body convulsed in her sister's arms.

Albert Lee and others ran to the scene and saw Mary holding Martha screaming hysterically as Martha cried out in pain. He walked over to Twiggy and slowly knelt down beside his wounded sister. "Who it was?" Albert Lee screamed aloud to a crying and terrified Twiggy. "Irene," Albert Lee then said lowly as he stared his wounded sister in the eyes. "Who shot you? Who done this to you and Mar?"

Twiggy knew exactly who had shot her and Martha. She reached out a bloody hand and grabbed her brother's hand. "K-Keisha! Keisha!" was all she said before she went unconscious.

People stared in shock at the scene. Twiggy and Martha, two of the most respected G-Queens in Ghost Town had both suffered gunshot wounds. Ne'Ne' and Dimples were crying heavily, worried that their aunt was going to die this day. Fourteen year-old Sandy grabbed hold of the twins and held them at her side as the three of them looked on at Martha and Twiggy laid out in the grass at the foot of the trail. Ghost Town had seen people shot, and even killed before, but seeing the way Martha and Twiggy were shot, and hearing the screams of pain coming from Martha brought things home for everybody out there—if it could happen to Martha and Twiggy, then it could damn sure happen to anybody else.

Instead of learning a lesson, however, quite a few youngsters were motivated to join Folk; namely Sandy Duncan. She didn't know why, or who shot the two women, but in her eyes, Twiggy and Martha were real gangsters. And if she was going to be in Ghost Town, Sandy wanted to become a G-Queen like the ones that came before her; besides, her mother was a G-Queen, so becoming a gang member for Sandy Duncan was only the next natural step in her eyes.

Twiggy and Martha were both rushed by ambulance to Jackson Memorial where they received treatment for their wounds. As they lay side by side in their respective beds, having completed surgery the night before, they watched the news together the following morning. They were both shocked to learn that Albert Lee, Clark Senior, and two other Folk Gang members from Ghost Town had been arrested after fleeing a murder scene the night before. Albert Lee had murdered Keisha, Keisha's seventeen year-old brother, and Keisha's forty-three year-old mother.

Keisha wanted revenge for the fight in Kroger's and for the murder of the V-Queens on New Year's Day in Washington District. She got her revenge against Ghost Town, but she paid with her life, and she also caused her mother and brother to lose their lives as well.

Albert Lee was apprehended with the murder weapon, which he also used to fire on officers as he tried to flee the scene, and was charged with three counts first degree murder and attempted murder on an officer. His actions would end the G-Queen wars, but it would cost him, Clark Senior, and two older Folk members their freedom.

Albert Lee didn't care, however; seeing his sister and his woman laid out in the manner in which they were the day before had driven the man over the edge. He reacted before he thoroughly thought out the entire situation. Still Ghost Town was avenged.

Martha was released from the hospital two weeks later. She had suffered a flesh wound to her side that had missed her vital organs. Twiggy was released a week after Martha. The thick, gold six-point star medallion she wore the day she was shot had prevented the bullet from fully penetrating her chest. It lodged in her sternum but doctors were able to treat the wound easily. Both females were lucky to be alive; and in spite of nearly losing their lives, Martha and Twiggy would continue to hold true to their Folk Gang roots. After surviving their gunshots, it was fair to say that Twiggy and Martha somewhat felt invincible.

Many people from Ghost Town, including Mary and Loretta, had attended Albert Lee, Clark Senior, and the two other Folk Gang members' murder trial a month and a half later. The state had a solid case against Albert Lee, Clark Senior, and the two other leaders. All four were found guilty. Clark Senior and the other two Folk members received life without parole. Albert Lee Charles, who was the perceived master mind, was sentenced to death. He would have to deal with numerous appeals for years to come.

Ghost Town had been dealt a serious blow. Not only did they lose their leader, but they had lost three ranking members as well. While Albert Lee and his crew were preparing to be shipped to Parchment State Penitentiary, Twiggy and Martha were home still recovering from their wounds.

Ghost Town was in a weakened state during this period of time and Twiggy and Martha both knew it; especially Twiggy. She had seen Ghost Town walk this path when her oldest brother Nolan was killed in 1976. As she lay on the couch crying over the fact that Albert Lee was now on death row, a week after he was sent upstate, Twiggy, with Martha at her side, knew the two of them now had the huge task of reorganizing the Folk Gang in Ghost Town.

CHAPTER 14
THE CHANGING TIDES

It was now August of '88, and Twiggy and Martha were back at full strength and preparing to take back to the streets. Their first priority was to pay Albert Lee a visit to find out who he would give leadership to in Ghost Town. Second priority was to realign the G-Queens, who'd been in a state of flux ever since the shooting. The street side of things would be handled, but after Martha was shot, she and Mary argued constantly about her gang affiliation and the arguments were beginning to disrupt the family. Mary was scared for her sister and often worried about Martha's welfare. The scene inside the Holland living room this hot and muggy evening in August had become all-too-familiar in the Holland home.

"Martha, you are twenty-nine. Twenty-nine years old! How long are you gonna keep playing this game?" Mary asked in dismay upon seeing a six-point star tattoo Martha had just gotten on her right arm and showing it off proudly inside her bedroom.

"This ain't a game, Mary! I'm tryna survive out here!" Martha responded as she rubbed Vaseline on the fresh artwork.

"I *been* surviving! And I was *never* part of any gang!"

"If it wasn't for me you wouldna never even sur—" Martha caught herself once she realized what she was about to say.

"Say it!" Mary screamed. "If it wasn't for you I would've

never even survived back here? That's how you see me? As helpless and incapable?" Mary asked as she turned and walked away, heart-broken that her sister would even begin to speak those words to her.

Martha ran out of her room and grabbed Mary from behind, turned her around in the hallway and said, "I was stupid for getting ready to say that, Mary. You know I did what I did out of love and not to rub it in your face."

"Then why say what you were about to say, Martha?"

"I'm sorry, Mary. I really am. Say you forgive me for even *thinking* of saying that! You, you raising two beautiful daughters on your own and you always keep them safe. You looked out for me when I didn't have a dime. You was my rock once upon time because that's what we do. We Hollands and we always look out for each other, and we do it outta love."

"I know Martha. I know you love me, and I love you. I'm hurt not for what you were about to say because I know you don't mean that. I'm hurt because I'm scared for you. You make me worry living the life you're living."

"I don't mean to, sister."

"But you do. You did so much for me in the beginning, so much for *us* in the beginning, and you still do things now. I appreciate that very much. Your talents, the attributes that you have could be used for something better. I see it. I just want you to see in *yourself* what *I* see in you, Martha. You're my heart—and this bond should be unbreakable. But your lifestyle is slowly breaking us apart. Understand? I just don't want that to happen."

"Folk is all I know, Mary. For the last eleven years it's all I know." Martha said somberly as she walked away from her sister.

Mary followed Martha into the living room and said, "You have a diploma, Martha. You can get a job at the Dairy Queen where I work."

Martha looked over to Mary, chuckled slightly and said, "Mary, please. I ain't had a job ever. Dairy Queen ain't my style and you know it."

Mary couldn't help but to smile herself upon realizing how ridiculous a suggestion she'd just put on the table for Martha. She knew her sister would never put on a uniform and name tag and say, 'Welcome to Dairy Queen. Can I take your order?' The mere thought had tickled Mary briefly, but she quickly regained her composure and expressed more of her emotions. "Martha, I'm scared for you," she said seriously. "All these young girls around here look up to you and Twiggy. Y'all should use that for the positive."

"Look where we at, Mary. What's positive about this place?"

"It's our home, Martha. And there is much to be taken from it besides what goes on in Ambush and with the Folks."

"Like what?"

"Like Ne`Ne` and Dimples. Have you been paying any attention to your nieces lately? If you haven't noticed, they are starting to get infatuated with what you and Twiggy are doing, Martha. You may not see what's positive about our home, but I do. And two of them are right here inside these walls. If you don't see something positive in yourself or Ghost Town, see it in your nieces. I know you care for them."

"I love my babies," Martha said with a proud smile as she picked up a picture of Ne`Ne` and Dimples from one of the end tables in the living room. "I would do nothing to hurt them."

"And you mean to do nothing to hurt me, Martha. But—but I can feel your pain." Mary said quickly before turning her head away from Martha in shame.

"What you said?" Martha asked in a stunned manner as she turned and stared at her sister.

"I never told you," Mary said as she raised her head and stared Martha in the eyes. "The day you got shot? I felt it!"

Martha stared at her sister as she briefly reflected on the day Donna Jacobs slapped Mary and she remembered the sensation she felt when Mary was slapped. Martha thought nothing of it over all the years, but she now knew and understood at that exact moment, just how much hurt she was causing her sister, and Mary's revelation had left her in stunned silence. Martha had no response.

"They not only hurt you that day," Mary said, breaking the brief moment of silence. "They hurt me that day, Martha. When you hurt? Sometimes I can feel it. More than you could ever know. I wonder if you can feel the hurt inside my heart right now because I really don't want to do this, but I have to. I love you Martha, you're half of me, I'm half of you, and I don't want to lose my half, but I also can't put my daughters at risk. If you don't want to change? That's fine by me. Just don't do it here, okay? For your nieces sake, live your life outside of here so I can give them a chance."

"So what you sayin', Mary?" Martha asked as she sat the picture of her nieces back onto the end table.

"I know what you are and I'm not judging you at all, Martha. But your nieces—my daughters—will not grow up being a part of that gang. I see the little six point stars they draw in their notebooks. The gang insignias, and I don't want that for them. I tell them that they can and will do better and not be a part of that life. Don't make it hard for me to keep them away from your gang. And you and I are all they have. We don't know where Naomi and Sam are and we are all *we* have. Maybe they've both gone on with their lives and have forgotten about us. I don't know the answer to that. What I do know is as of right now we don't have any other family. All we have is us. And if I lose you it would kill me. You hear? It would *kill me*!" Mary ended as she sat down on her couch and rested her arms on her knees and wiped away the tears that were forming in her eyes. This discussion was taking a lot out of Mary. She hadn't spoken this candidly to Martha in a long time, but she had to share her emotions with her sister to let her know how she truly felt about her lifestyle.

Martha said nothing as she stared at her sister and then sat down beside her. She leaned forward on the couch and picked up another picture of her eleven year old nieces and stared at the image real hard, thinking about the fact that the last thing she wanted was for Ne'Ne' and Dimples to get involved in what she was doing. "Damn, Mary," Martha said lowly, "I been so caught up in the life I never even thought about that. I'm sorry for everything. And believe me, I was glad to do what I did when we first got here." Martha said as she placed her hands underneath her chin.

"I was glad to be your inspiration, Martha. And right or wrong, I'll never go against you. I know what you are and it's fine by me. I can't live your life, but it would break my heart if anything happened to you, Ne`Ne` or Dimples. Maybe, and don't be mad at me, but just maybe things will be better if you were to move out. Please don't be mad. I'm just, I'm just—"

What Mary was now asking Martha to do was hard for her and she was at a loss for words at this point. The sisters had always been together since they could remember and Naomi said in her journal that they should never split up. Mary was struggling with how to balance the safety of Ne`Ne` and Dimples, the love she had for Martha, Naomi's request, and not really wanting to put Martha out. In the end, Mary put her daughters first, but she only asked that Martha move out, hoping she would respect her wishes, and even though she would only ask, it was still hard for to explain the reasons why.

Martha sensed her sister's apprehension and responded by saying, "I know what you tryna say, Mary. You only looking out for Ne`Ne` and Dimples and you have every right to do that. I respect that, sister. And believe me, I'm not mad at you for what you asking. I respect it and I understand. I actually saw this coming a while back. I believe things will be better for both of us." she ended as she pressed her head to her sister's head and the smiled. "I'm gonna be okay, Mary. Don't worry about me."

"You're not gone move outta town away from us are you?" Mary asked lowly.

Martha laughed to herself in silence. At that moment, she was glad God had given her Mary as her sister. Many people believe in the good twin/ bad twin myth. If that myth were true, it could be argued that Martha would have been the bad twin. Martha didn't see herself as being bad, however; she was only trying to survive the best way she knew how. She could have easily manipulated Mary and forced her to allow her to do as she pleased because she knew Mary did not want her to leave her life for good. She only wanted her from under her roof.

On this day, Martha could have easily threatened to leave forever and she knew it would have forced Mary to bow. But the hard truth was that Martha needed and loved Mary just as much as Mary loved and needed her. Martha could have been selfish with her love. She could have used her sister's love to her advantage, but Mary was family, and for Martha Holland, family was above all else. Ne`Ne` and Dimples were precious to her. She couldn't be without her nieces and Mary no more than Mary could withstand not having her around, and that is what would hold the two sisters together for all time. That's what Martha quickly thought about as she laid her head in her sisters s lap, proud to have a sister as loving, sweet, and caring as Mary.

"No I'm not going far, Mary," Martha said humbly. "Most likely, I'm going right across the street by Twiggy. That okay?"

"That's fine by me Martha. And you're still welcome here anytime. You know that right?"

"Thanks, Mary. Can you forgive me for almost belittling your plight back in the day?"

"Child, please. I manipulated you all the way from Tuscaloosa to Ghost Town, Martha. I was ready to leave the day Donna slapped me." Mary quipped as she sniggled.

Martha's eyes and mouth widened and she got up from Mary's lap and grabbed a pillow and hit her sister and the two fought playfully.

Ne`Ne` and Dimples were in their room with door shut, but they still heard the entire disagreement. When they heard the two sisters laughing, they ran from their bedroom into the living room.

"We don't like when y'all fight!" Dimples said as she sat on her mother's lap as Ne`Ne` jumped into Martha's lap.

The Holland females had an open discussion between the family and before long there was laughter and good feelings amongst the family. It was agreed that Martha would move out. It had been a long time coming, and the resolution had resolved the tension between the sisters. The family all piled into Martha's car and went to *The Sizzler* and had dinner. They then went to the mall and walked around as they drank milkshakes.

****

Mary was sitting at her dining room table looking through old photographs from back in the day about a week after the sisters had their last disagreement. She silently smiled as she reminisced about times past when she and Martha first landed in Ghost town. Martha had put many a smile on Mary's face back then, guiding the family towards respectability in a neighborhood where that particular attribute was hard to come by, but held in high esteem once accomplished. Ne`Ne` and Dimples, on this early Saturday morning, came out of their rooms after cleaning them up and sat at the table with their mother and shared in some of her earlier memories.

"Momma, why daddy don't never try and get in touch with us?" Dimples asked.

"Well, your daddy left us alone, sweetie, but I don't want you two to be mad at him. We were both young and foolish. Besides, you both are doing just fine now. I know I can't stop y'all from wondering, but the truth is, your father wasn't prepared to raise you two and take care of me at the same time."

"Why have intercourse and get pregnant? I don't understand that, momma." Ne`Ne` said.

"Sometimes, when you're young, Rene? You do foolish things and you live to regret them."

"You regret us, momma?" Dimples asked, her dark brown eyes displaying a hint of uncertainty.

Mary's heart grew warm. "Ohh no baby," she said as she hopped from her seat and hugged Dimples. "Never will I feel that way. You two are the most important things in my life and you always will be. I'm blessed to have two of the most beautiful daughters in the world. Come here." Mary said as she clutched both her daughters tightly in her arms. "Don't you two ever think that you were a mistake. You two are my reason for living, understand?"

"Yea. I love you too, momma!" Ne`Ne` and Dimples said in unison as they turned to one another and giggled. "We said the same thing at the same time! You did it again! Stop repeating me!" Ne`Ne` and Dimples said at the exact same moment before they, along with their mother, erupted into laughter.

"That is beautiful! Me and Martha haven't spoken simultaneously in years! Only once can I remember us doing that which was the day you two were born. But you two have it!" Mary said as she hugged both her daughters and laughed with them. "Come on, let's do something today!" Mary then said.

Mary and her daughters decided to rent some VCR tapes and pop popcorn and spend the day watching movies. They all dressed and headed to the video store. Mary never even bothered to ask for a ride from Martha because she wanted to ride the bus as it would give them more time to hang out together. She and her daughters walked through Ghost Town and waited in front of Chug-a-lug's on the corners of Casper Drive and Hanging Moss for the city bus to ride to the video store.

At the same time, Martha and Twiggy were walking through the trail leading to Ambush, almost stepping in the very same spot in which both of them nearly lost their lives. As they walked, Twiggy informed Martha that Sandy Duncan was about to get made this day. "I been wantin' ta' put that white girl down," Twiggy said as she and Martha walked side by side through the wooded trail. "She back there waiting on us. Eh, Albert Lee called, too. He said drop another C-note in his commissary. I'm puttin' in a hundred myself. Just let me know when ya' ready, Folk."

"Alright. I got it today." Martha replied as the two women traversed the trail, quickly approaching Ambush.

When they reached the clearance, they saw Sandy waiting in the circle at the end of White Street with Gina Cradle and three other females. Sandy was now fifteen; she stood 5' 7" and weighed around 135 pounds. The freckled faced, brown-haired, blue-eyed teen grew scared when mini-fro wearing dark-skinned Twiggy, standing 5'10" weighing 145 pounds, and Martha, with her jet-black hair braided into two thick plats, and standing 5'9" weighing 145 pounds, emerged from the woods in their wartime apparel. Sandy eyed the two thick gold bracelets Twiggy wore and told herself that someday she would be the top ranking female leader of Folk Gang in Ghost Town. She dreamed of wearing Twiggy's bracelets one day as Twiggy and Martha approached her.

Sandy guarded herself as Twiggy, Martha, Gina, and three other G-Queens surrounded her. She was scared, but she knew she couldn't plead for mercy. She swung at Twiggy and missed and before she knew what happened, Twiggy was all over Sandy, pounding her into submission. Martha and the other G-Queens jumped on her as well. The fight was an outright beat down, but Sandy, bloody mouth and all, swung with what little strength she had left, remembering the day when her mother was jumped in while continuously telling herself not to fall. The fifteen year-old back peddled and danced around as she took blows from the six females, but before long, Sandy was no longer fighting back. She stood and covered her head and face as Twiggy and Martha, and the other females pounded her head and body; still Sandy didn't fall. Twiggy stopped the beating all of a sudden when she realized Sandy wasn't going to take a knee until she was severely beaten to the point of having to be taken to the emergency room. She grabbed the weary teen and hugged her close. Martha and the rest of the females stood by and watched as Twiggy slowly raised her right hand and produced a pitchfork and said, "This Sandy Duncan, G-Queen, Folk Gang foot soldier, factioned to Ghost Town."

The year also saw Simon Charles, Jesse Green, and Clark Junior get made. The new recruits were young and ambitious, just the type of people Ghost Town needed at the time. Albert Lee had sent word a month after Sandy was jumped in that his brother Peter Paul was to lead Ghost Town. At the age of twenty, Peter Paul over saw forty-five members in Ghost

Town, including his nephew Simon Charles.

Martha had moved from her home into Twiggy's home towards the end of August 1988 and the realignment was going along smoothly; except for the fact that Martha and Twiggy felt that Albert Lee had made a mistake anointing Peter Paul as War Chief of Ghost Town. They felt that he should have anointed the two of them because Peter Paul was not a natural born leader. On top of that, he caused trouble just about everywhere he went. Peter Paul often got into fights with Vice Lords at the skating rink, or on the campus of Jackson State University, which was becoming a popular hangout during the late eighties.

Martha and Twiggy had prevented a major war over the actions of Peter Paul just before 1988 came to a close. And as 1989 rolled in, Peter Paul may have been the appointed leader of Ghost Town, but it was clear to everyone that Twiggy and Martha were pulling the strings. The two had spent nearly $23,000 of their money on Albert Lee's appeals, and by doing so, they gained even more street credibility by standing behind Albert Lee. The two only stopped when Albert Lee, realizing their attempts was in vain, told them to start looking after their families. He was preparing for his date of execution; although he never told Martha and Twiggy that he was doing so. The two females obeyed his orders, besides, they didn't have much money left. Slim had increased Mary's rent to $375 a month that year, and Martha, knowing what she and Twiggy were about to do next, had paid her sister's rent for the whole year; just in case something happened to her and Twiggy during their next joint venture—the cocaine drug trade.

Martha and Twiggy took their last $1000 dollars and the two took on the new venture with a connect coming out of Canton, Mississippi, a small town north of Jackson, that allowed them to reap a huge profit. By mid-summer of '89, thirty year-olds Twiggy and Martha were heavy into the crack cocaine drug trade and gang-banging had taken a second seat as the two were enthralled with the fast money they made from slanging the drug.

Martha was able to refurnish Mary's house and she also gave

her enough money to buy her nieces' entire wardrobe for the school year. Mary thanked her, tried to repay Martha, but she would always insist that Mary keep the money. Mary would always relent, but she would pay some of it back by taking Martha out to dinner and buying her gifts.

Martha also saw her family daily and things were going along smoothly ever since she'd moved out of the house a year ago. Mary, meanwhile, was trying as best she could to raise her daughters not to become involved in gang activity, but gangs were all around—at school and all through Ghost Town. The lifestyle was slowly seeping into the psyche of Ne`Ne` and Dimples, and Mary was beginning to have a hard time disciplining her daughters during the latter part of 1989 and early 1990.

Martha even began to notice the twins' subtle changes and she constantly scorned her nieces saying they weren't meant to be in a gang. But as the nineties got underway, both Mary and Martha saw that it was becoming harder and harder to keep the allure of the streets away from Ne`Ne` and Dimples—especially Ne`Ne`.

The Holland Family Saga Part Five

CHAPTER 15

A DAY AWAY

It was the summer of 1990 and Ne`Ne` and Dimples were at the curve in Friendly Lane just outside the entrance to the trail leading to Ambush. They had begun hanging out regularly with seventeen year-olds Sandy Duncan and Simon Charles. Ne`Ne` and Dimples, both thirteen, were slender, 5' 2" 125 pound caramel-skinned teens with dark eyes. They had thinly-haired bodies, and thick, jet-black coarse hair just like their mother and aunt.

Besides Sandy and Simon, fourteen year-old Jesse Green, and fifteen year-old Clark Junior hung with the twins. These six friends were real close, and though there were many other teens that hung in Ghost Town, these six friends were always together and in a world of their own. They had known one another since they were babies and now that they were coming of age, they looked forward to hanging with one another almost every day.

Simon was sitting behind the steering wheel of a 1971 navy blue drop top Chevy Impala on chrome Daytona rims and all white interior this hot sunny day. The car was Twiggy's car. She had purchased it from the profits she made from cocaine. Simon had gotten his license, and since Twiggy was always with Martha, she let her younger brother use her car whenever he wanted to—which was just about every day.

Jackin' For Beats, a rap song by the rapper Ice-Cube, blared from the car's stereo as Sandy, Clark and Jesse took turns passing a blunt back and forth while Ne'Ne' and Dimples stood beside the car talking to Simon Charles. Simon was a cool and calm husky seventeen year-old. He stood about 5'9" and weighed over two hundred pounds. He had a round face with thick sideburns and corn-rolled hair. The dark-skinned young man was adored by a lot of girls in Ghost Town, but they stayed away from him because Sandy Duncan, who was fast accelerating in the ranks of Folk, had already claimed him as her own. Sandy and Simon had broken each other's virgin when they were only fourteen, and although Simon slept with other girls, he never fooled around in Ghost Town because he knew word would get back to Sandy.

Jesse was a slender 5'8" 140 pound fourteen year-old. He was dark-skinned with short wavy hair; Dimples had a crush on Jesse.

Clark was a 5'7", muscular 155 pound fifteen year-old. He was light-skinned with a neatly trimmed Afro and thin mustache and he had taken a liking to Ne'Ne'.

When Martha and Mary arrived in Ghost Town, it was because of the fact that Mary was pregnant that the two sisters were discernible; but over time, Martha had taken on a more hardened look, she and Mary were now easily distinguishable. Ne'Ne' and Dimples could easily fool people at school, and most of Ghost Town as well; but Simon, Sandy, Jesse and Clark could easily tell them apart because of the simple fact that they had been around the twins for years. They knew their demeanor. Ne'Ne' was bold and daring and she talked loud. She was somewhat like Martha. Dimples was more fun-loving and easygoing, somewhat like her mother Mary.

"Simon," Sandy yelled aloud as she stood in the grass with Jesse and Clark smoking the blunt, "Simon, turn that shit up that's my mutherfuckin' song!"

Simon looked over to Sandy, shook his head and turned to the twins and asked, "So you and Jesse hooked up yet, Dimples?"

"Nahh man. That boy scared to even hold my hand, Simon." Dimples remarked before she began dancing to the music as

The Holland Family Saga Part Five

Simon leaned back in the seat and chuckled to himself.

"Simon!" Sandy then yelled.

Simon rose up quickly and yelled, "What mutherfucka? I ain't, I ain't turning that shit up! You wanna hear it come sit your ass in the car!"

"You gone learn ta' stop tryna' high-cap on a bitch 'round here!"

"I high-cap onna bitch 'round here whenever I get ready ta' cap onna bitch 'round here!" Simon said as he laughed aloud and turned the radio up. "Man, that bitch crazy as a mutherfucka," he yelled over the music as he turned back to Ne`Ne` and Dimples.

Just then, Martha and Twiggy pulled up on Friendly Lane beside Simon in Martha's drop top powder blue Cadillac. Martha had refurbished the car's interior and had placed 18" gold Daytona rims underneath. Even though the car was over ten years old, it was still clean, an Old School Classic. "Hey, what the fuck I told y'all two 'bout hanging in this cut right here!" Martha yelled at Ne`Ne` and Dimples as Simon turned the music down. Sandy quickly hid the blunt and she, Jesse and Clark remained silent in front of the trail.

This group of youngsters, like most young people in the neighborhood, all feared Martha and Twiggy. They all knew Martha and Twiggy had been putting in work since the late seventies and were dead serious whenever they confronted people in Ghost Town, or anywhere else for that matter. The younger people in Ghost Town believed they were only seconds away, or a few wrong words short of an ass-whipping whenever Twiggy and Martha were putting them in check— and a good portion of the time they were right.

Ne`Ne` and Dimples *knew* not to hang in front the entrance on Friendly Lane for the simple fact that Martha had been shot there. She and Twiggy would always worry that her nieces may get caught up in a raid, or maybe get mistaken for lookout soldiers and end up getting killed by the Vice Lords at the foot of the trail on Friendly Lane. Simon, Sandy, Jesse and Clark were waiting by the trail for Martha and Twiggy to finish selling their product so they could go back in Ambush and make some crack sales themselves this day.

Martha and Twiggy had Ghost Town on lock in 1990. No one could sell anything when those two were in Ambush—not even Peter Paul. When Albert Lee and the three other top ranking members went to jail, no one besides Slim and Chug-a-lug were strong enough to control Martha and Twiggy. Slim and Chug-a-lug, however, both had semi-retired from Folk Gang at the end of 1989. Slim got involved in real estate and Chug-a-lug began to open up more convenience stores. Slim and Chug-a-lug also knew they were being investigated by the F.B.I. for money laundering and racketeering, which could have them both facing thirty years behind bars. The feds were trying to prove that the two were actually using their businesses and properties as fronts to wash drug money brought in by various members of Folk Gang and for either of them to be seen with gang members would only enhance the feds' case.

Martha and Twiggy, knowing no male Folk member in Ghost Town outranked them, had grown in their own way as well. The two of them began manipulating Peter Paul and pulling rank on the younger G-Queens and male Folk members, all of whom were only in their early twenties or late teens. Martha and Twiggy could care less about gang-banging at this particular juncture of their lives. They had outgrown the lifestyle, but they were still top ranking G-Queens with Twiggy being the leader and Martha the co-captain. The two were now using their status to gain an advantage over other crack dealers, like Peter Paul, Simon, Sandy, Jesse and Clark. However, the main thing that kept Martha and Twiggy with the respect they commanded was the fact that they still put in work from time to time.

If a G-Queen had a problem, she knew she could go to either Twiggy or Martha, or both, and have her problem rectified either through action, like the time Twiggy and Martha bitch slapped a G-Queen's uncle in the middle of White Street for all to see for trying to perform an act of incest, or through council when they advised another G-Queen not to have an abortion. In that case, they gave the girl $3000 dollars and sent her to live with her grandmother in Little Rock, Arkansas. They received a picture from the former G-Queen and a thank you card from the girl's grandmother a month after the baby was born. They had saved that young teenager and her baby's life. So in spite of their manipulative ways, Twiggy and Martha were revered by all who ran the streets in Ghost Town. Much more than the immature and ignorant Peter Paul.

Peter Paul was 6' tall, 175 pounds with an Afro just like his brother, Albert Lee. He wore the sunshades like his brother as well and was the spitting image of Albert Lee, but that was all he possessed, Albert Lee's looks, because he had not the street sense or managerial skills of his older brother.

Whenever Martha and Twiggy left Ambush, Peter Paul would set up shop. Only his group, which consisted of low-ranking foot soldiers, was wild and loud. Peter Paul would pull up in Ambush in his blue Iroc Z-28, turn up the music, fire up a blunt and talk shit all day as he made sells out in the open. Whereas Ambush was deemed a place of business for Martha and Twiggy, and Simon and Sandy as well, it was playtime for Peter Paul.

Simon and his bunch never affiliated with Peter Paul when they were in Ambush. They wanted to sell their product as quickly as possible and get from around him and his rowdy bunch; and if ever the twins were to follow Simon and company into the drug circle, no one would stop them and Martha knew that to be a fact. And this is the reason that whenever she saw her nieces in front of the trail leading to Ambush, she would send them inside. She knew Simon and the rest of them were waiting for her and Twiggy to leave Ambush so they could head back there and she knew Ne`Ne` and Dimples would follow their friends into Ambush and she did not want her nieces hanging in Ambush at all, especially when Peter Paul was back there.

"Y'all get y'all asses in that house and don't even think about goin' back there in Ambush!" Martha said as she eyed her nieces.

Dimples headed home. Ne`Ne`, however, tucked her hands inside the back pockets of her jean shorts and remained in position.

Martha leaned back and eyed her niece sternly. "You heard me Rene?" she asked.

"We wasn't even doing nothing, auntie!" Ne`Ne` snapped.

"Hold up," Martha said as she removed her sunshades and blue bandanna, threw her car into park and jumped out from behind the wheel. "This li'l mutherfucka over there think I'm joking."

Sandy, Jesse, and Clark broke and ran through the trail towards Ambush and Simon started the car and crept away slowly. "Alright then, I'll hollar, Ne`Ne`." Simon said before pulling off.

"Man, y'all some hoes!" Ne`Ne` hollered as she watched her friends vacate the area.

Martha grabbed Ne`Ne` around the neck and forced her to one knee on the ground. "Watch your mouth! You think you hard? You wanna be hard, Rene?"

"Let me go! We wasn't even doing nothing!"

Martha snatched Ne`Ne` up and shoved her towards the yard. "Get in that damn house! You know I don't play that damn shit with you!" she yelled as Ne`Ne` walked ahead of her.

Dimples watched the scene unfold from the yard as Twiggy got behind the wheel of Martha's Cadillac and slowly followed her and Ne`Ne` back to Casper Drive. "Now you get your ass in that house and stay there! I better not never catch you back there, Ne`Ne`!" Martha screamed as people in the neighborhood looked at the scene unfolding.

Ne`Ne` walked into Mary's backyard angry and embarrassed, stomping pass Dimples and climbing the backstairs. She entered her mother's home and slammed the door, leaving Dimples behind in the backyard. Dimples stared at Martha without saying a word. Struck with fear and knowing not what to do, she stood in silence and awaited her orders from her aunt, who was staring coldly at her.

"Well," Martha asked as she widened her eyes and placed her hands on her hips. "What the hell you looking at, Regina? Take your ass inside and lock the damn door!"

Dimples immediately ran into the house and locked the door, doing just as her aunt commanded. Martha then turned to the people in the neighborhood who were now standing in the middle of Friendly Lane and ogled them angrily. "The fuck y'all looking at? Push out from 'round here ain't shit to see!" she yelled as the group began to slowly disburse. Martha then got into the passenger seat of her car and slammed the door. "Them some sneaky li'l girls. Especially Ne`Ne` with her hard-headed ass," she told Twiggy as Twiggy slowly crept away.

"Hey, that's Ghost Town for ya' ass." Twiggy remarked as she drove up Casper Drive slowly.

"I know Folk—but it'll break my sister heart if them girls was ta' get mixed up in this shit!"

Martha and Twiggy were now headed to Hibernia Bank's downtown branch where they each had a safe deposit box. The two women also had just over $7,000 dollars apiece in separate savings accounts at the bank and did not want to make any further cash deposits into the savings accounts for fear of arousing suspicion from the I.R.S. The safety boxes were now being used to stash their profits. As they rode to the bank, Twiggy couldn't help but notice the look of dejection on Martha's face. She watched in silence as Martha rubbed her eyes and covered them with dark, mirror-tinted sunshades.

"You don't like to do them like that huh, Folk?"

Martha looked over to Twiggy with her darkened shades covering her eyes and shook her head to say no. "I love my nieces, Twiggy," she said seriously. "I just don't want them involved in this shit. I don't know why, but it's hard for them to understand that—especially Ne`Ne`."

"Being where we at ain't making it easy for nobody back there, Martha. Loretta got the same problem with Sandy. Sometimes I wish we never jumped that li'l girl in. Sandy tell me all the time that when I retire? She gone get these bracelets and be top G-Queen. That's a helluva goal to aspire to. They just don't get the big picture. We don't bang no more—we straight hustle—and it's a big difference between the two."

"True. But they li'l young asses can't see that shit, Irene.

They infatuated with being in a gang—but half these mutherfuckas out here that gang-bang is straight cowards and they wouldn't do *shit* unless they had numbers."

"You right, Folk. I remember Kenyatta Branch and how much heart she had. That girl there would fight anybody by herself. Kenyatta didn't care about numbers."

"Yeah. Washington District fucked her around that day, but we got our revenge."

"We did. But it put Albert Lee 'nem in jail after Keisha came back on our ass."

"See," Martha said as she sat upright and took off her shades. "That was gangster how all that went down, Irene. These young ones not ready for that kind of drama. For every Kenyatta, and although she rode that five, I gotta say, Keisha was a gangster too. She came blastin' through Ghost Town by herself that day. Ain't had nobody with her but a driver. For every Albert Lee, Clark Senior, Kenyatta or Keisha, it's like ten or fifteen cowards that *call* themselves gangsters. Shit just ain't the same." Martha ended as Twiggy nodded her head in agreement and turned into the bank's parking lot.

When they left the bank, Twiggy had Martha drop her off at her man friend's home in Clinton, an upscale suburb about fifteen minutes outside of Jackson. "Y'all comin' out this way tonight?" Twiggy asked as she exited the car.

"Yea. Me, Mary and Loretta be through after dark."

"Loretta?"

"Yea, girl. Ole big thighs said she wanna climb a tree trunk tonight!" Martha said as she and Twiggy laughed.

Martha drove back to Jackson with the top down on her Cadillac. Her eyes were covered with her tinted sunglasses and she was wearing a blue bandanna around her neck, her thick, jet black hair braided into three thick pigtails. She brushed off a few cat-calls from young and old men alike as she traveled down the streets of Jackson, Mississippi, slowly making her way back to Ghost Town while blasting the song *Children's Story,* by the rapper Slick Rick. The whole time she drove,

The Holland Family Saga Part Five

Martha thought about her nieces and how she had treated them earlier in the day. Although she knew she was justified, it didn't prevent her from feeling a little remorseful over the way she'd talked to them—especially Ne`Ne`. The image of the dejected look on her nieces' faces made Martha feel bad at heart, even though she knew she was right for scolding them, and it was now propelling her to do something to make it up to her nieces.

While Martha was heading back to Ghost Town, Ne`Ne` and Dimples, meanwhile, were sitting in their mother's bedroom looking out the window at Sandy and Simon, who were now in front of Simon's house. They watched Clark and Jesse as they 'slap-boxed' in the yard, and eyed Sandy dancing to the music coming from Twiggy's ride.

"Sandy know she can't dance," the twins said simultaneously and burst into laughter.

"I told you to stop marking me, Dimples." Ne`Ne` said as she hit her twin with a pillow.

"I'm the oldest! You be repeatin' my words!" Dimples snapped as the twins play fought.

"Girl, you only got me by six minutes! That ain't nothing!"

"Six minutes!" Dimples yelled.

"Six minutes Dougie Fresh and you're on! On, on, on! On, on, on!" they then said in unison, singing Dougie Fresh's song *The Show* before they both erupted into laughter.

"I'm going get a soda pop!"

"Bring me one, Dimples," Ne`Ne` said aloud. "*I wonder what Sandy 'nem doing now,*" she then said to herself as she returned to the window.

Ne`Ne` looked out the window just in time to see Sandy and Simon making their way into the Charles' house. In her eyes, her friends were just hanging out and she wanted to join them.

"Here your soda can, Rene." Dimples said upon returning to the room.

"Thank you. Man, Sandy 'nem just chillin'. I'm going over

there!" Ne`Ne` said as she hopped from her mother's bed.

"Martha said stay inside!" Dimples remarked.

"They gone!"

"Ne`Ne`, nooo," Dimples whined as she blocked her twin from leaving their mother's room. "Come on now. Listen to auntie! She right! Simon and Sandy be selling crack in Ambush and we don't need ta' be back there."

Ne`Ne` sat back down on the bed and looked out the window just in time to see Simon emerge from the Charles' house with Sandy following close behind. Jesse and Clark soon followed the two. Simon and Sandy each held an AK-47 assault rifle in their arms as they slowly made their way to Twiggy's Impala. The twins watched as their four friends piled into the car and rode off towards Ambush.

"You saw them big guns Sandy and Simon had?" Dimples asked Ne`Ne`.

"Yea, man! They goin' get paid!" Ne`Ne` replied as she hopped from the bed and ran towards the back door.

Dimples gave chase and ran and stood before Ne`Ne` before she could exit the back door and pleaded, "Don't go by them, Ne`Ne`!"

"Dimples, get out my way!"

"No! Martha said—"

"I don't care what Martha said! I'm going in Ambush!" Ne`Ne` said angrily as she shoved Dimples aside and opened the door. She then quickly closed the door shut and said, "Martha outside," as she locked the door and ran to her bedroom.

"Go 'head and go in Ambush now!" Dimples remarked sarcastically with a smile on her face as she followed Ne`Ne` towards her bedroom.

"Forget you, Regina!"

The twins were in Ne`Ne`s room hanging up clothes when Martha entered the house and walked into her former bedroom.

"Hey what's up, y'all?" Martha asked humbly.

"Nothing, auntie," the twins replied lowly and in unison as they continued to hang up Ne'Ne's clothes.

"Look," Martha said as she stepped into the room and removed her sunshades, "I wanna say I'm sorry for doing what I did earlier—but I knew Simon and Sandy was headed to Ambush. That right there? That ain't for y'all."

"I know, auntie." Dimples replied.

"Rene?" Martha then asked.

Ne'Ne' knew Martha was right. Everybody that went into Ambush sold drugs. All she really wanted to do was hang with her friends this day, but seeing Sandy and Simon each toting an AK-47 while headed to the back of Ghost Town let her see firsthand that what went on in Ambush was serious business. She wasn't prepared for what went on back there and she knew it. "I'm sorry auntie. I was just hanging with my friends that's all, and you came and—"

"I know. I know. But your mother and I don't want y'all back there. My sister works hard to give you two the things Simon and the rest of 'em have ta' hustle ta' get. Hanging is cool, but not in Ambush my babies. Not back there y'all." Martha said as she grew teary-eyed and pulled Ne'Ne' and Dimples close to her and kissed the tops of their heads.

Ne'Ne' and Dimples hugged their aunt back tightly, witnessing her get emotional before their eyes. Dimples understood fully. If it meant that much that it would cause Martha to become emotional, she knew hanging in Ambush was the wrong thing to do. A dangerous thing to do. Ne'Ne' knew it as well, but the thought of hanging in Ambush would linger in the back of her mind always because the allure of the street life was a calling that was just too irresistible for her to ignore at this point and time.

"Your momma," Martha said as she held her nieces close, breaking the silence, "your momma would be heart-broken if anything ever happened to either of you. She loves you. I love you. That's why I'm hard on y'all because I don't want y'all to go through what I been through in life so far. Fighting. Shooting and gettin' shot. And running the risk of going to jail for the things I do now. The two of you deserve better, understand?"

"Yes, auntie," the twins said together as their grip tightened on their aunt.

They broke their embrace and Martha helped her nieces hang Ne`Ne`'s clothes and clean both their rooms. "Let's take a ride!" Martha announced the moment they were finished.

The twins immediately grew excited. They loved to ride in Martha's convertible. They each freshened up and grabbed their leather Louis Vuitton pocketbooks and followed their aunt out the door. Once Martha announced that they were all going for a ride, she could see the change in her nieces; they were all smiles as they walked out the back door. Just before she exited through the back door, Martha shoved Ne`Ne` gently. Ne`Ne` turned and tapped her aunt softly and leaned back into Martha as Martha pulled her close and rubbed her thick head of hair. "I'm sorry I embarrassed you, sweetie." Martha whispered in her niece's ear.

"I'm sorry I talked back, auntie." Ne`Ne` replied as the three of them headed out the door, got into the convertible and rode out of Ghost Town, far away from Ambush and the often alluring call of the streets that held sway over the place they called home. Jackson, Mississippi was more than just Ghost Town, more than just hanging in the neighborhood spending idle time. A day away from the 'hood was not only welcomed, it was needed by Martha and her nieces.

CHAPTER 16

DOING IT IN THE DARK

Mary was home sitting on her couch looking over newspaper advertising ads as she awaited her daughters' return from their outing with Martha. When she heard Martha's car pull into the driveway she got up to greet her family at the back door.

"Momma," Dimples said as she hugged her mother, "auntie took us to this big ole lake today."

"It's called the Ross Barnett Reservoir, Dimples." Ne`Ne` chimed in as she gave her mother a hug.

Martha hugged her sister and they all settled into the living room. Mary picked up the ad she was scanning and Ne`Ne` and Dimples both grew excited. They looked at one another and yelled aloud in unison, "School clothes!"

"Yes, school clothes. So what's the latest fashion?" Mary asked.

"Oooh, momma," Dimples said animatedly as she stood up, "they got these knee length silk dress outfits with the matching eel skin shoes and then, then, the new Air Jordan's is the sh—I mean, that's what everybody wearing. And Sandy said everybody in the high school getting Gucci attaché bags this year, either suede or leather."

"Yea. Them is some bags nice. And you know Polo shirts and Girbaud's with the Eastland shoes are always in style! They got new sweater dresses like the ones you be wearing sometime too momma, they real nice." Ne`Ne` added.

"All these name brands. Polo? Jordan's? Girbaud's? Silk, suede and leather? Y'all two gone get some Wrangler jeans and a pair of knickerbockers and be happy!" Martha said as she and Mary sniggled.

Ne`Ne` and Dimples laughed at Martha's remark and threw pillows at her and Mary. "Hey, hey," Mary said as she laughed, "how y'all gonna attack your own mother?" The twins then got up and went into Ne`Ne`s room, taking the insert ads with them so they could circle the clothing items they liked.

"You know them attaché bags cost like a hundred dollars apiece, right?" Martha asked Mary.

"A hundred dollars? Each?"

"Yea, but don't worry 'bout it. I'll get that, and their shoes and supplies too." Martha replied.

Martha always helped Mary with purchasing the twins' school clothes even though she never asked nor expected her to help out. Martha knew her sister would never ask her for anything, but she had the unwavering desire to help make things easier on Mary, who worked forty plus hours a week in order to take care of her children. Martha was proud of Mary because she was the type of parent that took care of her own. She knew Mary had put herself in a position to take care of home if something ever happened to her, and she was glad to know Mary was more than capable of surviving if she wasn't around. In spite of that fact, however, Martha would do whatever she could to make things in life less stressful on her hard-working sister.

"Hey, you still coming out tonight?" Martha then asked.

"Sure is. Speaking of, I'm going nap for a couple of hours."

"Alright, I'll be back around nine." Martha stated as she got up and went over to the Charles' house.

****

Shortly after nine, Martha, Mary, and Loretta climbed into Martha's car and drove to Clinton and picked Twiggy up and headed to a club in Vicksburg, about a forty-five minute drive west of Jackson. Mary had Sandy watch the twins on this night, and the twins, as their mother and aunt were clubbing in Vicksburg, were all over the house talking loud, cussing, and running back and forth to the kitchen for cookies, soda, sandwiches, cereal and anything else they could think of to put inside their bellies.

Thirteen year-olds Ne`Ne` and Dimples believed that because it was seventeen year-old Sandy Duncan that was watching them, it was just as if no one was supervising their actions. Sandy, however, took her job seriously. She respected Mary and Mary had entrusted her with the supervision of her daughters. Sandy was trying to watch TV, but the twins were getting louder and louder. They had the radio and the TV going in Dimples' bedroom and all the lights were on in the house. Tired of hearing herself repeatedly and politely asking the twins to quiet down, Sandy jumped from the couch and rushed into Dimples' room. "Sit down and shut up!" she hollered towards Dimples and Ne`Ne`.

"You ain't my momma and you can't tell me what to do!" the twins remarked in unison and then laughed aloud at their simultaneous remark.

"If I was I'd beat the ever-loving crap outta both of y'all!!"

"But you not our momma sooo—you can't touch this!" Ne`Ne` said as she broke out and began singing M.C. Hammer's song *You Can't Touch This* as she began doing the running man, a dance which had her running in place.

Dimples joined her sister and the twins did the typewriter, a dance which had them sliding sideways to and fro across the carpeted floor in the middle of the bedroom. Sandy stared angrily at the two from the threshold of the room as she shook her head in disgust. She ran into the room and the twins separated and scurried out into the hall. Dimples ran out the front door, but Sandy cornered Ne`Ne` in the hallway. The two struggled, but Sandy was stronger. She got the better of Ne`Ne` and shoved her into her room and told her to remain there and closed the door. She then went and locked the front door on Dimples and called Simon at his house and the two talked briefly. Sandy then returned to Ne'Ne's room and sat in the room with the twin, who was now angry that she didn't make it outside with her sister. Ne'Ne' and Sandy could hear Dimples running around the house tapping on the windows.

"Ne'Ne'! I'm free! I'm free! You gotta escape massa!" Dimples joked as she ran from window to window.

"Oooh, these some bad li'l heifers!" Sandy thought to herself as she listened to Dimples' taunting remarks.

Just then a volley of gunshots was heard echoing from the front side of the twins' home on Casper Drive and Dimples went silent. Ne'Ne' screamed aloud for her sister at that moment, scared something had happened to Dimples. Sandy let Ne'Ne' go when the two heard Dimples banging on the back door, yelling, "Ne'Ne'! Sandy! Somebody let me in!"

Ne'Ne' went to open the door, but Sandy grabbed her and held her down on the kitchen floor. "Let me go, Sandy! My sister out there!"

"She was hard at first! What happened to her?"

Another round of bullets thundered into the night air and Dimples began kicking the door hard. "Let me in! Rene! Sandy! Somebody open the door they shootin'!" Dimples cried amidst the gunfire.

"What? I, I, can't hear you over the gunshots, Dimples!" Sandy yelled from the kitchen as she held Ne'Ne' down on the floor.

"I said they shootin'! Open the door!" Dimples pleaded.

Sandy let go of Ne'Ne' and got up and opened the back door and Dimples rushed in with a face full of tears. She hugged Ne'Ne' as the two cried together and leaned against the washing machine and stared back at Sandy, who had a stern looked on her face. "Now," Sandy said loudly, "y'all each go to your room and stay in there! No more cookies! No loud music! I don't wanna hear nobody sneeze up in here! And turn them damn lights off back there too! You don't never know what's gone happen running outside this time of night!" she ended as the twins each went to their respective rooms and closed their door. Order had been restored in the Holland household, and before long, the twins were sound asleep.

Sandy had called Simon when Dimples first ran out the house. She wanted to scare her and teach both her and Ne`Ne` a lesson at the same time so she had Simon shoot her AK-47 into the ground in his backyard. That ploy worked because Sandy would not have a problem with either of the twins the rest of the night. She returned to the living room to watch *Def Comedy Jam* in the now tranquil domicile.

****

Meanwhile, in Vicksburg, Mary, who wore her hair pinned up with twisted curls hanging down on either side of her face, was sitting at the bar sipping a rum and coke as she swayed to fro, enjoying the sounds of The Mary Jane Girls' song *In My House*. She had on a cream, tight-fitting silk skirt that hung just above the knee with a matching cream and white three-quarter length silk coat and white knee length leather boots. Her nails matched her clothes and she had on a clear lip gloss. Martha's hair was styled the same as Mary's and she had the same outfit, but hers was all black, including the boots. Martha was out on the dance floor dancing with a man who'd recently bought her a drink.

Mary and Martha hadn't paid for a drink from the moment they entered the hole in the wall rhythm and blues night club, which featured low ceilings and a large dance floor with a long bar and plenty of stools. Small tables were up against the wall and they surrounded the entire dance floor, and that's where Twiggy and Loretta were hanging out. Thirty-five year-old Loretta Duncan, her brown hair pressed, dressed in a dark brown all-in-one silk dress with a slit on the right side than ran halfway up her thick thigh, with a pair of eel-skin black pumps on her feet, was sitting on the lap of a heavy set black man that was near her age as she sipped on her vodka and cranberry juice. The man's friend sat with Twiggy, who wore a tight-fitting navy-blue leather short set and navy-blue sandals with straps that wrapped around her calves. The man complimented Twiggy on her hairstyle, which was a neatly trimmed and lined mini-Afro that had been permed and curled. The four sat and talked after the men had offered to buy them drinks.

Mary was sitting alone at the bar when a slender gentlemen slightly taller than she sat beside her. "Care for another drink, miss?" he asked politely.

"Well thank you mister, umm,"

"My name is Vincent. But you can call me Vince." the dark-skinned medium-built man stated as he smiled.

"I'm Mary."

"I been watching you and your sister since y'all came in, Mary," Vince remarked as he ordered two rum and cokes. "She's kinda on the wild side. So that means you must be the good twin."

Mary laughed lowly. "We're both good—in different ways, Vince. Don't let the looks fool you. We are both, very, very good," she said seductively as she eyed the man and sipped her drink.

Mary was out for a good time on this night. She'd dated several men after Clark Senior was sent up state, but she never had anything serious going on, and that was the way she wanted things in her life. She never let anyone get close to her nor her daughters. Mary was fine with having a friend with benefits, but exclusivity was a requirement for her because once she became intimate with someone, that man and that man alone would be the only man she would have intercourse with during that time. She had turned down a couple of men who wanted to form a relationship with her in the past and they politely stepped aside. Mary chose her sexual partners wisely. She didn't want the drama-filled types that had three or more kids by two or more different women, nor did she want anyone who was a street thug, or unemployed. A few female friends at work had told Mary that she set her standards too high, but to Mary, the men she often turned down just weren't man enough to deal with what she required for a man to become her lover, and by being a "choosey lover" as one man friend called her, Mary saved herself many a bad experience with the opposite sex.

The Holland Family Saga Part Five

Before long, Mary and Vince were on the floor dancing. When a slow song was played, the two came together and there was an immediate spark—sexual tension was beginning to form. Mary loved the way Vince's body felt next to hers, he was a natural fit. Every curve in her body was complemented by his muscles. Another slow song was played and Mary could suddenly feel Vince's erection poking her navel. Vince could feel the heat emanating from Mary's body in return. They danced close together, grinding against one another as Vince let his hands slide gently down Mary's back to the top of her ass. When she did nothing to stop him, Vince gripped Mary's ass and rubbed it softly, producing a moan from her as she blew her warm breath onto his neck and laid her head on his shoulder and rocked in unison with this man who was stirring a sexual desire within her, a desire she hadn't felt in a long time. The song ended and the two returned to the bar and shared another drink and talked for almost an hour before Martha, Twiggy and Loretta announced that they were going to another club. Mary invited Vince to follow the females to the next club, and he agreed, if only to spend more time with Mary.

****

"You'll never make me stay…so take your weight off of me…I know you seduce every man this time you won't seduce me…"

Michael Jackson's song, *Dirty Diana* played loudly on the sound system inside *The Champagne Room*, a night/strip club on the outskirts of Vicksburg. The club was an upscale club that had a V.I.P. section, a large marble dance floor and a medium-sized stage for its dancers. Loretta, Martha and Twiggy were near the stage watching two female dancers and a male dancer perform to the song while Mary and Vince sat in a darkened booth towards the back of the club. Mary could see the performance and she slowly became entrenched in the erotic act that was unfolding on stage. The male dancer slowly dry humped the female that lay beneath him as the other female, who was dressed as a Dallas Cowboy cheerleader, complete with boots and a cowgirl hat, rode his back. The male dancer was lifting his body up and down in a slow, rhythmic pattern while the female on his back ground atop him and cracked a whip. The song's lyrics, coupled with performance, had the entire audience in a trance. The female below the male dancer then spread her legs and propped herself up with her elbows and began to thrust upwards, slamming her body into her male companion as the song played on.

"She likes the boys in the band she knows when they come to town...every musicians fan after the curtain comes down...she waits at backstage doors for those who have prestige...who promise fortune and fame a life that's so carefree..."

Mary was enthralled by the performance, and she didn't resist Vince when he slid his hand across her thigh. She also didn't protest when he leaned in and kissed her on the lips; instead, she returned the kiss with passion.

Out on the floor, Martha, Twiggy and Loretta were each clutching a bottle of Dom Perignon in one hand and had a stack of ones in the other as they hoot and hollered at the erotic dancers' performance. "That's what the hell I'm talking 'bout! Stud lovin'! Ride that damn stud!" Loretta screamed as she threw dollar bills onto the stage.

Martha and Twiggy were yelling and throwing bills as well. Loretta said she wanted a stud, meaning she wanted a black man to take her. Martha and Twiggy were not only there to help Loretta find a man, they were out to swing also.

Mary, meanwhile, now had a glazed over look in her eyes as Vince manually manipulated her pussy, making her soaking wet, and we he disappeared beneath the table, Mary knew what was coming. She blushed, looked around to see if anybody was watching, which they weren't, and waited in anticipation. Vince was setting off fireworks in Mary. When she felt her dress being raised she eased up from the leather seat and helped Vince pull her dress up to her waist. She then felt Vince's breath on her panties and waited in all eagerness to feel his tongue press against her neatly trimmed vagina. Vince pulled her panties tight and licked her through her panties and a stunned Mary let her hands fall to the side as she moaned aloud. She widened her legs and closed her eyes and slowly rotated her hips. What Vince was doing was stimulating, but Mary wanted tongue on flesh. She reached for Vince's hands and removed them from her panties and took her own hands and pulled her panties to the side, exposing her glistening vagina while rotating her hips and thrusting forward slightly, trying to find the warmth of Vince's mouth. She wanted his lips there, and Vince knew it. Finally, after several excruciating seconds had passed, Mary felt his tongue encircle her clitoris. She grabbed the sides of the table and shuddered with an immediate orgasm and then sat back and enjoyed the ride. She watched the rest of the show as she gently ran her fingers through Vince's thick head of hair as he gave her slow, hot head.

By the time the club closed, Mary, Vince, Martha, Twiggy and Loretta were all quite tipsy, but they still weren't ready to call it a night. Things were just heating up. Martha and Twiggy got two young male dancers to leave the club with them when it closed. The male dancers, both twenty-three years of age, were brown-skinned and over six feet tall and muscular. The young men grabbed two fifths of E&J Brandy and before long, all seven adults were partying in a huge suite inside the Hilton hotel in downtown Vicksburg directly overlooking the Mississippi river.

The two male dancers did a private show for Martha, Twiggy and Loretta while Mary and Vince went into the bedroom to finish what they had started. There were two king-sized beds in the bedroom, but Mary and Vince were the only two inside the bedroom at the time. They stripped off their clothes and Mary fell back onto one of the beds and Vince slid on a condom and was entering her in seconds. This was no sweet love-making between the two, it was pure lust, uninhibited passion and a need to have complete and utter fulfillment. The two were all over one another kissing, gently biting, rubbing cheeks and clawing at one another's flesh as Vince long-dicked Mary until she creamed, her legs were wide open when her juices shot out across Vince's dick and trickled down the crack of her ass and formed a small puddle on the satin sheets as Vince continued to slam into her, forcing Mary to scream his name as he ejaculated into the condom, bringing about another powerful orgasm. The two were entangled with one another, breathing hard, sweating and laughing as they kissed one another hungrily. "I need a break, baby. But we just getting started.

You were right." Vince stated as he grabbed Mary close and she sunk her head into his chest.

"Right about what?" Mary asked through heavy breathing.

"You are good. Very good. This is some of the best pussy I done had in my life."

Mary smiled to herself. She knew Vince was going to say that. She had heard it several times before. As Mary and Vince rested for a few minutes, the sounds coming from the living room told them that the party was heating up even more.

****

"Lines of people lined up inside and out...it's just one reason to rock the house...but in the daytime the streets were clear... you couldn't find a good freak anywhere 'cause...the freaks come at night...the freaks come out at night..."

Whodini's song, *The Freaks Come at Night* blared on the stereo in the living room as Martha, Twiggy and Loretta, all who had stripped naked and were sipping mixed drinks and smoking joints, egged on the two young strippers they had taken from *The Champagne Room.*

"Take it out! Take, take the mutherfuckin' schlong out and let me see it!" Loretta yelled aloud as she stood butt naked in front of one of the male dancers with a glass of Brandy.

The dancers' names were Herc, and G. Chocolate, and Loretta was drooling over Herc. He pulled his thong aside and when his thick tool dropped and dangled, Loretta grabbed for it.

"Stroke that mutherfucka!" Twiggy yelled over the music as she sipped her drink.

Twiggy was a sexy slim dark-skinned woman at 31 years of age. She had small breasts, a flat stomach and a shaved vagina. Her ass was flat, but when she bent over, it was one of the most beautiful asses a man could lay eyes upon as everything was fully exposed. Loretta was a thick bow-legged woman with large double-d-cup breast with large pink aureoles; and even at thirty-five, she still had a somewhat flat stomach, wide hips and a wide, firm ass. Martha and Mary were both sexy at thirty-one, tan-skinned and hairy with taut, pert rear ends and

The Holland Family Saga Part Five

"snapper" vaginas.

"I'm a get this man-cannon hard as a diamond! Watch this here!" Loretta said as she wet her hand with spittle and began to slide it back and forth over Herc's dick. Herc placed his hand on Loretta's ass as he gyrated, the two then lip-locked as Loretta stroked him with expertise. "This mutherfucka, ooh you sexy white mutherfucka, you gone make this dick come!" Herc said aloud as he gripped Loretta's bare ass tightly.

"Shoot that shit! Come on!" Loretta said with aggression as she flicked her tongue across Herc's nipples, causing his dick to erupt like a volcano. When Herc's fluid splashed out onto the carpet and Loretta's hand, she pulled the dancer into the darkened bedroom and pushed him onto the bed and straddled his body in reverse. "Momma want some tongue loving," she said as she dropped her vagina onto Herc's mouth and took his limp, semen soaked dick into her mouth and licked him clean.

Martha and Twiggy were still in the living room with G. Chocolate sitting side by side on the couch taking turns giving head to the young man.

Mary had heard all the explicit conversations and she looked up at Vince who was now focused on Loretta and Herc, who were locked in a raunchy sixty-nine. Mary was shocked, but turned on all the more watching the two go at it. Martha and Twiggy soon entered the room and Twiggy closed the door and pulled the curtains shut which caused the whole room to go dark.

"Why you did that?" Loretta could be heard asking.

"It's better in the dark. Just stay on your side of the bed shit! Me and Martha got our tree trunk over here!" Twiggy could be heard saying as she and Martha giggled.

Inside the darkness, Mary grabbed for Vince's dick to get him hard. He slid on a condom and rolled Mary onto her side and entered her as he tweaked her nipples. Before long, Mary's moans of passion could be heard by all.

"Mary doing the damn thang," Martha said to herself as she sat astride G. Chocolate and bounced up and down on his dick,

riding him at a rapid pace with her hands planted flat on his chest. Martha was really getting into her fuck when she felt hands on her ass. She knew it was Twiggy, but she didn't care, she was too entrenched in the fucking she was receiving.

"Ride that dick." Twiggy whispered sexily into Martha's ear.

"Aww shit!" Martha cried, "Aww, aww shit!" she yelled as she gyrated at a furious pace.

Twiggy then got behind Martha and pressed her small breasts to her back and tweaked Martha's nipples. Martha was so aroused, she grabbed Twiggy's hands and held them firmly against her breasts as she was driven over the edge towards an intense orgasm. "Aww, damn! Aww fuck! Nigga you gone make come all over this dick tonight!" she was heard yelling repeatedly.

Martha began shuddering and G. Chocolate soon began fucking upwards into her as he smacked her ass, driving Martha crazy, making her moan like a woman possessed. He leaned up, grabbed Martha's thick head of hair and drove his tongue down her throat in a forceful manner that only made her hungry for more. She pushed him back down into the mattress and leaned forward, placed his hands on her ass and demanded that he fuck her. G. Chocolate rested on one arm and leaned up slightly, "This what you want, baby," he asked, rather he proclaimed to Martha as he held a handful of hair and drove his dick deep inside Martha "You want the shit fucked outta you don't you?"

"Yeah," Martha screamed. "Fuck me! Fuck me like you mean it!"

G. Chocolate was nearly jumping up off the bed into Martha's pussy. "Come on you good pussy mutherfucka! Get this dick! Act like you want it!"

"I want it!"

"You want it?"

"Fuck me!"

"Take it!"

"I'm—oh my fuckin' god—oh my god!" Martha cried aloud.

"You nuttin? You comin' on my dick? Come on daddy dick, Martha!"

Martha shrieked and her body stiffened, but G. Chocolate was relentless. Even when Martha tried to climb off his rod, he held her down. "Uh, uh! You ain't done! You ain't done with this dick!"

"Please," Martha begged. "Please!"

"You here this shit, Herc? All that shit Martha talked at the club! Now she backing off the dick!" G. Chocolate said as he long-dicked Martha slowly. "Twiggy, I'm waitin' on you, woman," he then said.

Herc could only mumble inaudibly because his mouth was filled with Loretta's pussy. "He can't talk right now his mouth full." Loretta said, bringing about slight laughter and enough pause to allow Martha to climb off G. Chocolate. She was covered in sweat and breathing heavily, nearly out of breath from having been taken over the edge in style of fucking that reminded her of Albert Lee. G. Chocolate had nearly caused Martha to call Albert Lee's name, but she held that one back. She rolled off G. Chocolate and lay beside him.

Twiggy then straddled him and impaled herself on his thick cock and G. Chocolate laid back and moaned, "Oooh, shit. Wait a minute! Wait a fuckin' minute."

"Uh, uh, nigga! Don't bitch up now," Twiggy said as she rocked back and forth. "Pussy hot ain't it?"

"Oooh, Irene, Irene, Irene."

"That's right. Call momma name," Twiggy said as she high-fived Martha. "I got 'em for ya' sister."

Twiggy sat down on G. Chocolate's dick and gripped it tightly with her muscles and he came in under two minutes. She and Martha then began teasing him and he said Martha had him there already. "I'm a get you for that shit, Twiggy."

"Yeah nigga, whatever." Twiggy replied as she lit a joint.

Loretta was the loudest. Herc was dishing out a serious

pounding on the big fine white woman's pussy, but it was exactly what she wanted. "Take me! Ohh, yes, give me all that dick! All of it!" Loretta yelled.

The sounds of flesh slapping flesh was heavy in the room. As Martha lay on her back, she soon felt a pair of lips on her pussy. G. Chocolate was next to her toking on the weed, so she knew it was Twiggy. Neither Martha nor Twiggy had never done nothing like this before, but on this night, for whatever reason, maybe the alcohol, the marijuana, and the two young studs that were pure fucking machines, they both dared to explore a taboo form of sex that had suddenly intrigued the both of them.

"Mmm! Mmm!" Martha moaned as she ground against Twiggy's face, allowing her take her there. And since the lights were off, she knew no one besides G. Chocolate would know.

Loretta was somewhere in the room, maybe on the floor, but her screams were letting Martha know she was lost in a thorough fucking. Mary was repeatedly calling Vince's name; she, too, was lost in ecstasy. G. Chocolate knew what was happening beside him and it turned him on. He got up and fumbled on the nightstand for another condom and quickly slid it on and felt around until he found Twiggy's up turned ass and entered her slowly. Twiggy rose up and turned around and kissed him, he could taste Martha's pussy on Twiggy's lips. "Don't tell," Twiggy whispered in between kisses.

Martha then got up and began rubbing Twiggy's breasts while G. Chocolate took Twiggy from behind. She didn't return the favor, but she and Twiggy shared a long passionate kiss as Martha tweaked Twiggy's nipples and rubbed her clitoris until she came, moaning into Martha's mouth. G. Chocolate erupted into the condom and the three sprawled out onto the king-sized bed. Before long, Mary's moans subsided. She was done for the night. Everybody was done except for Loretta and Herc, who lasted for almost another hour.

Mary, Martha, Twiggy, Vince and even G. Chocolate wondered just what in the hell Herc and Loretta had going on as they listened to the woman enjoy having sex with a black man for the first time in her life. The last thing to be heard in the darkened room was that of Loretta repeatedly thanking Herc for giving her the best sex of her life.

"Thank you," Mary, Martha, and Twiggy all thought to themselves simultaneously, glad Loretta and Herc had finally settled down.

What happened in the darkened room would forever remain a secret between, Mary, Martha, Twiggy and Loretta. They all had spontaneous sex, but Mary and Vince had agreed that they would still get together from time to time because they enjoyed one another's company in and out of the bed. Martha, Twiggy and Loretta would continue to venture back to Vicksburg, sometimes with Mary and Vince, but they would never repeat what they had done the first time they went. Never again did Martha and Twiggy explore one another in the manner they did their first night out in Vicksburg. They talked about what happened the day after, and Twiggy said she was just high and curious.

Martha, in turn, admitted the fact that she was high and caught up in the heat of passion and it felt good at the same time. The two women would hold that secret forever because if word ever got out that Twiggy had ate Martha's pussy, their rep in Ghost Town and throughout Jackson would be ruined. That was something they could not let happen, and neither had lesbian desires. What happened in Vicksburg, in both their eyes, was just some freaky shit that had simply spun out of control and was to never get repeated again. Both women had put what happened behind them and out of their minds.

In the meantime, the rest of 1990 was a fun-filled barrage of sexual conquests for all four females. And as 1991 came into existence, the women slowed down. The frequent trips to Vicksburg had finally run its course; but every now and then they would venture into the town and 'unwind' as they began to call their trips to Vicksburg.

The Holland Family Saga Part Five

CHAPTER 17

FUNKY ASS DICE AND RIM JOBS

It was now September of 1991. Ne`Ne` and Dimples were fourteen and in high school now and Simon and Sandy had both graduated high school earlier in the year. They were among the first in Ghost Town to accomplish that feat. Twiggy and Martha's cocaine hustle was going pretty good and eighteen year-olds Simon and Sandy, and seventeen year-old Clark, and sixteen year-old Jesse Green, both of whom had dropped out of high school, were now holding down Ambush.

Martha and Twiggy not only hustled Ambush, but they also now supplied Folk members in other neighborhoods as well with the help of Peter Paul and Gina—who had become a hot item. Everybody knew Martha and Twiggy; and the streets respected the two off top because of their long street résumés.

Mary, meanwhile, was searching for a new job during this period of time because Dairy Queen was giving way to the numerous fast food chains opening up on Hanging Moss Drive. Her hours were beginning to get cut so finding another job for her was priority one.

On this clear warm night in September, Mary, her daughters, Martha and Twiggy were sitting in Mary's kitchen playing *Monopoly*. Mary had fixed chitterlings, collard greens and cornbread from scratch earlier in the day and everybody sat and ate. Now, the five females were engrossed in the game. Ne`Ne` and Dimples loved when Martha and Twiggy hung around the house. Their aunt and Twiggy were always busy, and times spent with the two were cherished by the twins.

Martha and Twiggy knew that, and although they would rather be out in the streets on this night, they both knew the twins really wanted them to hang with them so they kindly obliged when Ne`Ne` and Dimples literally begged them to spend the day with them. Martha hadn't spent a day with her family in weeks so she easily agreed.

The females were heavy into the board game when Ne`Ne` and Dimples looked at the clock simultaneously and saw that it was 7 p.m. They turned to one another and screamed as they ran into the living room and turned on the radio.

"What's wrong with y'all?" Mary asked.

"Momma, that new radio show we told you about come on tonight for the first time!" Ne`Ne` yelled. "Dimples it's on 105.9!" Ne`Ne` screamed as her sister twisted the knob to the right setting just in time to catch the show's intro...

..."*Five, four, three, two, one, diamond...Talk to me nah...Cruising down the street...real slow...what the fellas be yellin'...Marrero...Talk to me nah...Cruising down the street...real slow...what the fellas be yellin'...Marrero...*"

"I'mmm baaaacckkkk! Whoa! You know the voice! And you definitely know the station! 105.9 the super stud station that's ruling the nation! This the one and only Jammin Jazzy the diva of the den and I'm here with the certified Hot Girls Misses Jones the devil herself! Chanel Marie who's wickedly nice, and Miss Amanda Spanks the Latin Soul Sister.... And this...Is the Fantastic Fourrrrrrr!" Jazzy yelled in the microphone just as the lyricist's vocals came over the airwaves.

"*Now sit back and relax so you can hear what I say...and realize it's comin' from the T-H-I-C-K... I'm like 'Digg 'em... so give me a smack I'll smack ya back...react whack to my attack and get a cardiac arrest...stop breathing...heart a stop pumpin'...rhymes still kicking crowd still jumpin'...then dig inside ya' chest to see what's blocking them arteries...and they'll find the rhymes that's departing me...*"

The Holland Family Saga Part Five

Ne`Ne` and Dimples cheered and ran back into the kitchen. "That's The Fantastic Four Show, y'all! It's four of 'em and them girls is live! They from New Orleans!" Dimples said joyously as she grabbed the dice.

"I like Misses Jones! She funny!" Ne`Ne` said as she rolled the dice.

"Nahh. I think Sister Amanda Spanks gone be the best Deejay on that show!" Dimples snapped.

"Girl, you trippin'! Misses Jones gone run that whole show watch what I tell ya'!" Ne`Ne` snapped back.

Mary, Martha and Twiggy had to quiet Ne`Ne` and Dimples down because they were trying to listen to the rapper. His lyrics were smooth and the song had a nice beat they had to admit. "This show might be all right." Twiggy stated as she grabbed the dice and rolled them. She moved her wheel barrow four spaces and landed on Park Place which was owned by Ne`Ne` and Dimples, who were playing as a team.

"That's $1750 dollars auntie," the twins screamed.

"What!" Twiggy yelled over the music. "I knew I shoulda bought that spot! These ole funky dice selling me out, man," she said as she counted her money. "Y'all take checks Ne`Ne`?" she then asked as they all laughed.

****

Meanwhile, over in Ambush, Simon, Sandy, Clark and Jesse were listening to The Fantastic Four Show as well. Ne`Ne` and Dimples had all of Ghost Town listening to the Fantastic Four on this night because they had talked all week about the new show after hearing the show's commercials and promotions over the radio. Sandy was lying across the trunk of Twiggy's Impala, her head bobbing slowly to M.C. Thick's song as her body vibrated from the heavy bass permeating from the two 15" sub-woofers in the trunk of the car as she watched Simon shoot dice with some Folk members from the Queens section of Jackson.

Simon was losing his ass off this night. As M.C. Thick's song played on, Sandy, wearing a blue bandanna, dressed in a pair of blue Capri's, white tank top and white air Nike's, hopped from the trunk of the Impala and went over and pulled Simon back from the group. "You need ta' focus, man," she whispered. "Now I know you ain't gone let them fools from the Queens come way over here in *Ambush* and wreck shop! Come on! Talk to me nah!"

Simon began to get buck as he listened to Sandy's voice and the song blaring from Twiggy's car. These two were jam tight —childhood friends that had grown up together and turned lovers. They were Ghost Town's very own modern-day version of Bonnie and Clyde. They knew each other all-too-well and had one another's back at all times. Simon and Sandy were a silly couple, but they could also be down-right deadly as time would reveal.

"Come on, champ!" Sandy said as she rubbed Simon's back as if he were in a boxing match. The three folk members from the Queens stood by laughing at the two. "This real shit right here, y'all! Simon they got you on the ropes, champ! But we got 'em where we want 'em! Hard eight!" Sandy ended as she brushed her long brown hair back from her face and continued to massage Simon.

Sandy then began humming the theme song from *Rocky* as Simon jumped up and down and twisted his neck before he rushed back to the dice game as if he were entering the center ring of a boxing match. "Hard eight," he yelled as he picked the dice up and rolled them again, trying to land a hard eight, which was two fours. Sandy's little speech, her fluent massage and her humming of the *Rocky* theme song did nothing for Simon, however; he crapped out on the first roll—and the Folk members from the Queens grabbed the cash and hopped into their two door white Delta 88 on Tru rims and rode away laughing.

"Damn! We almost had that shit! We goin' out ta' Queens Friday and I'm a win my fuckin' money back! Funky ass dice wouldn't hit the hard eight for shit!" Simon remarked in a disgusted as he returned to making more crack sales, trying to recoup the $700 dollars he lost.

Friday evening had rolled around and Ne`Ne` and Dimples

had just exited their school bus to get set for the weekend. Mary was off today and she was in her yard pulling weeds when the twins arrived home. They ran inside and tossed their book bags, went into the backyard and kissed their mother and ran over to the Charles' house. The twins had seen Twiggy's Impala parked in the Charles' yard so they knew Simon and Sandy were home. Ne`Ne` and Dimples ran up the stairs and tapped on the door and twenty-three year-old Peter Paul answered.

"What's up, Peter Paul? Sandy here?" Ne`Ne` asked.

Peter Paul let the girls in and went into the bedroom where Simon and Sandy were. He opened the door and saw a butt naked Sandy, kneeling behind a butt naked Simon who was lying on his stomach, with her face planted in between Simon's butt cheeks, her head swaying gently from side to side and up and down. Simon was smiling with his eyes closed and writhing about on the bed. Peter Paul had seen this before; he caught Simon "rimming" Sandy out earlier.

All day the two were in the room "rimming" one another and fucking like rabbits. Peter Paul eased the door shut and walked back into the living room and eyed the two twins subtly. Peter Paul had slept with nearly every teenager in Ghost Town—except the twins.

Ne`Ne` and Dimples smiled back innocently at Peter Paul as they stood in the living room dressed identically in navy blue Guess Jeans, black Eastland shoes, and navy blue and white Polo shirts. He fantasized briefly about getting head at the same time from the two petite and sexy fourteen year-olds. Had they been anybody else, Peter Paul would have definitely tried the two, but he knew Martha would literally kill him if he even dared. Peter Paul relinquished those thoughts and told the twins that Sandy and Simon were in the room busy giving each other rim jobs.

"What's a rim job? What? They, they stealin' rims?" Ne`Ne` asked in a perplexed manner as she eyed Twiggy's Impala through the screen door.

Peter Paul laughed aloud and said, "I'm not getting in that shit right there! I thought y'all knew already. Go ask your momma first. Or Martha or somebody," while ushering the twins to the door. "They be out after while," he ended before he sent twins home.

"Why, or rather the word how, how would Sandy and Simon be doin' a rim job and the car is outside sittin' on rims already?" Ne`Ne` asked as the twins made their way back to their mother's home.

"He said we should go ask momma first. I think a rim job has to do with sex or something." Dimples replied.

"I don't know. Maybe, so, Dimples. But I always thought a rim job was when somebody stole rims off another car. Like a car-jacking or something."

"Let's go ask momma." Dimples answered as the twins broke into laughter and ran back home. "Momma! Momma!" Ne`Ne` and Dimples suddenly yelled as the two ran into the backyard and asked bluntly, "Momma, in sex what's a rim job?"

Mary had gotten an immediate sinking feeling in the pit of her stomach upon hearing her daughters' question. She was also a little embarrassed. She knew what a rim job was as she'd had it done to her on several occasions. *"This is one for the books!"* Mary thought to herself as she pulled off her garden gloves, removed her apron and hugged her daughters and walked them inside.

Ne`Ne` and Dimples would ask often ask their mother various questions about what happens during sex, "how babies get born?" "what's an orgasm", questions of that nature. Mary had answered those questions and many more and she often admonished the twins to wait until they graduated high school at the very least before they ever even *thought* of having sex; but it was always the understanding that if the twins ever had a question regarding their sexuality, they were free to ask their mother.

The twins knew they could ask their mother anything, but this particular question had caught Mary off guard as this was a question she'd never thought she would have to answer for her daughters at such a young age, and for that matter, in life.

Thirty minutes later, whilst Mary was schooling her daughters, Simon and Sandy had just finished dressing in preparation to ride out to Queens to try and win Simon's money back. Simon wore a navy blue Dickies outfit with a black pair of casual suede shoes with a navy blue bandanna tied around his head. He draped his diamond clad left wrist across the steering wheel and cruised out of Ghost Town thinking only of winning back the money he lost just days earlier.

Sandy was sitting right beside Simon. She had on a tight fitting pair of light blue Capri's, a white tank top and a brand new pair of white and light blue Fila's. She also wore a ten karat diamond cut gold six point star medallion around her neck with a light blue and white bandanna tied around her head. Her clear blue eyes were hidden by a pair of thin, mirror tinted sunglasses. Sandy had given Simon half of the seven hundred dollars he needed and was just as certain as he that he would win his money back this day. Simon approached a red-light half way enroute to Queens and let the top down on the Impala and turned the volume up on the song *New Jack Hustler*, by Ice-T. It was a perfect day. The sun was out and the sky was clear blue. The temperature was seventy-four degrees; unusually cool for this particular part of the south for September, but all-so-welcoming given the blazingly hot and muggy months of July and August.

The light turned green and Simon cruised through the intersection and continued on, he and Sandy riding like Cavaliers towards Queens—confident of themselves. They pulled up in front of a gang member by name of Frog's house and exited their car and approached a group of teenagers belonging to Folk Gang hanging out under the canopy in the driveway. The members greeted Simon and Sandy with the Folk handshake and they smoked a couple of blunts until Frog came out with a case of beer and started the dice game on the concrete underneath the canopy.

Simon started out by placing side bets with whoever was rolling the dice. Depending on who was rolling, he bet with the person or against him. Simon would always make money in that manner during a dice game; but when it was his turn to roll, he noticed that whenever he rolled an even number, everybody would bet him to roll a hard number. Simon knew he was unlucky when it came to rolling a hard number, but he also knew he could win a huge pot if he hit so the bet was tempting. If he bet against everybody and won, he would clean them out as they always bet real big on him not rolling a hard number.

Simon's turn to roll arrived and he grabbed the dice and shook them rapidly in his right hand. Sandy knelt beside him and stared at the concrete and waited with the rest of the Folk members. When Simon rolled the dice, they bounced across the floor and landed on 4-3. He grabbed his money and faded all bets and grabbed the dice again and began shaking them rapidly in his right hand. When the dice stopped, this time, a 6-3 was on display. Simon felt comfortable with a nine so he bet heavy against those who bet against him. After three rolls of five, eight, and ten, Simon rolled a five and four and won the bet. He grabbed the money down and Sandy began counting it as Simon shook the dice in preparation of another roll.

The dice scooted across the concrete and landed on a 6-4—an even number ten. All the Folk members quickly began to call for a hard ten against Simon. He looked over to Sandy, who merely shrugged her shoulders and said, "We got eight hundred. Our seven plus one. What you wanna do?" she asked as Frog handed her two cold beers.

Simon had won his seven hundred dollars back, plus another hundred dollars, but he now had a forty-nine hundred dollar bet before his eyes. He took the beer handed to him by Sandy, opened it, took a large squib and said, "Fuck it! Let's do it!"

Simon grabbed the money from Sandy and threw it in the pot and grabbed the dice. He rolled a 6-4 and a 2-2 before he rolled snake eyes and lost all he and Sandy's money again. "Fuck!" he yelled angrily as he stood up and walked away from the dice game as the other members laughed aloud and mocked him. "Let's get the fuck from 'round here, Sandy!" he said angrily as he walked towards Twiggy's car.

One of the Folk members from Queens had a brown '73 convertible Impala. He owned a detail shop and was fixing the car up for himself. The car had a white and brown interior and gold trimming on the outside. The only thing that was missing on the car was a set of rims. Twiggy had recently placed a set of gold Daytona rims on her car. Seeing an opportunity for himself, the young man offered Simon a single bet—if he rolled a hard eight before he crapped, he would get the brown Impala. If not, Simon would have to give up Twiggy's Daytona rims. Simon had no more money; he'd lost everything in Queens this day, but if he won the car, he knew he could resell it and get back on his feet. And all he had to do was roll a hard eight from the start.

Sandy sensed that Simon was considering the bet and she wasn't in agreement with it in the least bit. She suggested that she and Simon leave. "Simon look, we can get a front from Twiggy or Martha and stack another grip and just come back next week. Don't fuck with Twiggy rims, Folk. Let's just go back to Ghost Town."

Simon ignored Sandy's suggestion and took the bet. He walked back under the canopy and told everybody to stand back and give him space because he wanted to be alone whilst rolling the dice. He was sure if he had complete silence and was left alone, he could roll a hard number. He just had to concentrate. He shook his hands rapidly and threw the dice. The dice bounced across the concrete and Simon saw that he indeed had rolled a hard number, only it was the number two—Snake Eyes. He'd crapped out on his first roll and the young man went and Twiggy's rims off her car and placed a set of all black junkyard rims onto Twiggy's Impala in place of her gold Daytona rims.

"How the fuck I can't roll a hard eight?" Simon asked loudly as he drove with the top down back to Ghost Town once the guy had exchanged rims.

"Forget about your hard eight! Twiggy gone be mad as fuck with our asses! That was dumb, Simon! You shouldna never done that shit! You shouldna *never* went in Queens!" Sandy said angrily as she stared out at the scenery.

"What? It was your idea in the first place!"

"No it wasn't, Simon! And even if it was—I was in it with you up until the point you decided to play for Twiggy's rims! When we loss all the money we had we shoulda just left! I wouldna never gambled on Twiggy's rims! We in for a long mutherfuckin' night over this here shit! A *long* ass night!" Sandy said as she laid back in the passenger seat.

"That's the last time I listen to your ass! I shoulda *known*! Had me all bucked up at the beginning of this shit with that fuckin' Rocky theme music back in Ambush!" Simon stated as he reached out and hugged Sandy.

Sandy nuzzled up against Simon and grabbed his crotch and said, "This the real hard eight right here. We'll get 'em back—but we got this situation with Twiggy. Them dudes ripped us a new one."

"I know. Don't get too comfortable 'round this bitch. Get ready to make room for another one for Twiggy. Here we go!" Simon replied as he prepared to turn onto Casper Drive.

"Ehhh, umm, let, let me out right here, Folk. I gotta get something from Chug-a-lug's." Sandy remarked cooly as she jumped up and cracked opened the door as Simon slowed to turn into Ghost Town. Sandy was trying to remove herself from what she knew was going to be some serious shit involving Twiggy and Simon.

"Aww hell no! You in this shit right along with me!" Simon snapped as he sped up to prevent Sandy from exiting the car. Sandy closed the door, raised her right hand, and produced a pitchfork and broke into the Doobie Brothers' song titled *Jesus is Just Alright*, singing the song's breakdown...

"*Jesus...he's my friend...Jesus...he's my friend...took me by the hand...took me far...from this land...Jesus...he's my friend...*"

"What the fuck you singin' church hymns for and shit? Like we ridin' into our own death or some shit?"

"That's the Doobie Brothers not a church hymn, Simon! But never mind that song—we was talkin' about Twiggy back at the store!"

"So what? I loss the rims. Big fuckin' deal! When I get back on—my auntie gone get a *new* set of rims! Fuck it!"

"Simon? You know we talkin' 'bout Twiggy, right? Man, if we go down there, we fuckin' dead! We dead! We gotta get more rims for Twiggy before we ride down there!"

"Fuck it, brer! Twiggy gone have ta' understand! And I'm a grown ass man! Whatever happen happen! And I ain't got no money for no fuckin' rims anyway! And being that she my auntie? Twiggy gone show love and understand what we been through today." Simon said confidently as he tried to buck himself up.

Sandy leaned back into the passenger seat and said in a nonchalant manner, "Fuck it then! Let's do it!"

As Simon and Sandy rode slowly down Casper Drive towards Friendly Lane, they were both thinking how they would have to tell Twiggy, once she saw her vehicle without the rims on it, exactly how and why her gold Daytona rims, which cost her two-thousand dollars, were no longer apart of the vehicle. The two felt sorry for what they had done, but no one would be more heart broken than Twiggy. She and Martha were sitting in Martha's Cadillac on Friendly Lane right beside Mary's house sipping gin and juice when she caught sight of her car riding slowly down Casper Drive.

Twiggy's jaw dropped when she saw her car. Martha, however, couldn't contain her joy. *"Ooohh, they is dead! They dead,"* she said to herself as she chuckled. Martha knew from Peter Paul what Simon was up to; and when she saw Twiggy's car, she knew right away something funky had went down in Queens. Everybody that was out had soon focused on the scene unfolding on Casper Drive, which had caused Simon to grow hot under the collar and sweat profusely.

Sandy was shaking her head. *"We is so fuckin' dead!"* she thought to herself as she stared blankly out the passenger side of the car.

Clark and Jesse were out as well. They bent over at the waist and clasped their hands to their knees when they saw Twiggy's car, both knowing full well that Simon had loss the last of his money in Queens, had gambled and lost Twiggy's rims in the dice game and had loss, and were now about to be in deep shit with Twiggy—both he and Sandy.

"What the fuck happen to my shit," was all Simon and Sandy heard as they slowly passed Mary's house and turned into the Charles' driveway. Twiggy leapt from Martha's car and ran over to her home. "Where my rims, mutherfucka?" she yelled loudly to Simon.

"I lost 'em in a funky ass dice game!"

"You—you lost my rims?" Twiggy asked surprised. "You lost my mutherfuckin' rims in a *funky ass dice game*?"

"Yea, I'm sorry." Simon stated sadly as Sandy hugged him from behind.

Twiggy, Martha, Mary, Gina, Vince and Peter Paul were planning to ride down to Gulf Port, Mississippi and kick it on the beach for the weekend. Twiggy wanted to drive her car, but Simon ruined those plans. "Go get my fuckin' rims!" Twiggy commanded as Martha came across the street laughing.

"Ooohh Oui! This shit gone be good! Too damn good!" Martha said through laughter as she walked over and stood on the sidewalk beside an angry Twiggy.

"We ain't got no money for no rims!" Simon remarked as if he was annoyed by his aunt's request.

"I don't give a fuck what you gotta do, Simon Avery Charles! Go get me some fuckin' rims, li'l nigga! Today!" Twiggy commanded as she marched up the sidewalk leading to the stairs and entered her home.

Martha knew what was about to come. "She goin' get her gun," she told Simon. "Y'all better get the fuck from 'round here and go straighten this shit out."

"Man she ain't gone—" Simon was cut off when Twiggy came back onto the porch and fired four rounds at his and Sandy's feet.

"Go get my fuckin' rims!" Twiggy yelled as she fired the last two shots from a .44 magnum into the ground.

Simon and Sandy took off running back to Twiggy's car amidst the last two gunshots. Sandy didn't even bother opening the door. She hopped over the driver's side door and scrambled into the passenger seat as Simon jumped behind the wheel and started the car and put it in reverse. He then yelled for Twiggy to stop playing.

"Oh, these bitches think I'm Def Comedy Jam today!" Twiggy remarked as she stood in her front yard and reloaded her gun.

Simon quickly backed out of the drive-way and sped out of Ghost Town. He and Sandy rode over to the Galleria Mall where Sandy bought the Doobie Brothers' CD, *Toulouse Street* that had the song *Jesus is Alright* on it. She played the song repeatedly as the two rode back to Ghost Town. They made it back to the neighborhood an hour and a half later playing *Jesus Is Alright* in hopes of getting a reprieve from Twiggy; but Twiggy wasn't giving reparations on this day. She wanted rims back on her ride—immediately!

As the song played, Twiggy, who was sitting on her porch with Martha waiting on Simon and Sandy's return, leapt from her porch and opened fire again when she saw that Simon and Sandy didn't have any rims in their possession. "Get my rims back on my car, mutherfuckas!" she yelled.

Simon and Sandy sped out of Ghost Town whilst being shot at by Twiggy and people were bent over laughing, including Martha, Mary, Dimples and Ne`Ne`.

"No they didn't! They thought that they could play that song and Twiggy would forgive them?" Mary asked as she laughed in her front yard with her family.

Mary was a rock and roll fan and she knew the song well. She summed up what Sandy and Simon were trying to do and got a serious laugh out the situation as did everybody else who was out to witness the scene unfolding. Everybody in Ghost Town knew Twiggy never had intentions on shooting Simon and Sandy, she was shooting into the air, but Simon and Sandy knew right away that they would not have peace until they had a new set of rims for Twiggy.

When night fell, Simon and Sandy returned; this time they came in on Friendly Lane with the music off, hoping they could just go inside and go to sleep. Twiggy, however, was on the side of her house, and when she saw that Simon and Sandy still had no rims, she opened fired again as she ran and stood in the middle of Casper Drive and Friendly Lane and fired into the night air. "Don't come back in this bitch until you got my mutherfuckin' rims!" Twiggy yelled as she emptied her .44 into the night air as Simon and Sandy sped up Casper towards Hanging Moss where he made a quick right turn and drove out of Ghost Town.

"We gotta get some fuckin' rims quick-like if we ever wanna go back home!" Sandy said as she slid a clip into a .9mm Beretta.

Twiggy had just pushed Simon and Sandy over the limit; but she didn't care. She wanted rims back on her ride and she meant what she said. Simon and Sandy rode out to Tougaloo College, about fifteen minutes from Jackson. There, they picked up on a flashy car with an Indiana license tag being driven by a young man. By riding by his lonesome, in a somewhat secluded portion of the city, the young man appeared to be an easy mark for Simon and Sandy, who only needed a quick set of rims to get squared up with Twiggy. The Indiana license tag on the two door black Cutlass on chrome Daytona rims the two were trailing had Simon and Sandy under the belief that the young man was a college student from out of town; possibly with no family members in Jackson, Mississippi.

When the young man began to veer onto the freeway and head north on Interstate-55, Sandy looked over to Simon and said, "Tell me this guy ain't going back to Indiana tonight! Unfuckin' believable how much bad luck we been having all week!"

"I ain't letting this nigga go! He gotta stop for gas sometime. We gotta a half a tank. Let's see how far he gone go." Simon remarked as he merged onto the interstate.

The young man rode up the highway unaware of the danger his life was in. Two predators were out this night looking for an easy mark and he was on their radar. The car exited the interstate after traveling about twenty miles and cruised to the end of the ramp. The road sign at the end of the ramp had an arrow pointing to the right which was the four-lane road that led towards Canton, but the car took a left turn and crossed under the interstate and headed down a secluded two lane road bordered by a dense forest on either side.

Simon and Sandy quickly switched seats and Sandy followed the man for several miles, staying at a far enough distance so as not to arouse suspicion. She knew not where the young man was going so she looked over to Simon and said, "Simon, I know we need these rims, but Folk, we going way out in the boon docks. We like one more turn from being lost even if we do get the rims."

"I remember the way. I was waiting for a stop sign. The next time he slow down, or we get to a stop sign, just pull up right on side that mutherfucka." Simon remarked as he eyed the vehicle's tail lights.

Simon and Sandy trailed the young man for another three miles and a flashing light came into view, letting them know that they were approaching an intersection. The two cars ascended a hill side and soon as the young man stopped his car, Sandy was hitting the brakes on Twiggy's Impala. She pulled alongside the young man's car at the secluded flashing red-light in rural Madison County and Simon aimed his gun at the young man from the passenger seat and opened fire. The bullets from his .9mm shattered the window on the car and the driver fell over onto his right side. Simon then jumped out the Impala and shot the young man two more times through the driver's side window before he opened his victim's door and shoved the young man's body into the passenger seat, got behind the wheel and sped off.

Sandy followed him to a secluded place deep in the back woods of Madison, Mississippi, the next town over. There, with the corpse still inside the car, Simon and Sandy stripped it of its rims and placed them into Twiggy's backseat and trunk. The two then searched the dead young man's pockets and found $300 dollars, enough for a half ounce of cocaine. Simon and Sandy then stole all the young man's CDs and ripped out his CD player and doused the interior of the car with lighter fluid and set it ablaze; destroying the body and any evidence. They then drove back to Ambush and placed the rims on Twiggy's Impala.

It was almost five in the morning when Simon and Sandy entered the Charles' home, but Twiggy was still up. She was standing at the end of the hall fully dressed, her pistol still in her hand. "You in this mutherfucka," she said angrily as she stared Simon directly in the eyes, "you better have my shit back like it was, Simon!"

When Simon told her they had gotten her a new set of 18" chrome Daytonas, Twiggy asked him where did they come from. Simon looked at Twiggy and spoke not a word as he held his chin in the air. Twiggy stared back at her nephew as she began to pat her gun against her side whilst shaking her head up and down. She knew at that moment, that Simon and Sandy had killed someone this night. "You threw the gun away?" she asked lowly.

"Yea. Tossed it in a swamp under a overpass on the way back here."

"You did what you had to do, Simon. But don't ever put yourself in a position like that again. You should make money. Not be out there gambling your shit away," Twiggy ended before she went into her bedroom and finally went to sleep.

Simon and Sandy went into Simon's room and laid back on the bed and stared at the ceiling, neither speaking a word as they both contemplated on what they had just done. What started out as a friendly dice game in Ambush, had led to them committing their first murder. They had to kill another human being and pull of a "rim job" all behind a "funky ass dice game". They would not make this mistake again, but that "funky ass dice game and rim job", had ignited a fire within Simon and Sandy that would be hard to extinguish.

CHAPTER 18

FUKUTOO: MARY"S PRANK

It was now April of '92, about seven months after Simon and Sandy had car-jacked, robbed and killed a young man in Madison County, Mississippi. They were now back in pocket with Twiggy and she had resumed allowing them to use her car several months back. Martha and Twiggy were still selling cocaine, but they had stopped supplying Ghost Town. That job now belonged to Peter Paul and Gina Cradle. The reason being was because a month after the car-jacking and homicide, Simon and Sandy went back to Madison County to pull another lick. Simon had found out that the guy he killed had been a 'big timer' in Ridgeland, Mississippi. He and Sandy found out where his home was located and scouted the place for a while and surmised that a female and a toddler were the only two staying there; they waited until the woman left for work one morning and broke into the home and found a half-kilo of cocaine and $5,000 dollars in cash. The two kept the money and gave Peter Paul and Gina Cradle the half-kilo to sell and the four would split the profit. Peter Paul then set up shop in Ambush and he and Gina Cradle were now earning good money.

Simon and Sandy, on the other hand, would steal from, or rob other hustlers who had no Folk ties out of their drugs and money and give the drugs to Peter Paul and Gina to sell and they would all get a cut. Everybody was getting paid in 1992. Martha and Twiggy, who were scoring a kilo themselves, began supplying other customers. The two women mainly dealt with people their age or older. Original gangsters, ex-pimps, and 'hole-in-wall' night club owners who wanted in on the action from time to time. Their clientele was low-key and quiet.

Peter Paul, Gina, Simon and Sandy were the new breeds in Ghost Town. They came of age with the attitude of "live for today because tomorrow we may die". That attitude was fast over-taking the youth of this particular era in Ghost Town and every other neighborhood in Jackson, Mississippi and throughout the south. Albert Lee, Slim, Clark Senior, Chug-a-lug, Martha and Twiggy were the forerunners; and now only thirty-three year-olds Martha and Twiggy were still ranking members out of that group, and they were beginning to slow down themselves.

The baton was slowly being passed to Peter Paul, Gina, Simon and Sandy. And they would gladly except the street-baton from the players of the late seventies and eighties and continue to run the race and play the game of high risk/high reward, only this next generation was bolder, more violent, willing to do whatever it took to come out on top. Still, in spite of it all, they were young, and sometimes gullible. Mary's prank would bring that side of this next generation to life.

Simon and Sandy were returning from the Galleria Mall in early April of '92 after a shopping spree, cruising down Hanging Moss just about to turn onto Casper Drive and enter Ghost Town. "Eh", Simon yelled aloud as he slowed just before Dairy Queen. "What the? That sign say fuck you too?" he asked Sandy over the song *G-Thang*, by Snoop Dogg and Dr. Dre that was blaring from Twiggy's drop top Impala.

Sandy turned down the music and leaned forward and looked over to her left and noticed the sign. "Fuck you too? That's Fookootoo dumb ass! It's Chinese! Oooh we gotta Chinese Kitchen back here now," she said excitedly.

"Nahh. That shit say fuck-you-too! Hey, mutherfuckas? Fuck you too!" Simon yelled towards the workers as he rode pass the construction site with his middle finger in the air.

The Holland Family Saga Part Five

A month later, Mary was in her garden in the front lawn tending to her new-sprouting four 'o' clocks. It was May of '92 and school was nearly over. On this warm Friday morning, since Ne'Ne' and Dimples had passed all their exams and were headed to the tenth grade, they took the day off from school and hung out in the yard with their mother helping her tend to her garden and plants. Sandy came over later in the morning and greeted the family.

"Hey, Sandy," Mary said nicely. "I haven't seen you up this early in a long time."

"I know. But Fookootoo's opening today and me, Simon, Peter Paul and Gina going have lunch up there."

"Hmmphh!" Mary snapped.

"Why you say that, Miss Mary?" Sandy asked with a concerned look.

"It's nothing really. But ever since those fast food restaurants opened up on Hanging Moss, business been slow for Dairy Queen." Mary said sadly.

"For real?"

"Umm, hmm. I don't know how long I'll be working there."

"Aww. I'm sorry." Sandy remarked.

Mary already had a job lined up at Caro Food Services in the Human Resources Department. The job position was opening in June which was about a month away. She was planning on leaving Dairy Queen shortly, but during this period of time, Mary decided to have a little fun with Ghost Town. She knew people in the neighborhood respected her, and she also knew they respected Sandy as well. On this morning, however, Mary had decided to see just how far she could manipulate Ghost Town—and it would all start with Sandy Duncan. It was a wickedly delicious prank, and Mary meant no harm by it; she merely wanted to have a little fun with the young folk inside of Ghost Town.

Sandy stood by the fence and looked at Mary with a worried look in her eyes and asked, "Is Dairy Queen going under?"

"Yes. I don't know how long we gonna stay open. Especially since this Footookoo or whatever you call it opening up now." Mary said as she smiled to herself.

Sandy grew concerned for Mary. She brushed her brown hair from in front her eyes and quietly walked over to the Charles' house, thinking hard about what she'd just heard.

Ne'Ne' and Dimples heard the conversation themselves. "Momma, why you care about Dairy Queen and you got another job already?" Dimples asked.

"Babies, just sit back and watch this thing unfold and have a good laugh with your mother." Mary said as she hugged her daughters and chuckled whilst watching Sandy walking up Friendly lane.

Sandy tapped on the Charles' front door and Simon quickly answered. "What's up? You ready ta' ride up to fuck you too?"

"It's Fookootoo! Fookootoo! Dumb ass! And no! We got a problem, Folk!"

"What? Bitches trippin'?" Simon asked as he went for his .40 Glock resting on the coffee table.

Sandy entered the Charles' home and closed the door and told Simon about Mary's dilemma. "We can't eat there, Folk," she said seriously. "Mary can lose her job if we start eating at Fookootoo's."

Simon respected Mary off top, and if she was running the risk of losing her job, then he would not help out in that matter. "Well, you can't miss what you never had right?" he said as he and Sandy sat down on the sofa where he rolled a blunt for the two of them to smoke.

Sandy and Simon spread the word quickly about Fukutoo's, telling everybody that would listen that Mary's job was at stake. "Don't eat there," was the word on the streets of Ghost Town. Twiggy and Martha caught wind of the situation and they went so far as to encourage people in Ghost Town to eat at Dairy Queen more often. Mary didn't expect things to excel the way they had during this time, however; it was a harmless prank in the beginning, but it was quickly turning into

The Holland Family Saga Part Five

something reminiscent of a 1960's boycott. Hypocrisy, however, loomed just beneath the surface.

The twins' 15th birthday party had arrived and everybody sat out on the patio at Dairy Queen and ate hamburgers, fries, and drank milk shakes; although they would've rather had food catered by Fukutoo's. Ne`Ne` was able to phone into The Fantastic Four Show and was able to get Mrs. Jones to shout out to Ghost Town. Everybody was listening to the radio through the speakers on the Dairy Queen's patio when the Deejay began to speak.

"Alrighty then! We're back peoples," Mrs. Jones, said over the airwaves on this warm night in June of '92. "I wanna send a special dedication out to Ne`Ne` and Dimples! They identical twins y'all! And they are representin' Ghost Town up in Jackson, Mississippi! Mary? Your daughters say they love you with all their heart, and Martha, hey, they say thanks for being their aunt! They know you busy and they understand and they love you anyway! Happy fifteenth birthday to Rene and Regina! Everybody in Ghost Town, say it with me! Happy Birthday, Ne`Ne` and Dimples!" Rolanda concluded as the song *Tennessee by* Arrested Development was cued up over the airwaves.

A week after the party, Loretta was walking down the sidewalk on Casper Drive with a Fukutoo uniform on headed home toting a huge plastic bag, having taken a job at the Chinese kitchen. Everybody in Ghost Town knew and liked the bosom, bow-legged jovial woman, and no one said a word about her taking the job at Fukutoo's. Twiggy and Martha had moved their product to a safe house on the outskirts of Jackson near *North Park Mall*, so Loretta had lost her hustle. Although she had money stashed away, she didn't want to dip into her funds so she took the job at the Chinese kitchen.

Loretta bounced down the sidewalk waving at people who were hanging out this star-lit night and rounded the corner onto Friendly Lane and walked passed Mary's house, entered her yard and walked into her home where Sandy was inside bundled up on the couch watching *Def Comedy Jam*, her favorite show.

"Hey, baby. I brought home some shrimp fried rice, General Tso's chicken, and shrimp egg rolls from the job. You care for a bite?" Loretta asked Sandy.

Sandy knew Fukutoo was off limits to Ghost Town, but since her mother worked there, she was granted immunity. Right? That was her reasoning at least. Everybody in Ghost Town knew about the restaurant, a few families who'd distanced themselves from the Holland, Charles, and Duncan families ate there in spite of; but those that were close to the families respected their wishes. So long as the Holland, Charles and Duncan families didn't eat there, no one affiliated with the three families would eat there. Loretta worked there, however, and that set Sandy and her apart from everybody else. Sandy didn't think twice about digging into the food; and she was glad she hadn't because it was downright delectable. She had just eaten three shrimp egg rolls and had just flipped the lid open on the styrofoam plate that held a massive amount of General Tso's chicken when the phone rang. She licked her fingers and reached over with a mouthful of egg roll and answered, "Hello?"

"You coming out? You know we gotta do that thang for Frog in Ambush." Simon stated.

Sandy was caught off guard. She swallowed the egg rolls and said, "I'm coming, Folk. Give me a minute."

Simon could hear the chewing and was beginning to come to an assumption. "What you eatin' on? I know you not—never mind. Just come your ass on. I'm leaving out now and I'm coming over there."

When Simon hung up the phone, Sandy jumped up and ran into the living room and looked out the window. She saw the front door of the Charles' home open and Simon's silhouette appear in the doorway. "Oh, shit!" she said under her breath as she ran back into the kitchen and quickly ate, all the while looking over her shoulder as if she was being watched. She finished what she could and ran out the door and met up with Simon, who was just entering her front yard. "Let's go work this package, Folk," she said quickly as she swallowed the last remnants of the General Tso's chicken, never bothering to look

Simon's way.

"You ate that fuckin' food your momma brought home didn't you?" Simon asked as he followed Sandy out the yard.

"Nahh, Folk! I just got dressed and walked out here!"

"What the hell your ass was eating when I called you then?"

"A bologna sandwich, man! Why you worrying 'bout what I ate? Let's just go to Ambush."

"Give me a kiss, baby."

"Not with this bologna on my breath. Come on." Sandy replied as she began headed towards the trail leading to Ambush.

Simon nodded his head up and down slowly with his lips curled to one side as he eyed Sandy walking away. He didn't believe one word she'd said. The following day, Simon rode through the drive through at Dairy Queen with Sandy in the passenger seat. Mary was at the order taker's window when Simon ordered a double burger combo. He paid for his meal, smiled at Mary and slowly crept away from the drive through. When he left the drive, Simon threw the bag with the burger and fries in the back seat and rode quickly over to Fukutoo's.

"Hey? What the hell you doing?" Sandy asked as Simon pulled into Fukutoo's parking lot.

"Shit! I *donated* to Dairy Queen! Now I'm going get what I really want!" Simon replied as he exited the driver's seat.

"You a hypocrite!" Sandy yelled aloud from the passenger seat.

"Take one ta' know one. I know what your ass did last night so leave me and mines alone." Simon replied before he slammed the door and walked towards the restaurant. He came out with his order a few minutes later and drove over to Chug-a-lug's and got a brown paper bag and transferred his General Tso's chicken plate into the paper bag to hide his food.

"You fuckin' unbelievable, man! You going through all this shit to cover your fuckin' tracks?" Sandy asked as she shook her head in disgust. Never mind she was the first to cross-over and have a taste of the Chinese Cuisine.

Simon drove down Casper Drive in Twiggy's Impala in a very cautious manner. Normally, he would have the top down when it was warm out. This day, however, the top was up, the windows were rolled up and Simon had the radio turned off and was driving at a snail's pace as if he were transporting a nuclear bomb towards the White House. He was slumped down in his seat, his head swiveling back and forth, searching for any witnesses to his dastardly deed. Simon pulled into his drive and crept from the car with his plate of food. Peter Paul and Gina were in the house counting money in the kitchen when Simon and Sandy walked quickly through the living room and turned left, avoiding them both. The two went into Simon's room and locked the door, so they thought, as the lock on his door had been broken for months.

Sandy sat and watched as Simon opened his General Tso's chicken plate with shrimp fried rice and her mouth watered. She wanted some of his food, but she dare not ask. Instead, she ridiculed Simon for going against Mary's wishes in order to throw the heat off herself. Simon merely nodded as he ate, stuffing his mouth with food. "Damn. This some good shit right here," he said lowly as he bounced up and down on his bed.

Simon soon began taunting Sandy and she was beginning to get weak. She'd had tasted the General Tso's chicken and the shit was fire, nearly, no, it *was* irresistible. Simon piled food onto his plastic fork and pretended it was an airplane, passing the food in front Sandy's mouth at an agonizingly slow pace while making airplane engine sounds. "I can see in your eyes you want some of this shit. You already know how it taste because you had some last night, huh?"

"Forget you, Simon," Sandy answered, still unable to take her eyes of the food.

Simon did the airplane gesture again and this time, Sandy couldn't help herself, nor did she want to. She lunged forward and clasped the fork between her teeth just as Peter Paul and Gina burst into the room.

"Yea, bitches!" Peter Paul screamed aloud as he and Gina broke and ran towards the living room.

"I knew they had that shit in there, Pete!" Gina said aloud as two went and grabbed money off the kitchen table. "What I tell ya', baby? My black ass was right!" Gina could be heard yelling aloud through laughter as she and Peter Paul ran out the house.

Simon looked out the window and saw Gina and Peter Paul hop into Peter Paul's Iroc and speed off. He and everybody else knew they were going to Fukutoo's. The silent boycott was secretly off, only Twiggy and Martha weren't informed of this fact.

Martha and Twiggy rode passed Fukutoo's two days after Peter Paul, and Gina had went and ate there. Both of them believed that this 'neighborhood boycott' was ridiculous. They could smell the Peking duck, roasted chicken, shrimp fried rice and God knows what else they had inside that building, every time they passed the place. Twiggy was riding by slowly with a glazed look in her eyes, she and Martha both staring at customers happily going in and out of the establishment. Martha coughed and mimicked the words, "Turn left."

"Fuck it man," Twiggy cried aloud. "This ain't Montgomery, Alabama! And I ain't mutherfuckin' Rosa Parks!"

"Damn right! Let's go eat!" Martha yelled aloud as Twiggy swung the Cadillac into the restaurant's parking lot.

Both females got out the car and immediately scanned Dairy Queen to see if Mary was working. "She down there?" Martha asked.

"I don't see her! Come on, Martha!" Twiggy answered as she and Martha walked briskly into the building, careful not to be seen. Twiggy and Martha acted as if they were under surveillance by the F.B.I. on this day. They had to be quick, everybody in Ghost Town knew Martha's car so time was of the essence. "Give me the Poo-Poo platter and two shrimp egg rolls! Martha, what you gettin', sister?" Twiggy yelled as she walked to the front of the line. Other people were before Twiggy, but she wanted in and out. The boycott, remember?

They weren't supposed to be there.

"You gotta wait your turn!" a Chinese cook yelled aloud to Twiggy.

"Man, look—we, we ain't got time, Folk! I need a Poo-Poo platter!"

"And a General chicken plate!" Martha added as Twiggy slammed a fifty dollar bill on the counter.

"Keep the change! Just let me get my order right quick!" Twiggy told the cashier.

The two plates only cost fifteen dollars. Twiggy's fifty dollar bill and the large tip, however, superseded the rest of the patrons. The two women received their orders and instead of heading into Ghost Town, they went the opposite direction, away from Dairy Queen and Ghost Town. They would eat in a park this day.

Two days later, Martha called and asked if Mary had to work, Mary knew the reason why, and she informed Martha of the fact that she was not losing her job, just moving on. Martha and Twiggy were surprised to learn that Mary had pulled a fast one; they got a laugh out of it upon realizing how ridiculous they were acting. If they wanted Chinese, all they had to do was go there; Ghost Town was not supporting Dairy Queen, although Mary really had people believing that for a few days.

Ne`Ne` and Dimples even began to believe that their mother's job was at risk, in spite of what she had told them when the prank had started days earlier. The twins had devised their own scheme. They both knew Loretta got off around eleven 'o' clock on most nights. They didn't want to go to Fukutoo's and purchase a plate outright because their mother would see them, and even if she wasn't at work, Mary, the twins' own mother, had started the boycott so they couldn't go there, at least this is what they believed in their little happy-go-lucky hearts. They watched and watched nearly every day, plotting on how to get a taste of some of the food that Sandy, Simon, Peter Paul and Gina had all gotten a taste of.

Loretta left for work about 12:30 p.m. one sunny Tuesday

afternoon in late May and she was spotted by the twins, who eyed her walking pass their home from the living room. "Tonight we gone eat some Chinese!" Ne`Ne` said as she and Dimples pranced into Dimples' bedroom and began counting money.

Later on that night, Ne`Ne` and Dimples snuck out the back door and left it unlock. It was 11 'o' clock straight up. They waited in their backyard for about twenty minutes before they heard that swishing sound, the sound of a plastic bag that held styrofoam plates, and they knew it was Loretta headed their way. Ne`Ne` peeked from behind the four foot wall beside her driveway, and when she saw Loretta approaching, she and Dimples jumped out.

"What's up, Miss Duncan?" Ne`Ne` asked calmly as she walked around Loretta, eying her plastic bag.

"Hey, twin. What's up?"

Dimples emerged at that moment. She eyed Loretta and asked, "What's in the bag, Miss Duncan," as she, too, began walking around the woman in a circular pattern.

Loretta was made aware of the prank by Mary and she was now ever alert; constantly watching for those who tried to hide the fact that they liked the food from Fukutoo's. She knew the, twins had been watching her and it was just too funny to the woman that the youngsters in Ghost Town were doing all they could to hide the fact that they really liked Fukutoo's food. They were transferring food to different bags and containers and constantly searching to find someone else who was eating a Fukutoo plate to justify their own actions. Loretta, always jovial, decided to play the twins' game so they could finally get a taste of the food. "Well," she said as she looked to her left and right, eyeing Ne`Ne` and Dimples as they strolled around her slowly, "I got umm, Lo-Mein, mandarin chicken and beef fried rice, why?"

"Sounds good. But what happened to the shrimp fried rice, Miss Duncan?" Ne`Ne` asked.

"That's one of their best items. We sold out. Excuse me twins. I'm going home to enjoy my meal." Loretta said as she brushed passed the girls and loosened her grip on the bag she was carrying, all the while laughing to herself because she knew what was about to come.

"That's our food!" Ne`Ne` said as she snatched the plastic bag away from Loretta. At the same time, Dimples had stuffed twenty dollars into her uniform apron.

The two fifteen year-olds ran up the stairs of their home, entered, quickly closed the door and locked it and ran into Dimples room and locked the door and sat down and ate Fukutoo for the first time. They too, became enamored with the Chinese cuisine. "Oh—my—god!" Ne`Ne` said aloud through a mouthful of mandarin chicken.

"Momma gone be mad when she find out about this." Dimples remarked.

"You mean *if* she find out, Regina." Ne`Ne` replied as she and her twin dug into the food.

Loretta, meanwhile, had just walked to her front yard and was laughing aloud. She unlocked her door and Sandy quickly jumped from the couch rubbing her hands together; eager for a taste of the mandarin chicken. "Where the food, momma?"

"Girl, Ne`Ne` and Dimples jacked my ass for that shit! I tell ya' this here is ridiculous! If ya' wanna eat the food just go there!"

"But Mary said not to eat there because she can lose her job!"

Loretta said nothing, she merely laughed louder, bending over at the waist. She couldn't believe how gullible the youngsters were. She and Mary had been eating at Fukutoo's ever since the place had opened. The two women got their kicks out of manipulating the youngsters; and even Martha and Twiggy were fooled for a short time. The rouse kept the youngsters on a rope for almost a month, hook, line and sinker. They were trying their best to hide their passion for Fukutoo's, all for the sake of Mary's job. The rouse was fully uncovered when Ne`Ne` and Dimples busted their mother snacking in the kitchen late one summer night in the month of June. Finally, everybody was able to eat at the restaurant on their own free will, but they will always remember how silly they all acted during that short span of time.

CHAPTER 19

THE THREE MISTAKES

It was now July of '92, a month and half after Mary had caused a stir with her prank. Fukutoo's was now a mainstay in Ghost Town. It wasn't nothing to see people walking down Casper Drive eating out of a styrofoam plate, or on their way to get one of those styrofoam plates. Mary had left Dairy Queen and was now working at Caro Foods. She had also gotten her license and purchased a used two door 1990 Cutlass supreme. The car was gray with gray suede interior and Cutlass rims. Mary didn't have the pimped out ride like Martha or Twiggy, she only wanted something reliable to get her to and from work.

Ne'Ne' and Dimples were on summer break enjoying the weather and just hanging around the house from day to day. Simon and Sandy had established themselves as the neighborhood jack-artists; meaning they were heavy into the art of armed robbery. Peter Paul and Gina were still holding down Ambush and had Jesse and Clark working underneath them; all was good in Ghost Town during this period of time, everybody was happy, healthy, and bank rolling, but dark clouds were unknowingly looming.

Twiggy was in her car one hot July day a week after the Fourth of July holiday headed to the downtown Hibernia Bank. Martha was at their safe house near North Park Mall cooking up a half-kilo for Peter Paul at the time. Twiggy had an unusually large amount of cash on her this day and she was headed to the bank to deposit the funds in her safe deposit box. When she stepped into the chamber and retrieved her box, she noticed she didn't have enough room for the five-thousand dollars she was toting. She could only get about half of it in the box. Twiggy then tried to get another deposit box, but the bank manager informed her that all the slots were full. Unbeknownst to Twiggy, the bank manager lied to her because he was suspicious of the woman's activities.

Twiggy then decided to deposit the remainder of her money into her personal savings. The bank manager noticed the unusual amount of cash Twiggy was trying to put into her safety deposit box earlier, and when she decided to throw the rest into her savings account, he took it upon himself to investigate. Twiggy believed she still had $7,000 dollars in her savings, so she deposited the other $2,500 dollars—mistake number one. She did not bother to check her balance statement after making the deposit—mistake number two.

In Twiggy's mind, she now had $9,500 dollars in savings, still under the $10,000 dollar mark that would spark an I.R.S. investigation; but had she checked her statement, she would've noticed that interest had accumulated during the time she and Martha had been holding onto those savings accounts. Twiggy now had a total of $10,800 dollars, just over the limit for the I.R.S. to investigate.

Martha had $8,300 dollars with accumulated interest; she knew exactly what she had in savings, and she never informed Twiggy of the accumulated interest, assuming Twiggy always checked her statements; indirectly, this was mistake number three. Twiggy had "slipped" this day, and neither female had check stubs or W-2 forms to show for the money they had in savings. And at least twice a month they signed in and out for six different safe deposit boxes. The bank manager was keenly interested in the six deposit boxes, three that held the name Irene Charles, and three that held the name Martha Holland. He would need warrants and sufficient evidence for the deposit boxes, but he could work on Twiggy immediately. The man simply did not want his bank affiliated with illegal activity, the very thing he believed Irene Charles was involved in at the present time. The bank manager also saw the amount of money

Twiggy had in savings that day after she made her deposit and he immediately notified the I.R.S. An investigation was beginning to get underway on Twiggy.

****

Later that night, Sandy and Simon were sitting in front of Sandy's house smoking a blunt bobbing their heads to *The Ghetto*, a song by rapper Too Short that played low on Twiggy's Impala. It had been a week since Simon had gotten Twiggy's car last and he and Sandy were planning to ride around on this warm night. Martha had just ridden through and picked Twiggy up and the two of them along with Loretta, was headed out to Vicksburg to 'unwind'. Mary was home sleep as she had work the next morning, and Dimples and Ne`Ne` had just finished listening to the Fantastic Four Show. The twins went into the kitchen to find something to eat and it was then that Ne`Ne` heard the music outside. She peeked out the kitchen window and saw Simon and Sandy sitting in the car in front of Sandy's house and whispered to Dimples, "Let's go see what they doing."

"Momma said stay inside." Dimples replied.

"Aww girl, momma dead asleep. We just going right down the sidewalk."

Dimples thought for a few seconds, she knew Ne`Ne` was going with or without her so she went, just to keep an eye on Ne`Ne`. The twins giggled as they crept out the door and locked it. They crept low along the chain-link fence and scooted across the sidewalk, slowly approaching Simon and Sandy, who were facing the trail leading to Ambush as they sat in the car. When the twins got close to the rear of the vehicle they rose up and screamed loudly. Sandy jumped and turned around brandishing a chrome .9mm and Ne`Ne` and Dimples hit the ground.

"Ohh, shit," Sandy said in a surprised manner as she jumped out the car and went and helped the twins up from the ground. "Folk, you all right? Y'all all right?"

"We was just playing, Sandy!" Dimples whined.

"I know, Folk! But I thought y'all was some hooks we done robbed coming back on us! We can't play like that no more! Shit serious now!"

"What the hell y'all doin' out this late? Mary gone kick y'all ass for sure!" Simon then remarked.

"Our momma sleep. We just come to hang for a minute." Ne`Ne` answered.

Just then, Clark and Jesse walked onto Friendly Lane. Ne`Ne`'s heart fluttered when she saw Clark as she still adored the youngster. She eyed his fresh white T-shirt and blue bandanna he wore as he strolled up to the group looking flyer than ever with his sagging navy blue *Dickies*, diamond earring and thick herring-bone chain. "What's up, Folk? Y'all ready to ride?" Clark asked Simon and Sandy.

Simon, Sandy, Jesse and Clark were all planning on riding through the city and kick it for a while. Ne`Ne` wanted to ride and she expressed her desire. Dimples wanted to go along for the ride, too, but she was reluctant because her mother had told her and Ne`Ne` both not to go outside. She was standing on the sidewalk wondering what she should do when Jesse walked over and grabbed her hand and told her he would be glad to sit out and kick it with her if she didn't mind. Dimples felt more comfortable doing that; she and Jesse walked up to Fukutoo's to buy Chinese food and returned to Dimples' back porch and eat and chill.

Meanwhile, Simon, Sandy, Clark and Ne`Ne` were out on the town preparing to get into whatever. They rode up to Jackson State University campus and saw that it was packed. Simon approached the entrance and waited at the light and looked to his left and eyed the scores of teenagers and young adults that were perusing the area. Jackson State's campus was a medium-sized complex sitting on 245 acres of land and featured over fifty structures. Everybody mainly hung out along Gibbs Green-Memorial Plaza, which was a long walkway that was surrounded by residences, the dining hall, Science building and the music building. One would turn onto Luther G. Garrett Drive and ride about ¾ of a mile, make a U-turn and ride back down towards the main street, one long, narrow semi-circle it was. Cars would be parked on the right side of the curb all the way around the loop; finding parking was a time-consuming task and the ride through the loop was even longer. The ride, however, did give players time to shine, and Simon was shining indeed on this night. Twiggy's ride was clean, the black paint was shining from the wash that was put on it earlier and the interior was glistening from the Armour-all polish and the chrome Daytona rims were glistening from a coat of chrome polish. Simon turned onto Luther Drive and crunk up the stereo, blasting D.O.C.'s song *It's Funky Enough.*

Ne`Ne` was excited out of her mind. She had never seen this side of Jackson. Young people were everywhere, talking loud, dancing, laughing, and shouting out to one another. Some students wore fraternity and sorority t-shirts and hung out near the drum section that was out playing for the Greek squads, who competed with one another for show and status. Ne`Ne` was soaking it all in; she was enamored with the scene that lay before her eyes and she instantly fell in love with the night life. Simon looped around after forty-five minutes and eyed a spot next to one of the residences and pulled in right behind some Folk members from the Queens section and shook his head.

"What's wrong, Folk?" Sandy asked.

"You know that's them same mutherfuckas that took Twiggy's rims last year, right?" Simon replied as he shook his head from side to side in a somber mood.

"Play 'em again, Folk!" Sandy stated as she hopped out the car. Ne`Ne` quickly hopped out and followed Sandy and the two walked over to the group. "Yea, we back, mutherfuckas! Fade somethin'!" Sandy yelled aloud to the group of about nine male Folk members.

"Eh, take your partridge family looking ass back over in Ghost Town! You and your hairy ass side-kick," a Folk member yelled aloud.

Ne`Ne` knew the dude was only joking and she didn't take offense. "Fuck you! Kermit the frog looking ass!" she remarked through laughter.

"What the fuck you said, hoe?" the young man as he walked

over to Ne'Ne' with a look of aggression displayed upon his face.

"I ain't a fuckin' hoe! And I said I said fuck you! Frog!"

"You know me?"

"Yea I know your ass! You went ta' Callaway remember?" Ne'Ne' asked as she stretched out her right hand and gave Frog the Folk Gang's signature handshake.

Frog looked around confused as he completed the handshake. Who was this young tender trying to hold it down for Folk Gang in Ghost Town? He knew Sandy was over some of the G-Queens in Ghost Town, not to mention she and Simon both had a reputation throughout Jackson as being bona fide jack artists based on what happened the day Simon lost Twiggy's rims.

Sandy was surprised as well; she never saw that one coming from Ne'Ne', but she, too, was impressed. Sandy was one of only maybe a handful of white people out on this night. A great majority of people in the game knew she was a down female and the fact that she was white bothered no one because Sandy kept it real at all times. On top of that, she had earned stripes right alongside Simon.

Frog knew the story in reference to how Simon and Sandy went out the same night they lost Twiggy's rims and car-jacked another set of rims and murdered their victim in the process, and then went back and stole the cocaine. It was a gangster move in the purest form if Frog had to tell it. Frog had even put Simon and Sandy up on a couple of capers shortly thereafter, and they all broke bread together. Frog was a jack-artist himself, and he knew for certain that Simon and Sandy were serious when it came to the jack-play, and he, along with many other people from his crew admired Simon and Sandy's abilities. Frog surmised that Ne'Ne' was a rookie in training that was coming up under Sandy; so on the strength of Sandy, Ne'Ne' had gained his approval.

"You all right, li'l one," Frog said to Ne'Ne'. "Sandy," he then yelled aloud, "look out for shorty right there, she got heart." he ended as he popped the trunk on his black '89 T-top

Camaro and grabbed a couple of forty-ounce St. Ides and handed one to Sandy and Ne`Ne`.

Ne`Ne` had never drank before, but she didn't want to punk out amidst her peers. She grabbed the bottle, her left hand barely able to clasp the huge glass container, and cracked it open and she and Sandy guzzled the beer at the same time. Ne`Ne` found the beer surprisingly refreshing. To her it tasted like fresh, crisp-flavored water that was smooth and ice cold. She caught an immediate head rush and shook it off quickly.

"Eh, nigga? Where our forty?" Simon asked as he and Clark walked onto the scene.

"Got y'all right here, Folk! Say brer, let a nigga hold that D.O.C. disk," Frog said as he went into the cooler and handed Clark and Simon a forty ounce.

"Hell no! You gotta buy your own!" Simon remarked.

"When the last time *you* paid for something, mutherfucka?" Frog asked as he and Simon laughed and dapped one another off.

"Alright show me some paper! Dice game on over here," one of Frog's crew members yelled aloud as he cleared the side walk of females that were close by gyrating to the music coming from Twiggy's car.

"Hey, Simon? Twiggy ain't gone be mad if we take her rims again huh, Folk?" Frog asked.

"Hell yeah she gone be mad! And she gone shoot at his ass like she did the last time," another member of Frog's crew stated and the group laughed aloud.

"Y'all saw what happened last time. Bitches got they head cracked that night—so for public safety reasons y'all niggas might wanna think about lettin' me win." Simon said as he and Sandy counted their money.

"Fuck the public! All my Folk right here," another gang member remarked as the group broke into heavy laughter.

"I here ya', Folk. Fade the twenty." Simon stated as he threw down his money and knelt down on one knee.

Six other Folk members joined in and the pot was $140 dollars out the gate. Simon rolled the dice and rolled 6-2, an eight out the gate. "Aww you funky bitch," he yelled as he stood up and walked away from the group in disgust.

"Hard eight! Bet a hard!" members of Frog's crew yelled aloud as they laughed knowing that eight was Simon's unlucky number.

"What's wrong. Folk?" Ne`Ne` walked up and asked before she swallowed another gulp of the forty.

"He can't hit the hard eight and they wanna bet the hard eight. We can make a fuckin' small fortune if he roll that shit—but we can lose our ass off if he bet it and crap out." Sandy said as she stared back at the group.

"Don't bet the hard right now, Simon. Just win outright." Ne`Ne` said. "Here," she then added, "I got twenty on the eight outright."

"Me too Folk!" Clark then added. "Take them niggas down."

"Bet outright? You think that's the play, Ne`Ne`?" Simon asked.

"Yeah, man. You gotta get hot first. Then come back with the hard."

"What ya' think, Sandy?" Simon asked.

"Hmm, the last two times we bet the hard off top. Ne`Ne` might be right, cuz. Let's do that there because we tried the other way and lost twice. We really ain't got shit ta' lose if we try somethin' different. I agree with Ne`Ne`. Bet the eight outright, Folk."

Simon and company walked back to the game where Frog and his crew were all ready to bet the hard eight. Simon declined and bet the number outright. He rolled three times before he hit 5-3—eight outright. Money was made. Simon rolled again and hit seven two times, eleven once and rolled a six. Ne`Ne` whispered in Sandy's ear and Sandy pulled Simon back.

"Bet the hard six, Folk!" Sandy whispered as she took another squib of beer.

"I thought we was waiting on the eight."

"Nahh, the six! You struggle with the eight! Six is a better number! Bet the hard six! Come on, two threes and we paid!" Sandy said lowly.

"Alright, mutherfuckas! We going on the hard six! Everything!" Simon said loudly to Frog and his crew.

"Ev—everything? Boy is you crazy?" Sandy asked.

"What? Y'all said that's the number right?"

"Yea, man. But fuck—the whole kit and kabootle, Simon?" Sandy remarked.

"Roll that shit, man! Frog 'nem done kicked your ass twice! We win tonight we got over a grand!" Ne`Ne` said before taking a deep swallow of beer.

"Ne`Ne`? If we lose our money? I'm a have ta' do you like Twiggy did us that day." Sandy said as the whole group laughed.

"Shiit, we ain't losing! Roll that shit Simon!" Ne`Ne` said in a confident tone.

"Come here, girl!" Simon said as he grabbed Ne`Ne` and tucked her head under his arms.

Ne`Ne` smiled and wrestled lightly with Simon. "Come on, Folk! You messing my hair up!" she said through laughter.

"Nahh, you my good luck charm ta' night. I'm a rub ya' head like they do at the Apollo." Simon remarked as he rubbed his hands across Ne`Ne`'s thick, platted hair.

Ne`Ne` couldn't help but to feel as if she was becoming a part of Folk Gang in Ghost Town. She was out hanging with Simon and Sandy, Clark was at her side, she was sipping beer and even Frog had welcomed her; she was on an emotional high this night. And when Simon stepped back to the game and rolled a hard six on his second roll, and ran up and grabbed her and twirled her around in his arms as Sandy and Clark cheered, she fell in love with Folk Gang. Ne`Ne` was fast delving into a world she had always admired from afar; now she was becoming a part of it, and that sat just fine with fifteen year-old

Rene Holland.

Simon stood back and began to jump up and down. "Maestro! Music please!" he yelled as Sandy quickly started humming the theme song to *Rocky*.

Simon danced his way over to the group and picked up his money and 'gangster walked' through the group over to Frog's car and grabbed another forty ounce. The crew from Ghost Town hung with Frog and his crew for a while before they decided to leave Jackson State. Ne'Ne' didn't want to go because she was having too much fun this night; but Sandy knew she had to get her back to Ghost Town. Before they left, Simon and Frog exchanged CD's. Simon gave up his D.O.C. disk and Frog handed Simon The Ghetto Boys' *Uncut Dope* CD. Simon and company then left Jackson State headed back to Ghost Town. As they rode home, Sandy pulled out a bag of weed in a small yellow envelope and fanned it before Clark as she smiled and rocked back and forth in the front seat.

"Where you get that?" Clark asked from the backseat.

"From one of Frog people." Sandy answered as she turned back forward. "Simon, hit the next store, please."

After buying a pack of swisher sweets, Sandy hopped back into the car and began rolling a blunt and lit it up as they continued to ride. She shared the blunt with Simon and Simon passed it to the back seat after several tokes. Ne'Ne' went for it, but Clark grabbed it and passed it back to Sandy.

"What's wrong? Y'all don't want no weed?" Sandy asked as she turned around in the front seat.

"Nahh, y'all two be with that booty licking and shit. We ain't smoking that!" Clark replied.

"They both fuckin' virgins!" Simon said as he and Sandy laughed.

"If it ain't happen to you, you can't understand, Clark." Sandy replied.

"It feel good?" Ne'Ne' asked.

"Girl, please! That shit—to me? Fucking period is more

addictive than the crack we be selling in Ambush!"

Ne`Ne` had been soaking in Sandy Duncan's entire demeanor the whole night and had made up her mind that she wanted to be just like her. In the past, Mary believed Martha would become a bad influence on her daughters, but Sandy was not only telling, but she was showing, and doing things to and with Ne`Ne` that Martha would never have even dreamed of doing. Sandy was unwittingly becoming the conundrum in Mary's raising of her daughters, but neither Ne`Ne` nor Sandy saw what they were doing as a problem because they had been friends since the first day Sandy arrived in Ghost Town over eleven years ago. Ne`Ne` was the typical teen, prone to mischief, but the mischief that nineteen year-old Sandy Duncan often delved in was of a higher caliber and far more serious, and sometimes deadly.

Sandy knew what she was doing, though, but only to a degree. She knew full well that if Mary found out that Ne`Ne` was hanging around participating in gang activity, Mary would raise hell, but Sandy liked Ne`Ne`; she was cool. Sandy also believed that Ne`Ne` would eventually begin hanging out with other gang members who would get her hurt, or worse, and she wasn't going to let that happen. By allowing Ne`Ne` to hang with her, Sandy was somewhat keeping an eye on the fifteen year-old. She meant no harm and she truly cared about Ne`Ne`. And by keeping Ne`Ne` close to her, Sandy honestly believed she was helping to protect the young teen.

They reached Ghost Town about 1:30 that morning and Simon turned down the music and let Ne`Ne` out and he, and Sandy went over to the Charles' home. Clark got out and walked alongside a tipsy Ne`Ne`, who was also a little high from a few tokes of a blunt she and Clark had shared before they reentered Ghost Town. They reached the back door and Ne`Ne` turned and embraced Clark and the two shared a long passionate French kiss in her backyard. She then waited as Clark went and lightly tapped on Dimples' window and she awoke from her slumber and quietly unlocked the door. The two twins sat in Ne`Ne's room and shared their experiences that night. Ne`Ne` learned that Dimples had kissed Jesse as well; they both giggled when they realized they had both kissed a boy for the first time on the same night. An hour later they both went to bed.

CHAPTER 20

ANYBODY KILLERS

It was now mid-August, a month after Ne`Ne`s first night out with Simon, Clark and Sandy and for the past four weeks or so, she had been sneaking out of the house on weeknights when Mary went to sleep. Dimples and Jesse were often engaging in heavy petting inside a sleeping Mary's home and were getting ever closer to going all the way; Ne`Ne`, on the other hand, had been there and done that two weeks ago.

She had returned to Ghost Town one night after sneaking out with Simon, Sandy and Clark and for the first time, she went with them and hung in Ambush. It started to rain so they all ran over to Clark's grandmother's home. Clark's grandmother was a diabetic; he took good care of her, but the elderly woman mainly stayed locked in her room. That night was no different. As they sat on Clark's porch, and talked, the conversation turned to sex.

Before long, Simon and Sandy went into Clark's room and locked the door. Shortly thereafter, Ne`Ne` and Clark were inside sitting on the couch kissing. Soon, Ne`Ne`s leather shorts were unbuttoned and she felt fingers creeping inside her panties. Clark felt a hand grabbing his hard-on through his *Dickies* and opened his fly and Ne`Ne` wrapped her small, soft hand around his dick. Before long there were lips down there. Ne`Ne` got up a few minutes later and ran to the bathroom wiping her mouth when Clark was done. She wiped her face clean, and cleaned her vaginal area, and then tapped on Clark's door and got a condom from Sandy. She returned to the living room and handed the condom to Clark and removed her shorts and laid back and spread her legs. Clark began to open the condom, but Ne'Ne' stopped him. "Uh, uh," she said lowly as she sat back on the couch with her legs spread. "You have to do me like I did you before you put it in."

Clark got on his knees and lowered his face to Ne'Ne's crotch and tentatively stuck out his tongue and flicked it and she wiggled and squealed with delight. She raised her legs, slid to the end of the couch and exposed her bottom and pleaded for Clark to slide his tongue across her ass. Sandy had repeatedly told Ne'Ne' about the pleasures of oral sex, 'a thorough licking' as Sandy liked to call it. Clark stared at the fully exposed female before him, panting and pleading, rubbing herself. Ne'Ne's wanted her first time to be downright freaky and she wanted get freaky with Clark. Clark obliged and as he lapped at Ne'Ne's anus, she began to tremble; she then squirted a clear liquid that splashed Clark's face. The teen got up and wiped his face with his t-shirt. He thought Ne'Ne' had urinated on him until she told him she had shot-off and she wanted to do it again, this time with him inside of her. Ne'Ne' was a squirter; the sofa cushion was damp when she and Clark finished three minutes later. Neither lasted long during actual intercourse their first time out, but the sex was intense, and the feelings produced for both were incredible. Sandy gave Clark two more condoms and he and Ne'Ne' repeated their act two more times before they ended their first sex-session; although they would now get together whenever the opportunity presented itself.

Ne'Ne' reflected on her first time as she rode with Clark, Simon and Sandy headed back from Jackson State with the top down on Twiggy's convertible. Sandy was fumbling with the CD's as the convertible bounced down Beasley Road. All four teens were high and a little drunk when Ne'Ne' threw the last portion of a blunt out the car and dusted her hands clean.

"Y'all want another blunt?" Sandy asked, realizing all the cigars had been used.

"Nahh. I'm thirsty though! I gotta cotton mouth." Ne'Ne'

answered.

"You got a cock in your mouth?" Sandy asked through laughter.

"Not a cock! Not yet anyway!"

"Ooohh! Nasty booger!" Sandy replied as she laughed aloud.

"I got it from you, big sister! I said I'm thirsty!"

"Ohh, a cotton mouth! Alrighty! We can fix that." Sandy said as she came across The Ghetto Boys' *Uncut Dope* CD.

Simon had never bothered to listen to the CD Frog had given him weeks earlier so Sandy put it in and flipped through it. Most songs everybody had heard before like *Balls and My Word*, *Scarface*, and *Damn it Feels Good to be Gangster*. She skipped backwards and came across a song that started off with the voice of *Chuckie*, the murderous doll from the horror movies. "That's Chuckie talking!" Sandy yelled aloud as organs began playing and a thunderous base began blaring across the speakers as a rapper's voice exploded onto the song. Sandy listened with wide eyes to the psychotic lyrics as a rapper by the name of Bushwick Bill rapped on...

...*"Play pussy get fucked...means your better off dead...I wanted seafood so I fished in a child's head...mutherfuckas beware 'cause I'm sick...dead heads and frog legs, mmm, cake mix..."* Sandy began bucking in her seat. "That shit tight, Folk!" she screamed as she turned the stereo up loud.

Before long, everybody was bucking in their seats and laughing at the insane lyrics. The song broke down and Sandy swore she heard cows mooing in the background of the song. "That's a cow? That's a fuckin' cow he got in the background?"

"You high as fuck!" Simon said as he laughed.

"No! They put moo- mooing cows in there! Watch!" Sandy rewound the song and when the cows came into the background the four laughed aloud. The weed had all four teens with the giggles. Sandy put the song on repeat and they rode through Jackson playing the 'Chuckie' song over and over, laughing and bucking their seats.

Sandy then had Simon pull into a convenience store where she hopped out and asked Ne`Ne` to come with her inside. The lone cashier smiled at the two females as they burst through the door laughing. The stereo was still up loud and the two females danced down the middle aisle headed towards the beer cooler.

"We can't buy beer! I'm fifteen and you only nineteen!" Ne`Ne` whispered.

"Who said we paying for this shit? Come on. Grab a twelve pack." Sandy replied nonchalantly as she reached for a twelve pack of Budweiser. "We gone walk to the front and hook a left and run out this joint!"

The two females walked to the front of the store, Ne`Ne` picking up a large bag of potato chips on the way. The female cashier was unlocking the register preparing to ring up the girls, but when they cleared the aisle they both broke left and scurried out the store. The female cashier looked on in shock as Sandy and Ne`Ne` dashed out the front door and ran around the side of the building out of sight. The two hopped in the car and the four sped away. The cashier never got a look at the car, and although she got a good look at Sandy and Ne`Ne`, she never bothered calling the police. She was simply glad she didn't get robbed at gunpoint. Two other citizens, however, wouldn't be so lucky on this night.

A half hour later, after listening to *Chuckie* seven times in a row, and drinking some of the beer, Simon announced that he wanted more weed. "Let's go hit something!" Sandy chirped.

All four teens were now on an 'ill-trip'. Fueled by two blunts, cans of beer, and infectious music, they set out for more marijuana. Ne`Ne` was wearing Sandy's blue bandanna around her head and was lost in the moment, sinking ever deeper and deeper into Sandy and Simon's lifestyle. She watched as Sandy passed her .9mm to Clark and then came up with her beloved AK-47. Ne`Ne` looked and noticed that Simon was riding towards Tougaloo, a well-known Vice-Lord neighborhood. She grew nervous, but she believed her friends knew what they were doing—at least she hoped they did.

Simon rode towards an apartment complex on County Line

Road, just outside of Tougaloo College Campus and slowed the car down. He turned down the music and told Ne`Ne` to remove the headscarf before he entered the apartment complex and cruised slowly down the long drive through the huge two-story brick buildings. Halfway through, Simon spotted two lone men at the opposite end of one of the buildings inside complex who appeared to be in their early twenties. He turned down a short dead end drive and parked on the opposite side of the building, just out of sight and grabbed his Tec-nine from under the driver's seat. He and Sandy quietly exited the ride and Clark got behind the steering wheel holding onto the gun. Ne`Ne` stayed in the backseat watching the scene unfold.

Sandy crept across the grassy lawn on side the building and leaned her chopper against the brick wall and tied the blue bandanna she had gotten back from Ne`Ne` over the lower half of her face. Her blue eyes squinted and when she nodded, Simon could tell she was smiling. He smiled back as he covered the lower half of his face with a black bandanna and nodded to Sandy and the two tip-toed along the backside of the building.

Ne`Ne` and Clark, meanwhile, waited quietly inside the drop-top Impala. "You ever done this with them before, Clark?" Ne`Ne` asked.

"Umm, hmm. Them two right there though? They fools with it." Clark replied as he raised the top on the Impala and then reached for another beer.

"Give me one too!" Ne`Ne` whispered.

Simon and Sandy, meanwhile, were on a mission. They approached the edge of building at the opposite end and could hear the men talking and laughing. "Man it's slow as a bitch out here!" one male said.

"I thought Tougaloo had a game," the other said.

"They did—but it's away at Alcorn State. We shoulda went ta' Washington District, man. Vice Lords always out buying over that way," the first man stated.

"I know. Let's be out, homie. Eh, let's go hollar at them hoes we met the other night up ta' J-State." the other replied.

"For sho', nigga. Let's roll."

Just then Simon and Sandy ran out from the side of the building and cornered the men against the wall. "This only a jack-play niggas don't make it a homicide!" Simon stated lowly as he aimed his Tec-9 at one of the men.

Sandy had her chopper up against her shoulder pointed at the other man. The two men were frozen with fear. "Drop everything, mutherfuckas! Hurry up!" Sandy said lowly as she lunged forward with her gun.

"Hold up, alright? Just, just don't shoot," one of the men stated nervously as both men slowly began to empty all of their contents from their pockets.

The two men threw down a set of car keys, two sandwich bags filled with marijuana along with two knots of money wrapped in rubber bands. Sandy bent down to pick the money up, when she did, one of the men grabbed hold of her AK-47 and the other quickly grabbed hold of Simon's gun. The four wrestled on side of the building in near pitch darkness. Things hadn't gone according to plan. Sandy was tugging on her gun trying to squeeze the trigger, but she couldn't reach it. "Shit," she mumbled as she began kicking at the man and swinging her left arm. "Fuck, man! Let it go!" Sandy's voice echoed out into the darkness.

Simon was caught off guard by the sudden actions of the men, but he was 6' 1" 210 pounds, and was much stronger than his opponent. He quickly regained control of the gun, grabbed his victim around the neck, pulled him forward and immediately squeezed the trigger. "Fuck wrong with you, nigga?" he asked as he fired four bullets into the man's stomach. Simon's victim dropped to the ground immediately and was dead before his body could fully stretch out into the grass.

Sandy was still struggling with her victim, but he let go of the gun and tried to run when his counterpart went down. The gun fell to the ground and Sandy quickly picked it up and cut him down by shooting him in the back of his legs. She then ran up to the man and said, "Fuck wrong with you, nigga," just before she used her feet to turn her victim over to shoot the pleading man three more times in the chest—killing him instantly.

Clark put the car in drive after hearing the gunshots and then aimed his .9mm at the gap Sandy and Simon had traveled through waiting to see who would emerge first—either Simon and Sandy—or the two men who were Simon and Sandy's targets. Clark's hand was shaking slightly. He'd fired weapons before, but this time, he knew if Simon and Sandy didn't emerge from the gap, he would have to open fire and flee the scene and Simon and Sandy would be on their own.

Ne`Ne`'s heart was thumping and she was terrified out of her mind. She crouched in the backseat, hoping Simon and Sandy were okay and began wondering what would happen next. She and Clark both sighed when they saw Simon and Sandy trotting back to the car. Clark lowered his weapon and sped off as soon as the two were back in the car and made a beeline towards Interstate-20.

As Clark merged onto the highway, Sandy began to express exuberance towards she and Simon's treacherous act. Simon was pissed at Sandy, however; he said nothing as he reached over the front seat and slapped her across her face so hard, she fell against the side of the car, bumping her head against the window.

"What the fuck you hit me for?" Sandy said as she began to cry.

"As long as you live you better not never, *never* in your mutherfuckin' life use that word again!"

"What word?" Sandy cried.

"Nigger! You called him a nigger before you shot him!"

"I said the N-word? Shit! I'm sorry y'all! I didn't mean n-i-g-g-e-r, I said the other word, g-a, n-i-g-g-a!"

"Either fuckin' way—don't use it!" Simon said angrily.

"I said exactly what you said when you shot that other dude! I'm not a racist and you know that, Simon! Y'all," Sandy then said to Clark and Ne`Ne` as she grew worried that her friends were going to think she was prejudiced. "Ne`Ne`? Clark? As long as y'all been knowing me I never said that word. Right? Y'all know I'm not like that right?"

"I know you not like that." Ne`Ne` said.

"Simon, come on man. That's Sandy, brer. That's Sandy, Folk." Clark stated as he looked over at Simon.

Simon had known Sandy for over eleven years and deep down, he knew she wasn't prejudiced, and he believed she had never even uttered the word when he or any other black person wasn't around; but hearing Sandy say it just sounded wrong to him. Never mind the fact they had just murdered two men, Simon was pissed over the fact that Sandy had called one of the victims a 'nigga' before she killed him. He was more pissed over that fact than the homicide itself. He said nothing as he stared out the window.

"I ain't gone say it again, y'all! I promise!" Sandy stated. "Here," she said to Ne`Ne` as she handed her five twenties.

"What's this for?"

"Just for comin'."

"Here!" Sandy said as she handed five twenties to Clark. "I'm sorry!" she said again.

Simon turned around in the front seat and stared at Sandy and she, in turn, looked at her boyfriend with an apologetic look on her face as she cried. "I'm sorry! I'm, I'm not prejudiced and you know that! You know me, Simon!"

Simon reached out his right hand and he and Sandy did the Folk Nation handshake, "I know you not a racist. My bad, Folk."

"Thank you. Again, I'm sorry y'all." Sandy said as Ne`Ne` placed her hand to her cheek and gently wiped her tears. "Thanks Ne`Ne`." Sandy said lowly. "I can't believe I said that word." Sandy ended lowly through tears as the car traveled down the highway.

The four returned to Ghost Town and turned in for the night. Ne`Ne` crept inside after 2a.m. and met Dimples, who was worried sick about her sister, at the back door and hugged her.

The Holland Family Saga Part Five

"I thought you was in trouble, Rene," Dimples whispered.

"I'm cool, Regina." Ne`Ne` said lowly. "Come on, let's go to your room." Ne`Ne` didn't tell Dimples what all she had done and saw, she only told her about taking some beer. She had three left, and she and Dimples sat and drank the beer quietly as their mother slept. Dimples told her sister that she lost her virginity that night and Ne`Ne` then told Dimples about her first time with Clark. After drinking the beers and sharing some of their most intimate secrets, the twins turned in for the night, Ne`Ne` drunk and high, and Dimple' slightly tipsy.

That night with Simon and company had changed Ne`Ne`s life. She couldn't get the images of seeing Sandy and Simon disappear into complex, the hearing of gunshots, watching them jog back to the car, and the argument she witnessed. Ne`Ne` couldn't help but to think how nonchalant Sandy and Simon were about the murders. They argued instead, over the N-word. To Ne`Ne`, Simon and Sandy were true gangsters. She hoped to have their heart someday and the more she hung out with Sandy and Simon, the more she would take on their ways. Nearly all of her free time was spent with Simon and Sandy during the summer of '92, mainly on the weekdays while Mary was asleep and unaware of the mischievousness her daughters were sinking deeper and deeper into. Even Martha was unawares as she and Twiggy were seldom in Ghost Town as they were busy supplying their customers, and whenever she was in Ghost Town, which was during the day, the twins never let on that they were having sex, smoking, drinking, and participating in gang activities, and their friends never told. It would be a while before the twins' secret lives would be uncovered.

The Holland Family Saga Part Five

CHAPTER 21

IN AN INSTANT

It was now October of 1992; school was underway for Ne'Ne' and Dimples, so they couldn't hang out as much as they did during the summer. Most of their time was now spent around the house or on the go with their mother on weekends when she was off, and when Mary came home from work during the week. Mary's daughters were harboring secrets though; Ne'Ne' would sometimes sneak out on school nights to hang with Sandy and shoot her guns, and both twins would sometimes have sex with their boyfriends before Mary got home during the week. They had quickly learned how to hide this side of their life from their mother real well.

Peter Paul and Gina had moved into their own place not too far from the Queen section a few months back and the two of them were doing well with their cocaine hustle. Peter Paul, however, had to constantly scorn Gina Cradle about her spending habits and she was secretly beginning to resent his reprimands. Things were going along smoothly in Ghost Town overall—but as always, trouble lurked about.

Ne'Ne' and Dimples were out in front their home jumping double Dutch with their mother one warm October evening. Mary was jumping up and down between the ropes, her legs rapidly moving as her daughters turned faster and faster. "Momma you good!" Ne'Ne' yelled just as Simon and Sandy bent the corner onto Casper Drive.

Simon had gotten Twiggy's car repainted not too long after the double murder in Tougaloo. The '71 Impala was now jet black with a white rag top, and 18-inch triple gold Daytona rims and tan interior that almost matched the wheels. Simon had also placed hydraulics on the car. He could be seen riding up and down Casper Drive with Sandy Duncan on his side, the two riding in three-wheel motion. He would stop in front of Mary's home whenever Ne`Ne` and/or Dimples was out and make the car bounce up and down as he knew the twins got a kick out of seeing the car rise and fall. This warm October evening was no different. Simon hit the block and rode down Casper Drive in three-wheel motion with Sandy in the passenger seat and stopped in front of Mary's home. "Momma, that car tight!" Dimples remarked as Mary turned and eyed the car.

"How can they ride like that? With the car leaning to one side?" Mary asked as she and Dimples twirled the rope for Ne`Ne`.

"Eh, Folk!" Sandy yelled to Ne`Ne` just as Simon began to make the car pancake up and down, "We—we got y'all s—s—some," Sandy couldn't get her words out from the motion of the car. "Stop! St—stop, brer," she yelled aloud to Simon.

Simon said nothing in response as the car continued to pancake up and down. He just stared at Sandy seriously as he hit the switches on the car, getting his stunt on in the middle of Casper Drive and Friendly Lane. Sandy had a plate of food in her hands and she was trying to eat, but the food began spilling in the car.

"Y—you wastin' food in—m—my sister shit!" Simon managed to say as the car bounced up and down.

"Eh—F—Folk! I was eatin' be—before you, st—started pancakin'!" Sandy struggled to say aloud.

Mary and her daughters couldn't help but to laugh at the two. They watched from the sidewalk as the Impala bounced up and down in the middle of the street. Sandy was laughing loudly; she and Simon both looked as if they were having the time of their lives inside the car. Simon finally dropped the car low and pulled into the driveway to his home and the two went over by Mary and the twins. Sandy had bought them all Mandarin Chicken plates and they would hang out the rest of the day.

****

Meanwhile, Martha, Twiggy, and Peter Paul were at Martha and Twiggy's safe house out near North Park Mall. The two bedroom house was pimped out with two leather sofas, a "55 TV, two queen beds, two large closets that held some of Martha and Twiggy's wardrobes and one large oak table in the kitchen that held scales, plastic bags, pots and pans and razor blades. Martha and Twiggy rarely slept there; they spent most nights in Vicksburg at a suite inside the Hilton Hotel, but if they ever fell off they would at least have a furnished apartment to start out with.

Thirty-three year-olds Twiggy and Martha were supposed to be on their way to Vicksburg this evening, but Peter Paul had purchased a quarter-kilo that he needed rocked up right away as sales were good in the Queens. It would take about forty-five minutes, but Martha and Twiggy had delayed their trip to help Peter Paul out this day.

They were all sitting at the table watching Martha do her thing as they conversed. "You know Herc still be asking about Loretta?" Twiggy asked Martha.

"Girl, please. Loretta got her another tree trunk she climbing." Martha replied.

"What's a tree trunk?" Peter Paul asked.

"You, brother!" Twiggy stated as she and Martha laughed.

"Yep! You big hunka hunka man you!" Martha stated, adding to the laughter.

"Mar, you can't handle me!"

"Boy, please! I put this fuckin' snapper pussy on your ass," Martha said as she donned a face mask and began to sprinkle cocaine into a boiling pot of water, "I put this snapper pussy on your li'l young ass you be looking for me in the daytime with a flash light."

"Whoop! Whoop! Whoop!" Twiggy said aloud as she high-fived Martha.

"We own them young boys in Vicksburg. You better ask somebody, Peter Paul." Martha said in a confident tone.

"Y'all rocking like that?"

"Yes, sir. Them young boys do whatever we ask—in and out the bed." Martha said. "Got they minds gone with the game we run, ole boy."

"We used ta' play with your mind too when you first became leader in Ghost Town," Twiggy said.

"Shiit! I *let* y'all have Ambush!"

"Whatever!" Twiggy said as she rolled her eyes. "On the real though, Folk? We was mad at first when Albert Lee made you leader because you used to fight too much. When this 'caine hit though, you got right."

"Umm, hmm," Martha added, "nobody don't bang hardly. It's just Folk fuckin' with Folk, and V.L. dealing with V.L. Everybody tryna get money."

"Right, right," Peter Paul stated. "But every now and then—"

"The fuck jump off!" Twiggy stated, finishing Peter Paul's sentence.

Almost an hour later, Martha had finished cooking up the cocaine for Peter Paul. She went to wash up and just as she returned to the kitchen, the back door was kicked open. Peter Paul thought it was the police, but when he saw the ski-mask, he jumped and began to wrestle with the man in the threshold. Twiggy jumped up and screamed as a gunshot rang out and Peter Paul dropped to the floor. Another gunshot rang out and Twiggy fell onto the table and then hit the floor herself. Martha had her .9mm on her and she quickly grabbed it just as the man began to enter the home. He didn't see Martha as he walked through the door, but when he looked and saw her with the gun pointed at him, his eyes widened. Martha fired two shots that crashed into his skull and he fell on top of Peter Paul.

"My brother! He all right? Aww fuck! I'm hit in the body!"

The Holland Family Saga Part Five

Twiggy hissed threw clasped teeth.

"You all right?" Martha asked as she knelt down beside Twiggy.

"Fuck no! That bitch shot me, Mar! Peter, Peter Paul? Where he at?"

Martha looked over to Peter Paul and saw that he had been shot in the right eye. She could tell he was dead. She looked back at Twiggy and shook her head somberly. "Aww, shit! Aww, God!" Twiggy moaned as she sat up on the floor and grabbed her gun from her waist band. "I didn't have time ta' pull my piece, Mar! Take, take, the shit and get the fuck outta here! Call, call the ambulance for Peter Paul before you leave!"

"Twiggy, he dead. You need the amb—"

"Call the ambulance for Pee and get the fuck from 'round here, Martha!"

Martha knew if the ambulance and police came, they would find the cocaine along with the dead bodies and investigate. She had killed a man, and even if it was in self-defense, she felt she couldn't take the risk. Twiggy fired her .357 into the lifeless corpse of the intruder and dropped it just before Martha ran into the living room and dialed 911. When she got back to the kitchen she saw Twiggy had removed the intruders mask and both women stared Martha in shock when the realized that they knew the young man.

"Go see Chug before you move! Chug was his godfather." Twiggy hissed through heavy gasps of air.

"Alright," Martha said as she scrambled to remove the drugs from the scene. "I'm a meet you at the hospital. You sure you gone be all right?"

Twiggy raised her bloody hand and gave Martha the Folk handshake. "Just come see me at the hospital when you sort this shit out, Folk and let me know what's up," she said lowly as she grimaced in pain. "Go on Martha before they catch you."

Martha didn't want to leave, but she knew she had to. She grabbed the cocaine and stuffed it into a duffel bag. She shoved the scales, pots and pans into a plastic bag, clearing the table completely and ran to her Cadillac and fled the scene. She made it back to Ghost Town and pulled up in front Twiggy's home and quickly exited the car and let herself into the home and where she stashed the cocaine and paraphernalia. She then beckoned Simon and Sandy over from Mary's front yard and the three stood in the living room where Martha broke the news. Simon fell back on the couch and sobbed after hearing that his uncle was killed and Twiggy was wounded.

"Simon, be cool man. I got this here. Look, I need for you—"

"All my people keep getting taking away! First my daddy and momma, now my uncle and my fuckin' auntie! Albert Lee on death row! I ain't gone have *nobody* left!" Simon yelled angrily as he cut Martha off.

"You got me!" Sandy replied lowly.

"You ain't fuckin' family!" Simon yelled as he jumped from the couch and grabbed Sandy around the neck and began choking her.

"Simon!" Martha yelled as she began hitting Simon in the back of the head.

Simon then turned on Martha. He slapped her in the face and she began fighting back. They were all over the living room, knocking over lamps and pictures and rearranging the home's furniture. "Fuck wrong with you?" Martha asked as she held Simon in the head lock. "I'm Folk, nigga! *We* Folk! Me *and* Sandy! And you fighting *us*? We ain't hurt your people! Now focus!"

"Let me go!" Simon yelled as he broke free of Martha's grip. "My people," he then said lowly as he sat in a chair. "Not Twiggy, man. That's my fuckin' girl. That's my heart, Martha!" Simon and Peter Paul were cool, but Twiggy was like a mother to him. And for all the wrong he'd done in his life, Simon was having a hard time dealing with the shoe being placed on the other foot. He looked up at Martha as he sat in the chair and wiped his face and asked, "What we gotta do?"

Martha, upon realizing Simon had regained his composure,

gave him and Sandy the Folk handshake and the three stood close together in a small circle. Top ranking members in Ghost Town had fallen and Martha knew she now held the lead position for the time being; but she was more than up to the task at hand. "Simon," she said calmly, "I need you to go to the hospital and stay with Twiggy. Get all her belongings and stay there because she need you right now. Me and Sandy got your back alright?"

"I'm good. I'm good. Let me in on what's going down when you find out," Simon said as he wiped his face with his t-shirt, shook off what pain he could, and said, "I'm on my way to the hospital."

"Do that," Martha said as she watched Simon head for the front door. "And when I find out what the fuck happened I be right up there. Sandy? I need for you to go get that thang!" Martha then stated in reference to the AK-47 Sandy owned.

Sandy ran into Simon's room and grabbed her AK-47 as Simon ran and hopped into Twiggy's Impala. The car lifted from the ground and Simon backed out of the drive, aimed the car towards the main drag and burned rubber as he sped out of Ghost Town. That noise got Mary's attention. She was on her porch with her twins vaguely aware of the activity over at the Charles' home, but after seeing the way Simon sped from Ghost Town, she became worried about her sister. She left her porch and walked across the street to the Charles house. "What happened?" she asked worriedly as she met Martha and Sandy exiting the house. "What happened? Why Sandy carrying that gun? What happened?" Mary asked repeatedly.

Martha said nothing as she walked pass Mary. "Answer me dammit!" Mary yelled as her eyes welled up. "Where the hell are you going? What are you up to? The both of you?"

"Mary, go inside, lock the door and don't open it for nobody. Understand? I be back tonight."

"Martha, what happened?"

Martha didn't want to tell Mary anything, but for safety reasons she knew she had to do so. She opened the door to her Cadillac, looked Mary in the eyes and said, "Somebody from

Ghost Town set us up today. Peter Paul dead and Twiggy in the hospital. She got shot. I don't know who ta' trust out here besides Simon and Sandy, so go home, lock the door and don't open it. You hear? Don't tell nobody—not even my nieces. Nobody. Understand?"

"Okay! Okay! Ohh, God! This is a sad day! A sad day!" Mary stated lowly.

"Umm hmm," Marta replied as she got behind the wheel of her Cadillac and grabbed her .9mm from underneath her seat and cocked it, "but Twiggy gone be all right, and I got Peter Paul."

"Martha please don't—"

"I ain't tryna hear that shit, Mary! Niggas killed Peter Paul right in front his fuckin' sister? What if I was standing where Twiggy was? Fuck that! Folk gotta pay!"

"You'll be just like them, you—"

"Mary go home!" Martha screamed as she and Sandy pulled from the curb and swung her car around in the middle of Casper Drive and sped away from Ghost Town, leaving Mary looking on in shock.

Mary ran home, grabbed her daughters and ushered them inside and locked the door. Ne`Ne` and Dimples had asked her what happened, but Mary wouldn't tell. "Go and get ready for school, while I fix dinner," she said as she began reaching for seasonings inside her kitchen cabinets.

"But momma," Dimples replied anxiously, "Sandy had that big gun and Martha just—"

"Rene and Regina!" Mary screamed, cutting Dimples' statement short. "Do as," Mary paused and lowered her voice, realizing she was angry for no good reason at her daughters. "I'm sorry. I'm sorry for hollering, just, just do as I say, sweetie pies, please. Martha and Sandy will be fine," she ended somberly, rather, unconvincingly, as the twins slowly walked out of the living room; they, too, were now worried about Martha and Sandy.

****

Martha and Sandy meanwhile, had ridden out to Queens section over towards Chug-a-lug's house. The now forty year-old former gangster was sitting in his yard when Martha pulled up. Several young teens, all Folk members, were out and they watched as Martha and Sandy slowly emerged from the Cadillac. They eyed the chopper Sandy held at her side along with Chug-a-lug, who said calmly, "I hope thissa social call," as he stood up to greet Martha, all the while eyeing the AK-47 Sandy held at her side.

Martha stared at the young teens and said in an angry, commanding tone of voice, "Y'all young asses need ta' push out from 'round here! This grown folk business!"

The young teens all knew Martha, and seeing Sandy gripping the chopper let them know the two meant business. They looked at Chug-a-lug and he nodded his head—only then did they 'push out'.

"What's going on, Martha?" Chug-a-lug asked seriously.

"Eh, Folk? Your Godson? He told you about a hustle he had set up for today?"

"He said he had a li'l' caper set up for this evening. Why?"

"Who he said put 'em up on that?"

"Peter Paul and Gina Cradle had that set up for today. Why?"

"Gina *and* Peter Paul?" Martha asked as she looked back at Sandy in disbelief.

"Umm hmm," Chug-a-lug said as he rocked back on his heels. "Gina told him about a lick Peter Paul had set up for 'em at a house out by North Park Mall. He said Gina and P-Paul been watching the house."

"Was Peter Paul ever around here today? I mean were they together? Him and Gina?"

"Nahh. P-Paul left late this evening by his self. Gina came over here a few minutes after he left and told Frog it was on because she knew nobody was at the house."

Martha then read the whole play in an instant. She informed Chug-a-lug of the fact that Frog was dead and Gina Cradle was the reason she had to kill him. "You killed my Godson?" Chug-a-lug asked in a surprised manner as Sandy tightened the grip on the chopper, worried that drama was about to kick off.

"This the deal, Chug," Martha said, "Gina called me this evening asking me if she could ride to Vicksburg with us right? When I told her me and Twiggy was already on our way out there she said she'll catch us next time."

Chug-a-lug read the play near bout just as quick as Martha. "So you think Gina was planning on robbing y'all house while y'all was away," he asked.

"Yea. Only Peter Paul needed a package rocked up right quick. We met him on our block leaving the safe house and we doubled back. Now, I'm thinking Gina believed we was gone so she sent Frog out there to hit our stash."

"But why Frog shot Peter Paul?"

"Come on, Chug. You get caught robbing somebody house you know and you gone just take off your mask and tell 'em you made a mistake? Frog had ta' play it all the way no matter what because he was already in too deep. He had 'em, man. Peter Paul was out and Twiggy was down, but I came from the bathroom and pulled my Nina. I guess Frog didn't know I was in the house and I didn't know who he was because he had a ski-mask on. I ain't know who it was so I blasted. You don't ask questions in a situation like that, ya' feel me? Gina set the play up. Only we wasn't supposed to there when it went down."

"That bitch Gina got my people killed," Chug-a-lug said somberly as he looked to the ground and bumped his fists together in frustration. "Damn!"

"Trust me, Folk. Ghost Town don't wanna go ta' war over this shit, but we will if we have to. Let me handle Gina and squash this shit before word get out and all hell break loose." Martha said seriously.

"What about the fact that you killed Frog? How we gone straighten that shit out? 'Cause people gone wanna know."

"Nobody but me, Twiggy, Peter Paul, and Gina knew where

the house was at—put the word out on Gina after her body pop up. Tell 'em the truth. Tell 'em she threw Frog in the cross and got 'em killed, but she got hers as well so everything squared away. Just be sure to leave me and Sandy name out the shit when Gina body pop up. We go back in the day, Chug, and you know I'm not like that. I killed Frog true enough, but I didn't know it was him. Gina responsible for this shit." Martha said lowly.

Chug-a-lug closed his eyes and thought for a minute. In his mind, it could easily be argued that Martha, Twiggy, Peter Paul and Gina plotted against Frog and the drug deal went bad at their safe house; but the fact that Gina was putting Frog on a so-called 'lick' before anything ever went down could not escape his mind. On top of that, Chug-a-lug knew Martha and Twiggy weren't jack-artists. All roads did seem to point back to Gina and he told Martha to handle her business, figuring if Martha, Twiggy, Peter Paul, and Gina were conspiring against Frog, then Gina would not be harmed because if she were killed, then Martha would have had to been a heartless individual; and over the years he'd known the woman, Chug-a-lug had never known Martha to be so scandalous.

"Kill Gina Cradle, and we all even." Chug-a-lug stated as he gave Martha and Sandy the Folk handshake.

Martha returned to her Cadillac and left Queens section looking for Gina. The two women would not rest until they found the woman and dealt with the situation at hand. They rode to Peter Paul's apartment, but there was no sign of Gina. They then rode back to Ghost Town and went to Mary's home, who was so glad to see her sister was safe.

Mary had just finished cooking dinner. The deep-fried trout and French fries smelled delectable and when offered up plates of food, Martha accepted. She was both hungry and tired, but completing the mission was of the utmost importance.

"Simon called," Mary said lowly, "he said the doctors induced a coma on Twiggy. She unconscious, but she's gonna live." Mary said as she smiled and placed a plate of food onto the kitchen table before Martha.

Martha waited for Mary to fix Sandy a plate of food before she ordered her to head over to White Street and wait in Ambush for a sign of Gina. No one but Sandy and Martha knew what was transpiring at the time. Martha knew she had to find Gina on this night before word spread that Peter Paul was killed and Twiggy was shot. Gina had to disappear before that fact could be known, that way, it could be made to look as if Gina was also a victim of what went down and not the person who was killed in an act of revenge. Martha knew how to play the game well; she knew if she didn't find Gina before the word got out on Peter Paul and Twiggy, the bitch just may get away with her treacherous deed.

Sandy took her plate of food with her and ate as she walked down Friendly Lane headed towards the wooded trail leading towards Ambush. Shortly after Sandy left, Martha broke down and cried. "Twiggy," she said lowly. "That's my fuckin' girl, Mary. She can't die! Not like this," she said as she pounded the kitchen table repeatedly.

"She'll be fine. But I'm worried about *you*, Martha."

"Us too, auntie," two soft voices were heard sayin' in unison.

Martha looked up to see her two nieces standing in the threshold of the kitchen with teary eyes. "We, we don't wanna see you die, auntie." Dimples said lowly.

Martha leaned forward in her lap and heaved. "Come here babies!" she said as she looked back up and stretched her arms.

Ne`Ne` and Dimples ran and hugged their aunt and Mary hugged her sister as well. Mary and her daughters knew Martha was a gangster, but they didn't care. She'd never really let her street life intertwine with her family life; but on this night, Martha had no one left but her family and Sandy Duncan and she was just as scared for herself and Twiggy as Mary and her daughters were scared for her; but Martha knew what she had to do. And even though she wasn't a part of the street life, Mary understood why her sister was going through and planning on doing what she going to do on this night. Mary didn't condone it, she merely understood.

Martha sat and ate dinner with her family and the mood was

somewhat somber. Jokes were cracked to help ease the tension. Ne`Ne` and Dimples then turned on the radio and listened to the Fantastic Four Show for a while and Misses Jones, the Holland family's favorite host and Dee-jay, unknowingly brought laughter, but the laughter and happiness was brought down when the phone rang. Dimples answered the phone and her smile dropped when she heard Sandy's voice. She handed the phone to Martha with trembling hands.

Martha acknowledged Sandy and heard her say, "Folk? I found Gina. She was by her people house."

"Where she at now?"

"She in Ambush tryna make a few dollars."

"Bring that thang with you and wait for me by the trail on Friendly Lane." Martha replied calmly.

"I gotcha'!" Sandy said as she and Martha hung up the phones. Martha got up from the table slowly and washed her hands in the sink and Mary and her daughters hugged her one last time before headed out the door.

"Be careful, Martha. Please." Mary said.

"I love y'all. Don't worry about me, family. I'll be all right," Martha said as she stood at the back door. "This is just something I gotta do for Twiggy. Don't hold this against me, please."

"I'm not, Martha. It's your life. Twiggy is your friend, and me, Ne`Ne` and Dimples will always be your family—right or wrong. We love you. Just please, be careful." Mary ended as Martha kissed her cheek and walked to her Cadillac, got in and started the car and headed to Ambush.

The Holland Family Saga Part Five

CHAPTER 22

MARTHA'S MARK

Martha pulled up slowly onto White Street and rode to the cul-de-sac in Ambush. Her car slowly made a wide turn and pulled up beside Gina and she quickly discerned that Gina had a surprised look on her face. It was a look that told Martha that Gina was wondering what she was doing in Jackson when she and Twiggy were supposed to be in Vicksburg. Martha, who was now strapped with a .357 taken from the Charles' home, exited her car and walked over and spoke cheerily to Gina in order to loosen her up a bit. When Gina said to her that she thought she and Twiggy were in Vicksburg, Martha's assumptions were solidified.

"Twiggy had ta' double back to the house right quick." Martha replied in a carefree, unawares-type tone of voice, all the while in full tune to the deviousness of Gina's act.

"What? Back to the safe house by the mall?" Gina asked in a concerned manner.

"Nahh. She right up the street by her house. We headed back out though. I just came ta' grab another bag of weed. It's gone be a long night in V'burg." Martha stated happily as she asked Gina to sell her a bag of weed.

"I only got crack—but if you let me ride, I'll buy a sack of weed on the way to Vicksburg."

"Deal." Martha replied in a cool manner.

Martha was beginning to believe Gina was now trying to cover her tracks. She was getting inside of her mind. She pictured that Gina was thinking that if she was in Vicksburg with her and Twiggy, when they found out their house was broken into, she would not be a suspect because she would have been with them the whole time. After about five minutes, Martha announced that she was headed to pick up Twiggy and Gina began walking with her to her car. This was the test. Martha knew not if Gina had a gun on her; but if she was playing the same game as Martha, she could easily pull a gun and blast her inside the Cadillac.

The two approached the car and Martha requested that Gina sit in the backseat so Twiggy could hop right in and Gina obliged. Martha closed the door and got behind the wheel and adjusted her mirror to focus on Gina's hands resting in her lap as she clutched her .357 and began heading towards Casper Drive, knowing full well that she was putting herself at risk at this moment. Gina sat quietly; believing she was headed to Vicksburg, watching as Martha rode pass the Charles' home and turned right onto Friendly Lane.

"I thought you was picking up Twiggy," Gina said inquisitively just as Martha turned around with the .357 in her right hand.

Gina's eyes grew wide, but she managed to catch Martha by surprise when she quickly grabbed the gun. She and Martha began to wrestle, Gina in the back seat and Martha behind the steering wheel. Martha had the car aimed towards the wooded trail so she let go of the steering wheel and kept her foot slightly on the gas pedal as the car cruised down the street and slowly began to pull to the right. The car bounced up the curb just before the trail's entrance and Martha hit the brakes in front of the trail just as Sandy came into view.

Sandy saw Martha struggling with Gina and opened the passenger door and began hitting Gina with the butt of her AK-47, causing Gina to scream out loud in fear once the realization that she was being set up had sunk into her psyche.

Martha was able to wrap her finger around the trigger and she fired a single shot that struck Gina in the left arm. Gina let go of the gun and screamed as she grabbed her arm and Sandy quickly jumped in and closed the door and Gina's screams then went silent. Her pleas would go unheard because the windows were rolled up and the top was closed on Martha's ride. Gina was screaming to the top of her lungs and begging not to be kidnapped. Martha had to turn up the radio and Sandy hopped into the back seat and pushed Gina to the floor and laid on top of her to conceal the now terrified woman as Martha casually drove out of Ghost Town as if nothing happened. As if she and Sandy hadn't just kidnapped a woman and were now on their way to finish the job.

Sandy grabbed the .357 from Martha and placed it in Gina's face and ordered her to be quiet. She then removed her blue bandanna and stuffed it into Gina's mouth to conceal her low squeals as Martha rode north on Interstate-55 for about twenty miles out to the Ross Barnett reservoir and found a secluded spot to pull into on the Rankin County side where she and Sandy wrestled Gina from the back seat of the car. The three were now amidst tall, lingering oaks with branches hanging over the water and a three foot high bank. Bald cypress trees draped with moss rested in the water just off shore in this area that had a swampy appeal. The sun was beginning to set and flocks of blue heron took the air, seemingly aware of what drama ay beneath their feathered-bellies and flapping wings.

Martha grabbed her .357 from Sandy and pushed Gina up against the hood of the car. Weakened from the gunshot, she lay back on the hood stricken with fear as Martha approached her, her brown eyes reflecting the sun. "You got our fuckin' house robbed bitch!" Martha said lowly as she placed the gun underneath Gina's chin.

"Robbed your house? Folk! I ain't have nothin' to do with that shit! I been in Ambush all day!"

"You telling me the truth?"

"I swear! Frog did that on his own!"

Martha eased up a bit and apologized to Gina as she looked over to Sandy, who could only shake her head over the fact that Gina never even realized she had just given herself away.

No one knew Frog was the one who had robbed the house except the people who were in the house, and Gina was not one of those people.

"My bad, Folk. We gotta get you to the hospital," Martha said. "Eh, just tell 'em it was an accident alright? You shot yourself. Tell 'em you shot yourself." Martha requested.

"I will. That's what I was gonna do anyway." Gina replied as she stared at Martha and Sandy as she clutched her arm wincing in pain.

Gina was planning on telling the doctors and the police that Martha had shot her. She was prepared to roll over on Ghost Town if ever she made it to the hospital. Gina Cradle was once a loyal member of Folk Nation, but the money that was being made from selling cocaine beside Peter Paul had fueled a certain kind of greed within her that she could not control. Peter Paul knew of her spending habits, and when he cut her off, Gina resented that; her greed blinded her judgment to the point of betrayal. She figured she could take all of Martha's and Twiggy's cocaine and make her own money and no one would've suspected that it was another Folk member that had robbed the house. Gina never had any intentions on seeing anybody hurt, but by sheer fate, Martha, Twiggy and Peter Paul were at the house when Frog struck. Frog went on the lick alone since no one was supposed to be there, more money for him and Gina to split in his mind, but just like Martha had told Chug-a-lug earlier in the day, even though he knew the people in the house, Frog had to play it all the way through. Gina caused two people, two Folk members to lose their lives over a simple act of greed. Martha thought about all of that as she slowly walked away from Gina and asked her, "How you know Frog robbed the house, Gina?"

Gina then realized the error she made. "I'm sorry, Folk," she said lowly as she leaned back against the car.

"Don't give me that Folk shit! Peter Paul dead mutherfucka," Martha yelled.

"Nobody was supposed to be there, Martha!"

"Well bitch we were there! Pee dead and Twiggy in a coma

over your bullshit!"

"My arm. I need a doctor. Please! I'm sorry! I swear I'm sorry and I'll do anything you ask! Anything!"

Martha believed Gina never had intentions on seeing anyone get killed, but the fact remained. She also couldn't get it out of her head that if Frog had gotten the ups on her, she and Twiggy both would be dead right alongside Peter Paul. The bottom line was that Gina plotted against Ghost Town and she now had to pay.

Martha walked away from Gina, who began to plead as she knew what was coming. Sandy stepped aside and watched as Martha turned and opened fire with her .357, flipping Gina's body onto the hood of the car with a single gunshot. Gina coughed, gagged and spasmed as her body slid off the hood onto the ground. She was still alive, her body convulsing from the bullet lodged in her shoulder. Martha then took the AK-47 from Sandy, walked over and stood over Gina and fired four shots into her chest cavity, killing her instantly.

Martha Holland had hurt several people in her time and she had seen murders take place. She aided and abetted homicides early on, and she had also killed Frog, and act in which could be argued as self-defense. This murderous act that was perpetrated against Gina Cradle, however, was an outright murder fueled by revenge and Martha felt the least bit remorseful. She and Sandy threw Gina's body into the reservoir and drove to Greenwood, Mississippi to clean Martha's car and themselves. They would visit Twiggy the next morning after tossing the .357 into a landfill.

The Holland Family Saga Part Five

CHAPTER 23

THE LAST OF THE O.G.'S

"Police have no motive or suspects in what appears to be the murder of a twenty-seven year-old woman preliminarily identified as Gina Cradle. The woman's remains were found floating near the shore on the north side of the Ross Barnett Reservoir in Rankin County early this morning by a local fisherman. The man said he happened up on the body when…"

Martha was sitting in the living room of Mary's home watching the 12 'o' clock news a week after she had killed Gina. Peter Paul was buried two days before, only Twiggy couldn't make the funeral because she was still in the hospital and the doctors hadn't released her. Martha leaned forward on the couch and listened to the program intently. She saw the footage of the body bag containing Gina's corpse and bowed her head in shame. She felt bad for killing Gina, but she believed in her heart that she was justified. It felt strange watching the scene, somewhat surreal to Martha. She changed the channel, no longer able to watch the news reporter speak on the death of someone she'd viewed as a friend only days earlier. Just as Martha sat the remote down on the coffee table, Sandy knocked on the back door.

When Martha let her in the first thing Sandy asked was, "You saw that shit about Gina?"

"Yea. Eh, you did get rid of all those guns right?"

"Yeah, they at the bottom of the mighty Mississippi River.

Me and Simon tossed 'em the night after..." Sandy's voice trailed off. She was about to say aloud that Martha killed Gina.

"It's okay, baby. I know you ain't gone speak on that. We just had to purge all the weapons after something like that." Martha said as she patted Sandy's back and the two went and sat in the living room.

"I gotta get another chopper." Sandy stated as she and Martha began discussing where they could purchase new guns off the street.

****

Meanwhile, Twiggy was lying in her bed watching the news, having seen the story about Gina's murder a few minutes earlier. *"Them hooks shoulda threw her ass off the third floor in the mall that day instead of Kenyatta,"* she said to herself as she smiled slightly.

Martha had shared her secret with Twiggy the day after she killed Gina when she and Sandy paid her a visit and she was reflecting on the situation, admiring Martha's aptitude when two plain clothes detectives walked into her room.

"Irene 'Twiggy' Charles." one of the men stated matter-of-factly.

"Who the fuck are you?" Twiggy stated as she cocked her head to one side and cut her eyes at the two men.

"I'm detective Marvin Kettle and this is my partner Victor Bland—were homicide. We wanna ask you some questions."

"About what?" Twiggy asked as she raised her mattress to allow herself to sit upright.

"First of all," Marvin, a 6' tall crater-faced Caucasian began to speak, "about the man that shot your brother? You said Peter Paul and the intruder wrestled over the gun and the intruder shot your brother in the eye and then he shot you. At the same time you grabbed your .357 and shot the intruder."

"Right. That's how it went down."

"Wrong," Marvin said lowly. "You see? The bullets from your gun were planted in Clifford 'Frog' George's back *after* he was dead. Forensics says so."

"Fuck forensics! I took him down in my own house. That's self-defense all the way."

"Not denying that," Victor, a short, pudgy and bald Caucasian remarked, "but Frog also had a couple of nine millimeter slugs planted in his skull. Now that tells me that another gunman was in that house—and that person was the one who killed Frog. We also found traces of cocaine on the table in the kitchen. All of this seems to be painting a picture that says this was a drug deal gone bad. Your little self-defense testimony might not hold up in court."

"You charging me with anything?"

"Not yet." Marvin replied with a sly smile.

"Well until you do, I suggest you two ugly mutherfuckas get the fuck out my room! And next time, talk to my lawyer!" Twiggy said as the two men eyed one another, turned and walked towards the door.

Before he left, however, Detective Kettle turned back to Twiggy and said, "We'll be back. We know your whole family's violent history from your brother Nolan right down to this case here—and now it's your turn to catch a case. You're getting off easy though—can't say the same for Nolan and Peter. And Albert Lee ass isn't looking to good either. Now, we may not be able to send you to death row like Albert Lee—whose time is getting short mind you—but we *will* remove you from these streets, Twiggy. That we will do. By the way, if you don't want to take this entire rap? Tell us who killed Gina Cradle? Somehow she fits into all this right? We both know you covering for Martha Holland because that's your ace-boon-coon. Both of y'all was in that house and we know it! I suggest you save your own ass!" Marvin ended as he and Victor walked out the door.

Twiggy sat back and thought about what the detectives said. She had never dealt with the police before in her life and she wasn't about to do so now. She decided to call Martha and have her visit so she can run everything down to her so they could formulate a plan to keep themselves out of jail.

Martha was preparing to leave the Charles' home when the detectives left Twiggy's room so she had missed the call. She had an ounce of cocaine on her and was preparing to make a drop-off at *Mugsies* pool hall in North Jackson. She hopped into her car and as she rode away, her pager went off. She recognized the number as the number to the hospital, but rather than double back to the house, she stopped off at Chug-a-lug's to make the call from a pay phone.

Martha was dialing the number to the hospital when she was immediately swarmed by narcotics agents with guns drawn. She raised her hands into the air and was immediately handcuffed and rushed into the backseat of a squad car. Her car was then searched, but the officers found nothing. What the officers didn't know was that Martha had the cocaine stashed in the crack of her ass. She removed the powdered ounce and stuffed it deep into the backseat of the squad car. Some other unfortunate captive would wear that charge. Martha then believed she would be let go when the agents found nothing, but when she saw the F.B.I. pull up, she knew she was in deep trouble.

Martha was transferred to an F.B.I. agent's car and then taken downtown, and just as she suspected, she was charged with conspiracy to distribute cocaine and her bond was set at $100,000 dollars. She would have to sit for almost two weeks. She knew that because when she called Simon and had him notify Twiggy that she needed a bond posted, Simon told her that Twiggy would be out the hospital in a week or so and wouldn't be able to bail her out until then. Martha felt relieved, however; conspiracy would be easy to beat in her eyes because she figured the feds had much of nothing to go on. She knew from the streets that when the feds couldn't prove guilt outright they would imply that a person had intent, thus the conspiracy charge. She was preparing to fight her charges from the streets, but the feds had other plans.

Twiggy was released from the hospital a week and a half later and she went straight to the bank to retrieve enough funds to bail Martha out after she'd checked on her house and changed clothes. The bank manager was on hand this day and as Twiggy went into the private room to check her boxes, the

The Holland Family Saga Part Five

bank manager made a phone call. Fifteen minutes later, Twiggy had just finished counting out $10,000 dollars and was separating the remainder of her money evenly when she saw F.B.I. agents charging out of the corner of her eye. She tried to hurriedly shove the boxes back into their proper slots, but she was accosted before she could do so. She was handcuffed and the agents took possession of her funds, confiscating $71,000 dollars total. Twiggy was later charged with conspiracy to distribute cocaine and tax evasion and was jailed in the same facility as Martha. The two women were kept separate and Marvin and Victor went to work.

"Irene, Irene, Irene," Marvin said with a sly smile as he stood before Twiggy in a dimly lit small four-cornered room with no windows. "I told you I would see you again."

Twiggy merely stared at the man. "Y'all ain't got nothin' on me! Just a bunch of green backs," she said angrily.

"Oh yea? Well, your boyfriend Martha is saying otherwise. She said it was *your* cocaine she was selling out there on the streets. We can charge you with running a criminal enterprise, woman."

Twiggy only stared at Marvin with a look of wonderment on her face. "That bitch told you that shit?" she asked as she curled her lips to the side and stared back at the detective.

"Martha Holland," Victor said to Martha in another room at the same time pressure was being applied to Twiggy, "your friend Twiggy isn't the loyal woman she professes."

"What?" Martha asked lowly as she sat behind a table whilst handcuffed.

"Irene just rolled you over and fucked you with no Vaseline. She gave you up for killing Frog and also said you were responsible for killing Gina Cradle. Just like that!" Detective Bland said as he snapped his fingers.

"You lyin! Twiggy ain't a snitch! And if she did say somethin'? She lyin' on me because I ain't have nothing to do with Frog or Gina gettin' killed!"

"Tell us what happened, Martha. Make it easy on yourself,

woman!" Victor snarled just before he lit a cigarette and offered one to Martha.

Martha pushed the pack of unfiltered Camels back in Victor's direction and said, "I wanna see the charges! If you not charging me with murder, I ain't talking. Matter of fact, if you charge me with anything? I'm still not talking! Fuck you mister officer! Kiss my black ass why you at it!" Martha ended as she slumped back in the chair and closed her eyes.

Marvin and Victor tried for over nine hours to break the two women, but neither would cave in. The detectives had to admit that Martha and Twiggy were two rare breeds. They had used this routine many times before and they were successful ninety percent of the time, the other ten percent of suspects were innocent. As guilty as they were, Martha and Twiggy never rolled over on each other and were placed into general population a couple of days apart.

Martha was lyin in her bunk inside the huge 71 person dormitory when she was tapped on the leg. She rose up and saw Twiggy standing beside her bunk. It was the first time the two had seen one another in over two weeks. They knew not what to expect from the other, they only went on their gut instinct, and their gut instinct told them that neither would rat out the other. They'd weathered the storm and were now facing tax evasion and a conspiracy to distribute cocaine charge. Serious enough charges no doubt, but far less than the murder charges they were nearly hit with.

Martha was glad to see her friend. She rose up and hopped from the bunk and the two women hugged quickly. "I missed you, Mar." Twiggy said. "Folk, they tried to hem us up, but I stood solid. I didn't rat on you."

"Me either Twiggy." Martha said as she smiled at her friend. "We still got a lot of work to do to beat this conspiracy charge. I'm gone get us a lawyer."

"How?" Twiggy asked. "If anybody go near that money in the bank they gone just take it. That's another charge."

Martha had been holding onto the diamond necklace she had taken from the Jacobs' home in 1977 the whole time she was hustling because she believed early on that it would be valuable one day. Fifteen years later, her beliefs came true. Martha had over $75,000 dollars in the safety deposit boxes inside the bank, but she couldn't touch it. She thought about having Mary go to the bank and use her I.D. but she didn't want her sister to get into trouble. What Mary could do, however, was go to the bank and withdraw all of Martha's savings, nearly $9,000, and have the diamond necklace appraised and sell it.

Mary was home from work about 1p.m. the day after Martha and Twiggy were reunited in Hinds County Jail. She was so worried about her sister that she had been lagging behind at work and on this day, her supervisor sent her home early. She was sitting on the sofa in her home crying her heart out and thinking about how she'd often told herself that she was prepared for the day when Martha would no longer be around. Mary always believed Martha would be killed. She now knew that if something like that ever happened to her sister, it would tear her heart out because Martha was alive and well behind bars and she was still finding it difficult to function.

The phone rang in Mary's home a few minutes later as she sat crying on the couch and she ran and answered it eagerly, knowing the whole while that it was her sister calling. When she heard the operator, she eagerly accepted the call and wiped her tears and brushed her hair from her face and sat down and greeted her sister lovingly, telling her how much she missed her.

"I miss you too, sister. Mary, I never expected things to happen like this, but better here—"

"Than like Peter Paul." Mary said, finishing her sister's sentence.

"Right. How my nieces?"

"Fine. They're fine. They told me to tell you that they love you. They still in school. Call back after four today?"

"I promise." Martha said lowly.

Martha missed the warmth of Mary's hearth and home. The

day after she killed Gina, she had spent several nights in her sister's home and never once did Mary complain. She was just happy Martha was still around. Martha was beginning to realize what all she would be losing if she lost her case. Just to be home with her sister and nieces, to sit and have dinner, to play a board game, and listen to her nieces' favorite radio program; the simple things would be the things Martha would miss the most. Not the clothes, not the easy money, or the fine young men, Martha would miss time with her family—something she somewhat took for granted when she was on the outside.

"How'd you know I was home?" Mary asked Martha breaking, her brief thought and ending the short pause.

"Twiggy called Simon and he saw you pull up while he was on the phone. Mary, can you do me huge favor, sister?"

"Anything, Martha."

"Come and see me tomorrow. You, Ne`Ne` and Dimples."

"We would love to!" Mary said proudly as she twirled the telephone cord in her hands.

Ne`Ne` and Dimples were so excited to learn that they were going to visit Martha the following day that they had called their favorite radio show, The Fantastic Four, and shouted out to Martha and Ghost Town. "Hey caller, you got Mrs. Jones on the airwaves what's hatning?"

"Hey, Misses Jones! This Ne`Ne` from Ghost Town!"

"Ne`Ne`? Happy birthday Ne`Ne`!" Mrs. Jones yelled over the airwaves.

"It ain't my birthday Misses Jones! I wanna represent for my auntie Martha and all of Ghost Town!"

"Check it! So how's everything up in G' Town? I mean the family okay? Y'all alright up there?"

"Misses Jones? This is not the time for personal calls!" the voice of Sister Spanks said aloud over the airwaves.

"Girl, this one of my favorite callers! Don't hate 'cause people don't ask for you when they call!" Misses Jones snapped back as Ne`Ne` and Dimples laughed aloud. "What you wanna hear, Ne`Ne`?"

"Play Welcome to the Ghetto by Spice One!" Ne`Ne` yelled into the phone.

"We gotcha comin' up shortly, baby girl! Hey, who got the hottest show in Jackson, Mississippi, Ne`Ne`?"

"The Fantastic Four!"

"On?"

"Hot 105.9!" Ne`Ne` and Dimples yelled at the same time as *Welcome to the Ghetto* began to play over the airwaves.

Ne`Ne` and Dimples enjoyed the show and went to bed promptly at eleven and the next morning the two of them, along with their mother, were sitting in the visiting room talking with Martha. They spent all morning together, sharing breakfast and laughter. Martha eventually got to the heart of the matter with Mary. She told her sister of her intentions and Mary went to the bank that day and withdrew Martha's $9,000 dollars and had the diamond necklace appraised and learned that it was valued at $7,000 dollars. Mary then took the $16,000 and went to a lawyer that Martha and Twiggy had agreed on. Their trail date was a month and a week away and the lawyer quickly went to work on their case. Martha and Twiggy were in constant contact with their lawyer and he updated the two regularly. The charges were serious indeed, but the lawyer felt he could get a reduced sentence, something Martha and Twiggy didn't fully agree with at the time.

"A reduced sentence?" Martha asked the lawyer a week before the trail as they sat inside a small visiting room surrounded by gray steel walls. "What happened to all the fuckin' money we paid you? What about the fact that they ain't found shit but dust and paraphernalia?"

"What is key here is the fact that they found residue in you all's home. Frog had a drug possession charge and was a known gang-member. Twiggy was apprehended with over seventy thousand dollars in cash and she can't explain where she got it from. You're lucky they haven't issued warrants for your deposit boxes, Martha. These detectives are somewhat sloppy so I say let's go why we have a chance before things get bigger. Trust me, they really do have more dirt to find. You two are in this together. Your name was on the lease of the home as well as Irene's so you are just as guilty of conspiracy as Irene, Martha," the lawyer said matter-of-factly.

"What we facing?" Twiggy asked.

"Well, you're looking at thirty years. Now what we—"

"Thirty years!" Martha and Twiggy yelled at the same time.

"Man, they ain't got shit on us!" Martha yelled as she and Twiggy stood out of their seats side by side.

"They have wire taps from Peter Paul's phone. Phone calls he made to Twiggy discussing 'rocking up' product. They have pager numbers from Martha's beeper. Numbers that are in the names of known drug dealers; and if Marvin Kettle and Victor Bland take the stand, things could descend downhill very rapidly. A plea is looking pretty convincing ladies. Now, I can get full dismissals on everything and you can walk away scot-free today—but that means cooperation. You two will have to give up the names on the numbers they have. If you go to trial, you'll be at the mercy of the court. Getting found guilty will cost you two women thirty years a piece; but if you plea, then the two cops' testimony will not come into play and there will be no further investigation into those numbers. You two will have to take the fall for everybody involved, or this case will go on and on and the sentences will only increase. It's a gamble I know. Cooperating is guaranteed freedom. The plea will be a risk, but not a serious one. Going to trial with the evidence they have and can obtain will not be the smartest decision. They will delay this trial and gather further evidence and sink you ladies," the lawyer stated sadly. "I'm sorry, but this is the best I can do."

"What if we plead guilty? How much time we facing?" Martha asked as she and Twiggy paced the floor in the private visitor's room.

The lawyer smiled. This was what he was hoping for. Although Martha had put up $16,000 dollars, it wasn't enough to go to war with the feds, but the lawyer was able to work with what resources the money afforded him. "Well, you can get the thirty years cut in half, even less if the judge is willing to take into consideration that neither of you has a violent criminal past on record. I'm pushing hard for work furloughs and rehabilitation programs. This state judge that I can get you two before is a fairly lenient man, he grants second chances. Also," the lawyer added, "the feds will turn the case over entirely to the state if you take the plea. If you go to trail, it's highly probable that the feds will bust this thing wide open. There's no telling how they will play this case out. They want the big bust—you two are just low rungs on the ladder. Don't let the feds make this case bigger than what it is by going to trial. They will use those tax dollars to make sure they put you two away for decades for merely wasting their time. Both of you could be hit with a kingpin charge and be forced to do thirty years flat. No parole what-so-ever. Please, take the plea. I know you don't want to rat nobody out. The state charges, in my opinion, are the best way to go. At least, with the amount of money you two paid, I was able to find loopholes that would allow the feds to drop their case, but only if you plead guilty to the state. That's a good thing."

Martha and Twiggy stared at one another, ratting was not an option. The plea bargain would be a gamble, but they would rather take that chance than be labeled rats. After all they had done, Martha and Twiggy had become idols in Ghost Town, to go out as snitches would be one of the greatest twists of fate in the history of Ghost Town. Martha and Twiggy knew they were taking a huge gamble, but they would rather take their chances before a state judge than roll over on fellow gang-members and other drug dealers. They hinged their future on their lawyer's statements.

As they stood before the judge on their trail date, Martha and Twiggy were nervous as ever. They had put everything on the belief that their lawyer would get the judge to go low on their sentencing. The lawyer said he could get them a sentence of no less than two years, but no greater than ten years. The two thirty-three year-old women stood before the judge in their orange jumpsuits shackled down. Martha's hair was pressed, flowing gently to her shoulders. She had never adorned this look before, but she looked gorgeous as she stared forward at the judge, her sexy brown eyes had a look of mercy within them. She wet her lips slightly and wiped her watery eyes, her right hand flowing gently over the beauty mark under her left eye. Twiggy stood beside her friend in her orange jumpsuit as well. She had her hair done in neat stacks; her sexy, slender frame shook slightly as she was nervous as hell. She wiped her teary eyes as well because she, just like Martha, was hoping the judge would go low, just as the lawyer said.

Mary, Ne`Ne`, Dimples, Simon, Sandy, Jesse, Clark, Chug-a-lug, and other Folk members from different sets in Jackson were on hand to witness the sentencing. Mary and the rest of Ghost Town were worried sick, hoping the sentence wouldn't be too overwhelming. The others were on hand to see whether Martha and Twiggy would roll over. Everybody knew the two were facing jail time. The people from Ghost Town only hoped the judge wouldn't give them an absorbent amount of years. The others, however, were hoping there wouldn't be a stoppage to the proceedings before the sentences were announced because that would mean that Martha and Twiggy were possibly willing to cooperate with the law.

The judge sat behind his bench reading documents and then looked over to the two women, smiled slightly at the two, and called their lawyer and the state prosecutor before his bench. The three talked amongst themselves and when Martha and Twiggy's lawyer returned to their table he was sweating real hard and had a nervous smile on his face. Martha and Twiggy looked at their lawyer and he looked at them and said nothing. He patted Martha's back as the judge announced loudly, "Case docket number 144-6781, the State of Mississippi vs. Martha Holland and Irene 'Twiggy' Charles. On the charge of distribution of cocaine, how do you women plead?"

"Guilty." Martha and Twiggy spoke innocently.

Martha and Twiggy were both smiling inside now. The conspiracy charge, and the tax evasion charges against Twiggy went away, meaning they would only be charged with distribution of cocaine because the case was now out of the feds' hands.

The judge looked the two women over again, asking them were they promised anything in return for their plea and they both replied no. The judge then sentenced both women to eleven years in prison with time off for good behavior. If they partook of various programs within the prison system, they could both be out in seven or eight years.

Martha and Twiggy knew full well that what happened to them wasn't fair. The government had nothing on them really, but the threat of doing thirty years behind bars was too great a risk and Martha and Twiggy would both rather spend several years behind bars than forever be labeled as snitches and have their family name and reputation ruined. Before the bailiff took them back to the holding cells, they were allowed to hug their family members one last time.

Mary took it the hardest. She pressed her cheek to Martha's as she cried and said, "Call me, every day. I love you Martha," she said lovingly into her sister's ear as gang-members filed out of the court room after witnessing Martha and Twiggy take a blow to the chin. A blow that many of them would have gladly chosen not to take if they were in the same boat; but still, they came to pass judgment on Martha and Twiggy who were truly, the last of the O.G.'s.

"I love you too, Mary." Martha remarked as she embraced her sister and kissed both of her nieces good-bye.

"Sandy," Twiggy said, "look after my nephew."

"I got 'em, Folk." Sandy remarked as she wiped tears from her eyes.

"Hey? I guess, I guess you was right." Twiggy said as she smiled down at Sandy.

"About what?"

"When you said when I retire you were going to get those bracelets. They yours. Go to the property room. I released them to you, baby girl."

Sandy's eyes lit up at Twiggy's statement. She would be next in line to lead the females in Ghost Town. Her dream had come true, although it was bitter sweet. She hugged Twiggy tightly before the guards gently nudged the women back towards the holding cells. They were more than generous with the time allotted to Martha and Twiggy.

Mary, Ne`Ne`, and Dimples, along with Simon and Sandy, watched as Martha and Twiggy were led away. It was a sad day, but also joyful because Martha and Twiggy had survived the streets, kept their reputation intact, and had the hope of coming home in a relatively short span of time. Seven years was indeed a long time, but considering they had murdered people and had been selling drugs since the late seventies, Martha Holland and Irene 'Twiggy' Charles got off fairly easy.

CHAPTER 23

SENTIMENTAL SANDY

"When this trains ends...I'll try again, Lord...I'm leavin' my woman at home...Tuesday's gone with the wind...Tuesday's gone with the wind...Tuesday's gone with the wind...my baby's gone...with the wind..."

Lynrd Skynrd's song *Tuesday's Gone* blared loudly from the stereo in Simon's two door white on white drop top '77 Caprice Classic on a sunny evening in May of '93.

Twiggy's Impala was now often kept in Sandy's yard because both she and Simon liked the Caprice more since it was the newest ride on the block. Sandy was sitting beside Simon stuffing money into a brown paper bag as she puffed on a blunt. She soon put the weed out and turned the stereo down a little and leaned back in her seat and covered her eyes with sunshades. All day Sandy had been quiet while she and Simon made their pick-ups and drop-offs. Simon had noticed her somber mood early on in the day and he wondered what was going with his woman because she had been listening to slow, sometimes downright depressing rock and roll songs ever since the two of them had left Ghost Town in the early afternoon. Simon sensed that Sandy was troubled over something as she had never been this dejected in all the years he had known her. As the song played on, Sandy lay back in her seat and looked up towards the sky and shook her head from side to side. Simon, in an attempt to cheer Sandy up, asked if she want any Fukutoo's.

"Nahh ,Folk. I'm straight," she answered lowly.

"What the fuck wrong with you? You got the Mississippi Blues or some shit? Playing all these slow ass rock songs. Shit making me depressed!"

"I'm just thinking, man. I can't think with that loud ass rap music in the background. That's why I'm playing Skynrd—so I can think."

"What's been on your mind all day?"

"Life."

"What about it? What? You getting sentimental on me?"

"Boy? The way you whined when Twiggy went to jail?"

"Eh, I told you not to bring that shit up ever!"

"Why? Why you can get sentimental, and it's a problem for you when you see me get sentimental or down a little bit?"

"Because I don't like to see you sad. You got a problem with that?"

"Ohh, now who's getting sentimental?" Sandy asked as she raised her head and gently stroked Simon's arm.

"Come on, man!" Simon said as he brushed Sandy's hand away. "That's why I don't be tellin' you stuff like that! I get sentimental for one second and you go ta' turnin' the shit into a Street Car Named Desire episode!"

Sandy burst into laughter as Simon pulled her close and hugged her as he rode towards Ghost Town. "I was just thinking about Ne`Ne`," Sandy remarked. "Thinkin' about her and how much things done changed back in the 'hood since Martha and Twiggy went to jail. It's just not the same. Not as fun—and Ne`Ne`, man, she a handful out there sometimes."

"I know. She look up to you though, Sandy."

"I know That's why I was quiet. I care about that li'l girl. She my weak spot. You and Ne`Ne` both. And Martha made me promise. That's what's makin' it hard for me to resolve this issue—this promise to Martha."

The Holland Family Saga Part Five

"You doing your best, baby. Ne`Ne` kind of hard-headed. She used to do Martha the same shit."

"I know, man. I just wish she would see that this life ain't all fun and games." Sandy replied as she turned up the volume on the stereo just slightly bringing the music back within earshot, leaned back in the seat, closed her eyes, and continued thinking of fifteen year-old Ne`Ne`.

A lot of things in Ghost Town had changed since Martha and Twiggy went to jail and Peter Paul was killed. In early December of '92, Twiggy had given Sandy complete control of the G-Queens in Ghost Town and Simon was now captain over the neighborhood. The problem was that many of the kids in Ghost Town were either too young or too scared to join Folk Gang.

During the seventies and eighties there were plenty of gang members around, but by the early nineties most were dead or in jail. Only Simon, Clark, Jesse and Sandy were ranking members, and they hadn't been involved in Folk Gang for no more than six years. Martha and Twiggy alone had over thirty years combined; they were vets to the game. Simon and company were new breeds, however; the laws that Albert Lee enforced during his reign waned off when he went up state. Peter Paul's reign was loose knit. Simon's reign was no more than a loose affiliation with Folk Gang in Ghost Town. He only held true to the fact that only Folk members could sell in Ambush. They often allowed a few members from Queens to come and make a few sales to 'thicken up' the set a little bit with Clark and Jesse, but Ghost Town was now past its heyday. There was still money to be made in Ambush, however, although things had slowed down a great deal.

Simon and Sandy had taken over Twiggy and Martha's customers and now sold ounces the way Martha and Twiggy used to do. They only did drop offs and pick-ups and hung in Ambush from time to time to keep order and show others that Folk Gang in Ghost Town still had leadership.

Sandy had recruited a few young G-Queens, but neither had the heart she had when she first joined Folk Gang. The young teens wanted the reputation, but not the drama that came with being a part of the gang life in Ghost Town. Sandy didn't do much of nothing with the G-Queens because she didn't trust them in her affairs. Although they were a few, to Sandy they only meant numbers. One person, however, did gain a great deal of favor with Sandy Duncan—Ne`Ne`—but Sandy was now conflicted about allowing Ne`Ne` to hang around her.

The reason was because a month after Martha was sent up state, she asked Sandy to look after her nieces and keep them out of Folk Gang. Sandy had plans for Ne`Ne` before Martha stepped in. Her plan was to recruit the young teen, school her and have her as her second in command; but when Martha gave the order, Sandy obeyed. Sandy never jumped Ne`Ne` *nor* Dimples into the gang, but she still hung with Ne`Ne` more than any other female in Ghost Town.

Sandy was also doing the best she could to keep Ne`Ne` under wraps, but the fifteen year-old had grown wilder when Martha went to jail, and she wanted to be up under Sandy at all times. Sandy was cautious with Ne`Ne`, though; and she kept in mind the promise to Martha. She would often just ride around with Ne`Ne` until Mary got home from work around five p.m.

When Sandy caught Ne`Ne` in Ambush one school night back in March selling crack cocaine, she sent her home. That scenario had played out the entire month of March. Sandy didn't want to rat Ne`Ne` out to Mary, so she started standing guard whilst Ne`Ne` sold her rocks at night. During that time, Sandy had fully come to see the heart within Ne`Ne` and knew she was right about the youngster all along; she only wished Martha had not given the order to keep Ne`Ne` out of Folk Gang.

Sandy then decided to take the twin under her wing; promising herself she would let nothing happen to Martha's niece. Ne`Ne` wanted to join Folk Gang, but Sandy would not break her promise to Martha for nothing; besides, Ne`Ne` did things Folk members were allowed to do, so getting jumped in wasn't necessary like it was during Martha's time. Sandy thought about those mixed-up emotions of hers as Simon turned onto Casper Drive. The 19 year-old young woman was

The Holland Family Saga Part Five

doing the best she could with Ne'Ne', a fifteen year-old who was becoming a fast part of the streets of Ghost Town and causing a conflict within Sandy's heart, an organ that was rapidly growing in sentiment towards Ne'Ne'.

The Charles' home had now become a hangout for Clark, Jesse, Ne'Ne' and Dimples. Before Mary came home from work, the twins would be there having sex with Clark and Jesse freely and they would sometimes skip school and stay there the whole day. Sandy tried her best to keep them in line, and for a short while, she'd come to resent Mary, whom she viewed as naive to the plight of her daughters. She visited Mary one Saturday afternoon in late March of '93 not too long after Mary's 34th birthday when she spotted her out in her garden pulling weeds that day. Mary greeted Sandy nicely and offered her a cold drink, but Sandy declined as she stood in her yard staring pitifully at Mary.

Sandy remembered how Mary was all up in smiles that day. Dimples and Ne'Ne' had both made the honor roll and Sandy listened as Mary spoke proudly of her daughters. She could see the joy in the woman's eyes as she spoke. Sandy wanted so badly to tell Mary what she knew about her daughters, especially about Ne'Ne' selling crack, but she just couldn't bring herself to rat her friends out. She hen rationalized, telling herself that she would not allow the twins to hang at the Charles' house during school time. That idea worked because the twins started attending school regularly.

The next problem was the fact that Sandy was still going along with holding secret the fact that Ne'Ne' was sneaking out the house and making crack sales in Ambush at night, even though she always stood guard and made sure that Ne'Ne' went straight inside afterwards. This was the biggest conflict with Sandy. On top of that, to prevent the twins from getting pregnant, Sandy kept them supplied with condoms. She knew she was wrong, if only she could shift this problem over to Mary without snitching out her friends. Sandy was condoning the life the twins were leading outside of Mary's home and she just didn't feel right upholding their deeds. She was not living up to the promise she made to Martha and it hurt her every time she looked into Mary's face. It also hurt Sandy whenever Mary smiled her beautiful smile as she spent time with Ne`Ne` and Dimples because she knew the twins' dark side; and it was beginning not to sit right with Sandy Duncan who was becoming more emotionally mature as she approached the age of twenty. It wasn't too long ago that Sandy had killed a man with Ne`Ne` in the car. She had also stolen beer for Ne`Ne` and smoked weed with her quite a few times as well. Sandy couldn't believe she had done those things with Ne`Ne` in August of '92. Now, in May of '93, Sandy was becoming more sensitive to the things she did with Mary's daughters—especially Ne`Ne`.

Martha called on the regular and Sandy had her under the belief that everything was fine with her nieces as far as the streets were concerned. Truth was, Ne`Ne` was not being kept in check the way Sandy knew Martha wanted her to be. Dimples wasn't much of a problem; she only liked to have sex with Jesse on occasion. The twins were hiding their lifestyle well, but in Mary's eyes, they were ideal daughters. It wasn't that Mary didn't pay attention to her daughters, she was just a hardworking woman who trusted her daughters would do the right thing whenever she wasn't looking and the twins had her under that firm belief, but the truth was that they were simply succeeding at doing things behind their mother's back and no one, not even Sandy Duncan, was willing to make the woman aware.

Sandy noticed that most of the twins' mischievousness took place on school days when Mary was resting after a long day's work. The weekends still belonged to the unsuspecting mother and her daughters, however; she often had chores and errands for the twins do to on the weekends. And during breaks in the school year, Mary would take them to work with her to help around the office. The twins were good overall; they were polite and never sulked at their mother's requests.

Sandy had watched Mary closely since that day in late March, and by May of '93, she had learned a valuable lesson from the woman: you don't have to sell drugs or be a part of Folk Gang in order to survive in Ghost Town. Mary had been doing fine the whole time Martha ran the streets and she never had to run with a gang, sell drugs, steal, or hurt another person in order to survive. She was really a good mother in Sandy's eyes.

Sandy relinquished her thoughts as Simon pulled into the driveway of his home and turned off the engine. She was thinking real hard about Ne`Ne` now; she really cared deeply for Martha's niece. When Sandy exited the car, Ne`Ne`, who was in the yard with Dimples and Mary, called out and waved to her. Sandy waved back and smiled as she went inside. An hour later Ne`Ne` knocked on the door to the Charles' home and Sandy answered.

"What's up Sandy?" Ne`Ne` asked as she walked in and plopped down on the couch.

"Chillin'. Eh, don't go off in Ambush tonight. I'm tired today and I won't be back there so don't go." Sandy said as sipped a twelve ounce beer.

"Alright Folk. Hey, Martha called today. She told me to ask you to write her a kite."

Sandy knew right then and there that Martha wanted an update on her nieces. "Alright. How you making out in school, Ne`Ne`?"

"Going to the eleventh next year! Check this out!" Ne`Ne` responded as she went into the pocket of her Girbaud's jeans and pulled out a medallion with her name in it. "I got one for Dimples too. But I ain't gone give it to her until our birthday next month."

"That's tight right there." Sandy replied as Simon entered the living room.

"Ne`Ne? Tell Dimples nasty ass—if she don't stop leaving used condoms on the floor I'm gone mail them bitches back to Mary telling her to give Dimples her shit back," he stated as Sandy and Ne`Ne` chuckled.

"Hey, let me braid your hair, Ne`Ne`! Go get the grease and the combs out the bathroom." Sandy then remarked. Sandy smiled as she watched Ne`Ne` jump up eagerly and run to the back room to get the hair supplies. Sometimes, Sandy did things with Ne`Ne` just to keep her away from Ambush. She wasn't really tired this day, but she had been thinking hard about how she was dealing with Martha's nieces. By telling Ne`Ne` she was tired, she believed Ne`Ne` wouldn't go back there without her.

Sandy knew she was the last line of defense from keeping Ne`Ne` from going buck wild. She eased up a bit after reflecting on how the day was beginning to go and told herself that things weren't as bad as they seemed and she could work it out over time. When Ne`Ne` came back with the grease and combs, Sandy suggested that the of them two go over by her house where Mary and Dimples were working in the garden and she could braid her hair under the shade trees.

Loretta came out shortly after Sandy and Ne`Ne` sat down on the back stairs and she pulled her grill close by Mary's fence and the five females sat out and talked as Loretta grilled pork chops and chicken. It was just a regular day in the neighborhood for Sandy, who wished that everyday could go this smooth with Ne`Ne`. Better yet, Sandy wished everyday of her life could be as peaceful as the one she was having with her friends and family today.

"Hey Mary," Sandy asked, "can my momma pull the Impala in your yard so I can turn on the radio?"

"You're not going to play that vulgar rap music are you?"

"No ma'am. I got a Lynrd Skynrd disc in the car. We can listen to that if y'all want."

"I like that band. You got the one with Simple Man on it?" Mary asked.

"Yeah." Sandy answered as she smiled.

Mary moved her car and Loretta pulled the Impala into the yard and turned on the music. A melodic guitar was soon heard and before long the vocals to Lynrd Skynrd's song *Simple Man* could be heard loud and clear and Sandy, Mary and Loretta all began to sing along with the song...

..."*Momma told me...when I was young...to sit beside me...my only son...and listen closely...to what I say...if you can do this it'll help you some sunny day...*"

"That's a stupid song!" Ne`Ne` said loudly as she laughed.

Sandy stopped singing and braiding Ne`Ne`'s hair at the same time and said, "Listen to the lyrics Ne`Ne`. It's a song about life. About slowing down and taking your time." Sandy was subtly trying to send a message to Ne`Ne` at that moment. The fifteen year-old listened to the lyrics closely and understood the song, but she didn't think it applied to her and she told Sandy how she felt. Sandy shook her head and sung the song's chorus as she braided Ne`Ne`'s hair.

"And be a simple...kind of man...or be something...you love and understand...baby be a simple...kind of man..."

"That part when he say 'be something you love and understand'? He talking about being something that you proud of in life and knowing exactly who you are." Sandy told Ne`Ne`.

"I'm proud of myself for passing this year! And I know who I am! My name is Rene Holland!" Ne`Ne` replied as Sandy shook her head with a slight smile on her face and returned to braiding Ne`Ne`'s hair.

Dimples meanwhile, was dancing with her mother. She had heard the song many times before and she liked it. Sandy watched Dimples from the back porch, wishing Ne`Ne` had her demeanor. Ne`Ne` was more like Martha, however, and Sandy knew, just like Martha, Ne`Ne` would do whatever she wanted to do, whenever she was ready. She finished Ne`Ne`'s hair and the females talked as they waited for the chicken and pork chops. They ate and before long it was after ten 'o' clock. Mary and her daughters helped Loretta and Sandy clean their yard and they all turned in for the night. Sandy slept at her mother's home, something she hadn't done in a long time. They sat and drank beer at the kitchen table and talked as mother and daughter.

"Sandy," Loretta asked as the two sat at the table drinking beer, "how are things going for you out there? Are you okay?"

"I'm fine, momma," Sandy replied, sitting right beside her mother.

"What do you plan on doing, baby? You can't be a gangster for life."

"I know, momma. I'm saving money. This guy Mugsy? He owns a pool hall in North Jackson. He said me and Simon can buy in after a while. I mean, he just mentioned it to me in passing, but I'm thinking hard about that."

"You know your father, he umm, he ran a pool hall in Paducah."

"Ohhh, Lord. What happened?" Sandy asked as she shook her head, knowing her father's story had a bad outcome.

"He was selling amphetamines out his place. The police raided and he was taken into custody. Now here's where it gets sketchy because your father, as courageous and ignorant as he was, had enough sense to not fight the police. As the story goes, when they were transporting him to county lock-up, he tried to escape. Your father was a thin man like yourself, he may have slipped out of the handcuffs, but I doubt it. Paducah lawmen had been trying to capture your father for years and they wanted him dead. I think they pulled over and shot him on side the road and removed the handcuffs."

"What was done about it?"

"I was in jail at the time and couldn't do nothing. I had taken an armed robbery charge for your father. Took the rap for robbing a drug house when I was picked out of a lineup."

"Why?"

"I was there and I got fingered. I wouldn't roll on your father though because I loved him. Plain and simple. The police were after him then. They offered to let me go if I gave him up but I refused. Had I known I was pregnant? I would've gave him up. I think he woulda been okay with that, too, because he wanted me to have his child so bad. He woulda did the time and came home to me. But since I'd already been given time, he was going to take care of you until I got out, but when he died, the state took you in because my mother and father never wanted anything to do with you and I—and they still don't."

"I know."

"How you know?"

Sandy looked to the floor and her eyes welled up. She felt where her mother was coming from. "I always thought you were lying about my grandparents and the rest of the family in Lexington. I called them after I found their number in your purse like, like five years ago and I called and told them," Sandy began crying at that moment because she was really hurt by the way her grandparents had treated her. "I told them I was their granddaughter. 'I'm Sandy Duncan,' I told them. I was happy too, momma. 'I'm Loretta Duncan's daughter how y'all doing'."

Loretta began crying herself. She'd called her parents when she first arrived in Ghost Town and they told her to stay there and not call them anymore. "What did they tell you, Sandy?"

"They said that I would grow up to be a loser just like you and to never call them again. Fuck those people! They don't know you and me, momma. And look how they treat us."

"Now you see why I never talk about them goody-two-shoe assholes? For all they're worth they have no souls. I never wanted money from them—just their love. And they couldn't give it. So like you say—fuck those people!" Loretta said as she raised a beer can and she and her daughter toasted and continued drinking and talking until well after midnight when Loretta finally went to bed and Sandy went and turned on the TV.

****

Sandy was up watching *Def Comedy Jam* at about one-thirty in the morning the same night when she saw a quick flash out her living room window. She peeped out to see Ne'Ne' running towards the wooded trail. *"I told that li'l hard-headed mutherfucka not to go back there,"* she said to herself as she threw on her tennis, grabbed her AK-47, and headed out the door.

Sandy jogged through the trail holding her chopper at her side and was only a couple of minutes behind Ne'Ne'. When she stepped into Ambush she could see Ne'Ne' with her head inside the driver's side window of a customer's car already making a crack sale. Clark, Jesse, and three G-Queens, fifteen year-old Paulette and fourteen year-old Sidney, who were sisters, and their friend, fourteen year-old Urselle, were out as well. Sandy eyed the five as she ran over to Ne`Ne` and quickly pulled her away from the car. Ne`Ne` was just about to make the deal; but she dropped her money into the driver's lap and the driver of the car quickly drove off with her money and her crack when Sandy pulled her away from the car's window.

"Drop my money, Folk!" Ne`Ne` yelled. She took off running behind the car, but Sandy had caught up with her and grabbed her and pulled her back. "Sandy, they got my money and my cocaine!"

"Go home Ne`Ne`!" Sandy ordered.

"Fuck no! I want my money!" Ne`Ne` yelled as she eyed the car speeding up White Street towards Casper Drive.

"They gone! I'll give it back to you! Just go inside!"

"You ain't my momma! And stop tryna do me like Martha used ta' do back in the day!" Ne`Ne` snapped, bringing about jubilant laughter from Paulette, Sidney and Urselle. Ne`Ne` saw them smirking and she, too, laughed. "You can't make me do nothing!" she then said, knowing her friends were watching and getting a kick out the way in which she was talking to Sandy.

Ne`Ne`, Paulette, Sidney and Urselle were all laughing loud as Clark and Jesse shook their heads somberly, knowing full well that Ne`Ne` was wrong for disrespecting Sandy. Sandy looked around at Paulette, Sidney and Urselle and walked over to them and stood amongst the three.

"That shit funny, Sidney?" Sandy asked calmly as she pulled her brown hair from her face.

"No!" Sidney quickly answered.

"Paulette? Urselle? Y'all see something funny out here tonight?"

"No, Sandy." Paulette and Urselle responded at the same time.

Sandy then went silent. Everybody was silent as they watched her. Sandy stared coldly at the three teens for a few seconds and then suddenly and quickly used her free hand and swung at the three girls. "Get the fuck from back here!" she yelled as the teens took off running.

Sandy gave chase, swinging and kicking at the young teens as they ran up the stairs and out of Ambush. She then walked back to Ne`Ne`, still clutching her chopper and said, "Stay back here if you want to! Fuck it! I don't care no more!"

Sandy stared at Ne`Ne`, who was no longer smiling, for what seemed like an eternity and shook her head in disbelief before she walked off. Had it been anybody else, Sandy would have seriously hurt the person; but she had so much love for Ne`Ne` that she just couldn't bring herself to do her any harm. Ne`Ne` thought what she did was funny up to that point, but she could now see that Sandy was surprised and hurt over the way she had disrespected her. Sandy had never expected this behavior from Ne`Ne`. She was trying to look out for her, but Ne`Ne` only continued to play games. Sandy wasn't playing, however, she cared enough to do what she was doing and now it seemed as if Ne`Ne` was taking her kindness for weakness.

Ne`Ne` really *was* Sandy's weakness, but she couldn't let that fact be known to Ne`Ne`, or anyone else for that matter because she had to show strength at all times. Her lifestyle called for it. Sandy was trying to show Ne`Ne` through actions just how much she cared, but Ne`Ne` had missed the whole point up until this moment. Realizing the mistake she made, Ne`Ne` yelled aloud to her friend, "I'm sorry," as Clark and Jesse walked up the stairs and out of Ambush, leaving her by her lonesome. "Sandy, I'm sorry." Ne`Ne` yelled again just before Sandy disappeared into the wooded trail leading back to Friendly Lane.

Ne`Ne` now stood alone in Ambush. She wanted to be back there in the beginning, but now she was alone and felt like a fool. She walked over to the trail leading to Friendly Lane in complete and utter shame with the full understanding of how wrong she was for doing what she had done to Sandy. She walked back through the trail and knocked lightly on Loretta's door, but Sandy didn't answer. "I'm sorry." Ne`Ne` said lowly as she ran home.

For over a week Sandy had stayed away from Ne`Ne`. Before, when Sandy and Simon returned to Ghost Town after making their pick-ups and drop-offs, they would pull up in the yard and Ne`Ne` would soon find her way over to the Charles' home and was always welcomed. Now, whenever Sandy saw Ne`Ne`, she would have Simon drop her off in Ambush. Ne`Ne` knew not to go back there now, she also knew Sandy was mad at her. She would page Sandy often, but Sandy would never call her back. She saw Sandy in her mother's yard when she got off the school bus two weeks after she had disrespected her in Ambush and tried to speak to her, but Sandy merely walked inside and slammed her door shut. She was avoiding Ne`Ne` at all costs. To realize that Sandy Duncan no longer wanted to be around her began to stress Ne`Ne`. She and Sandy were cool once, but she had fucked it up and knew not how to repair the damage she'd done. She stayed inside with Dimples for days on in after the day Sandy walked into her home without responding to her friendly gesture. Dimples noticed that her twin was now studying for tests and hadn't been sneaking out at night. She also stopped having sex with Clark.

"You not right without Sandy around are you?" Dimples asked in concerned manner.

"I miss her, Regina." Ne`Ne` said as tears dropped onto her study sheet.

Dimples hugged her sister as she cried. "It'll be okay." she told NeNe`.

When Mary came home, she saw her daughters had on their night clothes and were sound asleep. That was a relief as it had been a long day. The weary mother fixed spaghetti and meat sauce, took a shower, had a cup of coffee and watched the evening news. Before long, she, too, was asleep.

Ne`Ne` was awakened by a soft tap on her shoulder hours later. She stirred awake and sat up on Dimples' bed; it was now after eleven. "Come on." Dimples said lowly.

"Where we going?" Ne`Ne` asked her twin.

"In Ambush by Sandy right quick."

The twins left their mother's home in their night clothes and walked through the warm air and entered the trail leading to Ambush. They stepped into the clearing and Ne`Ne`, who was in front of her sister, saw Sandy sitting inside the Impala with the top down, it's hood pointed towards the trail. She paused when Sandy eyed her. Ne`Ne` could also see that the same people were out the night she had disrespected Sandy; and a few male members from Queens section were out as well. Dimples nudged Ne`Ne` forward towards Sandy before she went and stood beside Jesse and Clark and began chatting with the two.

Ne`Ne` walked slowly over to the Impala and said in an apologetic tone, "Sandy, I'm sorry." Sandy looked at Ne`Ne` and turned her head and continued to bob her head to the song *Life is Too Short*, by the rapper Too Short as she sat in the driver's seat. "I said I'm sorry!" Ne`Ne` then yelled over the music, causing everyone to look in her direction.

"Go home," was all Sandy said as she exited the car and brushed pass Ne`Ne`, headed towards the stairs.

"You not my friend no more!" Ne`Ne` suddenly yelled. Ne`Ne` wasn't making a proclamation towards Sandy Duncan, to the contrary, the fifteen year-old had a realization that she had lost favor with Sandy and was saddened by that fact.

Sandy knew exactly what Ne`Ne` meant because he could hear and feel the sense of loss in her voice. *"I'll forever be your friend little girl."* Sandy said to herself as Ne`Ne` walked slowly back down the trail towards her mother's house.

The Folk members from Queens section started to sniggle and Clark shut them up quickly before they hopped into their car and left Ambush.

"You saw that? Man, Ne`Ne` getting all sentimental." Sidney then said.

"Baby got her heart broken tonight!" Paulette sulked in a teasing manner.

Jesse, Clark, and Dimples then split up. Dimples went after her sister, and Jesse and Clark headed up the stairs out of Ambush just as Sandy erupted. "Don't fuckin' laugh at her! She got more heart than all three y'all coward bitches put together!" Sandy yelled as she charged the three females, running them off again.

Sandy then ran and jumped into the Impala and sped up White Street, turned onto Casper Drive and sped up to Mary's house. She got there just as Ne`Ne` was entering the backyard and could hear her crying her heart out. She jumped from the Impala and ran and grabbed Ne`Ne` from behind and turned her around.

"You not my friend," Ne`Ne` cried. "You said you don't care no more! I'm sorry! That's all I wanted to say to you ever since that night was I'm sorry!"

Sandy hugged Ne`Ne` tightly and rocked the two of their bodies. "I just want you to listen to me," she said in frustration. "If something was to happen to you back there in Ambush, it'll kill me! Why won't you listen to me? Just listen to me! I'm tryna help! You out here slangin' crack? I'm worried you gone get pregnant! And I'm scared you gone *die*! Stop scaring me! Just listen to me because I'm only tryin' to help!" Sandy said as she too cried.

"I just, I just wanna be like you that's all." Ne`Ne` replied lowly.

"I'm nobody to want to be like, Ne`Ne`! Do something else with your life! Be better than me!"

"Thank you for sayin' that, Sandy," a soft voice then spoke out from the backyard.

It was Mary. She had awakened when she heard the Impala's tires screeching beside her home and got up to use the restroom and looked into each of her daughters' bedrooms to check on them and saw that they were gone. She was going to look for them when she heard Ne`Ne` and Sandy outside her backdoor.

Dimples ran up in time to see Sandy and Ne`Ne` crying underneath the light emanating from her mother's kitchen as they stood in the yard. "Momma, we was just—"

"Regina don't try to explain," Mary stated sadly as she opened the screen door and walked down her stairs and hugged Ne`Ne`. "You could have told me those things, Sandy. Rene? Why can't you be like me? I'm your mother. Why not want to be like me?" Mary asked as she began to cry. "I work hard every day to take care of you and your sister and you having sex and selling drugs behind my back? Why?"

"I don't know why, momma. I'm, I'm fuckin' up! I'm sorry! I'm sorry to everybody!" Ne`Ne` screamed as she hid her face and cried into her mother's bosom.

"I forgive you. And we're going to get through this. I never knew." Mary said as she looked over to Sandy.

"Martha made me promise to look after them both whenever they was outside. I was trying. I didn't know how to tell you. I didn't wanna—"

"Be labeled a snitch?" Mary asked, cutting Sandy off from her statement and then continuing by saying, "This here is different from what Martha and Twiggy did in that court room last year. These are my *daughters*, Sandy—not some gangsters on the street who would retaliate if you rat them out."

"I know, Miss Mary. I'm sorry for not saying nothing."

"You were only doing as you were taught by Martha, Twiggy and the rest of the Folk Gang, but these two are not going to be a part of that. When it concerns them, you tell me everything you know, okay?"

"Yes ma'am." Sandy replied as she looked to the ground.

Mary then ordered all three females inside where she made coffee and they sat and talked. Ne`Ne` and Dimples both confessed what they had been doing and they promised to change their ways, but it didn't prevent Mary from grounding them both during the whole summer. They would have to go to work with her everyday once school ended. In the meantime, they would remain on school grounds until Mary picked them up after she got off work.

"Momma," Ne`Ne` spoke softly as she sighed and shook her

head, "I'm not mad. I'm glad you know now because it's like a load off."

"For me too, momma." Dimples chimed in.

"Momma? Can Sandy still be our friend?" Ne`Ne` asked.

Mary sipped her coffee slowly, sat it back down on the table, eyed sandy and said, "So long as Sandy doesn't behave the way she behaved before. And only if she wants to."

Sandy was out there. The opportunity to end her, Ne`Ne` and Dimples' friendship had suddenly presented itself and she thought long and hard about that fact; but the love she had for the twins was just too great. She wanted to hang with them just as much as they wanted to hang with her. With Mary in the picture now, the twins would bring some normality from the madness inside her world. "I'd be glad to still be their friend Miss Mary," Sandy said with a smile. "It's other things to do besides selling drugs and having sex and that's what I was trying to show and tell them. I guess I messed that up. I'll be glad to do those other things with Rene and Regina from time to time."

The four females all smiled at that moment. A resolution had been formed. Sandy was relieved. Mary was informed. And the twins were set straight. The conflict between Sandy and the twins had finally come to an end to the delight and sentiment of all involved.

CHAPTER 24

PROUD MARY

"And then every night they had a big fireworks show auntie! Man, Disney World was the most fun place we ever been! Right Dimples?" Ne`Ne` asked towards her sister as Martha flipped through a stack of photos she was handed.

Ne`Ne` and Dimples were sitting in the visiting room of the Grenada County Jail, about two hours north of Jackson, Mississippi straight up Interstate-55, with their mother and Loretta Duncan. Martha and Twiggy were previously held at a facility only fifteen miles from Ghost Town in Pearl, Mississippi, but they weren't allowed to have visitors there. They were deemed low risk inmates so they were moved to Grenada County Jail in early March of '93 and that sat fine with both women. The jail had better facilities and a more laidback group than the state prison just outside of Jackson. When they were in Pearl, Mississippi, Martha and Twiggy were constantly running into people they knew from the streets who were still carrying on in the same lifestyle while the both of them wanted to remove themselves from that way of life. The move to Grenada was a blessing, the only problem was that they were two hours from home, but they couldn't have visitors when they were just fifteen miles from Ghost Town; and even though they were two hours away, they could now have visitors. They had put in their requests for visitation rights when they first entered Grenada County Jail, but the jail facility had to get them enrolled into state inmate worker programs first. It took four months for the women to get placed on the jail's farm. They were ditch diggers or 'irrigation technicians' as they often joked in reference to themselves. They didn't mind though, and if they performed well, they could transfer to other programs; and all the while they were earning credit towards their freedom.

Grenada County was a true rehabilitation facility, not just a prison. Martha and Twiggy were both lucky to have been sent there. The never asked for it, but they were glad they got the reward; they were still cellmates as well. Prison life wasn't so hard for either woman; they only wished they were free, but they were working towards that every waking day of their lives.

They got their approvals for visitation rights in late July of '93 and Mary, Ne`Ne`, Dimples and Loretta were the first ones to visit both women. Sandy and Simon would visit in the upcoming days. They had taken the trip to Disney World with Mary and her daughters and decided to stay another week. When Mary called down to Florida and told them the visitation papers had arrived, the two cut the week short. They were driving back to Mississippi the day Mary, Loretta and the twins visited.

Martha listened with a wide smile as her nieces' told her about their trip to Florida, their eyes teeming with joy the whole time they replayed their experience. Mary still had the twins under punishment the whole summer; but she had seen the complete change in her daughters. They were sincere in their endeavors. They had turned sixteen in late June, and they didn't sulk when Mary didn't do anything special for them outside of cake and ice cream. They told their mother they understood and they never really expected anything, not even a cake. They were proficient in their tasks around the home and also on Mary's job at the food distribution warehouse and both were now eager to learn how to become a woman from their mother. The twins often helped to prepare dinner at home. They made their first dish on their own, a meatloaf and mash potatoes when Mary let them stay home one day in early June. It was a test, and the girls had passed. Mary did it four times, and each time, Ne`Ne` and Dimples only got better.

The Holland Family Saga Part Five

Mary remembered the last time she left her daughters home alone, which was the twins' sixteenth birthday. As Ne`Ne` and Dimples talked with Martha, and whilst Loretta chatted with Twiggy, Mary's thoughts drifted back to the day of the twins' sixteenth birthday which was just over a month earlier...

...The twins had prepared a pork roast and gravy and rice with string beans and Mary had come home tired that day. She thanked her daughters for making dinner and told the twins not to expect anything for their birthday outside of the cake and ice cream she sat on the table and they told their mother they understood. When Mary fell asleep on the living room sofa watching the evening news, she was soon awakened by a tickling of her feet. She woke up and looked down to see her daughters rubbing her feet and washing them with warm water. They painted her toenails and finger nails and also fixed her hair. Mary grew teary eyed as she smiled proudly upon her daughters before she got up to fix dinner plates for everyone. While they were at the dining table eating dinner, Mary noticed that Ne`Ne` kept staring at her.

"What's wrong, Ne`Ne`?" Mary asked as she cut into her slice of pork roast.

"Nothin', momma."

"You sure, baby?"

"Well," Ne`Ne` said as she sat her fork on her plate, "remember that night when you overheard me and Sandy in the backyard?"

"Umm hmm," Mary answered, growing worried that Ne`Ne` had more to confess.

"I felt stupid for saying I wanted to be like Sandy after you heard me say that. Sandy my friend true enough, but I see I was wrong for wanting to be like her, and she was right for correcting me. When you asked me why I didn't want to be like you, I didn't know how to answer back then. I'm ready to answer that question now, momma." Ne`Ne` said as she bowed her head slightly.

Dimples listened. She and Ne`Ne` had talked about this

matter before and Dimples had encouraged her sister to tell Mary how she truly felt.

"Okay, I'm listening. Why don't you want to be like me?"

"I could never do what you do, momma."

Mary donned a puzzled look on her face. "What do you mean, Rene," she inquired.

"Well, we never knew our daddy. Some girls at school? They talk bad about their daddy. And these two sisters that stay on White Street named Paulette and Sidney always say that their daddy a good-for-nothing MF 'er. I asked them how they knew and they said their momma tell them that almost every day. I never heard you complain once about our daddy not ever being around. You been our everything. Our momma *and* our daddy. Our friend. A doctor. Litigator. Chef. Spokesperson. The police. Fire department. Helicopter pilot," Ne`Ne` said as she and Dimples started to sniggle. Mary chuckled as well, but she knew Ne`Ne` meant majority of what she was saying. Ne`Ne` was speaking from the heart, but she was also trying to embellish a little humor to make her mother laugh. She'd succeeded. "For real though, momma," Ne`Ne` said seriously, "you are a great woman. I hope to be great someday, but even if? I could never be as great as you," she ended as she eyed her mother meekly.

"You are a great daughter right now, a great person, both of you are great daughters." Mary said as she eyed Dimples, causing her to blush. "You two will grow into great women someday. Thanks for thinking I'm great, but I'm just a mother who has been blessed with the two most precious daughters in the world." Mary stated as she squeezed Ne`Ne`s hand.

"Tell her the rest! Tell her what you told me in the room Rene!" Dimples said as Ne`Ne`s eyes started to well up.

"What? What else is there to say, Ne`Ne`? You've said it all."

"No. Momma? I just," Ne`Ne` began to cry because she'd been overcome with emotion at that point. She briefly thought about the wrong she had done in the past and was glad she had a mother who cared. Most teens in Ghost Town, like Paulette,

Sidney, and Urselle, all three of whom Sandy often had to run out of Ambush, had mothers who didn't care one iota about the welfare of their daughters. Ne`Ne` was grateful to have a mother like Mary. "I just wanna say that, that," when Ne`Ne` couldn't find the words to express what she was feeling she grew frustrated at herself and hid her face and heaved.

"Come on, baby. You can tell me anything." Mary said in earnest, pulling for her daughter to say what was on her mind.

Dimples reached out and rubbed Ne`Ne`s back, and Ne`Ne` clutched her sister's hand tightly and rubbed her face its palm. She looked at her mother, her face wet with tears, slowly closed her eyes and held her head down as her face wrinkled from the emotion that had overtaken her as she shook her head from side to side. Her body was steadily heaving when she eyed her mother and said, "I'm glad you momma! I'm just, I'm just glad you *my* momma!" Ne`Ne` finally said lowly as she cried, dropped to her knees and laid her head into her mother's lap. Mary and Dimples both broke into tears at that moment and the three all held one another inside the kitchen and expressed the love they had for one another. That phrase, 'I'm glad you my momma', was echoing through Mary's mind as she sat at the table inside the visiting room. She would often replay that night, and today was no different. 'I'm glad you my momma' was the most precious thing anyone had ever said to Mary. It was one of the sweetest moments of her life and a memory to be forever cherished...

"...Momma! Momma!" Dimples said as she shook Mary, slowly breaking her train of thoughts.

"What happened?" Mary asked as she was brought back to the present.

"Martha was asking you about that man Vincent you used to date." Dimples replied.

"Vincent?" Mary didn't want to talk about Vincent, she was reliving some fond memories, beautiful memories, and Vincent was the furthest thing from her mind. "That man? I haven't seen him in over a year. Last I heard he bought a tractor and was working out west somewhere, child. California or somewhere I don't know. I been dealing with these two. Men aren't my main focus right now and never have been."

"Shiit! Girl, when I get out this place, mankind in some serious trouble!" Martha remarked as Twiggy agreed whilst laughing. "For real, Irene. I'm hot—ass—hell! I'd give my *right arm* for nice rock hard—"

"Twiggy look like you put on weight! No offense. You just look real beautiful with your new figure." Mary said as she cut Martha off before she went too far.

Martha realized her mistake and squeezed Mary's arm. Mary tapped her sister's hand and donned a look that said 'bad little girl' and she and Martha smiled at one another.

Twiggy kept the conversation moving forward by saying, "Thank you, Mary. I added that weight on purpose. I thought we was going to hard labor so why we was in Central Prison, I was trying to bulk up. This place here is like a resort though." Twiggy remarked.

"For real, huh," Martha said. "We got a radio in our cell but they won't let us have a TV. We be making wine, ham and grill cheese sandwiches and read a lot of books. Y'all still listen to the Fantastic Four?" Martha then asked her nieces.

"Almost every-single-night!" Mary answered for her daughters as they laughed.

"You like them auntie?"

"They was cool, Ne`Ne`, but we don't get them way up here."

"Aww man! They be tripping hard on there." Dimples replied.

"That damn show? Sandy listen to that show. I be hearing her kee-keeing all night!" Loretta chimed in.

"These two do the same thing, Loretta. Listening and laughing at Misses Jones. That's their favorite host on the show." Mary stated to Martha.

"And I'll take my answer off the air!" Ne`Ne` and Dimples stated at the same time quoting one of Rolanda Jones' most hated statements at the time as they laughed aloud.

The Holland Family Saga Part Five

The visit to Grenada was very uplifting for everyone that had visited this day. Martha talked to her nieces alone seriously about what they had done in the past when Mary, Twiggy and Loretta became enthralled in conversation. She pulled them over to an empty table and sat before them and said, "I'm living proof that that life is not all it's cracked up to be. You either end up here, or where Gina is today."

Ne`Ne` and Dimples knew Martha had killed Gina Cradle and began wondering why she'd brought this particular subject up to them. Martha leaned back in her chair and let what she said soak in for a few minutes. She waited for a reply as she studied her nieces' faces, which displayed a look of wonderment. She leaned forward and said lowly, "You wonder why I bring that up about Gina, right?" she asked as her nieces shook their heads in agreement. "What I'm trying to tell you is that there are people like the person I used to be still out there in them streets. People even worse than me. Don't become me, and definitely don't become like Gina is today. See? In that life? What they like to call now-a-days 'the game'? You either end up dead or in jail. I'm lucky to be in jail. Your momma always believed I was gone get killed out there. The way your mother worried about me? Shoot! I know I took ten years off your mother's life, but when I came here she got 'em back. Because she no longer had to worry about me getting killed. Don't take ten years from your momma, understand?" Martha asked as the twins nodded. "Ain't no walking away from the game without consequences. That's why I was hard on you, Ne`Ne`. You got just a small taste. Was it worth it?"

"Not at all. I be talking to Sandy a lot now. She always say she not happy with her life. She say she looking for a way out, but until then, she gone stay in the game. When my momma found out about me and Dimples, auntie? I slept better at night afterwards."

"Sandy been out there in that world. She can handle that life. If she wanna stay out there in the game, let her be, just don't neither of you follow in her steps. Understand," the twins nodded again to say yes. They were really heeding Martha's words this time. Mary's guidance, coupled with Martha's candidness was making strides with Ne`Ne` and Dimples; their resolve to stay out the streets was growing stronger. "When I look in your mother's eyes," Martha said, breaking the silence, "I see nothing but joy. Don't hurt my sister. Mary the sweetest woman I know. Y'all should be glad she y'all momma. Honor her by doing what's right."

"We will, auntie," the twins said at the same time.

"Cool beans. Keep doing what you doing. I saw ya' momma daydreaming while she was rubbing your back Ne'Ne'. She proud of the fact that you changed your ways. Me too. I'm proud of both of you young women." Martha ended just as visiting hours came to a close.

The group all exchanged hugs, somewhat saddened by the fact that they had to leave as time had flown by. Martha and Twiggy were pleading for them to come back and they all promised to do so every other weekend. Mary stood before Martha smiling proudly as other visitors were walking out of the room.

"Why you smiling like that, Mary?"

"Before you went to jail you had a rugged look. Now you back sexy like me." Mary answered with a smile.

"Like you? Girl, you know you look like me!" Martha stated as she laughed.

"No, child. I always been the sexy twin. You had a hard look. You had to come here to get sexy!"

"Ooohh Mary! I looked hard out there?"

"Martha? With them plats and them sunshades? The bandannas you used to wear? You was 'thugged out' as the young people say now-a-days."

"Tryna talk hip!" Martha said as she tapped Mary's arm.

A li'l somethin' somethin'!" Mary said, forcing a snort out of Martha that embarrassed her briefly. "I love you, Martha. I'll put some money in your account before I leave. Twiggy you need some money in your account?" Mary then asked towards Twiggy.

"Nahh, thanks Mary. Simon and Sandy got me straight,

thanks anyway."

Mary turned back to Martha, and said, "I'm so proud of you Martha."

"For going to jail?"

"No. For wanting to change. I can't wait until you get out. I miss you!"

"Me too, Mary. I'll be over forty by then or close to it by the time I'm let go. Shame I waited until I got in my thirties to go to jail. My grown ass." Martha said as she looked to the ground.

"Either way, we'll manage. You still have money in the bank. When your time's up you can go get it right?"

"I don't know. Just keep paying the slots for me. At least I'll have something to work for, a purpose when I get out."

"Right. Stay positive. Well, we'll see you in a couple of weeks okay." Mary said as she stretched her arm to shake Martha's hand.

Martha laughed and pulled her sister to her and hugged her, they touched cheeks and they both exhaled. Having not touched one another in almost a year, it was refreshing to be close to one another again. Mary handed Martha the stack of pictures to put in her and Twiggy's cell; pictures of her trip to Disney World, and also pictures taken in Ghost Town around the house. Martha placed the picture of Mary in between her daughters, all three wearing Mickey Mouse ears and t-shirts on top, stating that it was her favorite picture and she would hang that one first. Mary watched with proud eyes as her sister was then escorted back to her cell. She was missing Martha no doubt, but the calls were regular and now they had visitations; and with Martha doing alright in jail, and her daughters on the right path, everything in Mary's life was going along good. She rode back to Jackson a proud and happy woman on this hot day in July of '93.

The Holland Family Saga Part Five

CHAPTER 25

HIT 'EM UP

"Ooooh baby I love you…what more can I say…ooooh baby I love, love, love, love you…what more can I say…ooooh baby I need your sweet loving…I miss you more… and more everyday yay yay…"

Lynrd Skynrd's' slow, melodic and bluesy song *I Need You* blared from Simon's drop top white on white Caprice as he and Sandy sat inside the car in front the trail on Friendly Lane. It was about 55 degrees out and Simon and Sandy were both dressed alike in white and blue Emmitt Smith Dallas Cowboy jerseys and white Girbaud's jeans and blue G-Nike's and wearing blue Cowboys skull caps. The cold air whipped across the convertible as the two sat waiting for Ne`Ne` and Dimples' school bus to arrive in Ghost Town with the car was idling and they had the heat on to keep them warm.

Sandy had been on a serious rock and roll kick ever since the month of May and she now had Simon hooked on the rock music as well. The two sat in the car smoking a blunt and sipping gin on an overly cool day in November of '93. Sandy was deeply entrenched into the song and reflecting on her and her mother's relationship, which was odd one to say the least in her eyes. For a brief moment, Sandy asked herself why her mother allowed her to do as she pleased. Loretta was home this day and she had seen her leave the house with her AK-47 and she didn't say a word. Sandy's best guess was that Loretta was a gangster when she was her age so she had no problem with her doing as she pleased. She reflected as the song neared its ending, telling herself that she wouldn't stop doing what she was doing even if Loretta asked her to; in fact, she would only get mad and leave. She told herself that so long as she came home every night, then Loretta should be happy with that and just stay out of her affairs. She relinquished her thoughts as the song came to its conclusion and then played it again.

Sandy at the age of 20, was a slender 5' 9" 135 pound brown-haired, blue-eyed female. She had a hardened look to herself in her young age and her appearance wasn't a façade or a gimmick because behind the image lay the truth and the real. A product of her environment and upbringing, this youngster only did what came natural. And what came natural for Sandy Duncan during this period of time in her life was the art of homicide. Since the summer, she and Simon had completed three hits for Chug-a-lug and their names were now ringing throughout the underworld. Many people knew and feared both Sandy and Simon and they were propelling themselves towards the top of not only Folk Gang, but the underworld throughout Jackson, Mississippi in its entirety and they were already legends in Ghost Town, just like the ones who came before them.

After showing great love for Ne'Ne' and Dimples, making sure those two were all right and staying out of trouble, Sandy began focusing more on her street game. She and Simon's last hit, the robbery and murder of a drug dealer from San Antonio, Texas, had put them on big time. They earned $15,000 and a kilogram of cocaine and had put Jesse and Clark on major after that. Ghost Town was slowly returning to its glory days towards the end of summer and money was being made once again.

With money to blow, Sandy and Simon had taken a trip to New Orleans in early September as Sandy had wanted gold teeth. The two were going to drive to New Orleans and were planning on taking Ne'Ne' and Dimples, but Mary objected outright. The twins begged their mother without success and had to stay behind. Neither twin wanted gold teeth, they only wanted to visit the cast of the Fantastic Four Show inside the studio. The twins were angry at their mother's refusal; but they knew their deceit from days long past had prevented them from taking the trip.

Sandy had gotten six gold fronts from First and Claiborne, the popular dentistry in New Orleans that specialized in placing gold fronts in peoples' mouths. Her grill was 'gangster' as everybody called it when they eyed the dental work. Sandy was thugged out by the fall of '93, and Simon, now 20 as well, and standing 6' 2" weighing 220 pounds and sporting a thick, but neatly trimmed beard with braided hair, had to often ward off other males that tried to approach Sandy. A gangster white girl was rare in Jackson, Mississippi so Sandy drew attention where ever she went after she had gotten her gold fronts. She may have been white on the outside, but she was just as Black, and just as gangster as Martha and Twiggy were when they ran the streets of Jackson, Mississippi.

Now, on this cold day in November, Sandy and Simon were out on guard. A situation went down in Ambush earlier in the day while they were out making pick-ups and they were waiting to make sure that Ne`Ne` and Dimples would get off the school bus and go straight inside. Sandy was bobbing her head to Lynrd Skynrd's song when she looked up and saw the twins' school bus turn onto Friendly Lane and make its way towards the trail. The bus rounded the curb and Dimples yelled aloud out the window; but when she saw the chopper lying across Sandy's lap, she quickly raised it back up.

As the bus made its way to Casper Drive, Sandy donned a Dallas Cowboy starter jacket trench coat, grabbed her chopper, and hid it underneath the zipped trench coat and walked towards Mary's house where the bus would stop and let the twins off. Sixteen year-old Sidney and fifteen year-old Paulette was on the bus as well; they saw Sandy walking onto the sidewalk just as Ne`Ne` and Dimples were exiting the bus and yelled out to her. Sandy nodded her head and ordered the two teens off the bus with Ne`Ne` and Dimples. The driver wasn't supposed to let Paulette and Sidney, who were the last two students on the bus, off at this stop, but when Sandy stepped into view and told her the sisters were with her, the driver, who had seen Sandy many times before in the neighborhood, let Paulette and Sidney off before she turned onto Casper Street and headed out of Ghost Town.

"What's up, Sandy? That's a fly trench coat right there!" Dimples said as she eyed the chopper poking from the right sleeve of Sandy's coat.

"Thanks." Sandy replied as she stared down at the twins, Paulette and Sidney. "Y'all saw Urselle today?" she then asked the girls, who all replied no.

"I ain't seen her since last night. She wasn't in school either." Sidney said aloud.

"You wanna why?" Sandy asked.

"Why?" Sidney questioned.

"Because she got killed today at about eleven 'o' clock this morning!"

The four teens looked at Sandy in shock. "You see why I kept running y'all from Ambush? This shit ain't a joke out here! Urselle shoulda had her ass in school! Clark and Jesse was out there but she ran her li'l ass up to this car and tried to make the crack sale." Sandy said angrily as Ne`Ne` reflected on the night she and Sandy fell out, remembering that she had done the same thing. "Ne`Ne`," Sandy then said, "it was the same car that sped off with your money that night. They been doing that shit in other spots throughout the whole city and done made their way back 'round here after all this time. It's two of 'em. Urselle ran after the car when they snatched her cocaine. She was holding on to the passenger door just like you was about to try and do before I stopped you that night when the man in the passenger seat blasted her young ass in the face with a li'l thirty-eight snub nose. She was only fuckin' fifteen, and now she dead! Them dudes that killed Urselle was from Vernon District. We thinkin' they might come back today so I'm tellin' y'all to go home and stay inside. You understand me," the four teens nodded to say yes. Sandy then looked at Sidney and Paulette with concerned eyes. She knew the sisters' mother was a heroin addict and they rarely had food in their home. "Y'all girls ate today?" she asked Paulette and Sidney.

"We had lunch at school. We got some pork and beans and wieners inside for dinner." Paulette replied.

Sandy grew angry on the inside. She looked off to nowhere in particular and shook her head somberly. Sidney and Paulette were good girls at heart; they were just being neglected by their mother. Sandy remembered how Martha and Twiggy looked out for the younger G-Queens, and following in their steps, she decided at that moment to have an active role in Sidney and Paulette's life. "Y'all ain't eating no damn pork and beans and wieners," she said as she used her free hand to dip into her jeans pocket to pull out two twenties and hand the money over to Sidney. "Go up to Fukutoo's and get whatever you want! Make sure y'all girls just eat and get full okay? If you ever need money for food or anything else, when you see me, just ask me for it alright? And keep the change." Sandy said seriously.

Sidney and Paulette looked at the forty dollars with wide eyes. No one had ever given them that amount of cash before. The two girls hugged Sandy and thanked her. "I got y'all alright? You and the twins is straight. Y'all should look after one another."

"Okay! Thanks Sandy! Bye Dimples! Bye Ne`Ne`! We gone call when the Fantastic Four come on!" Paulette stated as she and Sidney ran up Casper Drive towards Fukutoo's.

"Bye, y'all!" Ne`Ne` yelled.

"Get y'all food and come right back here and go inside!" Sandy yelled aloud to Sidney and Paulette.

"We will!" Sidney and Paulette replied as they turned and ran up Casper Drive in a euphoric state.

Ne`Ne` and Dimples then walked into their yard and began discussing Urselle's murder. They knew Urselle, but they never really hung with the young teen the way Paulette and Sidney did; still the twins were dismayed by the sudden death of another young teen that lived in their neighborhood. Sandy called the twins back as they walked towards their back door. "Y'all all right? Y'all want some Fukutoo's or something while I'm out here waiting on those two?"

"Nahh, we good. We fixed a baked ham and macaroni last night. Want some?" Ne`Ne` asked.

Sandy accepted, but not before giving the twins twenty dollars apiece. They thanked her and welcomed her in, but Sandy waited outside for her plate of food as she was on the lookout. Dimples warmed Sandy's plate and she walked back to the car with her meal. Simon noticed the plate of food immediately and said, "Ain't this a bitch? You go down there to talk to the twins and 'nem and you come back snacking! Where mine?"

"Go get it. Folk!" Sandy replied as Simon got out the car and walked down to the twins' home and asked for a meal.

A short while later, Jesse and Clark were sitting on the stairs in Ambush. They noticed Paulette and Sidney toting four plastic bags and running inside just as a Ford station wagon entered into Ambush from Ghost Street, which was the thick wood-lined gravel road leading into Ambush. The car crept up the road and Clark and Jesse ran up the stairs into Clark's grandmother's home before they were seen and paged Sandy. When her beeper went off, she looked at the number and saw Clark's grandmother's home number followed by 187. The code had been given. Sandy hopped from the Caprice, dropping her plate of food and leaving the door open and the car running in the process and ran up the middle of Friendly Lane towards the intersection on Casper Drive with her chopper in her hands.

Sandy reached the intersection of Friendly Lane and Casper Drive just as the station wagon was nearing the corner and spotted the car approaching from the left. She aimed her rifle and opened fire, causing people that were inside to take cover on the floors of their homes because of the thundering gunshots that were being fired in rapid succession. The wagon sped up, but Sandy only continued firing her thirty round clip as she stood in the intersection of Friendly Lane and Casper Drive. AK-47 shells penetrated the windshield and shattered the passenger side windows as the car sped by. Sandy guided her rifle with precision, following the car and steadily releasing shells as it sped passed her. She knew she hit both men as they sped by once the car veered to the left and crashed into the two foot brick wall lining Casper Drive. Sandy eyed her handy work for several seconds before she took off running down Friendly Lane headed back towards the Caprice.

The twins had taken cover on the living room floor as Simon grabbed his .9mm and ran out the front door. People began to come out of their homes after the gunfire seized and upon hearing screeching tires, and then the crash. Sandy pulled up to Casper Drive with the Caprice and Simon hopped in the passenger seat and the two quickly sped up Casper Drive headed out of Ghost Town. The Caprice slowed for a brief moment in front of the crashed station wagon, and people screamed and scattered as Simon unloaded his .9mm into the interior of the wagon from the back seat, making sure that the two men who had robbed and killed Urselle were dead. Sandy and Simon then sped out of Ghost Town.

The twins had witnessed Simon shoot the men, and they knew Sandy had shot at the men with her chopper. Her words, *"This shit ain't a joke out here",* echoed through both their minds as they stared at the car wedged against the brick wall containing the corpses of two dead men.

Mary entered Ghost Town an hour later, returning home from work only to find that she was being guided pass her home on Casper Drive by city police towards Friendly Lane. As she rode pass the street leading to her home at a slow pace, Mary could see the police had Casper Drive blocked from Hanging Moss to Friendly Lane and ambulances and police cars were parked up and down the street. Mary rounded Friendly Lane and pulled into her yard and got out of her car and saw her daughters standing with Loretta on the corner in front her home. When she reached the front of her house, Mary caught sight of the wrecked car and was informed by her two daughters that somebody had killed two people inside the wrecked vehicle.

"That fuckin' daughter of mine is a psycho-path!" Loretta thought to herself, knowing full well Sandy was involved because she had witnessed her daughter walking out of the house with a gun in her hands just over an hour ago.

The Holland Family Saga Part Five

Everybody in Ghost Town either knew, or had an idea concerning who was responsible for the double murder, but no one said a word. Urselle was killed by those two men and they dared to return the same day. Sandy and Simon had put nearly everyone in Ghost Town on notice that they knew who'd killed Urselle. They told the girl's mother and anybody that would listen, so when the drama went down, nobody felt remorse for the two men who were in their early forties because they had killed a fifteen year-old little girl. Sandy and Simon held court on this day, and for Ghost Town, for Urselle, they placed both men on death row and had executed them both. Sandy and Simon, although they laced the streets of Ghost Town with crack cocaine and gang activity, the very thing that had caused Urselle to lose her life in the first place, were respected in the neighborhood for the simple fact that they didn't prey upon their own; instead, they looked out for people in Ghost Town. And that in itself held a lot of weight with a great majority of the neighborhood's residents.

The murder of the two men would turn into a cold case. The police tried to solve the murders, but the people in Ghost Town would not cooperate. They left it up to the police to solve the crime; besides, no one had ever connected the two men to Urselle's death. If the detectives had found out who had killed a fifteen year-old little girl, they would not have two more dead bodies on their hands. After Urselle was killed, the police should have been patrolling the area hourly, instead, they scooped her body up and kept rolling. Only Simon and Sandy were on patrol, and when people like them were policing the neighborhood, it only meant more bloodshed, and that is exactly what happened on this cool crisp evening in November of '93. The Vice Lords from Vernon District never retaliated against Ghost Town for the double murders. The two men resided in Vernon District, but they weren't gang members so Sandy and Simon were in the clear.

****

The rest of the year went about unhinged. Ne'Ne' and Dimples had a great Christmas that was spent it in Grenada with Martha and Twiggy. Mary and her daughters, Simon, Sandy and Loretta were allowed to bring two baked turkeys into the visitation room during the visit. Mary brought one for her and her family and friends, and one for the prison staff. The staff was delighted by the gesture; no one had ever done anything like that for them. Mary told the staff she was just grateful that they allowed her sister and her friend to come to their facility. Martha overheard her sister and she laughed to herself because Mary was standing their thanking the very people who were holding her sister captive; but Martha knew Mary was just glad she was still alive and had a chance at freedom in a relatively short span of time.

Martha asked loads of questions about her nieces the whole time. She wanted to be sure they weren't misbehaving. She and Twiggy then got an update on the streets from Simon and Sandy, who were modest with themselves; Loretta, however, gave the two women the full score. Martha and Twiggy sat and listened without passing judgment as Loretta detailed some of their activities using coded talk and low tones. If Martha and Twiggy thought they were hard when they were out there, they knew for a fact that Simon and Sandy was the shit and then some after hearing some of the stories Loretta had related to them.

Before the term spread throughout the south in the mid-nineties, as '93 was coming to a close, Simon and Sandy had been labeled 'gorillas' by Martha and Twiggy. The two were ahead of their time in Jackson, Mississippi. Martha and Twiggy had heard that term from a fellow inmate who was from Memphis, Tennessee, the place that gave birth to the term, 'gorilla'. Before the term ever became popular in the south, Simon and Sandy had already earned that title.

"Loretta," Martha then asked lowly as Simon and Sandy chatted with Twiggy, "don't take this the wrong way, but, how you feel about Sandy and what she do?"

Loretta bowed her head and said softly, "Everyday I fear for my daughter, Martha. I'm glad you asked. I'm glad somebody asked me. I know she ruthless, but when she come through that door at night, she stays home now," Loretta said happily and continued with her thoughts, "she used to stay by the Charles' house all the time, but she comes home every night now. I, I ran away when my parents tried to correct me and I know I hurt them badly. I don't want Sandy to stop loving me. I know she loves me now, and I don't want her to ever stop. I'm always scared that if I say something, she gone stop loving me."

"You know she ain't going nowhere without Simon." Martha stated.

"I know. But I don't want her to stop loving me. Understand? I know my daughter, Martha. And she would walk pass me as if she never met me because that's who her father was in the way he treated people and that's what I did to my family. I don't care about the people she hurt because they would do it to her if they had the chance. Sandy, you know Sandy—she loyal, and she has a good heart, she cares about those who care about her and she's fair. I was like her before I went to jail and part of the time while I was in there. When I got jumped into Folk Gang I realized after I rode to Yazoo City that I was sinking back into my old ways. Still, knowing I knew better, I held drugs for you and Twiggy. I was a bad parent, Martha. But when Sandy joined? I backed away from the gang life and started working an honest job. I tried to show Sandy through action that people can change, but she took to the streets anyway. So, now it is what it is. I never spoke out to reprimand her and now she's too far gone to start correcting her now. I just pray she come home to me every night. When I hear gunshots in Ambush I jump. Sometimes I jump awake from my sleep worrying if she's okay. It's hard living this way, but I make due." Loretta ended sadly as she squeezed Martha's hand, never making eye contact.

Martha grabbed Loretta's hand to reassure her, understanding her plight. She'd stated that she was a bad parent but Martha didn't agree; on the other hand, she didn't disagree. And even upon being given such a bleak and pathetic answer to her question, Martha didn't judge Loretta either. The way Martha now understood things, Loretta had never corrected Sandy because she feared losing the love of her daughter. She then thought about how Mary dealt with her nieces. Mary never had that fear; she did whatever she had to do to keep her daughters in line and knew not the fear of having her daughters not love her because it was something unfathomable. Hollands never stopped loving Hollands, at least that's the way Martha saw things in her life and in dealing with her family. Martha could see that Loretta knew that fear because she had lived through it herself and she had rebelled to the point that she ran away from her family. She feared losing Sandy's love and that was the reason she never chastised her daughter. Martha had just gotten to the bottom of the matter as to why Sandy was permitted to do what she did. Something she had been curious about for a long time, and she now understood; didn't make it right what Loretta was allowing her daughter to do, but she understood. She changed the subject and before long, she and Loretta were back laughing as they shared turkey and dressing before visiting hours came to a close and the group all said their goodbyes.

****

The New Year came in and months passed without much ado. Simon and Sandy were still doing their thing, and Ne`Ne` and Dimples had passed the eleventh grade. Dimples was trying hard to achieve a scholarship to Grambling State University and wanted to become a pediatrician. Ne`Ne` was interested in becoming an accountant. She liked what her mother did and wanted to advance what she was learning even further; maybe even becoming a corporate accountant. Ne`Ne` had her mind set on attending Grambling State as well. That way, she and Dimples could go through college together and share in their studies.

By mid-July of '94 Mary was doing real good on her job. She was working hard in order to save money to give her kids a head start in life when they graduated the twelfth grade in June of '95. The twins were at work with their mother on this summer day in July of '94 helping her do payroll when Ne`Ne` noticed that one of the workers' hours was incorrect and asked could she go and ask the man about his time sheet.

"Uh, uh, Rene. You not going out there by all them men," Mary said to now seventeen year-old Ne`Ne` as Dimples giggled.

"You gone let me get married one day, momma?" Ne`Ne`

asked jokingly.

"Yeah, when you're about—about forty!" Mary replied, causing Dimples to burst into laughter.

"Momma!" Ne`Ne` said in a shocked tone as she laughed along with her sister.

Mary laughed and exited her office with the time sheet and walked towards the dock worker's post. She noticed that a truck driver who was getting his truck unloaded stared at her for an unusual amount of time and in an odd way as she walked by the man and it somewhat unnerved her. She chalked it up to loose-fitting grey work slacks and a the tight-fitting top with a pair of five-inch heels that had her legs looking long and lovely, and her rear end sitting up real high as the reason why the man had stared at her for so long. *"I know I'm gorgeous, mister truck driver,"* Mary said to herself, smiling on the inside.

Mary was a knockout and she knew it. She dressed professionally, but her outfits always had sex appeal. She was wearing dark red lipstick and had her hair and face made up nicely. Her dark eyes looked alluring, her breast pointed, revealing just a hint of cleavage, but leaving much more to the imagination. The perfume she wore lit up the docks; workers eyed her rear end and stared into her face and inhaled her scent as she walked by. Mary brushed her shoulder length black hair from her face, all-the-while growing hot, but not in a sexual nature. She was growing hot because she could feel all the pairs of eyes boring into her flesh. She had made this walk many times before and had never let it get to her, but something about the way this one particular truck driver at the dock just beside her office stared at her made her feel uneasy, even if she did appreciate the attention.

Mary found the warehouse worker emerging from the food distributor's large deep freezer on a forklift and flagged him down and got the information she needed and returned to her office. She had to pass that man again, and once again he made her feel uneasy with his staring. She was glad she went instead of allowing Ne`Ne` to go as the stares from the men on the docks would make just about any female feel uneasy sometimes. She sat back down at her desk, and the man, who appeared to be in his early forties with Jehri-curled hair, continued to stare. *"If he wants a date, he has no chance, especially with that big Jehri-curl! What? That went out in the eighties? The early eighties!"* Mary thought to herself as she began to correct the worker's time-sheet, fully aware that the man was still staring at her. Feeling his boring into her face, Mary hopped up and closed her blinds so she and her daughters could work in peace.

About thirty minutes later there was a knock on Mary's door. She opened it to see one of the dock workers, who explained to her that the truck driver at the dock beside her office wanted a word with her.

"Tell him I'm not interested." Mary said and closed the door. A few minutes later, there was another knock and Mary this time opened her blinds only to see that truck driver again. "I'm taken!" she said loudly.

The man had said something, but because of the forklift traffic, the noise in the office and Mary's inattentiveness, she couldn't hear him. She went to close her blinds, but the driver tapped the window lightly and held his hands up to stop her. Mary watched as the man wrote something down on a sheet of paper. She was prepared to tell him again that she was taken until the man held up the sheet of paper with the name Sam Holland on it followed by a question mark. Mary stared and her eyes grew wide. She opened the door and asked, "How do you know him?"

"Are you kin to him?" the man asked.

"That's my brother! I, I never got to know him, but I know he's my brother."

"Oooh! I thought you knew him because I was gone ask you to say hi to 'em, but never mind."

Mary stopped the man and grew nice, apologizing for being rude as she explained to the man that she got hit on by drivers all the time.

"Apology accepted ma'am."

"When was the last time you saw Samson and where?" Mary asked as her heart pounded.

"He had a club, Persia's they called it. I last saw him in '82, but I moved away to Richmond, Virginia that year. You kind of favored him so I just had to ask. Man, your brother and his wife had it going on back then. I'm still looking for a club like that. I guess you can tell by the hair." the driver joked.

Mary chuckled, then asked, "Where's this club?"

"New Orleans. It's on Ferdinand Street in an area they call the ninth ward down there."

"What happened to Sam?" Mary then asked the man.

"I don't know. That's why I had to ask if you knew him or was kin to him because I wanted to know what he was doing right now. I don't have any friends or family back down there to let me know what's going on like Marvin Gaye song says. I got out the military in '81 and spent a few months in the 'Big Easy'. I stumbled upon that club one night and for the next four or five months I was there almost every night. His wife was a singer with a real good voice."

Mary reached out and hugged the man tightly. He grew surprised and said, "Hey, baby, I'm married. If my wife saw this she would have a hissy fit."

"I'm sorry, mister. You don't understand. It's a long story, but thank you. Thank you. There's a cafeteria here, let me buy you lunch and you can tell me what you know about my brother."

"Okay. I don't know much. Except that he had a wife that could sing. I can't remember her name though. I remember Sam because we had a conversation or two."

Mary didn't gain much insight into her brother's life from the man, but she now knew at least one whereabout of her brother from someone who knew him personally for a short span of time. The man hadn't seen Sam in twelve years, but in eighty-two, Mary knew Sam would have been about twenty-four or five. She now knew her brother had survived childhood and was now a grown man and it gave her hope. Mary began to make immediate plans to go to New Orleans and meet her long lost brother face to face and she couldn't wait to tell Martha the good news. She told Ne'Ne' and Dimples the news when she returned to her office after having lunch with the man.

"Our uncle Samson? You found him, momma?" Dimples asked in shock as Mary held back tears.

"I know where he last was in '82, but that's a big help. A great big help!" Mary said as she hugged her daughters tightly.

"Man, an uncle with a club! Momma, let us go with you to New Orleans when go down there and hit 'em up!" Ne'Ne' said.

"Hit 'em up," Mary said as she laughed, "Yeah, you two *can* and *will* come when I go and see if we can find your uncle and hit 'em up."

The Holland Family Saga Part Five

CHAPTER 26

THE TRUTH ABOUT SAM AND A DEN OF VULTURES

Mary and her daughters were now on their way to New Orleans just two days following the day she had learned of her brother's existence and whereabouts with Sandy tagging along. Mary had taken off from work, citing a family emergency. Sandy knew a little bit about New Orleans from when she and Simon had taken their trip to the city the year before and she knew how rough the city was; she and Simon saw all types of players when they went down there. They toured uptown, riding around neighborhoods and they quickly realized that they could be easy marks riding through different neighborhoods with a Mississippi license tag; on top of that, Sandy was white, she stuck out in the predominately black neighborhoods like a sore thumb. Still, Sandy went because Simon wanted to stay behind and continue doing the pick-ups. He felt safer making the pick-ups instead of allowing Sandy to do it on her own. Besides, they were on their way to meet Sam Holland, Mary's long lost brother; surely they would be all right once they found the man, which was everyone's thinking at the time.

The group made it to New Orleans on a sunny Thursday afternoon during the middle of July in '94. Mary had gotten directions to Ferdinand Street from the many city-wide atlases at her job. The street was located easily, but there was no club named *Persia's* to be found. They rode slowly up and down

Ferdinand Street in Simon's white Caprice. Sandy had the top up on the car as it was hot and muggy in New Orleans that day. Mary sat beside Sandy growing disappointed that the club the man had told her about maybe didn't even exist. She sat in the car with her shoes off staring out the window as they traversed the neighborhood that was filled with junked out cars and dilapidated houses.

People were everywhere throughout the neighborhood. Liquor stores were on just about every corner. Cars passed by blaring music and young men and women talked loud, often cussing each other as they stood on nearly every corner. Most were smoking blunts or cigarettes and nearly every young male they saw had a forty ounce bottle in his hand. Graffiti was everywhere and trash littered the sidewalk. Sandy stared at the organized chaos that her crystal blue eyes were gazing upon.

Ne`Ne` and Dimples were looking out the windows from the backseat at the scores of people. To them, Ghost Town could fit into the ninth ward at least five times over. The neighborhood was huge, and crowded. Despite its rundown condition, the people in the Ninth Ward, if Dimples and Ne`Ne` had to tell it, seemed happy to be where they were. The twins, as well as Sandy, also noticed that a great majority of the young people, both male and female had gold teeth in their mouths. No one from Ghost Town, except Albert Lee and Sandy, had ever had gold teeth, but down in the Ninth Ward section of New Orleans, gold teeth were just as common as the trash that littered the ground.

Sandy circled through the neighborhood looking at the names of the streets. She soon found her way back to Louisa Street, which seemed to be the main street through the neighborhood. Sandy was now on the corner of Higgins and Louisa Street, having just passed G.W. Carver High School and was sitting at the red-light when Mary stuck her head out the window and asked a man, who appeared to be in his thirties, did he know where club Persia's was located. The man leaned down and looked into the car, eyed Sandy, laughed and walked off.

"What the hell was his problem?" Mary asked.

"They might think Sandy the police." Ne`Ne` said from the

The Holland Family Saga Part Five

backseat as she and Dimples, along with Sandy chuckled.

Sandy then made a right turn onto Louisa Street and rode slowly. They approached another club and Sandy pulled over at Mary's behest where she again asked a group of older grey-haired men who were standing out in front of the building did they know where club *Persia's* was located. One of the men said the club had closed down in '84 and burned down in '88 as he pointed to the empty lot where Persia's once stood.

"Do you know a Sam Holland?" Mary asked.

"No!" the man replied quickly and walked away. The man was once a patron of Persia's, however; he knew Sam Holland was dead, but he wasn't about to tell a group of strangers, especially a group that were riding with a white girl, what he knew about Sam. The people in the Ninth Ward were not willing to cooperate with Mary on the grounds of Sandy Duncan being in the car. Sandy made the people feel uncomfortable, but she really felt right at home. She had been around black people for most of her life and had never even once considered that it was because of her presence, the group was being shunned. White people rarely entered the Ninth Ward, and the ones that did were almost always cops. If only the people had talked to Sandy, they would have come to know that she was a cool female, not an undercover cop, which the people in the neighborhood were beginning to believe was the case with her and the people she was riding with. The people that were questioned simply didn't trust the four females.

Sandy, Mary, Ne`Ne` and Dimples had traveled into a den of vultures and neither of them knew it; still, they continued searching for Sam Holland. Ne`Ne` had made the joke about the people thinking Sandy was a cop, but the statement was true unbeknownst to Mary and company. "These people aren't nice down here in the Ninth Ward," Mary said lowly as Sandy rode slowly down Louisa Street.

Sandy was now ready to leave, but seeing Mary's sadness had fueled her. She sped up a little and came across a park that was on Benefit and Louisa Street where she saw a bunch of people hanging out so she swerved her car around and headed back to the park. She pulled up to the curb and got out and walked up to a group of men standing on a basketball court and asked boldly. "We looking for a Sam Holland! Anybody know where this man at? His name is Sam Holland!"

The men all looked at Sandy, who was dressed in a pair of navy blue Capri's, white tank top and white sneakers. They looked at her gold teeth, her freckled face turning flush under the hot sun and one of them asked, "Who the fuck is Sam Holland? Ain't *nobody* named Sam back here! Take your country ass back to tha' trailer park! Wanna be black ass," he stated as the group laughed.

"Fuck you, cuz!" Sandy said as she backed up towards the car while eyeing the group of men with a snarl. The young teen then went up under his shirt. "Pull that mutherfucka, cuz!" Sandy yelled as she walked back to the driver's side of the Caprice where her .9mm under the seat.

Sandy was going for her gun, but Mary intervened. "No! No! We, we not from around here!" Mary yelled aloud to the men.

"I know that, bitch! Take y'all asses back ta' the country." the young teen said to Mary as Sandy reentered the car.

Mary said nothing to the young teen as she stared at him coldly. Ne`Ne` was about to speak out, but Mary shushed her. *"He lucky he got that gun, or I'll beat his face for cursing at me."* Mary said to herself as she eyed the young teen as Sandy pulled away from the curb. Mary could hear the group of males laughing at her as Sandy pulled back into the traffic flow. She was mad she had been cursed out by a teen younger than her daughters.

Sandy drove off grabbing her .9mm from under the seat. "These mother—, these people down here is *crazy*," she yelled as she pounded the steering wheel in anger. Sandy then swerved right onto Pleasure Street. She didn't know where she was going, and the ride was getting deadlier and deadlier for her, Mary, Ne`Ne` and Dimples.

Sandy drove to a stop sign and paused then sped through the intersection straight into the Desire project. She was riding up the street, the car bouncing furiously as she drove faster than normal with two cars approaching from the opposite direction.

"They not gone stop!" Dimples said from the backseat. "They not stopping! Sandy get over!" she yelled aloud.

Sandy was outraged, however; all Mary wanted to do was find her brother. They were in the same neighborhood where Sam Holland once owned a bar, but no one who Sam Holland was? Sandy *knew* they were all being lied to and it was hurting her to have to see Mary have to tolerate getting cursed out and having to risk her life in order to try and find her brother. Sandy thought about those things as she pulled over, Ne`Ne` and Dimples pleas from the backseat, and Mary's urging helping her to remain focus. Sandy clutched her .9mm as a money green Cutlass with a gold grill and triple gold Daytona rims rolled by slowly. The man behind the steering wheel eyed Sandy from beneath a pair of mirror tinted sunshades and had a cold-hearted look on his face that displayed only one question, *"What the fuck you doing back here?"*

Sandy stared back and clutched her .9mm tightly as the man rode by, staring back at her. She was so close to them man she could see her reflection in his sunshades. Mary eyed the man as well, and he in turn stared at her for a few seconds before he spat on Sandy's 18" chrome rear wheel and continued riding by. Sandy knew she was being provoked, but for Mary and her daughter's sake, she let that one slide, besides that, there were two car loads of people rolling by. She clutched her .9mm, making sure the man in the first car didn't stop and open his doors. If he did, Sandy was ready to open fire on the man. The second car then came into view, a navy blue four door Park Avenue, and Sandy eyed a muscle-toned man around her age with thick braids and tattoos and a mouth full of gold teeth.

"Get the fuck from back here white girl before you get you and the rest of them people fucked up!" the man yelled.

Sandy said nothing as she stared straight ahead, her legs shaking furiously as her nerves were bad. She eyed the man out the corner of her eyes. If he got out his car, Sandy would open fire.

"Manny! Leave them people alone! Hurry up man, Oscar leaving us!" a young female teen yelled causing Sandy to relax a little.

"Say, say, Katrina," Manny replied as he stopped his car. "Chill out! I got this right here! I'm looking out for people!"

"Why you helping them? Let Oscar do what he do, Manny!" another young female teenager remarked from the backseat.

"Tanaka? You gone make me bat the piss out your skinny black ass today! Shut the fuck up!" Manny yelled before he turned his attention back to the people in the white Caprice. "Country girl," he said with a smile, "they plotting on ya' baby! Get the fuck outta here! Straight up that way and go left at the end of this street! You go to the right, they gone fuck over ya' big time! They want that car! Don't go right I'm tellin' ya'!" Manny ended as he turned up his stereo and rode slowly pass Sandy.

"He told that girl he gone bat the piss out her!" Ne'Ne' remarked as she and Dimples giggled at the man's remark.

Mary nudged Sandy's shoulder and she pulled off. The group from Mississippi didn't know it, but they had just stared death in the face. The man driving the Cutlass was named Oscar Henderson, a well-known serial rapist and a killer. He was driving Mary's nephew, her brother Sam Holland son's car this day. Mary didn't know that she had a nephew and she would remain ignorant to the fact that she had just crossed paths with the people who knew of Sam Holland, and ran with Ben Holland, her brother's son. Oscar and Manny would have gladly led Mary to Ben had all the information been known to them, but on this day, Oscar was planning on car-jacking, in his eyes, not family members of Ben Holland, but just a group of four females whom no one in the Ninth Ward knew. He was also planning on kidnapping and raping Sandy before he killed her; he wanted 'the white girl'. Oscar knew they were from out of town so they were easy marks to the man.

Manny had told Oscar that they were probably lost, but Oscar said he didn't care. If they made a right turn and crossed Benefit Street, he was going to car-jack Sandy, Mary, and her daughters and take Sandy somewhere and do her dirty. Lucky for Sandy, or maybe lucky for Oscar, because Sandy was strapped and ready to fire, Manny was on hand this day to prevent the drama from unfolding, telling Oscar to wait until they circled around. Sandy actually had planned to make a right turn onto Desire Street and travel through the project. Manny didn't agree with 'killing the white girl and car-jacking a grown woman and two kids, maybe the black lady's kids. He'd given the people in the Caprice fair warning; but that was about all he would do, because if they went to the right, he wasn't going to stop Oscar from going through with his plan.

Manny watched over his back seat as 'the white girl' rode up the street quickly and made a left turn and headed out the project. He then smiled to himself, knowing he'd done a good thing, even if he didn't know the people whom he had saved. Satisfied that 'the white girl' was leaving the Desire project, Manny continued on down Pleasure Street going on with rest of his life.

"They not gone help us. We gotta find another way because if we keep circling this neighborhood, we gone get ourselves killed." Sandy said as she left the Desire Project.

Mary then had another idea. She hated to, but she had Sandy drive back to the burned out lot the grey-haired man had pointed out earlier and wrote down the real estate company that owned the land. She tracked the company down and pleaded with the agent on duty to give her the names of the people who once owned or leased the place, explaining her situation to the man and he went into the company's data base and printed out a copy of the owners. Mary scanned the short list and saw her brother's name. She found an address and the agent gave her directions to a street in New Orleans East.

Mary was now all smiles. Being from Ghost Town, where most of the people were friendly, well hell, they even had a street named Friendly Lane, back in Mississippi, Mary, and Sandy as well, thought they could just ride down to the Ninth Ward and ask someone if they knew Sam Holland and they would gladly tell them. The Ninth Ward, as Mary and her daughters, and especially Sandy, had come to learn, was a den of vultures. They had come real close to being killed, but all-so close to finding out the truth about Sam Holland's son as well. If the people that knew Sam had a son named Ben Holland had only cooperated on this day, the Holland family's course of history could've been greatly changed in July of '94, but the family would have to wait for that day to come, if ever it would arrive.

Mary talked about the things she'd witnessed and experienced the whole ride as they made their way out to New Orleans East. "God, those people back in the Ninth Ward were terrible! Why be so mean?" Mary asked.

"Mary, look like they got it bad back there and they stick to their own kind. If they don't know you, you on the outside. They not crazy, they just, they just doing what we do back in Ghost Town. Somebody ride through asking for y'all, I'll say the same thing—I don't know nothing. I wouldn't do like they did, bouta shoot people and all that, but still, I wouldn't tell a bunch of strangers I knew y'all."

"I understand Sandy, but you not like them. You not like them."

"You kidding me? I'm exactly like them, Mary!" Sandy said through laughter. Sandy didn't know how Mary took the statement she just made, but what she truly meant was that she could be just as ruthless as the people in the Ninth Ward. Sandy knew she had just ridden through a gangster set and to her, the Ninth Ward was just like Ghost Town and many of the other neighborhoods in Jackson that she often hung out in, only bigger.

"So, Ne'Ne' and Dimples, what's the first thing you gone say to your uncle when you meet him?" Mary turned and asked her daughters as Sandy let the top down on the Caprice.

Ne'Ne' and Dimples quickly huddled together. Mary watched as her daughters came up with a statement to ask their uncle when they first lay eyes on the man. They giggled under the hot sun and turned and said at the same time, "Where you been, Unk?"

Mary burst into laughter. Sandy chuckled, but she wasn't as excited as Mary and her daughters because she had seen the neighborhood in which Mary's brother once owned a club and had a different take on the matter. In her eyes, the place was hard-core. Sam's club was destroyed. The Ninth Ward was violent in her eyes, and if Sam had a club down there, it was a good possibility he was a player and had met a tragic fate. Sandy knew how the game went, and her gut instinct, based on the place where Sam Holland once hung out, told her that Mary's brother was either dead or in jail, but in spite of her silent objections, Sandy still hoped for the best right along with Mary and the twins because she believed on her heart that the family deserved a happy ending to this episode.

They rode down Haynes Blvd and found the street where Sam resided and pulled up in front of the address Mary had found and Mary jumped from the car like a little girl and ran up to her brother's door and tapped lightly. The neighborhood was a nice upper-middleclass neighborhood with huge homes and neatly kept yards. Mary stared at the area with an appreciative look upon her face and came to the realization that her brother was a success. He was a homeowner, owned a club once, and resided in a nice, quiet neighborhood, which was a far cry from the place she called home back in Jackson, Mississippi. Sam Holland, in Mary's eyes, was doing great things in life.

Sandy, Ne`Ne` and Dimples were impressed as well. They had never seen such beautiful homes up close. Homes that reminded them of the houses at the opposite end of Ghost Street where the white people resided. "My uncle rich!" Ne`Ne` said aloud as she and Dimples bounced in the backseat.

Mary rung the doorbell repeatedly, when she got no answer she looked around the neighborhood. Remembering that a petite, young, black female had pulled up to the home directly across the street and exited a Mazda 626 and entered the house across the street when she and the group first pulled up, Mary decided to walk over and ask if the people inside that home knew her brother. The people in this neighborhood seemed less aggressive than the people she'd encountered in the Ninth Ward and she felt more comfortable walking over and asking about Sam Holland.

Mary walked up the sidewalk and rung the doorbell once and waited patiently. Before long a young black man opened the door and asked, "Can I help you?"

Mary could see right away that the young man had been

crying, but she just had to ask about Sam. "Yes," she replied with a smile, "my name is Mary Holland. I was wondering if you knew the whereabouts of Sam Holland? He lives across the street over there."

The young man seemed as if he had to think for a minute before he recalled who Mary was referring to. "Sam, Sam, ohhh *Gabriella and Sam*." he then stated.

"Gabriella?" Mary asked.

"Yea, that was his wife."

"Calvin, talk to me!" the young petite woman Mary had seen earlier yelled as she had returned to the living room. Mary then knew that the two occupants of the home were arguing and quickly sensed that she was intruding, but she just had to find out about her brother. Out of respect, and not wanting to upset the young man further, Mary asked, "Did I come at a bad time?"

"Actually you did," the young man replied as he stared back into his home. He then turned to Mary and said, "But umm, Sam, his wife Gabriella, and their daughter was killed in January of 1984. They got killed. They all dead."

Mary screamed in shock then began to cry. "Oh my God! I'm, I'm sorry for bothering you mister."

"How you related to Sam?" the man asked as Mary walked away.

"He was my brother!" Mary replied as she ran back to the car.

The man stared at Mary as she ran back to the Caprice. He'd forgotten to mention Ben Holland and Ben's aunt Henrietta; he knew them both, but he hadn't seen them since a week after Sam and his wife and daughter were killed in 1984. He also wasn't thinking clearly because he was arguing with his wife, who had cheated on him and he had no time to entertain a woman who was asking about a family who had died ten years ago; but when he remembered Ben, he stepped out his door to tell Mary that Sam had a son, but Mary and company had already left. The man's wife reentered the living room just as he was closing the door and the two of them returned to their own business, going on with the rest of their lives.

As Sandy rode away, Mary broke the news. It was devastating news for everybody. Sandy was hurt, but she wasn't shocked. The Ninth Ward had taken Sam's life. Mary found her brother's obituary from an old news article at the public library. It was true. Sam, Gabriella, and Samantha Holland were all listed as being dead; having perished outside a motel in Kenner, Louisiana. Samantha Holland, who was only three days old at the time, had been listed as being burned to death inside the motel room and the article didn't list any survivors. The reason being was Ben Holland's aunt, Henrietta Jenkins, feared for her and her nephew's life. Henrietta knew who had killed her brother-in-law and her sister Gabriella and her niece Samantha, and she didn't want the man to track her and Ben down. And Mary didn't know that Sam's sister-in-law Henrietta, and Sam's son Ben Holland even existed in 1994 because the obituaries listed no survivors. And at the same time, neither Henrietta, nor Ben Holland knew that Samantha Holland had actually survived the fire and had been kidnapped by Sam and Gabriella's killer.

Samantha Holland was living in Kansas City, Missouri in 1994 with her parents' killer. Henrietta was leading a life separate from Ben Holland in New Orleans; the two of them were on bad terms. Mary and her bunch were residing in the state of Mississippi, and Naomi Holland was nowhere to be found in 1994. The entire Holland family was scattered during this period of time and the survivors knew not of the other's existence in some cases, and knew not the whereabouts of the ones in which they knew existed.

Mary rode back to Jackson, Mississippi a heartbroken, and disappointed woman and her daughters were hurt as well. The family all wished they had never learned the truth about Samson, especially Mary, because for her, not knowing the truth had kept Sam alive in her heart and mind. As long as Mary was living, to her, so was her brother Sam. Learning the truth had taken away the images inside of Mary's mind of what she perceived her long lost brother to be like. It would take a while to get over the entire scenario that had transpired during the trip to New Orleans.

The Holland Family Saga Part Five

CHAPTER 27
THE FOOLISH ONE

Ne`Ne` and Dimples were roller-blading down Casper drive on a hot summer afternoon in August of '94, a month after their mother had learned that her brother was dead. Martha had received the news when the group from ghost Town visited and it pained her heart so bad she couldn't sleep right for over a week. She'd stayed in from work for two days straight and the next couple of weeks were hard on the woman. Twiggy was a big help during that time; giving encouraging words, and sitting up with Martha during those times. Martha then began praying to God that Naomi was all right, because in her eyes, if Sam, the only male Holland family sibling had suffered a terrible fate, and she was behind bars, then how good could Naomi's situation be? Mary was the only one of the Holland siblings doing okay. Martha had hit a low point in August of '94, but she still pressed on, looking forward to the day she would be released and she would be reunited with her sister and nieces. Martha then decided that if Naomi hadn't been found by the time she got out, she would work to get her money back from the bank and search for her older sister.

Ne`Ne` and Dimples had a hard time dealing with the fact that there uncle was dead as well. To cheer them up, Mary began to teach the girls to drive. Ne`Ne` and Dimples had both gotten their learner's permits just over a week ago and would sometimes take turns driving their mother's Cutlass to and from Chug-a-lug's and Fukutoo's, and Sandy had also allowed them to use the Impala a few times with Mary's approval to drive to Kroger's Grocery Store, which was nearby the neighborhood. The twins loved the Impala, it was a drop top, and it had hydraulics and a killer sound system. They rarely drove it; but if they asked Sandy, and their mother agreed, they could use the car for an hour or two.

Mary had also taken the twins to the shopping mall the weekend after she got back from New Orleans. She had to buy their school clothes anyway, and it was during that time that she had purchased three sets of roller-blades. For almost three weeks, Mary could be seen gliding down Friendly Lane, her daughters following close behind. They would skate up to Dairy Queen and sit there and eat ice cream, before long, the twins had gotten over the disappointment of not ever even had the chance of knowing their uncle. It was a sad time for the Holland family, but Mary had helped her daughters get over what happened to Sam, and during that time she too healed; and Mary, just like Martha, began to wonder about Naomi and her whereabouts.

Resources and information concerning lost relatives were scarce during the early nineties, and Mary knew not where to begin to look for Naomi. She hoped that someday, somehow, just like the man she had come across that knew her brother Sam, that somebody who knew Naomi would ask her if she was Naomi's sister. Mary didn't know how Naomi looked; but she hoped desperately that she looked like Naomi so someone could see the resemblance and ask. At various times, she would walk down along the docks, making sure truck drivers noticed her in hopes that someone would ask did she have a sister named Naomi. Mary only got ogles, and asked out on dates, the same looks and questions she received before she found out about her brother, but she too, like Martha, kept pushing on through life with the hope that someday, Naomi would be found.

Ne'Ne' and Dimples, both dressed alike in blue jean shorts, and blue tank tops with their hair roller wrapped and wearing identical helmets, knee pads and elbow pads, laughed aloud as they glided down Casper Drive speaking to people they knew. The twins' we were replicas of their mother and aunt, only darker and a little shorter. They stood 5'6" and weighed 135 pounds. Their short and sexy frames swayed back and forth to the delight of some of the older men in the neighborhood as they glided down the street, their pert, firm-looking bubble butts bouncing and jiggling as they paraded on their skates. Their toned caramel skin glistened in the hot sun, and there sexy, dark eyes teemed with joy as their pouty sexy lips parted revealing pearl white teeth. Seventeen year-olds Ne`Ne` and Dimples were a delightful sight to behold as they skated down the middle of Casper Drive through Ghost Town, laughing loud and immersed in peace and innocence as they made their way over to Sidney and Paulette's house, the only two girls they now hung out with in Ghost Town.

Fifteen year-old Sidney and sixteen year-old Paulette had stopped hanging in Ambush after Urselle was killed. The two sisters were doing the best they could to stay out of trouble, but they were having a hard time just making it in life because their mother was a severe heroin addict. When Ne`Ne` and Dimples realized a while back that Sidney and Paulette didn't have any summer clothes, the twins went to Sandy and told them of the girls' plight and she agreed to help. Sidney and Paulette were embarrassed at first when Ne`Ne` and Dimples had told them what they'd done, telling the twins that they didn't want to have to keep asking Sandy for things. They told Sandy how they felt about the matter also; but Sandy still took it upon herself to buy the sisters some summer clothes anyway.

Sidney and Paulette were grateful to Sandy, and to show their appreciation they began to do all they could to please Sandy, which included staying out of Ambush and going inside early. Although she was running the streets, Sandy wanted better for the twins, Sidney *and* Paulette because they were the only ones in Ghost Town that she could seem to reach and she was having success in her endeavors. Sandy Duncan could have been an excellent social worker or child therapist, but she had already made her career choice and she didn't want the four teens to follow in her footsteps. She often told the four teens that "shit ain't a joke out here", and the four teens bore witness to Sandy's words in November of '93 with the death of Urselle and when she and Simon murdered the two men who'd killed the young teen the same day. Sandy was like a big sister to Ne'Ne', Dimples, Sidney and Paulette and to make her proud was what they wanted to do most, especially for Sidney and Paulette, who's needs were now being met by 21 year-old Sandy Duncan.

As they rounded the curb and skated onto White Street, the twins' smiles quickly dropped when they saw a girl named Latasha Scott standing with Sidney and Paulette in the sisters' yard. Latasha Scott was Sidney and Paulette's cousin. She was from Philadelphia, Pennsylvania and she had come down to Jackson two weeks earlier to live.

The moment Sandy saw the sixteen year-old she knew she was going to be trouble.

"How you know she mean bad?" Ne'Ne' asked Sandy one night during the latter part of August after the twins and Sandy had first met Latasha, who was a 5' 7" 145 pound red-boned female with short curly hair and big round brown eyes. Latasha was a cute female, but her disposition is what made her ugly. She had a condescending attitude towards others, often talking down to people as if she was above them all; and since she was from a bigger city up north, she viewed the people down south in Ghost Town as slow and country. Latasha failed to realize that the people in Ghost Town may have been country, but they weren't slow. The people running the streets in Ghost Town just had a more laidback "it's a done deal already" type of attitude when it came to matters of the streets. They had their *own* style of hustling. Ghost Town and Jackson, Mississippi itself did the same things that people in Philly did, sometimes worse, albeit on a smaller scale. People like Sandy Duncan and Simon Charles could survive just about anywhere, and they could care less about where you were from—to them it was where you were at in their eyes—and Latasha Scott was now on Ghost Town's home turf.

Sandy pondered those thoughts before she answered Ne'Ne's question that day, two weeks earlier and responded by saying, "Because Ne'Ne', Sidney and Paulette momma hooked on heroin. She barely home, and she spend all day gettin' high and shit."

"And?" Ne'Ne' asked.

"They momma on heroin! She not takin' care of her *own* two daughters and now she got another mouth to feed? I'm tellin' ya' that bitch Latasha running from *somebody* or *something* back in Philly! And now she run her stupid ass down here and she gone fuck it for everybody! I should just get her dumb ass out the way!" Sandy stated angrily.

Ne'Ne' and Dimples knew Sandy was thinking about killing about Latasha, but they didn't quite understand what she meant that day when she said Latasha was "gone fuck it up for everybody"; but they soon understood what Sandy was trying to say concerning that matter because Latasha wasn't in town a week and she had stolen a car and tried to get her two cousins and the twins to ride with her, but they'd all refused. The next day the car was found behind Fukutoo's. Since then, nearly every other day a stolen was car was found in or around Ghost Town. The 'hot spot' had made the news and Latasha bragged on what she had done. Latasha, to put it simply, did foolish things in the streets. Everybody else that ran the streets in Ghost Town was trying to get paid, but Latasha was out there trying to get a reputation as being a 'bad ass', but to the people in Ghost Town, however, she was just foolish. Nobody cared about the fact she was from Philadelphia and the people in Ghost Town didn't operate the way Latasha Scott operated; still, she kept up with her foolishness until Sandy checked her, in Ambush one day, telling her to stop stealing cars leaving them in the neighborhood, "Your ass makin' it hot around here for everybody," she said to Latasha's face. Latasha stopped stealing cars, but she quickly began doing other things outside of Ghost Town and no one cared or paid her no mind. So long as she didn't make it hot in Ghost Town again, no one cared what Latasha Scott was doing.

The twins skated over to Sidney and Paulette's yard and asked them were they ready to skate. Latasha stared at the two seventeen year-old twins before she laughed aloud and said, "Yesss indeed. Y'all two bitches seventeen and still skating? That shit played out in the eighties!"

"We wasn't asking you! And if you get smart with ya' mouth

again I'm a bat the piss out your ass today!" Ne`Ne` snapped as she held onto the sisters' gate, repeating a statement she heard during her trip to New Orleans.

"Your country ass Ne`Ne`? Everybody country around here man! And you and Dimples is still some li'l girls. Seventeen and still roller skating and shit? When I was in Philly we used to—"

"Nobody don't care about what you did in Philadelphia, Tasha!" Sidney snapped as she and Paulette began walking out the yard.

"They can't skate anyway 'cause they ain't got no skates!" Latasha snapped to the twins.

"Sandy didn't get y'all skates?" Dimples asked.

"No, man. She was supposed to been back so we could ask her again, but she and Simon still out." Paulette replied.

"Say, y'all? Let's go page Sandy and ask her and my momma can we use the Impala and go to the mall and buy the skates ourselves!" Ne`Ne` suggested.

The four teens giggled as they began making their way back to the twins' house. Latasha heard they were about to ride in the Impala and she wanted to ride with the girls. "Let me ride out with y'all to the mall, Folk!" she said aloud.

"We ain't Folk!" Dimples remarked.

"We li'l girls remember?" Ne`Ne` chimed in. "Why you wanna hang with li'l girls?" she then asked as the four teens laughed and skated and ran away from in front the house, leaving Latasha all by her lonesome. "Stay ya' happy ass right there!" Ne`Ne` concluded as she and 'Dimples' skated away, Sidney and Paulette running to keep up with the two as they rushed to the twins' home to call Sandy and Mary.

Latasha walked up Casper Drive all the while hoping her cousins and friends could not ride in the Impala. She was 'hatin'' on the twins and her cousins at that moment. Her hopes were dashed when she saw the black Impala slowly emerged from Friendly Lane. Latasha was near the corner of Friendly Lane and Casper Drive when she eyed the Impala.

Ne`Ne`, who was driving, spotted Latasha walking up the sidewalk with a begging look in her eyes and she hit the switches and made the car pancake up and down as she turned onto Casper Drive.

Latasha quickly grew envious of the twins and her cousins as she watched them ride out of Ghost Town. "Okay," was all she said under her breath as she continued walking up towards Friendly Lane.

Meanwhile, Ne`Ne` and company had to go over to *Mugsies Pool Hall* and meet Sandy, who had Sidney and Paulette's money. They pulled up to the pool hall in North Jackson and saw Simon standing out front with a few gang members from the neighborhood. He slapped boxed with the girls playfully and watched the car as all four teens went in to see Sandy. The teens entered the dimly lit structure, *Creepin' Onna Come Up* by Bone Thugs in Harmony blaring across the juke box in the nearly empty pool hall and saw Sandy, wearing Twiggy's gold bracelets and dressed in black baggy Girbaud's jeans, and a black wife beater wearing a blue bandanna and blue Adidas Forum tennis shoes, sitting at the bar with a stack of cash laying before her on the bar's counter. The girls knew not how much money Sandy had in her possession, but the pile of hundreds, fifties and twenties let them know that it was a vast amount. An AK-47 lay beside the money along with a bottle of Kentucky Bourbon.

"You know them li'l girls, Sandy," the bartender, a mid-fifties black man who did business with Martha and Twiggy back in the day named Mugsy, asked as he eyed the front entrance.

Sandy looked and smiled when she saw the teens and she beckoned them over. Sandy was at the height of her criminal career in August of '94. She and Simon were making plans to buy *Mugsies Pool Hall* soon, as Mugsy was retiring, and go legit. The two had found their ticket out the game and were making plans to marry soon after they bought the place. Sandy was getting close to realizing the dream she and Simon had for themselves and she was giving back to Ghost Town unconditionally in the process. Her crystal blue eyes lit up as the teens approached and she brushed her shoulder length brown hair from her face and stretched her arms and gave each girl a hug.

"Awwww! These my *babies* right here!" Sandy said aloud to Mugsy then asked, "So, y'all enjoying the Impala?" The teens all answered yes.

"Umm, Sandy," Sidney then asked shyly, her dark eyes peeking from beneath her neatly braided hair, "school coming up and me and Paulette, well, if you don't wanna do the skates? Me and Paulette could use some new outfits for school —if you don't mind. If not we'll just take the skates—but we just thought we'd ask because with school coming up and all, the people be laughing at us and if you don't dress right they be—"

Sandy reached into her pile of money and did a quick count and cut Sidney off by saying, "Here! This six hundred dollars. Get some clothes *and* the skates! That's all I can let go right now, but at least y'all will have something to wear when school open. Where Latasha retarded ass?"

"She back in Ghost Town." Paulette answered.

"Good! That foolish bitch right there? She gone fuck it up for everybody, man! Y'all stay outta Ambush and stay away from Latasha ya' hear me?" Sandy asked as she eyed the teens with stern eyes. The teens nodded and Sandy grabbed her AK-47 and walked them out of the pool hall, leaving her money on the bar counter.

"Sandy, your money!" Dimples said as they walked to the door.

"Nobody don't mess with nothing up in here, Dimples! We damn near own this place! Y'all go straight to the mall and head back to Ghost Town. I'm a see y'all later."

The four teens play-fought with Simon again before they hopped back into the Impala and went on to the mall where it took a little more than two hours for Sidney and Paulette to finish shopping. They then drove back to Ghost Town, arriving a little after 5p.m. The sun had went down a bit and the twins were planning on dropping off Sidney and Paulette's clothes by Clark's house so their mother wouldn't steal and sell the items, and then skate until the sun went down completely.

When they passed the twins' house, however, the girls saw Mary and Loretta running up and down Friendly Lane. Somehow the chickens had gotten out of the chicken coop. Loretta's gate was left open as well and Mary and Loretta were trying to chase down over a dozen chickens. The teens joined and quickly helped capture the birds, all-the-while believing they knew who had done the deed. Once the birds were all rounded up, the girls told Mary and Loretta their beliefs. Nobody had ever touched the Duncan family's birds all the years they'd been living in Ghost Town until Latasha showed up. All fingers were pointing to the Philadelphian, but Loretta, Mary and the four teens had no proof, so they had to let that one slide. The four teens did get to skate that day, in spite of the mishap, and they did so throughout the remainder of the summer and most of the school year until the weather grew cold.

****

In January of 1995, just after the Christmas and New Year's break, Latasha had finally gotten enrolled into Callaway High; but even there, she caused trouble with her foolish behavior. She was suspended in February after being caught stealing from the girls' locker room. One of the girls who Latasha had stolen from took the matter to heart; she also knew she was kin to Sidney and Paulette and because she couldn't get to Latasha, she and her gang of girls took their frustration out on Sidney and Paulette, beating the two sisters bad enough that they had to go to the hospital where Sidney received stitches over her left eye and Paulette had bruises on her back from where she'd been stomped on when she was knocked to the gym floor. From that point forth, the girls who'd beat up the sisters, started to pester Ne`Ne` and Dimples, who were close to Sidney and Paulette.

Ne`Ne` and Dimples often exchanged words with the girls and stood their ground avoiding fisticuffs, but Latasha, fearing a beating because she had no backup, quickly dropped out of school half-way through the month of February. It was during this time that Latasha began to delve into another criminal venture, the very same venture that had forced her away from Philadelphia, PA. Just as Sandy said, Latasha was "fucking it up for everybody".

Latasha recognized and understood fully the fact that she was making life difficult for the twins and her own cousins, but she didn't care. If they weren't with her, they were against her in her mind. She returned to her old hobby and was getting away with it without fail. She had plans on showing Ghost Town how they did things up north in Philadelphia. She had big dreams, anxious to show-off for her cousins and the twins and show-up Sandy Duncan at the same time. Latasha Scott didn't know it, but her stealing from the locker rooms in school, her returning to her old hobby, and the ambition to pull rank on Sandy Duncan, would have devastating repercussions not just for Ghost Town, but the city of Jackson, Mississippi itself.

CHAPTER 28
MARCH 22, 1995

"So umm, the concert is coming up tomorrow in J-town on the campus of Jackson State University, we want everybody up there to come and out and show love for TLC and especially my girl, Bree!" Misses Jones stated over the airwaves during the 7 'o' clock hour of the Fantastic Four Show.

It was a warm night, March 20, 1995, two days before Mary and Martha's 36th birthday and the day before the night of the TLC concert and Ne`Ne`, Dimples, Sidney, and Paulette, who all had tickets to the event, were sitting in Dimples' bedroom listening to the radio show and eating Fukutoo's. Sidney and Paulette's were sponsored by Sandy, and Mary had gotten her daughter's tickets the day they went on sale. The girls were having a good time in Dimples' room, eating Fukutoo chicken plates and listening to the music and discussing the topics amongst themselves. Ne`Ne` had been trying to talk to Misses Jones the whole week, and on this night, the phone was ringing.

"Hey caller, you on with Misses Jones! Who this?" the Deejay asked as the song Tootsie Roll by the *69 Boyz* played in the background.

"This Ne`Ne`!"

"Happy Birthday Ne`Ne`!" Misses Jones yelled over the music.

"You always do that! My birthday is in June! June!"

"Alright li'l sister! No need ta' get feisty! So what's hatning?"

"Nothing, I just wanna shot out ta' Ghost Town and ask could you play TLC song Red Light Special? And I'll take my answer off the air!" Ne`Ne` said laughingly. The four teens knew Misses Jones hated that statement so Ne`Ne` decided to say it so she could get a reaction from the Dee-jay. When Rene hung the phone up Dimples turned the volume up on the radio to see what Misses Jones would say.

"Now see! Stop the train! Stop the damn train!" Misses Jones said as the background music faded out, "Ne`Ne`," she continued, "see Ne`Ne` and her gaggle of hens done just triededed me! Let me get them straight right quick! You don't call here, make a statement and then hang up Ne`Ne`! Or, or take your answer off the air, Ne`Ne`! You lucky I ain't able to make it out there this weekend 'cause if I was, I'll hunt you and your gaggle down and ruffle y'all feathers! Don't call my show ask a question and then, take it off the air. And what the hell you know about a Red Light Special anyways? I'm a tell ya' momma! Ne`Ne` momma? They listening, they umm, hold up…that is a hot jam! Shot out to J-Town!" Misses Jones said as the four teens burst into laughter just as TLC's song Red Light Special began to play. "This here for my home girl Ne`Ne` and her posse up there in J-Town and they gettin'—as all y'all up there in J-Town should be doing—they getting ready for the concert at Jackson State University this weekend starring TLC and featuring my girl, Bree! I'm Misses Jones and you're listening to the Fantastic Four!"

The twins and their two friends were on the floor laughing. Misses Jones had shouted them out big time and they were simply thrilled. When the radio show ended at eleven, Sidney and Paulette returned home. When they got there, they saw Latasha sitting in their bed room with a huge garbage bag filled with marijuana resting between her feet rolling a blunt that was as thick as an adult index finger. She had given the cousins' mother some of the marijuana and the woman quickly left the house to sell it so she could buy heroin and get her fix. Latasha was also planning on selling some of the marijuana in Ambush. She offered some of the weed to Sidney and Paulette and the two sisters refused and walked out of their room as Latasha called them cowards.

Sidney and Paulette would never tell what they had seen on this night. They stayed away from Latasha the whole night, sleeping by Clark's house on the sofas. The next morning, Sidney and Paulette and the twins were waiting for the school bus and Latasha was out there with them, mocking the girls by calling them nerds. They ignored her taunts just as they heard a rumbling sound coming down Casper Drive. The girls looked up the street and saw a black convertible Mustang being driven by Sandy. The four friends cheered as Latasha rolled her envious eyes. Sandy got out and showed off her new '95 Mustang 5.0. The car had a white rag top, gold Daytona rims and all white interior with black trimming. The sound system was nice as well.

"Sandy, when you get this car?" Ne'Ne' asked as she sat behind the wheel briefly and eyed the interior.

"Last week! I got it out the shop this mornin' though! Fresh ain't it?" the four teens all gave Sandy her props on her new whip. "Hey," Sandy then said, "I'm a drive this, and y'all momma said y'all can use the Impala tonight!"

The four teens cheered aloud and clapped their hands. They were even more surprised when Sandy tossed them the keys to the Impala, announcing that Mary had allowed them to drive the car the entire day since they'd gotten their license a month earlier. Today was a special day; the four teens were going to their first concert and were going to have a fresh ride, and new outfits to wear. They could hardly wait until school was over. They ran to Loretta's yard and jumped into the Impala, leaving Latasha standing alone with the other school kids before she left as she was being ridiculed at the bus stop by the other kids, who'd all witnessed how Sandy had acted as if she had never even known her. Latasha walked away sadly, the seventeen year-old felt embarrassed and had nothing to do except to go home and get high.

****

The Holland Family Saga Part Five

It was now two hours before the concert and the four teens, wanting to get there early, were getting dress by Mary's house. Mary had to work the following morning and she had a dinner date this evening. Since the concert was scheduled to start at 7:30p.m., and conclude at 10p.m. Mary asked her daughters if they would like to eat some cake with her when they returned and they agreed. By 6p.m. everyone was ready and they were now standing in Mary's backyard preparing to leave. The twins were dressed in high, but loose-fitting white jean shorts, blue and white 'G-Nikes' with ankle high socks, white blouses and wearing their gold medallions. They had never worn them before, but on this day, they went all out. Mary smiled at her daughters and took their picture in the backyard. She then took Sandy's picture and Sidney and Paulette's picture and took group photos as well. It was an exciting night for the twins and their friends.

"Don't forget, we eating cake when you girls get back so don't get too full of that concert food." Mary stated as she watched her daughters run to the Impala. "Okay momma! Love you!" they yelled in unison while hopping into the Impala, Ne`Ne` behind the wheel.

Sidney and Paulette ran towards Sandy's mustang. "I got the front seat!" Paulette yelled as she hopped into the front seat.

"Man you beat me! I was gone call for the front seat!" Sidney said through laughter as she jumped into the backseat of Sandy's drop top.

"Sandy, take care my babies!" Mary ran and yelled before the five females pulled off.

"Don't worry Miss Mary. We going see the show and come right back!" Sandy yelled from her convertible Mustang.

The crowd at Jackson State was huge this night. Ne`Ne` and Dimples followed Sandy down the drive leading onto the campus blasting *Creep* by TLC as they hit switches on the car. Teenagers, and college students alike were trying to hollar at the twins and Sandy and the two sisters as well. People were everywhere, females were out in daisy duke shorts, doing raunchy dances, trying to attract the males' attention, and the males were pulling up in fresh whips, dressed in their most expensive outfit and wearing all the jewelry they possessed, looking to take a female home or to the motel for some fun after the concert.

The twins weren't there to get picked up; but when they found a parking spot beside Sandy, they did take a few numbers. So did Sidney and Paulette, who were dressed the same as the twins, only they wore all blue with white on white 'G-Nikes', their hair neatly braided. Sandy wasn't interested in numbers. Simon was her baby. She thought of him most of the time, wondering where he was on this night. She knew Simon wasn't going to attend the concert; he and Clark were going to hangout outside the auditorium and maybe shoot dice and meet up with the girls back in Ghost Town. TLC really wasn't they boys' flavor for a concert, but they were out and about scoping females and just kicking it with fellow Folk Gang members.

The concert got underway on time and the five females were a few rows back to the left of the stage on the football field with a good view. They watched the singer Bree perform first and she was real good. "That's the next Janet Jackson!" Sandy said into Dimples' ear as Bree sung an up-tempo version of *Again*, originally sung by Janet Jackson.

Bree warmed the crowd up, and TLC came on and closed the football field down. When they performed the song *What About Your Friends* and had the Jackson State Tigers cheerleaders on stage with them doing a hype dance routine, the girls in the crowd went wild. TLC sung songs off their two albums and closed out with the song Waterfalls, where sprinklers beside the stage shot water into the air. The water cascaded down onto the stage gently, wetting TLC and their dancers, who all wore tight silk dresses, and giving them true sex appeal throughout the extended, sensual version of the song they were doing.

When the concert ended Sandy and the girls looked around briefly for Simon. Sandy thought about paging him from the dining hall, but the crowd in and around the building was massive; looking for him would take a while and she'd promised to bring the girls right back. She would catch up with

Simon in Ghost Town was her reasoning. As Sandy and her group walked back to their cars, they were approached by another group of girls and one of them ran up and snatched Dimples' medallion off her neck. Dimples grabbed her neck checking for blood while trying to find out who snatched her chain. Seconds later, she saw the same girl that Latasha had stolen from earlier in the year at Callaway High School.

The girl, named Sasha, told Dimples that was "for hanging with them two bitches and they thieving ass cousin", referring to Sidney and Paulette and Latasha. Dimples wasn't hearing that shit, she charged the girls, so did Ne`Ne`, along with Sidney and Paulette. A crowd soon encompassed the girls and some people scrambled to get away from the ruckus. Dimples knocked Sasha down to the ground and Ne`Ne`, Sidney, and Paulette got the better of the other two females just as a crew of G-Queens who hung around *Mugsies* with Sandy approached the scene, along with V-Queens from Sasha's neighborhood.

The girls separated and joined their respective gang and began taunting one another. Sandy knew this episode could end badly, and rather than engage the girls and have the G-Queens fight, she pulled the twins, Sidney and Paulette back.

"Sandy this shit ain't over! I got you and your girls! I best not catch them hoes by they self!"

"You ain't gone fuck with us, bitch!" Ne`Ne` yelled.

"I'm a kill you and your sister!" Sasha yelled.

What Sasha said at that moment was a statement Sandy could not let slide. She walked back through the G-Queens and said, "You fuck with anybody from Ghost Town you gone have ta' deal with me!"

"Who the fuck is you?" a V-Queen around Sandy's age asked angrily.

"The bitch that's gone bring an end to all the high-cappin' y'all ugly hoes talkin' over there! It's best you ask somebody!"

"Come on, sisters," another V-Queen who knew of Sandy's reputation said. "Now ain't the time or the place," she ended as she wrapped her arm around Sasha's neck and whispered in her ear, "Let's go call your brother."

Sandy was busy trying to gather up her girls because security was now approaching the scene. The fight had died down, but Sandy had missed the play with Sasha and the other V-Queen talking. Had she seen the two, she may have been more alert and played things out differently on the college campus; but instead, that one unwittingly lack of attention would change the course of life for many people.

The girls cautiously made their way back to the cars, ever on the lookout for Sasha and her crew. Dimples had found her chain and was trying to repair it along the way. The girls made it back to their rides safe and left Jackson State undisturbed and headed back to Ghost Town, arriving just before 10:30p.m. Sandy pulled over at Chug-a-lug's and told them all not to speak on what happened and had run into Simon at the same time.

"How the concert was?" Simon asked as he and Clark leaned up against the white Caprice smoking a blunt and drinking a couple of forty ounce bottles of Crazy Horse malt liquor in front of Chug-a-lug's.

"It was good, Folk. Hey, I got something to tell you," Sandy said in reference to the fight. "Let me get my girls situated and I be right back up here. Save me some weed, too."

"Better hurry up!" Simon replied through light laughter as Sandy and the girls pulled off.

Mary was inside putting the finishing touches on her cake when the two cars pulled up onto Friendly Lane. Sidney and Paulette hopped out and began walking home, telling the twins that they would talk about what happened at the concert the next day. Sandy hugged the two and went into her home to use the bathroom whilst Ne`Ne` and Dimples went to check in with their mother. When the twins entered their home, they saw their mother putting icing on the vanilla cake she had baked. "How long on the cake, momma?" Dimples asked as she opened the cabinets and grabbed three saucers.

"About, about fifteen minutes. I want the icing to sit for a little bit," Mary replied before she licked icing from her fingertips.

Ne`Ne`, upon hearing her mother's answer, returned outside and sat in the Impala and listened to the last portion of the Fantastic Four Show. She thought about calling in to tell Misses Jones about Bree and her performance, but Sandy had rushed out and called her inside Loretta's home.

At the same time, Mary had just realized that she had no candles for the cake. She'd prepared to ask Ne`Ne` to ride her up to the store, but when she looked outside the screened back door, she saw that Ne`Ne` was gone. Not wanting to take her own car, because it had been running hot all day, Mary and Dimples decided to walk to Chug-a-lug's and buy some candles.

Meanwhile, inside Sandy's house, Ne`Ne` stared at the scene that lay before her eyes. The home had been ransacked. The two walked through the area looking at the damage in wonderment. Clothes were everywhere, furniture was upturned. Somebody was obviously searching for something. Sandy ran to her room where she had her money and AK-47 hidden in the vent at the base of the wall behind her bed had saw that it had been shifted slightly. Whoever was searching wasn't strong enough to move the bed; that was Sandy's assumption, and right away she had an instant moment of clarity concerning who was behind the act. She slid the queen-sized bed from against the wall, opened the vent and began grabbing neatly bundled stacks of money.

Ne`Ne`, still standing in the living room, had witnessed Sandy run out the room with the money and disappear into her mother's room before quickly returning empty handed. "Help me hide this money again real quick Ne`Ne`." Sandy said lowly.

Ne`Ne` had never seen so much money in her life. She knew Sandy had money, but she never figured Sandy had such a large amount hidden in her home. They each made two more trips before the money was transferred. Having hid the money elsewhere in the house, Sandy grabbed her AK-47 and ran back to the living room to use her house phone to call Simon at the pay phone up to Chug-a-lug's. The pay phone outside Chug-a-lug's began to ring and a female answered.

"Hello," the female said.

"Eh who this?" Sandy asked in a desperate tone.

"Who this?" the female asked in return.

"Never mind! Just ask if Folk out there!"

"What?"

"Just ask if that got Folk out there!" Sandy yelled.

"They got Folk out here?" Sandy heard the woman ask.

Simon heard the woman asking the question and looked her way. "Yea, yea," he answered as he walked over to the phone. "Thanks Folk," he added as the woman walked away. "Hello?"

"Simon?" Sandy asked.

"Yeah, what up Sandy, girl? You better come and get some of this weed before smoke all this shit," Simon said jokingly, flabbergasted off the weed he'd smoked.

"Eh look—that bitch—that bitch Tasha broke in my momma house and I'm goin' back there and kill that bitch tonight!" Sally yelled angrily.

While Sandy was explaining to Simon what transpired, Mary and Dimples walked up to the entrance of Chug-a-lug's. Dimples spoke to Clark as he gave directions to a white male. When Dimples noticed Bree, the lady who sung at Jackson State, walking towards the store's entrance from the opposite direction, she tugged on her mother excitedly and said, "She was singing tonight! She a star momma!"

Mary smiled at the woman, who held the door open for her, and the three females walked inside. "Bree, how long you been singing?" Dimples asked excitedly, unable to believe she was in the presence of a professional singer.

"Just about all my life! You enjoyed my performance?" Bree asked Dimples

"Hell yeah! My friend Sandy said you the next Janet

Jackson!"

"Tell her I said thanks for the compliment! Ohhh, they got fun-dip and watermelon now-laters in here! Girl, this candy is taking me back to when I was in elementary school and used to sneak out of class!" Bree said as she grabbed a handful of now-laters and a fun dip.

Mary, Bree and Dimples then walked around the store, Dimples in awe of the singer, who gave up her real name, Brianna Stanford. Dimples kept asking Brianna about TLC as she loved their music.

"TLC is like the title of their latest album, girl—crazy, sexy and cool. All three of 'em is laid-back and I like that about them. That's how the south roll, you know? We laid-back like that. I love they music, too! I was lucky to get these gigs with them given how popular they are." Brianna replied.

"You on the road with them?" Dimples asked.

"Umm hmm. We got Atlanta and Memphis coming up next week." Brianna remarked just as Mary found the candles and the three females walked towards the counter.

"Man, wait until I tell Sandy 'nem! I'm a say to everybody 'I met the next Janet Jackson'!'" Dimples stated as Brianna paid for the items she purchased and Mary's candles as well.

"Well, that was nice of you Bree." Mary stated.

"Not a problem. Your daughter and her friend made my night! I love Janet Jackson! And to be compared to *her*, in *my* eyes? Is the *highest* compliment! Here," Brianna then said to Dimples as the three females headed out the door, "this is my upcoming CD. Let me sign it for you."

As Brianna, Dimples, and Mary stood in the doorway of Chug-a-lug's, and whilst Sandy was explaining over the phone to Simon that she was headed over to Sidney and Paulette's house to confront Latasha—gunshots erupted from a red drop top Cadillac Brougham that had pulled up in front of Chug-a-lug's.

Mary saw the gunfire erupting from the guns and she turned and screamed as she shielded Dimples. She fell forward and felt a sharp burning sensation, then pain in her back.

At the same time, over one hundred miles away in Grenada, Mississippi, Martha, who was sound asleep, leapt from her bed, sat upright, clutched her back and screamed aloud in pain, "Mary!"

Martha knew at that moment that something had happened to her sister. Mary had told her years ago when Martha was shot, that she had felt Martha's pain and now Martha was experiencing what Mary had once told her. She just knew something awful had happened to her sister, but was helpless to do anything about it.

Twiggy leapt from her bed and knelt down before Martha. "What's wrong, Mar," she asked worriedly.

"My sister!" Martha cried as she stared Twiggy in the eyes. "Mary! Somebody hurt Mary!"

"Guard! Guard!" Twiggy cried out.

Corrections officers approached Martha and Twiggy's cell and she said aloud, "She clutching her back in pain! She need a doctor!"

The guards opened the cell and rushed Martha to the infirmary, nut she was still in a state of flux. "My sister! Twiggy! Somebody hurt Mary! She my sister! Somebody call my house! Marrryyyy!" Martha screamed as she was ushered away.

Twiggy was now concerned. She knew of the twins' sharing of pain, and something about this night was beginning to take on an eerie feel up in Grenada, Mississippi. Twiggy hoped for the best, but the manner in which Martha had freaked out told her that it would be a long and arduous journey to make it to daylight—and only then would Martha's fears be denied or confirmed.

****

While Martha was being taken to the infirmary up in Grenada, back down the road in Jackson, Sandy Duncan and Rene Holland could hear the gunfire coming from the beginning of Casper Drive. Sandy dashed out the door with her

AK-47 in hand. "Come on Ne`Ne`!" she yelled as she ran to her Mustang.

Sandy got into her car and peeled off, with Ne`Ne` following close behind in the Impala. As she approached Chug-a-lug's, Sandy recognized the red Cadillac, and could clearly see the shooters, who sped off when they saw the two cars approaching from Casper Drive, believing reinforcements from Ghost Town were arriving on the scene. Sandy pulled into the parking lot, Ne`Ne` following close behind, and she began screaming Simon's name aloud before she even got out her car. Sandy was screaming hysterically as she hopped from her Mustang and ran towards Simon, who was laid out on his back next to his white Caprice.

The discombobulated young woman knelt before Simon and stared in stunned silence as her jaw hung low. Sandy could see brain matter oozing from Simon's cranium. Simon had run from the payphone when the gunfire erupted and was attempting to retrieve his .45 Glock from the front seat of his car when he was cut down. Simon Avery Charles died in Ghost Town on the corner of Casper Drive in front of Chug-a-lugs at 10:47p.m. on March 21, 1995 at the young age of twenty.

Ne`Ne` jumped from the Impala and walked over to Chug-a-lug's entrance in utter shock. She could hear her sister screaming, and had seen Clark clutching his side in pain as he ran past her, "Vernon District! Them niggas from Vernon District hit us up, Folk!" Clark yelled to Ne`Ne` as he ran down Casper Drive back into Ghost Town. Clark would later be taken to Sacred Heart hospital and undergo surgery.

Ne`Ne` walked over to the entrance to Chug-a-lug's and knelt down and her eyes began to water. "Momma," she cried. "Regina what happened?"

"Ne`Ne`! Oh my God! They shot momma! They shot momma!" Dimples yelled as she lay beneath a non-responsive Mary.

Sandy ran up to the entrance of Chug-a-lug's and when she saw Mary laid out, she turned away and shut her eyes tight, clutched her fists and held back tears. *"Not Mary!"* she said to herself. "Mutherfuckas!" she then yelled as she regained her composure, turned and ran back towards Mary and the twins and heard Mary gasp. "We gotta get her to the car," Sandy quickly stated to the twins. "Y'all momma still alive!" she yelled as she gently rolled Mary over off of Dimples. "She still alive." she then said lowly.

Mary's eyes were open, she had blood around her lips and she was trying to speak, but every time she did, she only choked on her own blood. "My, mmmy, ba, mmmy babies," Mary said as she coughed up blood and her body began to tremble.

"We right here, momma!" Ne'Ne' and Dimples said simultaneously.

"Let's take her to the hospital! Come on!" Sandy yelled, her loud voice snapping the twins from their shock. The trio carried Mary to the Impala and Ne'Ne' got behind the wheel with Dimples in the back seat begging her mother not to die. "Hurry up Rene!" Dimples screamed as she and her sister peeled off in a desperate attempt to save their mother's life.

Sandy got in her Mustang and was preparing to follow the twins to the hospital. It was then that she heard the pleas of two men begging her for help. "Help us! Help!" one of them men yelled just as Sandy was about to pull off. Sandy looked back and saw that it was the lady from the concert on the ground clutching her neck as blood trickled between her fingers. *"She fucked up!"* Sandy thought briefly about pulling off, but she knew the young woman needed help and she was going right to the hospital anyway.

"Cuz," Sandy yelled aloud as she threw her car in park, "Put her in here," she said as she got out and pulled the front seat of her Mustang forward. "Come on man!"

The men hurried the singer Bree to the car and placed her in the backseat and Sandy quickly got behind the wheel and sped towards the hospital. Sandy was an emotional wreck at this moment. As she rode, hearing the men's pleas for the singer Bree to remain calm, the singer's legs kicking her backseat furiously as she was obvious pain, Sandy thought of Simon, knowing he was dead and grew angry. She then thought about

The Holland Family Saga Part Five

Mary and Clark, who'd ran off to God knows where. She also thought of the person responsible for breaking in her home, and ultimately, the shooters who'd opened fire on innocent people. The singer kicked Sandy's seat so hard once more, it snapped her from her trance.

"Y'all was at J-State tonight huh?" Sandy asked as she approached the hospital.

"Yea that was us! All she was doin' was singin'! We got lost! Why they shoot up the fuckin' corner? What they was shootin' at us for?" one man asked from the backseat.

"They wasn't after y'all cuz—they was after me!" Sandy replied just as she swerved into Jackson Memorial Hospital emergency room's entrance.

Mary, meanwhile, had already been rushed into surgery by the time the singer Bree was removed from the Impala. Dimples was outside of her mother's operating room with a face full of tears and frantically asking the many nurses that were going in and out of the room was her mother still alive. She thought Ne`Ne` was beside her, but when she noticed her sister was missing, she screamed Ne`Ne`s name aloud and rushed to find her twin and tell her to stay with her and Mary. Dimples ran out to the front of the hospital and saw the Impala, the doors wide open and the backseat coated with Mary's blood, parked in front the entrance—Sandy's Mustang, along with Sandy and Ne`Ne` were nowhere to be found.

"Nooo!" Dimples screamed through her tears as she looked around before realizing Ne`Ne` had left with Sandy. "Ne`Ne`! Nooo!" she yelled before she ran back into the hospital, distraught out of her mind.

****

Sandy Duncan and Rene Holland were now headed towards Vernon District. Sandy was behind the wheel of her Mustang explaining to Ne`Ne` that the shooters were two of the girls they had fought at Jackson State. Another shooter was a male.

Sixteen year-old Sasha and her girlfriend, seventeen year-old Anita, and Sasha's nineteen year-old brother had retaliated.

Sasha told her brother, who was a high-ranking Vice Lord from Vernon District, that Sandy and her crew had jumped on her and knocked her out; and that fueled her brother's desire to retaliate. Sasha knew where the girls were from and she'd guided her brother towards Ghost Town. The three rode past Fukutoo's and Dairy Queen headed towards Casper Drive and when they saw the group of people out in front of the store they assumed they were all Folk members. Zeke, Sasha and Anita opened fire with three Mac-11 semi-automatic sub machine guns and shot at everything and everybody in sight before they sped away—but they battle wasn't over just yet.

Sandy had just turned down a side street and pulled over in the middle of the block. She reached under the driver's seat and came up with a .9mm and popped the trunk and jumped from the car and went and grabbed her AK-47 and several clips from a secret compartment and ran to the passenger side and had Ne`Ne` drive as she armed the weapons. Sandy was making Ne`Ne` use a lot of side streets so as to avoid the police as she guided her towards Vernon District. As she guided Ne`Ne`, Sandy began duct taping two banana clips. She then armed the .9mm and placed it Ne`Ne`s lap and said, "Just point and shoot that mutherfucka when we get there," before she jumped into the backseat with her AK-47 and continued guiding Ne`Ne` to Vernon District.

Ne`Ne` turned onto a gravel road just before the railroad trestle leading into the neighborhood and followed the trestle's descent. The gravel road ran into a two-lane road where Sandy instructed Ne`Ne` to make a right turn, cross over the railroad tracks and drive towards the YMCA. "If you see that red caddy, let me know," Sandy said just before she laid down in the backseat.

Ne`Ne` crossed the tracks, but she was driving a little too slow as she entered the neighborhood. "Speed up just a little Ne`Ne`. Just be cool and act like we just riding through." Sandy whispered as she lay on the back floor board of her mustang with her locked and loaded her AK-47.

Ne`Ne` had been driving Sandy's mustang with a nonchalant look on her face the whole time. The teenager was feeling pure rage. All was on her mind was that somebody had shot her mother. She clutched the nine millimeter in her lap and scanned the block, the mustang's engine humming lowly as it cruised down the street.

At the same time Sandy's heart was racing. She thought about how she loss Simon, having never said good-bye. Never even thinking he would die so suddenly. She was heart-broken knowing the last image she would remember of the life she had with Simon would be that of him lying dead with his skull blown open. Sandy also couldn't get the image of Mary with blood running from her mouth out of her mind. She'd seen the shape the humble woman was in before she was taken to the hospital and she squinted her eyes and shook off the thought of Mary, who would never hurt a soul, having been killed just for walking to the store with her daughter. Sandy knew what she and Ne`Ne` were about to do on this night—but fuck it! This was something she felt needed doing. Sandy was close to exiting the game, but from this episode she could not walk away. Somebody had to pay this very night. There was no way Sandy was not going to retaliate for what happened to Simon and Mary.

"Nobody in front of the Y?" Sandy asked lowly.

"This whole block empty."

"Alright, take the next right and roll pass that store on the corner." Sandy remarked as she shifted on the backseat.

Ne`Ne` drove the car towards the store steadily thinking about her mother. She also felt that she should have stayed at the hospital with Dimples, but she wanted to kill the people who had shot her mother more than anything else. Ne`Ne`s eyes watered as the red Cadillac came into view and she thought of her mother, whom for all she knew, could be dead now, and it fueled her anger. Rene Holland was now staring directly at the people responsible for shooting her mother in the back and without notifying Sandy, she raised her arm right, aimed the .9mm, and opened fire, releasing a volley of bullets into the night air as the car cruised slowly pass the corner store.

Sandy heard the gunfire and she rose up from the backseat

and unloaded with her chopper. Sasha tried to jump from the backseat of her brother's Cadillac, but Ne`Ne` hit her two times in the right side and once in the back, cutting her down before she could escape. Sasha fell over the side of the car, her body convulsing from the bullet wounds.

Her brother Zeke was struck multiple times by Sandy's AK-47 in his right shoulder, the right side of the neck and in the back of his head. He fell over dead in the front seat behind the steering wheel of his car. Anita was inside the store buying blunts when the gunfire erupted and she and the cashier had taken shelter behind the counter.

Ne`Ne` rounded the curb in Sandy's Mustang and Sandy continued shooting at everything and anything in sight from the backseat. Bullets from her AK-47 cut through the night air at a fast and furious pace and the gunfire was so intense Ne`Ne` could literally feel the Mustang vibrating from the firepower unleashed from Sandy's AK-47. "Slow the car!" Sandy yelled, causing Ne`Ne` to bring the car to a slow roll in front of the store.

There was a dead silence for a few seconds as Sandy flipped the clip over to reload the rifle and opened fire again. AK-47 shells spewed onto the floorboard and leather seats of Sandy's Mustang, burning the seats and carpets as Sandy shot up the Cadillac, bursting its tires, shattering the glass on the store front, and unloading another round of shells into Sasha and her brother. Sasha died on the scene a few seconds after her brother passed away, half of her body lay outside the car and her legs were still inside the car on the backseat, she was nearly cut in half by the bullets from the AK-47. The sixteen year-old's blood flowed profusely onto the concrete. Brain matter from her brother's torn skull and her guts were splattered throughout the car's white interior and their blood began to pool together on the car's carpet.

Sandy and Ne`Ne` then sped back to Ghost Town, but when they got there, they saw the police had Friendly Lane and Casper Drive blocked off. Ne`Ne` quickly turned into the neighborhood before Ghost Town and Sandy, who was still shocked by the loss of Simon and the possible death of Mary, paid it no mind as the two approached the back entrance to Ambush.

Ne`Ne` turned onto Ghost Street and was halfway to the cul-de-sac when two males dressed in all black stepped out from the woods on the right side of the road. Sandy saw them first and she opened fire over the top of the windshield as Ne`Ne` slammed the car in park and hopped out and began firing the .9mm. The two men laid down flat and Sandy took the time to make her way from the car just as the men opened fire on her and Ne`Ne` again. Shots were ringing out violently in the back of Ghost Town, and Loretta, who was home trying to figure out what happened to her home, and making phone calls to the hospital to find out about Mary's condition and the whereabouts of her daughter, grabbed her heart when she heard the gunshots coming from Ambush. She quickly ran from her home screaming Sandy's name as she headed towards the wooded trail.

At the same time, Ne`Ne` was back peddling as she shot her weapon, but the moment she ran out of bullets, she saw a bright flash and everything suddenly went black. Ne`Ne`'s body stiffened and she dropped the gun and fell to the ground on her back, her arms spread wide and her eyes closed.

Sandy, meanwhile, had cleared the two shooters, but she heard one of the men yelling aloud to the other to finish off Ne`Ne`. Those words hit Sandy Duncan, who was in the clear and home free, way too hard. All she had to do was run alongside the wooden fence she was hiding behind and disappear back into Ghost Town, but she just couldn't find it within her heart to leave Ne`Ne` behind. Sandy knew Ne`Ne` shouldn't have even *been* with her on this night. She also knew she should have waited instead of retaliating; but her anger had blinded her judgment to the point of error. With that in mind, Sandy quickly made the decision to go back for Ne`Ne` and stepped into view just as one of the gunmen aimed his weapon at her friend.

"Leave her alone!" Sandy said as she aimed her weapon at the two men.

The first man froze, his gun still aimed at Ne`Ne`, who lay

motionless.

"Where my fuckin' weed bitch?" the man asked as he pointed his weapon at Ne'Ne'.

"I don't have no fuckin' weed! I don't even fuckin' know you!"

"How 'bout give us our shit and we even?" the second man remarked in a heavy Jamaican accent.

"I don't know what the fuck you talkin' about!"

"Sandy?" Loretta yelled aloud as she tripped over an unknown object at the foot of the trail leading into Ambush before she hopped up and continued running towards the cul-de-sac.

Loretta's voice only increased the tension between Sandy and the two unknown assailants.

"We can deal with this shit later, cuz! Let her be!" Sandy yelled, her eyes darting and back and forth quickly as she watched both men.

"You shoot him I shoot you! You let him kill that blood clot and we even!" the man with the Jamaican accent propositioned.

Sandy wasn't about to take that offer, however; she opened fire with her AK-47 and killed the man standing over Ne'Ne', but his counterpart opened fire on her in return. Sandy was running to her left blasting back at the second man when she saw quick flashes and everything suddenly went black.

Loretta emerged from the wooded trail a few seconds later and ran up Ghost Street towards her daughter's car, which was idling softly with the headlights running, top down, the windshield shot out and both doors wide open. The distraught mother stood before her daughter's car and shook her head from side and pleaded to God that what she saw in her mind and felt in her heart was not on the other side of the car blocking her view. She walked slowly, crying, repeatedly telling herself she was dreaming, having a nightmare. Loretta cleared the rear of the car and fell to her knees and screamed aloud when she saw her daughter lying on her side motionless.

The horrified woman could see her daughter's intestines hanging out her back as she scampered over to Sandy desperately, begging God for mercy and screaming aloud. When she got there, however, Loretta could see what terrible shape her daughter was in. Sandy was not moving and was turning dark. Loretta then looked over to Ne'Ne', who lay still on her back, her chest stained with a dark-reddish hue, and could only scream in agony over the carnage that lay before her eyes as she called out for help. Ambulances were soon on the scene and Ne'Ne' and Sandy were quickly transported towards Jackson Memorial Hospital.

****

"What happened?" Ne'Ne' asked herself as her eyes slowly opened.

Rene Holland now found herself staring up at a bright light. A thick plastic tube was inserted into her esophagus, she could feel hands on and inside her, beepers from equipment that was all around her were sounding off in rapid succession, and people were yelling orders and telling her to fight. *"Fight for what? Where am I?"* Rene Holland wondered.

"Rene! Don't die I love you! Rene! That's my sister let me go!"

"Dimples?" Rene asked herself.

"Why she telling me not to die? What happened?"

"Get her outta here! Rene, hold on baby! Just hold on for me!" another female voice, that of the doctor's, said in a desperate, but caring manner as she tried to place a clamp onto one of Ne'Ne' severed arteries.

Ne'Ne' was still unaware of the situation she was in, but she was slowly beginning to figure it out. *"Hold on for what? What happened? We was riding home and then—"* Ne'Ne' then slowly remembered what happened. She remembered shooting a girl, then shooting at a man who was shooting back at her. She then remembered she saw a flash then everything went black. *"I got shot! Oh my God! I got shot!"*

The realization of what happened to her had caused Ne'Ne' to grow scared, and to go into shock. *"Somebody shot my momma! Where my momma? Momma! Mommmaaa! Momma..."* would be the last thought that she would ever have before her eyes slowly closed and heart stopped beating. Doctors tried for over six minutes to revive the teenager for a second time, but it wasn't meant to be. The realization and shock of what happened to her was just too much for her body to bear. Rene was pronounced dead at 12:53a.m. on March 22, 1995, having died on her mother's 36th birthday after suffering a single gunshot wound to the chest from a Glock-11. Rene "Ne`Ne`" Holland, was only seventeen years-old.

Sandy Duncan's fight was still on-going. She lay naked on the operating table covered in her own feces. She was urinating and defecating uncontrollably. Doctors were rinsing and wiping her body free of blood and bodily wastes as they tried to stabilize the young woman, who was writhing about on the operating table fighting for her life. Sandy knew exactly what happened to her; but she also had the pressure of knowing Simon was dead, witnessing Mary get shot in her back, and ultimately witnessing Ne`Ne` get blasted in Ambush on her mind, on top of the trauma she herself had suffered. *"I shoulda waited. I fucked up. I shoulda waited. That bitch Tasha. We shoulda never went home that way...I'm sorry Ne`Ne`..."* would be the last thought that Sandy Duncan would ever have. Her crystal blue eyes watered, she slowly stopped moving, the sounds grew fainter and suddenly—everything went black.

Doctors tried for almost eight minutes to revive Sandy Duncan because she was moving her eyes and she was somewhat responsive during the ambulance ride, but in the end, she, too, lost the fight for her life. She died with her eyes open at 1:01a.m. on March 22, 1995 after suffering five black talon hollow tip bullets to her abdomen from an AP-9 semi-automatic. Sandy Duncan, was only twenty-one years old.

The Holland Family Saga Part Five

CHAPTER 29

NEVER AGAIN

Dimples had been sedated the night before after seeing Ne`Ne` being brought into the emergency room and learning that she had passed away. The seventeen year-old was lying in a bed next to her mother, who was in critical but stable condition as she lay in a bed beside her daughter. Mary could hear, but she couldn't speak. She knew something terrible had happened because she heard Dimples' repeatedly crying and asking God why.

Mary's face was twitching uncontrollably. She wanted to speak but couldn't. She had so much to say to her remaining daughter, knowing she had lost Ne`Ne` over the manner in which Dimples was crying and saying how much she was going to miss her sister. The heart-broken mother wanted to know how and why she had lost one of her offspring because both were well before she was taken to the hospital. The loss of Rene Holland was the only thing keeping Mary alive. She knew she had to be there for Dimples because if she were to die, Dimples would be a seventeen year-old parentless female growing up alone in a harsh place called Ghost Town. Mary was fighting hard not to let that happen. *"Momma's here baby, just, just hold on,"* she thought to herself as she listened to the incessant sobs emanating from Dimples' mouth. The pain of hearing Dimples cry and the loss of Ne`Ne` hurt Mary more than the bullet that had once been lodged in her upper back; and for Dimples' sake, Mary was doing her best to hold on.

The Holland Family Saga Part Five

Loretta Duncan was at the police station at the time. She, too, was reeling from the death of *her* daughter. The woman was in shock over the events that had transpired the previous night. Seeing her twenty-one year-old daughter laid out with her guts spilling into the streets would be an image forever impressed upon Loretta Duncan's mind. The pain of what happened to her daughter was too much to bear. Loretta was planning on moving away from Ghost Town and the state of Mississippi entirely as she sat and waited to be interviewed by the authorities and to identify a possible suspect that was apprehended near the scene.

Meanwhile, in Grenada County Jail, Martha Holland had just been released from the infirmary. She had spent the night there, and believing that something had happened to Mary, she called home but got no answer. Martha and Twiggy soon rejoined one another and Twiggy called her home but she herself got no answer. Twiggy then called Loretta's house and had got no answer there either. It was then time for breakfast. The local news usually started at 8a.m. so Martha and Twiggy weren't paying any attention to the TV until they saw that the seven 'o' clock national news had been replaced by the local news crew in Jackson, Mississippi. Both women turned their attention to the TV as they listened to the report with the rest of the prisoners.

"We're going live to Jackson, Mississippi to cover a shocking and very tragic news story," the reporter began. "In what has to be one of the bloodiest nights in the history of our beloved state since the Jackson State killings of 1970 where two people were shot and killed and twelve wounded, nine, I repeat *nine* homicides in a span of four hours took place in various parts of our state's capitol. Police and citizens are outraged at the violence overtaking our state's capitol and local pastors, and angry citizens alike are all calling on the local police and state politicians to step up and in, to put an end to the senseless violence."

As they listened to the reporter, both Martha and Twiggy just had a gut feeling that Ghost Town was somehow involved in the violence. Martha had the feeling the night before, and seeing the breaking news only confirmed what she had been feeling. The two women watched and listened as the news team shifted to Jackson Memorial Hospital where another news team member gave another live report.

"What we know so far is that all of these homicides are related. Police say it all started with a fight after a local concert featuring the hit R and B trio, TLC. That fight led to a shootout on a corner in a notorious neighborhood known on the streets of Jackson, Mississippi as Ghost Town. In that shootout, an up-and-coming singer from New Orleans who goes by name Bree, and a local woman named Mary Holland, were shot and both women sustained serious injuries. Police tell me that the doctors are saying that both women are expected to survive. Twenty-one year-old Simon Charles was pronounced dead on the scene of the violent shootout and another male was transported to Sacred Heart Hospital and is listed in good condition. Police say the group of people were all just—"

Twiggy yelled aloud, drowning out the TV as she leaned forward and pounded the table. Martha, at the same time, screamed after learning of Mary's plight and got up and leaned against the brick wall and grabbed her arms as she stared back at the TV with a face full of tears. Prisoners stared at the two realizing they were related to the people involved in the homicides and some began surrounding the two and offering their condolences.

The news team then shifted to Ghost Town where another reporter began to tell what transpired in Ambush. "It is here, on this lonely gravel road that seventeen year-old Rene Holland and twenty-one year-old Sandy Duncan's life came to a tragic end," when Martha heard her niece's name, she went hysterical, screaming her niece's name as she pounded the concrete wall before turning around and sinking slowly to the floor in a state of shock and disbelief. Guards soon entered and removed Twiggy and Martha from the tier. They needed not to find out about the fate of their family in which the manner it was being presented to them on this day.

Martha was allowed to call Jackson Memorial and check on Mary and it was there that she made contact with Dimples, who told her that Mary was okay, but Ne'Ne' had died on the operating table. Simon Charles and Sandy Duncan were dead as well. Sidney and Paulette, along with their cousin Latasha had been killed also. Martha hung up the phone crying heavily and broke the news to Twiggy, she was glad Mary and Dimples were okay, but losing Ne`Ne` was a crushing blow, and Twiggy had to face the fact that her nephew had been killed along with Sandy. Both women would lay in their cell in total silence and faces full of tears the duration of the day.

The city police along with detectives were still trying to tie in all the pieces. Sandy Duncan had died believing Latasha had gotten her and Ne`Ne` killed—and she was right; but Sandy didn't know the full story and she wasn't alive to tell what she believed. Sidney and Paulette knew part of the story as well; but they were also deceased. After interviewing Loretta, and Clark, who lay in his hospital bed, and statements given by a few residents from Ghost Town who knew the families, homicide detectives filed their report and began an investigation. People everywhere were talking about the shootings; authorities had the official report, but the story on the street went as follows...

...Two days before the concert, the day Ne`Ne` and Dimples were skating, Latasha had broken into a home in the neighborhood behind Ghost Town. She had done it once the day before and she went back to break into another home the following day, which was the day the twins were skating. There she found a trash bag full of marijuana. It was the same marijuana she had tried to get Sidney and Paulette to smoke with her the day before the concert. What Latasha didn't know was that she had broken into the home of some Haitians from Miami who were planning to set up shop in Jackson, Mississippi.

Latasha Scott had stumbled upon fifteen pounds of marijuana. It was the biggest lick of her life, but she would pay dearly. The two men weren't stupid. They knew Ghost Town was a rowdy neighborhood and before they expanded their search, they scoped out Ghost Town. On March 21, 1995, the night of the TLC concert, the two men walked down into Ambush and saw Latasha posted up selling drugs. Sandy and the four teens were at the concert along with Clark and Simon, so Latasha was in Ambush by herself that night trying to sell the weed she had stolen. The men recognized their product after Latasha had sold them a bag of weed and drew weapons on her, asking her what was she doing selling their product. Latasha, scared for her life, lied and said "that white girl in the Mustang" had stolen it and gave it to her to sell.

The men asked for the name of the girl who'd stolen their product and Latasha told them "Sandy Duncan". The men had heard of Sandy, she was going to be their competition in Jackson so she was already being watched. The men then asked who else was with Sandy and Latasha then lied on her cousins. Latasha was forced to take the men to her home and they were going to wait on Sidney and Paulette. They got her to tell them where Sandy lived while they were waiting and one of the men went and ransacked Sandy's home searching for his product as the other held Latasha hostage. When he didn't find his stash, the man returned to the sisters' house and saw that his counterpart was raping Latasha.

The men then took turns raping the young female, using her mouth and vagina to their satisfaction as they waited for the sisters. Latasha had thrust herself into a living nightmare, and in a final attempt to save her life, she told the men that Sandy had taken the stash and gave it to her cousins. "My cousins know where it's at! They moved it to Sandy boyfriend's house!" Latasha screamed through her vaginal assault.

"Where that nigga stay?" the man asked as he hopped off Latasha.

"I don't know for sure! He stay where Sandy stay!"

"We went there! No marijuana! Where is our marijuana, blood clot!" the man asked as he raised a machete before Latasha's face.

"I don't know! I don't know! Mister, please!" Latasha begged for her life without success. The two men slit her throat and hacked her body with the machete and left her naked on the bedroom floor to bleed to death.

When Sidney and Paulette entered the home, seventeen year-old Paulette was taken and made an example of to instill fear into her sixteen year-old sister. Paulette was hacked to death in the living room in front of her younger sister as the men asked repeatedly where Sandy's boyfriend resided. Sidney led the men to the Charles' home and they had searched that home as well, without success. By then the police were all over the front of Ghost Town processing Simon's murder scene after he'd been shot by Sasha and her group. The men walked Sidney back through the trail leading to Ambush and there they waited for someone who knew where Sandy Duncan's boyfriend was located to step into Ambush. The men never knew Simon was already dead and his death was the reason the police cars were out in front of Chug-a-lug's.

For over an hour the men waited with a terror stricken Sidney until she saw Sandy's car traveling up Ghost Street. Hoping she would be spared, Sidney pointed to Sandy's car. One of the men then hit Sidney in the neck with the machete, nearly decapitating the sixteen year-old's head. She was dead before she hit the ground. It was Sidney's corpse that Loretta had tripped over as she ran towards Sandy.

The men then ambushed Sandy and Ne'Ne', but they shot back at the men under the belief that they were being retaliated against by Vice Lords from Vernon District. They never knew the shooters they had encountered had nothing to do with what transpired at the concert, nor the shootout in front of Chug-a-lug's. These attackers were after the marijuana Latasha had stolen two days earlier. This tragic situation was started a month earlier when Latasha got caught stealing from Sasha inside the girls' locker room. That was mistake number one.

The second mistake came when Latasha started breaking into peoples' homes in the next neighborhood, only she had entered the wrong house the day before the concert. Latasha never figured the people in the home would find out who stole their drugs, but her foolish actions had caused the death of Simon Charles, and had caused Mary and a person who merely got caught in the cross-fire to be injured; but the repercussions of her actions weren't completed. Latasha then lied on her cousins and Sandy Duncan—mistake number three—as it led to the deaths of not only Latasha herself, but that of her two cousins, along with Sandy and Ne'Ne'.

The Holland Family Saga Part Five

Sandy believed she and Ne`Ne` were drama-free after killing sixteen year-old Sasha and her brother. Only Latasha had more secrets that went unbeknownst to just about everyone on Ghost Town at the time. Only Sidney and Paulette knew Latasha's secret, and had the two sisters told Sandy they had seen Latasha with a trash bag full of weed from the get-go, Sandy may have been able to prevent everything from happening and thus save her own life, Ne`Ne`, Sidney, Paulette, and even Latasha's life as well. Sidney and Paulette didn't want to rat on Latasha, however, even if she was wrong. Their inexperience prevented them from making the right decision. They should have told Sandy the moment they learned Latasha was breaking into people's homes in the next neighborhood.

Sandy, Ne`Ne`, Sidney and Paulette had nothing to do with what went down with Latasha Scott and the Haitians, but because she had lied and stole, she not only got herself killed, she caused the death of her two cousins, Rene Holland, and Sandy Duncan. Just as Sandy had said over and over again, Latasha Scott had indeed, "fucked it for everybody", and even *she* paid with her own life. Never again will Ghost Town see such a rash of brutal, horrific violence.

****

A week later, Dimples and Loretta pulled together to bury Rene, Sandy and Simon, all of whom had just enough insurance to cover expenses. Sidney and Paulette were buried by the city in a potter's field the same day since their mother had no life insurance on her daughters. Loretta, having found the money Sandy stashed away in their home, which totaled just under $47,000 dollars, and learning the manner in which Sidney and Paulette were buried, paid for the sisters' headstones. Martha and Twiggy weren't allowed to attend the funerals because Ne`Ne` and Simon weren't considered immediate family members. They were devastated by that fact. They sat in their cell the day of the funerals reminiscing; before long they were laughing as they relived some of their fondest memories. A prisoner had snuck the two some homemade wine and they got drunk as they talked about the Fukutoo Prank Mary played, the rims Twiggy forced Simon and Sandy to steal and how Ne`Ne` had given up the streets.

They were laughing on the outside, but inside, both women were torn apart by the loss of their family members. Together though, they would heal as they had both suffered similar losses at the same time.

Mary, meanwhile, couldn't make it to the funerals either as she was still in intensive care; but she knew, she just knew she had missed saying good-bye to her daughter. She would lay in tranquility, patiently awaiting the day when she could get up and run to her daughter's grave and say all she had to say to Rene Holland.

A news reporter was on hand at Sandy, Simon, and Ne`Ne`s funeral. The 31 year-old reporter, a black female named Georgette Grayson, seemed to take a sincere interest in Dimples' plight. She knew Dimples had lost her identical twin and her mother was still in the hospital in intensive care with a bullet wound to the back. Georgette had asked Dimples how she felt about the things that happened to her family as she sat beside her. Dimples was reluctant to speak, so Georgette acted if she ordered her camera men to shut off the cameras and said consolingly, "Just tell me how you feel, baby. Only us two will know. I know you have so much to say, and I want to help."

Seventeen year-old Dimples bowed her head and said through her tears, "My sister was my best friend. She made me laugh. Ne`Ne`, she, she was real good at expressing how she felt, you know? I always had a hard time doing that—but just to hear Ne`Ne` speak, when she got emotional? I mean, when she spoke, she said what *I* was feeling. I don't remember the last time I told my sister, well, before she died I told her I loved her. She shouldna had to been dying for me to say that. I loved my sister! She was my best friend! And now she gone!"

Georgette sat in the chair next to Dimples and the seventeen year-old lay on her shoulder and cried and hid her face in Georgette's bosom as her body heaved and she screamed to the top of her lungs calling out to Ne`Ne`.

Georgette broke down herself; she grabbed Dimples and held her close, telling her it was going to be all right. The cameras were secretly rolling, but Georgette waved her hands for the crew to stop filming. The news reporter was only supposed to get a story out of Dimples, but Dimples had opened up her heart to the woman. Georgette was a mother herself. She also had a mother and a younger sister that was still alive and well. The woman couldn't imagine having to witness her mother getting shot, and losing her sister so violently all in the same night. How did Mary feel? Did she even know her other daughter had died? What will happen to Regina? What will happen to this family once their plight is no longer reported on the local news? Those questions ran through Georgette's mind just before she said to her camera crew, "I can't, I can't go through with this! This family is hurting terribly and I refuse to exploit them," all-the-while as she held onto Dimples tightly, in a motherly sort of way and shed tears with the grief-stricken seventeen year-old. After the funeral services, the reporter took Ne`Ne` back to the hospital to see her mother and Dimples returned home later that evening. She was happy Georgette had taken to see her mother, and even happier that Georgette had stayed with her to make sure she was okay. The reporter had asked Dimples would she like to spend the night at her home, but Dimples declined, telling the lady she was going to go over to Loretta's home and spend the night with her. Georgette left Dimples her number and told her to call her if she needed anything.

When the Georgette left, Dimples went into her room smiling, but that's when reality hit—she was now all alone. She walked back out of her room and looked up and down the hall as tears began rolling down her face. She then walked and stood in the threshold of Ne`Ne`'s room, which was exactly the way she'd left it the day of the concert, her dirty clothes thrown in the corner at the foot of her bed, make-up all over her dresser, and several outfits she'd tried on before deciding to wear what she'd worn to the concert.

Regina knelt down beside her sister's bed with a face full of tears and grabbed the last item Rene had ever touched, which was a pair of Capri pants, and placed her hands on the exact spot where Ne`Ne`'s hands were as she broke down. Going on without Rene would be hard to do, but Dimples still had a mother in the hospital. Although grieving, she had managed to gather her emotions and went about straightening the house before packing clothes to go over to Loretta's home and spend the next few days. From there, she would began to put her life back together, but things don't always go as planned.

****

"*Now I feel wind blow...outside my door...I'm leaving my woman...at home, yeah...Tuesday's gone...with the wind... Tuesday's gone with the wind...*"

While Dimples was packing clothes to go and stay with Loretta, Loretta was sitting at her table listening to one of Sandy's favorite songs, *Tuesday's Gone* by Lynrd Skynrd and reading a letter as she opened an envelope containing her last paycheck. She'd learned that she'd just been let go from Fukutoo's, who were closing down and relocating according to the letter. Loretta had had enough of Ghost Town and was preparing to leave for good. Dimples had told her she was coming over to spend a few nights, but not even that fact could deter her decision. The grief-stricken mother had had all she could take, and the final straw was losing her job, in spite of the money her daughter had left behind. It was blood money to Loretta, worthless paper that could not buy nor restore what she'd loss, nor could it make her happy.

Loretta cried as she stared around at her trashed home, which hadn't been touched since the night her daughter was killed, as Lynrd Skynrd's song played on. Pictures of Sandy at various points of her life were spread about on the table and a single black candle was lit, creating a miniature shrine in memory of the only family member who truly loved Loretta. She'd called her parents the morning after Sandy had been pronounced dead to tell them what happened and they couldn't even remember their granddaughter's name. They never asked Loretta how she was doing, did she need help or said anything of the sort to ease her pain. The old, set-in-their ways rich duo only added to Loretta's hurt by taking turns telling her that it was probably her fault that her daughter was dead and to take care of herself before abruptly hanging up. She'd tried. Loretta Duncan really did try to raise her daughter right, but Sandy's death had, in Loretta's eyes, proved her parents right. She really was a loser. So was her daughter, and her daughter's father, both of whom were dead. Might as well join them. Loretta picked up a nine millimeter and said, "I love you, Sandy," before she got up and lit a fire in the sink and placed the gun to her chest and shot herself through the heart.

Dimples entered the home a few minutes later and smelled the smoke and heard the music playing. "Loretta your house is smoking!"

There was no reply, only the sounds of Lynrd Skynrd's song emanating from the kitchen...

..."*Train roll on...I'm many miles from my home...I'm riding my blues...away...Tuesday you see...she had to be free... alright...somehow I got to...carry on...Tuesday's gone with the wind...Tuesday's gone with the wind...Tuesday's gone with the wind...my baby's gone...with the wind...Train roll on...*"

Dimples covered her nose and entered the kitchen as the song approached its ending only to discover that Loretta had taken her own life. She lay face down on the kitchen floor, the gun laying on the floor beside her in a poodle of blood. The fire in the sink had forced her out of the home as it had grown too big to extinguish.

Dimples was near the point of having a nervous breakdown because she'd witnessed so much drama in such a short span of time. While firefighters were bringing the blaze under control, Loretta's body still inside the house because the flames had become too large before authorities arrived on the scene, along with Sandy's money, Dimples sat at the table in her home crying her heart out. She was just beginning to come to grips with what had happened in Ghost Town, but witnessing what she'd seen at the Duncan household was more than she could bear. She, too, now wanted a way out.

The Holland Family Saga Part Five

CHAPTER 30

THANK YOU

Georgette was sitting with Dimples in Mary's hospital room two months after the funerals and Loretta's suicide. The news reporter went to the school daily and got Dimples' homework and brought her a fresh change of clothes from home because Dimples feared going back to school because of potential threats from those affiliated with Sasha, and she feared going back into Ghost Town after discovering Loretta's corpse inside the burning kitchen, something that haunted her frequently whenever she tried to sleep. By her mother's side was where she wanted to be as it gave her comfort and made her feel safe, even though Mary was helpless during this period of time. Dimples had called Georgette the same day she'd given her number and she hadn't been back to Ghost Town since.

Georgette was a big help to Dimples, and she wanted to do something big for Ghost Town so that the violence that the people suffered would never take place again. The reporter's dream would unknowingly be realized years later, however; but as she and Dimples sat and talked inside of Mary's room, a real surprise and blessing was about to take place on this beautiful spring day in May of 1995.

Dimples was relating to Georgette how Ne`Ne` used to love to antagonize Rolanda Jones by quoting one of Rolanda's most hated statements. "The day before the concert, she, she,"

The Holland Family Saga Part Five

Dimples was all laughs this day as she sat with the reporter, "Ne`Ne` called and requested a song, and then said, 'and I'll take my answer off the air'. Misses Jones hated those words, Miss Georgette! And Ne`Ne` knew it! Misses Jones ragged us all night about that." Dimples said as Georgette smiled widely as she listened to Dimples.

"Thank you," a voice then said lowly and softly. Georgette and Dimples looked around for the voice they had just heard. It was Mary. She had awakened. Still sore, but able to speak.

"Momma, you talking! She talking, Miss Georgette!" Dimples said with joy as she walked up and hugged her mother lightly. "Momma!" was all she said repeatedly as she cried openly, "I, I'm not hurting you am I?" Dimples asked as she held onto Mary.

"Baby, your touch is the greatest sensation I have ever felt." Mary replied with a smile as she grabbed hold of Dimples and looked towards Georgette and said to the woman in a soft voice, "My, my sister's in jail. All Regina had left was me and I was defenseless. Thank you for doing what I couldn't do." Mary said to Georgette through half-opened teary eyes.

"It was my pleasure, Miss Holland. She's a special child."

"You're a special woman. Thank you again."

"Momma. Rene? She—"

"Shhh. Shhh. Baby, I know. I know." Mary said lovingly as she hugged Dimples with what little strength she had at the time.

Georgette watched as mother and daughter held one another and cried together, knowing the whole time that Mary and Dimples were crying for Rene Holland. Mary rested her chin on Dimples' head and looked out towards the bright morning sun and gave a long, distant stare. It was a stare of wonderment and disbelief that was planted on the grief-stricken mother's face as she exhaled, opening her mouth wide and closed her eyes and let out a heartfelt sigh. "Regina," Mary screamed. "Oh, oh my God! We lost Ne`Ne`! Rene!" Mary screamed, unable to hold back her emotions any longer.

The Holland Family Saga Part Five

"Momma! She, she and Sandy! They—"

"I couldn't speak inside that car that night. I wanted to tell you both that I was going to be okay but I couldn't speak! I just knew Rene was going to do something that night. What happened to her?"

After two months, the police and the news crews had the full story on what transpired on March 22, 1995 and Georgette gave a full report to Mary.

"I can't believe Loretta did that to herself," Mary said as she held onto Dimples, who lay next to her mother cuddled up like a new born baby. "That girl Latasha brought death to people's door step. Sandy never liked her. She was right. Latasha messed it up for everybody. I hate that place now. When Martha was running the streets I disliked it for a long time, but Martha, Martha," Mary paused at that moment because the truth of the matter was that she didn't have anything good to say. Martha was a gang banger and drug dealer, she'd also killed people. There was no justifying anybody's behavior that ran the streets of Ghost Town in her eyes, but none of them deserved to die the way they did—especially Ne`Ne`, who only got caught up for a split second after seeing her mother get shot. And Sandy just didn't have enough time to make the changes she wanted to make in her life and those two sisters' lives. Mary kept those thoughts to herself because she didn't want to come out as judging the people she considered family. She loved them as if they were her own blood and only wished they'd made different choices on life; maybe things would have turned out differently for all involved.

"Are you okay, Mary?" Georgette asked, shaking Mary from her thoughts.

"Yes. I'll, I'll survive. But Ghost Town is an ugly to me place now. The place I once called home took my daughter from me."

"Miss Mary," Georgette said with a bright, optimistic smile, "I'm now working for change back there. You won't have to live amongst the violence anymore. You'll be able to walk the streets freely and get those candles on your birthday like you were going to do before those tragedies took place."

Mary only smiled. She knew what Georgette and Dimples didn't know. She had news to share as well. "Parts of that bullet is still in my spine, I can't walk anymore." Mary stated lowly.

"Momma!"

"It's all right, baby. I'm alive. And that is what matters, okay," Mary said as she caressed her daughter's cheeks. "With training, maybe it'll happen again, but I'm alive. Georgette, I thank you, and I implore you to do what you can so we don't lose any more of our youth. But, I don't plan on being in Ghost Town much longer. As soon as I can, I'm taking my daughter and going as far away as I can."

****

A week later, Mary, who was now confined to a wheel chair, was sent home. She had told Georgette that she was planning to move away, but she had lost her job and was now receiving minimal disability benefits. Mary had never expected this to happen; and although she was wheel-chair bound, she could still perform her duties at work, but the company had released her anyway, not wanting to cover her on-going medical expenses. The once proud and hard-working woman now had just enough money every month to pay the rent, keep the lights on, pay Martha's slots at the bank and buy food. On top of that, her medical care was subpar because she had no benefits. Mary also watched as renter after renter moved away, and owner after owner slowly sold their property to the city. She wanted to leave Ghost Town herself, but she had not the money or resources. Sometimes, Mary couldn't even afford to buy stamps and envelopes to write Martha. Loretta Duncan, whom Mary had hoped to reconnect with, was gone, having taken her own life and what remained next door was only a burned out hull that was once the home of two dear friends. With so much death and tragedy left behind in its wake, Ghost Town was slowly beginning to live up to its name. It was becoming just that—a Ghost Town.

The houses that were bought by the city were being

demolished, and by April of 1996, the tall trees hiding the trail leading to Ambush had been cut down. Ghost Town had become brighter without all the trees around, but the place was steadily being vacated. Mary had plans for her and Ne`Ne`, but her being confined to a wheel chair and receiving subpar medical attention had sent her over the edge into a bout of depression. Thoughts of Rene Holland plagued her psyche often and the abundance of hope for the future and the remainder of her life when she sat inside that hospital room when she first spoke to Georgette was diminishing rapidly and the pitifully sad state was beginning to take its toll. Mary had never visited Rene's grave either; but she had her reasons. Reasons she would share with no one; not even Dimples, who visited often, just to shed tears because she couldn't afford flowers. Mary knew exactly what she wanted to do the first time she went to say her good-byes to Rene. She believed she would walk again someday, and she would not be right until she was able to stand before her deceased daughter and say all that she had to say. This was Mary's dream once upon a time, but all was hopeless by April of 1996. Thirty-seven year-old Mary Holland didn't know it at the time, but all she had to do was hold on.

Martha Holland, in the meantime, was writing home constantly, telling Mary that things would be great when she got out and the sisters were reunited. That day was years off and Mary knew it; she also knew not if she had the strength to keep fighting. The only thing keeping Mary from losing it completely was her daughter Regina, who had graduated high school, but had to forgo college for the time being in order to tend to her mother's needs. The Holland family, in April of 1996 was at one of its weakest points; but unbeknownst to Mary, Martha and Dimples, help was on the way. All the family had to do now, was to just hold on.

The Holland Family Saga Part Five

CHAPTER 31

YOUR MOTHER'S DAUGHTER

"Just the other night...I thought I heard you cry...asking me to come...and hold you in my arms...I can hear your prayers... your burdens I will bear...but first I need your hand...then forever can begin..."

A black and chrome Peterbilt semi-tractor-trailer turned onto Casper Drive and cruised slowly down the street on May 14th in the year of 1996. Traversing deeper and deeper into the rundown neighborhood in the semi-truck, the driver stared sadly at the dilapidated domiciles that were obviously in the process of being torn down as Michael Jackson's song titled, *You Are Not Alone*, played at a comfortable level inside the eighteen-wheeler.

The woman driving the huge rig reached into her overhead compartment and grabbed her .44 magnum and set it on the dash of her rig as she sang along with the song playing on her CD player while staring on at the dilapidated neighborhood, unable to believe that people actually resided in such a rundown place as the 18 wheeler cruised slowly down Casper Drive and stopped in front of an address, 2213 Casper Drive.

The woman saw that the house was boarded up, but she still jumped out of her truck with her weapon in hand and shifted her ten gallon cowgirl hat as she looked around sadly. No one was insight. All the houses seemed to be empty or torn down, or in the process of being torn down. She got back into her truck and prepared to drive to Grenada, Mississippi as she continued listening to Michael Jackson's song.

"You are not alone...you're not alone...I am here with you...I am here with you...Although we're far apart...You're always in my heart..."

The song played on as the woman guided her rig slowly pass the house on the corner of Casper Drive and Friendly Lane and it was there that she saw a woman sitting in a wheel-chair in the backyard with a young teenage female nearby leaning down tending soil. The woman in the wheelchair looked up at the rig and then shifted her attention back to the garden.

"Ne`Ne`, those are tomato plants you're pulling, baby." Mary said.

Dimples didn't correct her mother. It bothered her that Mary sometimes called her Ne`Ne`, but ever since she'd corrected her mother a couple of months back and she screamed at her until her lungs nearly burst, telling her that she will be whoever she says she is, Dimples had become afraid of her mother, who was slowly losing her mind before her very eyes. "I'm, I'm sorry, momma," Dimples replied as she started crying.

"Do it right this time, Rene! Ever since you could walk you've worked the garden with me, Rene so act like you know what you're doing!" Mary snapped as she wheeled closer to Dimples, who stood up and stepped away from her mother, afraid to let her near her.

"Rene, come here!" Mary hissed as she pointed to where she wanted "Rene" to stand. "You should have stayed," Mary then cried. "You should have stayed!"

"Momma, please," Dimples said as she covered her lower face and cried. Dimples didn't know her own mother anymore. This was not her mother. This was a deranged woman stuck in grief and she powerless to help her. "I'm, not Rene. I'm your daughter Reg—"

"Regina's fine! She's fine! She's inside preparing dinner and Rene you are alive and well! Right here with me," Mary said as tears streamed down her face, all the while staring at

The Holland Family Saga Part Five

Dimples.

The woman driving the truck's eyes grew wide. She could make out that two females seemed to be engaged in an emotionally charged discussion as she stopped her truck and slowly opened the door and emerged from the tractor-trailer once again. "Mary!" she yelled aloud as her lips trembled. "Mary?"

Mary whipped her neck around and her brown eyes immediately grew wide as she screamed and began wheeling her chair over the gravel driveway.

The woman driving the tractor-trailer began to cry as she ran across the street, yelling the whole time, "I found you! I finally found you thank God! Thank you God!"

"Momma! Momma!" Mary screamed as she tried with all her might to wheel her chair across the gravel.

"I'm your mother's daughter! My name is Naomi Holland! I'm your oldest sister, Mary! I'm your oldest sister!"

The closer Naomi got to Mary, the weaker her legs grew. She began to wobble and fell to her knees, literally crawling in her attempt to reach Mary. Dimples was assisting her mother across the gravel with tears filling her eyes. Mary was crying hysterically with her arms stretched forth, ready to embrace someone she'd nearly forgotten. Naomi was crying uncontrollably. And when she reached Mary, the two held onto one another for dear life and sobbed heavily. "My sister!" Mary screamed.

"Yes! Ohhh, Mary! Mary my God sweet Jesus! What happened to you?"

Nothing was said for a few minutes as Naomi and Mary cried on one another shoulders while Dimples stood by, crying uncontrollably herself. It was just three females, outside in a back yard all alone, crying their hearts out and thanking God, barley able to breathe.

Naomi soon let go off Mary as she perched herself on her knees and grabbed Mary's face with both hands. "You still look the same, Mary." she said through a tearful smile. "Do you remember me?"

"I, I can't remember so well. I remember we were in a car and you gave us some sheets of paper and we never saw you again. Where did you go? Why did you leave us?"

"I didn't leave you all," Naomi said low and soft. "They took you all away from me! I was trying to keep us together! But they took us away and split us up!"

"Martha, in jail!"

"I know. I know! It's over! It's over now!"

"No, it ain't over! Look at me!"

Naomi felt guilt for her sister's plight, but it wasn't Mary's intentions to make Naomi feel guilty. Truth was, Mary had problems that she had to face; both physical and mental, and neither Dimples nor Naomi knew exactly what Mary meant at the time.

"I'm going to help you. We'll never be apart again, Mary. I promise." Naomi said as she pressed her face to Mary's and hugged her again, rubbing her back gently. "My baby sister," she said lowly. "God I love you, Mary. And I've missed you all my life. You, Martha, Sam, everybody. I've missed you all my life."

Naomi then looked up at Dimples and said, "You are a Holland female. Where's your twin?"

"She's dead! Our brother Sam is dead too." Mary answered as Dimples wiped her watery eyes.

"Nooo! God what happened to all of you? What happened?" Naomi asked as she sat back down on the gravel in a defeated state.

Naomi Holland had just felt the full impact of growing up unable to protect her younger siblings. This was not the reunion she had dreamed of for years by a long shot. She had hoped that everything was fine—that she would find her brother and sisters all living happy, healthy lives, bearing children and living well; but she should have known better when she learned Martha was in jail. The woman was just hoping for the best; but life is not always fair, and dreams don't always come true. It was a reality of life Naomi herself knew all-too-well. And the reality for Naomi was that she had a sister in jail, one confined to a wheel-chair, a brother who was deceased and also a niece who was dead as well. Thinking about the outcome of her family and remembering the start they'd had back in Alabama before she'd witnessed the death of her mother, Naomi grew angry all over again. Angry at the white man for destroying her family. Angry at herself for failing to find her siblings in time—the tools she'd been using for years to justify her actions and the life she'd built for herself and her family now meant nothing. Naomi had a family. A family she loved. A family she wanted to share with her long lost sister. Those thoughts warmed her heart and she knew what good lay ahead for her surviving family and she was willing to share what all she possessed. She regained her composure and told Mary and Dimples what Nituna had told her in 1962. "This is not your home anymore! Baby," she said to Dimples as she stood up, "what's your name, sweetie? I'm sorry for not acknowledging you sooner."

"It's okay, Naomi. I'm Regina, Regina Holland." Dimples replied as she hugged Naomi tightly. Dimples felt in her heart that things were about to get better. She'd taken in Naomi's appearance as she and Mary talked. Well dressed, albeit denim and cowboy boots, fancy earrings in her ears and a thick platinum chain around her neck, a big diamond rock on her left index finger, and a shiny watch like none other clad to her wrist, a watch that made Twiggy's once-coveted gold bracelets look like mere toy store jewelry. Naomi emanated success to Dimples. Strength and power. And she was a Holland who had it in her heart to search for her mother. The way Naomi carried herself upon meeting her mother made it known to Dimples that she had an aunt who truly cared about family; and Dimples couldn't be more happier, not only for herself, but more so for her mother, who was on the edge of insanity.

"Okay, Regina. Get whatever medications your mother needs and a change of clothes. Leave everything else behind. We're leaving this place for good! Mary, will you please, please come home with me? Let me take care of you and Regina. Start a new life in Oklahoma? Far away from this place."

"My daughter's here."

"She can come too. I would never leave Regina."

"Not her," Mary said as she lowered her head. "Ne`Ne`! My other baby. She's buried here. I can't leave her."

"Mary," Naomi said as she got down on her knees. "What would your daughter want after living here? I think she would—"

"She would want me to be right here! Right here in Jackson, Mississippi where she is bur—" Mary caught herself, heaved heavily and continued, "she was callin' for me! I, I, couldn't help my child! And those thugs! All she wanted to do was go to a concert and she was killed for that? Why God let that happen? Why he put me here?" Mary asked as she beat her hands against her wheel-chair. "What did I do in life that was so bad to be put here? To be taken from my family? To have, to have *my family* taken from me? Why? Why God do that to us, Naomi?"

"Don't blame God, Mary. Don't you *ever* blame God. You don't see? It was God that brought forth this day! You've weathered the storm, Mary. Now, God is extending his hand," Naomi said as she stretched out her hand before Mary. "Through me He's working. Take my hand, and through me, let God help you. Please, sister. I'm begging you, we can't, *I* can't let you stay here. I promise to help. I'm only trying to help, please, I'm beggin." Naomi said as she remained on her knees and placed her hand against Mary's cheek and stared her in the eyes with a face full of tears.

Just then Dimples came out the house toting a duffle bag and was all smiles. She was ready to leave Ghost Town—for good. "I got my momma medicines and her prescriptions, some soft slippers, a pillow and some clothes too auntie!" she said excitedly as she jumped down the stairs.

Naomi stood up and grabbed Dimples and held her close. "That's right baby, I'm auntie. I'm your blood." she said proudly.

"I know! I'm just glad you never gave up on us. We was alone out here, but I just felt something was going to happen, something good! Everybody, well, when they was around, they called me Dimples." Regina said as she smiled up at her aunt.

Naomi couldn't help but to smile back. "You have dimples like me!" she and Regina said in unison before they burst into laughter.

Mary smiled slightly. She wasn't quite ready to leave because she still had something she wanted to do; but seeing how happy Dimples had gotten once Naomi arrived had broken her resistance and she didn't protest when Naomi began wheeling her towards the truck.

Naomi and Regina helped place Mary inside and Dimples ran and locked the door and hid the key over the door sill. They would later call the new landlord and tell him of their intentions. With Mary by her side, and Dimples on her knees in between her aunt and mother staring out the windshield of the truck with a wide smile on her face, Naomi's 1995 Peterbilt truck began to rumble forward. Naomi placed her ten gallon hat back onto her head and placed on a pair of shades and said, "Let's go home, family!"

"Where we going auntie?" Dimples asked with a wide smile as Naomi's truck cruised pass what was once the trail leading to Ambush.

Naomi reached over and rubbed Dimples' thick platted hair and said, "Oklahoma, Dimples! Ponca City is the name of the town nearby, but before we head there, we have to go see Martha. Would you like that?"

"Yeah, I miss her. Since the car been broke, we ain't been able to go. Not to mention we didn't never have enough—" Dimples cut her statement short, embarrassed of the fact that she and her mother were living poorly.

Naomi knew her niece and sister were struggling, but she didn't acknowledge the fact, she only stated that everything was going to be all right. "We going home, baby. You two will be just fine! Just fine! Right Mary?"

The Holland Family Saga Part Five

Mary didn't respond, she only gazed out the window and was feeling a mixture of emotions. She was happy Naomi had found her and Dimples, but she would not be complete until she set out to do what she had wanted to do ever since Ne`Ne` had been buried. Mary would hold that secret to herself for the time being.

The trio had arrived in Grenada after visiting hours so they spent the night at a motel and early the next morning they went to the county jail to visit Martha, who was unaware of the events that were transpiring. When Martha heard her name called for visitation, she was expecting to see Mary and Dimples. *"They finally found a way to see me? They could've saved that money though."* Martha thought to herself as she waited in line to enter the visiting room.

Martha was behind a plexiglass window and could see the people filing into the visiting area as she waited in line. When Mary came into view, Martha smiled. She then saw Dimples pushing her mother in the wheel chair and her smile grew wider; but when she saw the bosom woman walking behind Dimples, Martha screamed aloud, "Naomi!" Other prisoners looked around at Martha in a confused manner. "That's, that's my big sister!" Martha said as she began to push pass other prisoners, trying her best to get to the front of the line.

Prisoners were beginning to get agitated and they shoved Martha as she fought through the crowd. The guards grabbed her and tried to hold her back but she broke free and said, "Y'all don't understand, Ms. Singleton! That's my big sister! That's who I been talking about!" Martha cried as the guards tried to hold her back.

Martha pulled away from the two guards holding her, but Ms. Singleton, the lead guard who knew the woman's story, held the other guard back and the full-figured red-haired woman could only watch in happiness as Martha emerged from behind the plexiglass window and ran to Naomi in a desperate and urgent manner, knocking aside chairs in the process. Martha's voice echoed through the visitor's room. "I knew you were still out there! I knew it!" she screamed as she ran up and hugged Naomi tightly, crying on her shoulder the way a little girl cries after missing her mother for an extended period of time.

"I'm sorry. We was just tryna survive you know?" Martha said through tears. "Mary, Mary not like me! Don't be mad at me for being in jail! Don't be mad! Say you not mad at me!" Martha pleaded.

Naomi grabbed Martha just beneath her jaws, clasping both hand to Martha's face with a death grip and said, "Never! Never will I be mad at you for trying to survive, Martha! They beat us once—never again! You hear me? Never again!" Naomi said angrily as she held Martha's face in her hands and shook her head rapidly before hugging her tightly.

Martha held on to Naomi for dear life. Her face planted in sister's neck, hiding her face, not out of shame, but out of love. And the love that these sisters had for one another, even after being apart for over three decades, had never wavered nor failed. Instantaneous was the bond—the essence of a true Holland—a family whose love remained intact no matter how far, or how much time passes by. That is what makes one a bona fide Holland. And these sisters were Hollands through and through.

The four sat a table and Martha and Dimples began to tell Naomi many stories, the good, the bad, and the ugly stories that had unfolded throughout their lives. Naomi, however, revealed little about herself, she mainly listened to the events that transpired in Ghost Town. At the time, Naomi didn't speak on what she knew happened on the farm and at the orphanage and also how she got to Oklahoma.

Martha, Mary, and Dimples, however, continued to share stories. They talked about what happened with Rene and it pained Naomi. Mary didn't say a word during that time, and it was during the reunion inside the county jail as the family discussed the death of Rene Holland, that Naomi began to discern what was troubling Mary. She wasn't too sure, but she believed that the truth would be revealed once the family reached Oklahoma.

Naomi learned that Martha was getting her time cut short by working in the state programs that were offered and she was now inside of five years. Naomi was prepared to fight for Martha's freedom, but Martha said she was fine. "Just, please, just take care of Mary and Dimples. Let me know where you are and I'll come home when I'm done here. Just, Naomi, please, just don't forget about me back here."

"I'll never do that, Martha. I haven't forgotten in all this time, and I won't do it now. Mary and Dimples, my beautiful sister and my lovely niece, they will be fine. We'll have everything ready for you when you come home to Oklahoma. Whatever you want, just say it." Martha then remembered the seventy plus thousand dollars she had stashed at the bank. She told Naomi about it and Naomi assured her everything would be all right. Martha was both sad and happy to see her two sisters and niece leave, but she just knew they were going to be okay; and someday, she, too, would join them.

Naomi then drove back to Jackson, headed for Martha's bank. When she placed Mary inside a motel with Dimples, and she begged for her not to leave, Naomi had to repeatedly reassure Mary that she was coming back. Mary cried the whole time Naomi was gone, only relinquishing her tears when Naomi returned three hours later holding a check. The woman had bribed the bank manager, who knew of Martha's safety deposit boxes, with ten-thousand dollars cash. The three then set off for Dallas to deliver the load of frozen corn, which was a week late and had cost Naomi thirty-five hundred dollars in late charges, but Naomi didn't care about the money; she was reunited with her lost family members and knew the outcomes of all her siblings. As far as Naomi was concerned, despite the many tragedies, all was right within the Holland family.

As Naomi rode through the town of Ponca City, Oklahoma, to her place of residence, two days after she had visited with Martha, Martha was in Grenada opening mail and had just received a checkbook with a balance statement of $73,000 dollars. It would a secret she would keep to herself for the time being. Naomi had kept her word to Martha and all Martha had to do now was bide her time.

At the same time, Naomi was thinking of a way to bring Mary back from her bout of depression; she believed in her heart that the place she had just outside of Ponca City, Oklahoma would be the therapy her sister needed to return to a normal state. Naomi had an inkling what needed to be done, but before she would do it, she had to know for sure, because if she was wrong, the move she had in mind could send Mary over the edge for all time.

The Holland Family Saga Part Five

CHAPTER 32

OUR LAND, OUR HOME

Mary and Dimples looked out of the windshield of Naomi's rig in awe at the sight that lay before their eyes. Naomi resided on a huge ranch and the land went on for what seemed like miles. As they rode down a dirt road, bordered by a white fence on either side, they stared on in amazement. Naomi's ranch consisted of a vast hilly plain that held what seemed like hundreds of cattle. The cattle were gently grazing under the warm morning sun. Horses ran about freely and birds flew lazily across the land. Nature, and the land itself, seemed to be speaking that morning as if they were welcoming the trio that rode inside the rig; its engine humming lowly, never stirring the tranquility that the three had rode into that morning.

Far off in the distance to their right, Mary and Dimples noticed a two-story colonial style home that was partially hidden by trees. There was a hill behind the home and what appeared to be a creek that ran in between the rear of the house and the hill. To the left of the home was another hill lightly topped with beautiful red-leaved trees and also white-leaved trees.

"What are those beautiful trees there?" Mary asked as she pointed towards the hill beside the colonial home.

"Those are called Summers Red Maples, and the white ones are Cleveland Pear trees. That is our guest house over there beside the hill."

"Guest house?" Dimples stated in surprise. "Auntie, it's huge! And if that's the guest house—"

"We all reside over there." Naomi said, cutting Dimples off.

Mary and Dimples looked to their left and saw a four-columned brick home twice as big as the guest house.

"Auntie, this is beautiful! Everything feel like, feel like—"

"Fells like you belong here, sweetie?" Naomi asked as she cut Dimples' statement off and cupped her niece's chin.

"Yeah, man! I wish Ne`Ne` could see it." Dimples said lowly then added. "This place is, this place is like—"

"I would like to go over there to the guest house, if I may." Mary said lowly, as she cut Dimples off.

Naomi looked over to Mary and nodded. "You like that place over there, Mary?" she asked.

"Yes," Mary said as her eyes watered. "The trees, the way the sun shine casts a shadow over the hillside, and that lovely hill on the left of the guest house and those Summer Maples, that's what they are right?"

"Yes, Mary, there called Summers Red Maples."

"Yes, Red Maples. They are beautiful. That place looks peaceful. I want to go there."

"Okay. We'll have to travel by cart because the road leading there isn't big enough for the rig." Naomi stated. "There's people waiting to see you two as well. Look." Naomi added as she pointed to her left.

Mary and Dimples looked out Naomi's side of the rig and saw five black horses approaching them. A young boy rode one, and four girls rode the other four. Dimples let out a low gasp when she saw the figures atop the horses. Two of the females were riding separate horses and each were toting smaller females. An older male had a young male riding with him while two more females rode individual horses. The five horses, approached the gate and turned and rode alongside Naomi's rig. The children were laughing and yelling aloud at random, "Welcome! Welcome Mary! Welcome Regina!"

Naomi sped her rig up a little and the horses kept pace and Dimples and Mary could see for the first time that the six females were a trio of twins. Naomi had three sets of female twins and two sons. Mary, who had been distant ever since Naomi had entered her and Dimples' life, even let out a small smile. Naomi noticed her sister's subtle delight and said, "Mary, my youngest son is anxious to see you and Dimples. When he learned," Naomi started to cry as she, too, had become overwhelmed by the welcoming sight, "when they *all* learned that I had found you, they wanted to do something special. This is their gift to you and Dimples. They practiced hard and wanted to escort you and Regina home. That was their words, 'escort you and Regina home'." Naomi ended proudly through tears.

"What they did is very beautiful." Mary said lowly before she turned her head and looked towards the guest house.

Naomi rubbed Mary's shoulder and continued on towards her home. She turned left down another dirt road and pulled into a large parking area where a medium-sized warehouse sat, along with two other trailers and a semi-truck and exited her vehicle. When she walked around to assist Mary from the truck she saw her eight kids running towards her yelling and laughing aloud.

"Hey, don't leave my youngest two behind!" Naomi yelled to her kids in reference to her two youngest daughters, the youngest of her eight kids at age five.

The kids slowed, but they were so eager to greet their aunt and cousin. Naomi's oldest son continued on to help his mother and his cousin with his aunt. "Welcome home! Momma always said she had a sister! To learn we had a cousin was a bonus. I'm Dawk!" the twelve year-old stated as he smiled at Dimples.

"Hey Dawk. I'm Dimples. And this my momma—"

"Mary Holland! I know! My momma always talked about Mary and Martha!" Dawk said, cutting Dimples off.

All morning Dimples had been unable to finish a sentence and she couldn't help but to laugh to herself. She was overjoyed to be far away from Ghost Town, but Naomi's eight seemed just as excited as she was; only Mary was still detached from what was transpiring. Naomi was giving Dimples and Mary a new lease on life, only Mary seemed to be missing something. Naomi noticed it, so did Dimples.

Mary and Dimples were greeted by all of Naomi's kids and took in all of their names. Some had nicknames, but all of their birth names were truly unique. Dimples grew to love her eight cousins immediately. She couldn't wait to get to know the lively little bunch. Naomi explained to Mary and Dimples that she her youngest five kids, 'the young five' rather than say all of their names repeatedly as she began loading Mary into golf cart with the assistance of her oldest son Dawk.

"My husband, his name is Doss Dawkins," Naomi explained as she guided the cart towards the family home, which sat atop a gently sloping hill. "He's in Chicago working now. He left early this morning, but he'll be back in a couple of days. Until then, let's make ourselves at home and really, really, get to know one another." Naomi stated as she cruised towards her huge ten bedroom mansion.

Once inside, Mary and Dimples toured the place. Naomi told the two that a kitchen, eight bedrooms and a great room was upstairs along with six bathrooms, a music room, a classroom and two observation rooms. Three extra bedrooms, a den, separate offices for Naomi and Doss, offices they termed 'situation rooms', a library, along with another gourmet kitchen, over-sized living room, study room, theater room, and laundry area were in the downstairs portion of the overly large mansion, or *Ponderosa* as it would eventually become known to Mary and Dimples.

Naomi wheeled Mary through the home with Dimples and her kids following closely, all jockeying for position, each wanting to be close to Dimples and Mary as they walked across the wooden floors. Dimples felt very welcomed, very blessed to have an aunt like Naomi; not because she was wealthy, but because she truly loved her and Mary. And Naomi in turn wanted to do the utmost to make her niece and sister feel at home. Dimples was quickly being drawn in, and Mary, no matter how much she tried to resist, no matter how much sorrow she had in her heart for the things that happened in Ghost Town, especially losing Ne`Ne`, she, too, was beginning to feel at home, as if this land was where she was always meant to be.

Mary only wished Naomi had come into her life earlier; maybe Ne`Ne` would still be around to witness and experience what her sister was experiencing. Mary didn't want to dampen the mood, so after touring the downstairs, the overly large kitchen, twenty seat theater, sunken living room with its huge fireplace, she asked lowly could Dimples please take her to the guest house. Naomi and Dimples drove Mary to the guest house in a golf cart and Naomi, after assisting Dimples in placing Mary back into her wheel chair, went back to *Ponderosa* to check on her kids and prepare a huge dinner.

Mary didn't say it, but she wanted to be alone with her thoughts. Alone to digest how rapidly her life had changed, to come to grips that Rene Holland would forever be alive only in her memory. As she sat with Dimples in the guest house, Mary silently replayed those final days, the final minutes, and the moment she felt Ne`Ne`s spirit slip into the afterlife. She began to cry again, quietly, wishing she had moved away before her world was turned upside down and one of her daughters was taken away. Mary felt she should have seen the writing on the wall. *"I never thought allowing her to go to a concert would get her killed!"* she said to herself as tears streamed down her face. Mary then broke down and screamed aloud which caused Dimples to run to her side.

"Momma, you okay?" Dimples asked.

"Get away from me!" Mary screamed. "I don't want to be here!"

"Momma! We gone be all right from now on! Naomi gonna —"

"Why you let her leave? Why didn't you stop Rene from leaving the hospital with Sandy?" Mary asked Dimples as she cried.

"I was worried about *you* momma! Ne`Ne` and Sandy was gone when I made it back out front!" Dimples replied as she began to cry. "Anyway, I thought you was about to die!"

"I was fine! I was just fine! You should've stopped your sister from leaving!"

"How you think I feel? Nobody was there, for *me*! You was laying there 'bouta die! What was I supposed to do? I did the best I could! And you blaming me for Rene being dead? Momma, how could you say that?" Dimples said as she covered her face and ran from the guest house.

"Regina? Regina?" Mary called out. "I'm sorry." she then said lowly as she heard the door slam.

Regina ran back towards *Ponderosa* crying her heart out, having been crushed by what her mother had said to her. For a long time Dimples always blamed herself for her sister's death, but she kept those thoughts bottled up and to herself. To hear her mother basically blame her for Rene's death had caused her to feel guilty all over again. Just when she was beginning to heal, Mary had taken Regina's joy away, but it wasn't her intentions. The grieving mother just didn't know how to cope with the loss of one of her daughters, nor was she able to at the present time. Lashing out was her way of grieving.

Regina ran her heart out, her dark eyes pouring water, her twin plats flapping in the morning air. She ran at a furious pace, causing the cattle and horses to scatter as she ran past them. "I love my sister!" she yelled aloud. "I love my sister! It wasn't my fault! Rene I'm sorry! I'm sorry!" Dimples screamed as she fell to the earth and pounded the ground with her face planted in the soil.

Naomi had just squeezed the trigger on a sixteen gauge double barrel shotgun and had planted two slugs into the dome of a cow she was preparing to slaughter. She and four ranch hands were just about to fire up electric saws to cut a line in the massive bull's skin before they hung it up to let the blood drain before ripping it clean when she saw something moving out the corner of her eye. "What the hell is that in the upper field?" Naomi asked as she laid her saw on the ground.

"You want me to go and check, Senorita Holland?" a trusted ranch asked.

Naomi didn't answer right away. She went over to her golf cart and grabbed a pair of binoculars and focused in on the object writhing about on the ground in the middle of the upper field near *Ponderosa* and saw Dimples struggling with herself in the field. She sanitized her hands and said, "Flacco, go ahead with the slaughter. I'll be back shortly," as she climbed into the cart and rode over to Dimples.

"What happened? Dimples what happened?" Naomi asked upon her arrival.

"I killed my sister! I shoulda stopped her! Momma right, it's *my* fault she dead!"

"*Mary! What are you doing to your child?*" Naomi asked herself. "Shh, shh," she then said as she knelt down and scooped Regina into her arms. "Come on now, niece. I heard what happened that night. You did right staying with your mother. Ne`Ne` made her own choice that night and it's not your fault that she's dead. Look at me, Regina," Naomi said as she clutched her niece's face and stared into her eyes. "You just keep doing what you are doing. You are just fine. And this is home now. Ghost Town is no more. This is *our* land! *Our* home! And you are going to be just fine right here in Oklahoma. Understand?"

"I know, auntie. But my momma said I shoulda stopped Ne`Ne`! I didn't see her leave! I thought she was right there with me outside the emergency room!"

"I know, baby. I know. Look, go inside Ponderosa and clean up. Go clean up, get with your cousins, because they are really fun to be with," Naomi said through a proud smile. "Tell them I said to walk you around the ranch and show you the goat pen. Watch how much fun you have with them. Just walk out here on the land and enjoy it. It's ours. It's yours. Be at peace baby, and tonight when you go home, be as nice as you can be to Mary. Don't worry about what she says, just, just make sure she eats and washes her body, and starting tomorrow, I'll help your mother get back on track." Naomi said as she held Dimples close. "God I can't imagine what all you two have been through emotionally since your sister died; but I'm gone make it better, I promise, okay?"

"Okay," Dimples said as she wiped her tears and got up and walked slowly to Ponderosa where she was assisted by Naomi's big three.

"Okay, Mary," Naomi said under her breath as she hopped into her golf cart and rode towards the guest house, "enough of the pity party, sister. You're a Holland. And we are way stronger than what you are being now."

Naomi walked to the guest house and there, she saw Mary sitting in the living room knitting. A huge ball of yarn lay on the floor next to her wheel chair. Naomi knew not to ask was Mary okay because she knew the answer to that question after mere minutes of her arrival in Ghost Town. How to get Mary to open up was a question she believed she had the answer to, however; but that would take time. Naomi had her plan mapped out—she knew what she wanted to do—if only Mary would cooperate. With those thoughts in mind, she sat beside Mary, who was aware of her presence, but never acknowledged it as she knitted at a furious pace. Naomi picked up the ball of yarn and held it for Mary and asked, "What are you making, Mary?"

"When she was four, Ne`Ne`, she, she loved these little knit hats I used to buy for her. I was making her one."

"Ohh, I see. Mary? There's this doctor in town, real good doctor. Tomorrow I was thinking we can go see him. I know he can help you run. That's what you really want to do right? Run?"

"She, she told me once that she was glad I was her momma. I'll never forget those words."

"That's sweet. My li'l rascals never say anything like that to me. Spoiled they are."

"It's not because it was *Ne`Ne`* who died. I love them equally. I love both my kids the same, but this pain? This pain is like nothing I've ever felt! And the way I lost her? Never, never said good-bye. She did tell me she loved me. 'We right here momma!' That was the last time I heard her voice. It shouldn't have been the last time I heard my daughter speak! And I, I still had so much to say because I thought *I* was going to die."

Mary said through tears as she continued to knit the small hat.

"Well, let me help. Trust me Mary, it's been thirty years, but it seems like it was just yesterday when I witnessed you and Martha ride away in that station wagon. Please, let me help." Naomi said lovingly as she rubbed Mary's shoulder.

"This doctor," Mary said as she clutched Naomi's hand, "How you know I'll be able to run?"

"He fixed a child that went to school with Walee leg once. If he can fix a child, I know he can help a grown woman to run again."

"Run again." Mary said. "If he can only make me run for one day? I know where I'd run to."

"I do too, Mary. And I promise, you will run to that place." Naomi ended as she sat the ball of yarn down and got up and stood behind Mary and gently stroked her thick head of platted hair.

"Naomi?" Mary called out softly.

"Yeah, sweetie?"

"Tell, tell Regina I never meant what I said today, or in the past after we lost Ne`Ne`. I know it wasn't her fault. And," Mary paused.

Naomi was looking towards the ceiling with her eyes close, happy that Mary was opening up. When she heard the pause in Mary's voice, she opened her eyes and looked down at her, "And what?" Naomi asked.

"No matter how much time has passed, it takes a special sister to remember what happened to our family. Thank you for caring about us. I'm glad you my sister." Mary had partially quoted to Naomi some of the things Ne`Ne` had said to her. Ne`Ne`'s words were still as strong and lasting to Mary than the bond of love and hope that had been within Naomi's heart since 1966.

On this day in May of 1996 on a ranch in Oklahoma, the bond that had been missing for thirty years between two siblings was beginning to solidify. Mary rested her hope in Naomi, she said she would help her run and she believed in her sister's words. Mary didn't know it at the time, but when she was able, she would make the run of her life, and finally, she could say all she had to say to Rene Holland, the daughter whom she had lost in the twinkling of an eye.

CHAPTER 33

RUN LITTLE BUMBLEBEE, RUN

It was now July of 1996, almost two months after Mary and Dimples arrived on the ranch. Dimples was now working for Naomi on the ranch. She was in charge of feeding the cattle in the early morning hours, earning $600 dollars a week. Dimples simply loved her new life. She felt free, she felt connected to the land as if she always belonged there and she had come to appreciate her new morning routine.

Naomi, who had given up truck driving to help her niece and sister adjust to their new life, would arrive at the guest home at 4:30 a.m. She would let herself in and began to prepare breakfast for Mary and Dimples. Dimples would awaken around 5a.m. and join Naomi in the kitchen where the two would hold many an interesting conversation about their lives.

In the beginning, Mary stayed in her room until Dimples left the home. She would be up when Naomi entered her room around six and Naomi would help her bathe and then dress her and the two of them would have breakfast. Naomi would then take Mary to the chiropractor in downtown Ponca City where Mary would be in therapy for five hours. The therapy was by no means easy or cheap, but Naomi had paid the expenses in full.

A few weeks after she'd started therapy, Mary called down for Naomi and Dimples with joy in her voice, something they hadn't heard in Mary's voice in a long time. Just the way she'd called for them had made the two happy. Naomi and Dimples both took off running up the stairs happily and when they got there, they saw Mary sitting up in the bed smiling as she removed the covers on and pointed to her toes and wiggled them. "I woke up this morning and when I stretched? They moved! I can control them! And I have feeling up to my ankles! It's a miracle!"

"Momma, you gone run again." Dimples said lowly as she hugged her mother.

On this day, during the month of August, Mary had made significant progress, physically and mentally. After therapy, she and Naomi returned home and a dinner in celebration of Mary's progress had gotten underway. The family in Oklahoma always had a reason to celebrate. With eight kids and two adults, a ranch hand friendly to the family and a host of family and friends from Chicago who visited on occasion, there was always a birthday, a visit from up north, or a holiday or achievement that warranted celebration year round. Mary's progress was the reason for this particular family gathering.

Naomi's husband, Doss, and her son Dawk were grilling beef steaks and her oldest two daughters were making a huge pot of chili with thick chunks of potatoes. Naomi's middle two daughters were baking a huge cake, and her youngest three kids were back and forth, getting in the way, but trying to help at the same time.

Mary felt honored by all that the family was doing on her behalf and it was fair to say that she had fallen completely in love with her family by August of 1996. Never had love felt so good to the 37 year-old woman; she just had to tell Martha how things were turning out on the ranch. She wrote her sister, and sent copies of the numerous pictures they were taking down on the ranch and Martha was glad to know that all of her people were doing just fine back home in Oklahoma. She couldn't wait for the day she would be able to join them all and get to know her true blood.

The summer of '96 was a great one for the family. Dimples had even learned to ride a horse, during that time and things were going along smoothly, but Mary's struggles weren't over just as of yet because during the winter she had suffered a setback. The cold weather pained her ankles and her knees, which now had slight feeling. On real cold days, the temperature could drop into the teens, sometimes the single digits, and those days were excruciating for Mary. Some days, she couldn't even get out of bed. The winter of 1996 was brutal on her, but eventually, with medication and encouragement she was able to push on. And by early June of 1997, she had fully recovered.

Mary's therapy had cost just over $229,000 dollars, but it was worth every single penny. The month before, Naomi had made a trip to Mississippi to put the next phase of her plan to help her sister overcome the death of daughter. Mary thought Naomi was only going to see Martha, but when she awoke on a sunny morning four days later, she saw Naomi throwing dirt into a grave at the top of the hill on the right side of the guest of house as she stepped out onto the front porch.

When she saw what Naomi was doing, Mary understood why Naomi had gone back to Mississippi. Naomi finished what she was doing and got into her golf cart and rode through the Summers Red Maple trees and the Cleveland Pears which were now in full bloom. The grass on the hillside was a lush green and Mary could hear the water babbling softly in the creek behind the house. It was such a beautiful, peaceful day. Naomi emerged from the woods' trail in her golf cart and rode over to her sister with a wide smile on her face. She knew Mary had regained full use of her legs, and she hoped that what she had done would be the icing on the cake for Mary. She knew she was right when she saw Mary, who was now sitting atop a yellow Honda four-wheeler, smile at her then ask, "Is that who I think it is?"

"You're not mad?"

"Of course not. I, I never said so, but I wished for it." Mary said lowly.

"Well, now when you are ready, you can run." Naomi said as she smiled at Mary and extended her arm back towards the hill.

Mary stretched her arms and beckoned Naomi and she got up

and embraced her sister. She had every intention of making it to the hill top. She could have run this day, but no, Mary wanted to do something special. She'd waited almost two weeks, fighting the urge to get up and run up the hill until the day she had waited for had finally arrived.

For whatever reason, Mary was nervous this morning. She walked upstairs and went into Dimples' room and saw that she was gone from the guest house. Mary figured she was out in the field working. The date was June 22, 1997, Regina and Rene's twentieth birthday, and on this morning, Mary had baked a vanilla cake. She then sat patiently, looking at pictures of Ne`Ne`, knitting, and reading the journal Naomi had given her and Martha over three decades ago. The ringing of the bell in the kitchen a couple of hours later shook Mary from her trip down memory lane and she began readying herself. She went into the kitchen to remove the cake from the oven and let it cool. Moments later she grabbed a spatula and her eyes grew watery as she slowly began to spread vanilla icing onto the cake and reflected on the last night she spent with her daughter Rene, March 22, 1995. The day, in Mary's mind, was replaying in slow motion and the voices were echoing...

..."Momma, how these Nike's look on my feet?" Mary remembered Ne`Ne` asking her.

"They look nice, Ne`Ne`."

"Hey momma, you heard Misses Jones calling my name over and over? She know me! Man, I like that lady!" Mary could see the joy in her daughter's eyes as she reflected on that night. Ne`Ne` was really excited about driving the Impala and going to her first concert.

"I sure did, sweetie. Now, who's this group TLV?"

"It's TLC, momma! You need to get hip, woman!" Ne`Ne`s voice echoed as Mary imaged her standing in front of her mirror putting the finishing touches on her hair.

"Child, please! You and Dimples don't know nothing about being hip! I put the –i-p in HIP! Look at this here! Regina! Come see momma boogie, baby! I bet TLC can't do this!" Mary said as her daughters danced with her briefly, the trio moving about in slow motion inside Mary's vision.

Several minutes later, Rene and Regina dashed from the house. "Don't forget, we eating cake when you girls get back so don't get too full of that concert food." Mary remembered saying as she watched her daughters run to the Impala. "Okay momma! Love you!" she could hear the twins yelling in unison while hopping into the Impala, Ne`Ne` behind the wheel.

"Sandy, take care my babies!" Mary heard herself saying.

"Don't worry, Miss Mary. We going see the show and come right back!" Sandy's voice echoed through Mary's mind as she replayed that fateful night. As Mary put the finishing touches on the cake, she imaged in her mind Dimples talking to that singer in the candy aisle, the three walking towards the store's exit just as she heard the gunshots…

… "We right here momma! We right here momma…We right here momma…" that one phrase, the last words Mary ever heard Rene Holland speak now echoed through Mary's mind and brought tears to her eyes as she placed candles onto the cake, the same flavor of cake she'd baked the night she lost her daughter as the realization of what she was about to do and had been wanting to do for over two years finally sunk in.

Naomi, meanwhile, was on her mansion's balcony with a pair of binoculars. She wore a black skirt with a black sombrero this morning. *"Mary, come on baby, this is your day."* she said under her breath.

Naomi waited a few more minutes and grew disheartened. She was now headed over to the guest house to talk to Mary to see what was wrong, but as she walked towards her French doors, she saw a bright flash of yellow far off in the distance. She quickly turned and aimed her binoculars towards the guest house, and it was there that she saw Mary running towards the hill. Mary was dressed in a tight pair of black spandex, wearing a tight yellow tank top and yellow sneakers and she was holding a white cake.

"Yes," Naomi said lowly. "Run little bumblebee, run!" she then yelled happily.

Mary heard her sister's voice echo across the land and she ran with all her might as she held onto the cake, her thirty-eight year-old legs striding strongly across the land and up the hillside. Mary began to cry as she ran, and before long, she'd dropped the cake she held in her arms, and just cried aloud and ran full force up the hillside through the trees. She ran through the wooded trail and called out Ne`Ne`s name loudly. "Ne`Ne`, I'm coming! Momma's coming!" Mary yelled as she ran through the woods.

Mary cleared the trees and stopped at the top of the hill and leaned her body against a Red Maple and stared at her daughter's grave as she breathed heavily. The heartbroken mother was now alone with her daughter and was finally able to express what hadn't been said the night Rene Holland died. Mary walked shyly to her daughter's grave, knelt before Rene and said, "I wanted to tell you to wait in the lobby for me. I was going to be all right. Your friend Sandy? She died. Paulette and Sidney? Their cousin Tasha? And Simon? They *all* passed away, Rene. I never saw this coming you know? I was going out, you and Dimples had the concert. I was back home early and so were you all. I needed candles from the store for the cake we were going to share and me and Regina was coming right back and then—" Mary paused and patted her hands against her thighs in frustration. "Aww Rene! This is hard for me! Why? You didn't have to do that, baby," she said lowly. "I could have just left the candles off the cake that night you know? I should have done that. But I didn't know that was gonna happen, Rene. I baked another cake today! But I dropped the silly thing on my way up here!" Mary said and then laughed. "Dimples misses you. We all miss you. I just know you were calling for me. I can't imagine how scared you were laying there on that operating table with a bunch of strangers around you. You probably didn't even know what was happening. I wanted to run to you that night, just so you can hear my voice, maybe then you would've had enough strength to keep fighting. You were just a baby, *my* baby! And when you needed me most, I let you down." Mary spoke through tears. "If you hear nothing else from earth," she then said, heaving dramatically, "I ask God in Heaven to let you hear this—I love you, Rene Holland! My *daughter*. My *heart*. You were my *life*, Rene! You and Regina are my life! And the day you died a part of *me* died. A part of *Regina* died. A part of Martha died. A part of the Holland *family* died, baby! We love you Rene, and my child," Mary said as she balled her fists and held her hands on either side of her head as her voice reached a crescendo. "My *precious* child! Rene Holland? You, you will never, *never* be forgotten! You lived once," Mary said, pointing to her daughter's grave with tears streaming down her face. "I *knew* you! And I *loved* you! Still do! And always will! You were *beautiful*! Rest in peace, Rene Holland, because not only your mother and your sister have returned home, *you* baby, are now *home*. You're a part of our land and a part of *us*. I love you, Rene." Mary ended as she got up and turned away sadly, only to be startled to see Naomi and her husband, surrounded by Regina, and Naomi's eight kids.

Everybody was dressed in black and they all held flowers. Naomi walked over to Mary and stared down at Ne`Ne`s grave. "I laid her this way so the sun can rise on her face and shine down upon her all day and set at her feet. You like it?" Naomi asked lowly as her husband, eight kids, and Regina approached and stood behind her and Mary.

"This is beautiful, Naomi. Thank you, thank you all." Mary said lowly as she stood up and turned around and leaned into Naomi and wept. "I *miss* her! I just, I just miss her so much."

"We all miss Rene, momma." Regina said lowly as she hugged her heavily crying mother from behind.

Mary reached back with her right hand and clutched Regina's right hand tightly. "I love you Regina, I love you all! Forgive me please, but I, I just *miss* her!"

"We know, Mary. We know, sugar. Come on now shh, shh," Naomi said as she gently rocked her sister.

Soon the whole family surrounded Mary and Regina and they all embraced and shed tears for Rene Holland. A ceremony was then held and Mary and Dimples began to imagine exactly how they would fix up Rene's grave site. It would later strengthen the bond between Mary and her surviving daughter.

The Holland Family Saga Part Five

After the ceremony, a large feast was held in memory of Rene Holland, and in celebration of her surviving twin Regina Holland's twentieth birthday.

On June 22, 1997, over two years after suffering the loss of her daughter, Mary Holland had completely healed. She was over the pain, moving on with her life, but she would never forget 'her baby'; the daughter that if no one else knew had ever existed, Mary Holland knew she once had a daughter named Rene Holland—a person in whom Mary felt honored and blessed to have known and loved once upon a time. The next few years were peaceful for the Holland family; the only person missing was Martha, and she was due home in a few short years.

CHAPTER 34

GOING HOME

Martha was in her cell sitting beside Twiggy rubbing her friends back as she in her bunk crying softly. It was November of 2000 now, and both Twiggy and Martha had been down for seven years. Twiggy was crying for two reasons, she was about to be released and Albert Lee had just been executed the week before. The moment was bitter sweet for Twiggy, who'd earned her freedom, but had lost her brother at the same time. She never got to visit or say good-bye, only learning of his death via a message sent through another prisoner whose brother had known the man. Irene 'Twiggy' Charles was now the last surviving member of the Charles family. The forty 41 year-old woman had not a sole family member left on earth, as both her parents had died behind bars in Illinois, her brother and nephew taken by streets, Twiggy grieved her brother's death and she took it hard, but she knew that someday Albert Lee was due to have his day with destiny, just not in the manner he which he was taken, without any fanfare, nor final farewell.

Martha had been Albert Lee's lover years ago, and she, too, was saddened by what happened to him, but Martha's mind was far removed from Mississippi, the forty-one year-old had her mind set on going to Oklahoma. Martha had been telling Naomi about her friend and she had offered Twiggy the opportunity to move to Oklahoma with her as Naomi had approved, only Twiggy didn't know exactly what she was going to do. She was angry and confused just before her release. She talked about returning to Ghost Town to make some money and just disappear altogether. Martha didn't want that for her friend, however, and she told Twiggy to just hold on until she was released and they would be okay. Twiggy was not in her right mind when she was released from Grenada County Jail in March of 2001 and Martha knew it. She was worried to death about her friend when she left the prison.

In May of 2001, Martha had received a few pieces of mail for her 42nd birthday. She had gotten a letter from Mary and pictures of the family—Naomi's eight, Mary and Dimples and Dimples' son, Tacoma, and Dimples' husband, Takoda. Dimples had met Takoda when she had gotten a flat tire after dropping Naomi's middle daughters off at school in 1998. She had married the man in the summer of 2000. Martha now had nine nieces and nephews, and a great nephew. She was as eager as ever to be released from jail as life was going along at a rapid and exciting pace on the family ranch. Martha had also received a birthday card and a letter from Twiggy with her mail on this day.. In the letter, she learned that Twiggy, who had gotten a CDL license while in jail, was working at Caro Foods as a yard jockey shuttling trailers from the drop yard to the dock door and back. She also had an apartment and seemed to be doing okay. Twiggy said she did return to Ghost Town, but the place was different…

…*"I can't really describe it to you Mar,"*, the letter read, *"all I have to say is that you got to see it for yourself. I know I was angry when I left, forgive me please. I just miss my family. I know how you feel about going to Oklahoma, and I wish you well with that. I don't know if I'll go with you. To be honest, I don't know if I'll ever see you again Mar, because if something don't change down here soon, I'm going away forever. I been thinking about Loretta a lot. I'm lonely, and I'm alone. All I do is work and go home, have a drink and watch TV and reminisce about the old days you know? We were the best out there; but hey those are days long gone right? Well, write me back Mar, I miss you, Love 'Twiggy'."*

Martha wrote Twiggy back and invited her to Oklahoma one

more time and told her to "just hold on sister", worrying that she was going to go out in the manner in which Loretta Duncan had escaped Ghost Town. Martha never received a reply from Twiggy and it worried her nerves constantly, but as depressing as Twiggy's letter was, Martha wasn't about to give up because she had plenty to live for. She was released in early August of 2001 and the first thing she did was return to Jackson, Mississippi where she had over $70,000 dollars in the bank, money in which he used a portion of to purchase a new 2000 Chrysler Sebring convertible. The car was champagne with white leather seats and custom chrome wheels. Martha drove her car off the lot and went over to Sprint and purchased a cell phone. She then headed towards Ghost Town to visit the old neighborhood. She was surprised to see that Ghost Town had been transformed into a park. It was now Jackson Memorial Park. Chug-a-lug's, the old Dairy Queen where Mary once worked and Fukutoo's had all been torn down, along with several other businesses.

Casper Drive was no more. Friendly Lane was no more. The whole area had been flattened and transformed. The park ran from Hanging Moss Drive in between where Casper Drive and Friendly Lane used to be and traversed the entire length of Ghost Town all the way to what was once White Street. Martha parked her car and walked and stood on land that was once Casper Drive. She looked at the huge pond in the center of the park that now covered what she knew was once the intersection of Casper Drive and Friendly Lane. She walked along the sidewalk towards the pond, passing benches and small statues and staring at the beautiful oak trees and shrubbery that lined the sidewalk and various areas of land off the trail along with numerous ducks and geese walking about and squirrels that gathered and ate nuts. Ghost Town was transformed into a very tranquil, beautiful place; a far cry from the violent, drug and gang-infested neighborhood it had become by the mid-nineties.

Martha walked through the huge park, proud of its transformation, but sad at the same time. There was a lot of history underneath the soil that her feet walked upon. Martha thought back to the first day she met Twiggy in 1977 and a few of the events that transpired during the sixteen years she spent in Ghost Town. In spite of the bad things that happened, Martha couldn't deny she missed the place. It was the only place she ever called home. She walked along the trail pass the pond towards the rear of the park and found herself staring at a huge statue of an angel that had water spurting from its mouth.

The statue was about seven feet tall, surrounded by a circular pool of water. Martha looked around and realized she was standing in the center of what was once Ambush. The canal had been covered over and the land had been raised. She walked over to the left side of the statue and saw five cement monuments standing about four feet tall. She looked closer and saw names on the podium-like monuments. The monument in the center had Rene Holland's name on it. The one to the right had Sandy Duncan's name on it and the monument to the far right had Simon Charles' name on it. The monument to left of Ne'Ne's monument had the name Sidney Childers and the one on the far left had the name Paulette Simpson. The monuments had the group's birthdates and day of death and the phrase *'Never Again'* was on the bottom of each statue. Martha stared sadly at the monuments and read the brief passage underneath that gave the reason for the memorial: NEVER AGAIN— THIS MONUMENT IS A SOMBER REMINDER DEDICATED TO THE LIVES THAT WERE TAKEN IN ONE NIGHT DURING TRAGIC EVENTS THAT OCCURRED HERE ON MARCH 22, 1995—NEVER AGAIN

"MARY! You're walking!" a woman called out to Martha, breaking her trance.

Martha whipped her head around and said softly, "My name is Martha miss. Mary's my sister. Oh hey, you're a news reporter, right?"

"I was, Martha. I'm in State Congress now and I represent this area. My name is Georgette Grayson."

"Miss Grayson," Martha said as she walked over and hugged the lady. "My niece spoke very highly of you while she was in the hospital with my sister. She said you was the only friend she had during that time."

"Yea, they were gone by the time I got in office. Tell me, where are they?"

"They're in Oklahoma now. I'm headed that way myself me and my friend Twiggy."

"Twiggy, oh yes! Irene Charles is her real name right?"

"Yeah, how'd you know?"

"Well, the police department spoke badly about the Charles family. I feel sorry for her. I know she's the last of the family. She still works at Caro last I heard."

Hearing those words was a relief for Martha. She just may be able to contact Twiggy before she left for Oklahoma. "I was wondering about her. I haven't talked to her in a good while."

"Me neither. Tell her I said hi, when you see her. I know you're going to go," Georgette said through a slight chuckle.

Georgette Grayson had developed a sincere interest in the welfare of people after what happened on March 22, 1995. So much so that it fueled a passion within the woman to serve the public. She ran for congress on the promise of reducing crime and gang activity, ridding the area of drugs and providing after school programs for youths and she won hands down. She kept her promise when she got into office and now had a bright political career underway. The district she resided over, which included Ghost Town, had seen a double digit percentage decrease in crime and drug areas were nearly non-existent. She explained those things to Martha and Martha was impressed with the woman's work.

"That day, we call it March 22nd, that day forever impressed on me the need to do something for our young people. Your niece, Regina, I admit," Georgette said as she grabbed Martha's hand and the two women walked and sat on a bench and talked, "when I first met your niece I was only supposed to get a story, but she was such a beautiful child. She spoke openly, and it hurt my heart. I could only imagine how close Regina was to her sister, and to lose an identical twin had to be devastating. Her mother was shot, aunt in jail, I got to thinking, 'I can't exploit my people'. I wanted to do something to help you know? I got funding to build new single family homes throughout the city that low-income families can actually own and not rent. Once the remaining people in Ghost Town had been placed into their new homes, the gang bangers came back. There were stolen cars everywhere, lots of shootings and a few murders. I got the city to buy up the land from the land lords and got the banks to foreclose on the abandoned properties. This is my way of helping, do you like it?" Georgette asked as she spread her arms towards the park and the statue. Georgette's eyes had a worried look, she knew Martha lived in Ghost Town once and she hoped she wasn't mad at her for having her home destroyed.

"Georgette? This is the most beautiful thing I have ever seen in my life, besides the day my older sister Naomi walked through them prison doors. I'm glad somebody really cares. And I'm glad that someone that's working *inside* government actually cares about the little people. I'm glad you remembered my niece too. Rene was an angel, just like the statue, she was, she was—"

"She was a daughter, a sister, and a friend that left too soon." Georgette said as she placed an arm around Martha and the two women just sat and talked.

Martha and Georgette, after about two hours of laughter, walked slowly to front of the park hand in hand. "Martha, girl I never knew that there was so much activity on this small piece of real estate! Loretta? And her chickens? Sister? Sandy's mother sounds like she knew how to skin a bird!"

"Sure did. But Mary was the best cook in Ghost Town. I can't wait to see my sister." Martha said with proud eyes as she approached her car.

Georgette gave Martha her address and phone number and the two promised to keep in touch and Martha would let Mary and Dimples know as well. Martha now had one more stop to make before she left, she had to visit Twiggy and see if she still worked at Caro Foods and find out if her old friend wanted to take on a new journey.

Martha, giddy after learning from another driver exiting the premises, that Twiggy was at work this day, cruised slowly into the huge parking lot of Caro Foods and got a visitor's pass and walked along the front of the docked trailers in search of her friend. Men eyed her adoringly, dressed in a pair of khaki Capri's wearing a white tank top and white sandals. Martha's tan skin glistened in the warm afternoon sun. She had her hair in one long pony tail that hung just below the nape of neck and she wore a pair of thin framed dark sunglasses. At 42 years of age, Martha looked years younger and had a physique that would put most twenty-something's to shame. She no longer had the hardcore appeal she had before she went to jail in 1993. By August of 2001, Martha had made a complete transformation. She looked every bit the strong, sensual woman she had come to be.

As Martha walked, a white truck pulling a trailer pulled alongside her and blew the horn and the driver yelled aloud, "You lost or something, woman?"

Martha smiled as Twiggy, dressed in a baggy pair of denim jeans, with a light blue uniform shirt and low top black boots, hopped from the truck and hugged her tightly. Twiggy at forty-two, had gained a little weight. She was a 5'10" 145 pound slender and sexy 42 woman who now wore her burgundy-dyed hair in a crop. Twiggy wore burgundy lip-stick and had a bright wide smile as she stared at Martha, realizing Martha was pleased with her transformation. "You like my new look?" she asked as she twirled around in front of Martha.

"Yea, you look gorgeous, chick!" Martha responded. "Come on! It's time to go home!"

"Martha what did I tell you? I *am* home! I'm not going!"

"What? But Twiggy you said—"

"I never answered that question! I can't leave here! I got a good job! I work twelve hours a day five days a week, sometimes six! I get off, I go home, I smoke a joint or two and sip my gin and go to bed and do it all over again the next day. Now why would I wanna leave that, Martha?"

"You know what Twiggy," Martha asked as she lowered her eyes and placed her hands on her hips. "You know what? I thought better of you! You have a golden opportunity before you and you choose to stay here and work sixty hours and then go home and do nothing? You all alone here! If you wanna stay, stay! I'm going home!" Martha ended as she walked off.

"Fine!" Twiggy yelled before hopping back into her truck.

"Fine!" Martha replied. "And don't call me ever! I can't believe your ass! Don't call me!"

"I won't! Bye!" Twiggy stated as she started the truck.

"Bye!" Martha yelled as she brushed Twiggy off, never looking back.

Twiggy pulled off and began backing the trailer into an open dock as Martha left the yard and headed towards her car. Twiggy then got out and walked around the front of her truck and searched for Martha, looking on with worried eyes when she saw no sign of her friend. She walked to the rear of the trailer to open the doors and when she returned to the front of the truck, Martha pulled up in the convertible with the top down. "Girl, get your ass in this car and stop playing so we can get outta here!" Martha said as she and Twiggy burst into laughter.

"Sixty hours a week, Martha? Girl you think I wanna be out ta' this mutherfucka? What the hell took you so long?" Twiggy asked as she turned the truck off and walked towards Martha who was exiting the car.

The two women were like little girls as they ran and hugged one another, this time the tears flowed. "I missed you, Mar! It was hard being alone you know? But I held on, I held on sister, just like you asked me to."

"Me too Twiggy! We made it! We out!" Martha said as she and Twiggy broke their embrace.

"For real?" Twiggy asked. "I mean, you actually wanna leave this city and start over?"

"Hell yeah, Twiggy! Since 1977 we rarely been apart, making money together. And now we can go and do it again! Only this time we can do it legally. You game?"

"Big time, Martha! Let me clock out and let them know I'm leaving. Can I leave my stuff?"

"Irene? I got over $40,000! Money ain't a thang!" Martha ended as Twiggy took off like a little girl and informed her manager. The manager was mad, but Twiggy didn't care. She knew she and Martha were about to do something great in life and she wasn't going to let nothing stop it. She returned with a duffle bag she had taken from her locker that contained her personal hygiene items and walked towards the car, instinctively walking to the driver's side of the car.

"What you doing?" Martha asked.

"Come on, nah! You know I always drive, Mar!"

"This 2001, woman! Get in and kick back!" Martha stated as she got behind the wheel and Twiggy sat beside her. Once they started to head out of the yard, Martha suddenly stopped the car and said, "This don't feel right!"

"Told your ass! Get over here and let me drive! That's one thing that hasn't changed." Twiggy said as she and Martha changed seats. Martha pulled out her atlas and she and Twiggy got onto Interstate-55 and headed north towards Memphis, the two of them never looked back once the city of Jackson was at their backs because their future lay directly in front of them.

Martha and Twiggy rode for nearly six hours until night fell. They were just outside of Little Rock when they came across a country western store and decided to go shopping. Martha had plenty of pictures of her sisters and nieces and nephews. She and Twiggy saw how the family dressed in Oklahoma and they wanted to fit in when they got there. As they shopped, Martha had used her cell phone to call and talk to her family and give them the time of her arrival the next day. Everyone was excited.

Naomi was planning a huge dinner for Martha and Twiggy. Twiggy was a little nervous about meeting Martha's family and she wondered if they would accept her, especially Naomi. After talking to Naomi for about thirty minutes, however, and realizing that the woman was down to earth and welcomed her there on the strength of Martha, Twiggy was put at ease.

Naomi assured Twiggy that she was now a part of the family and she was just as welcome as Martha. Naomi had a big heart and if Martha trusted and loved Twiggy, so would Naomi and her family. Mary and Dimples already had love for Twiggy and they were excited that she was coming to the ranch with Martha as well.

After about two hours of talking on the cell phone and shopping, Martha and Twiggy got a hotel room and went and sat in the lounge and had a couple of drinks. The two friends talked constantly about the past and made plans for the future. Martha was planning on buying a truck and she and Twiggy could drive over the road for Naomi. That was their plan for the future, but on this night, Martha and Twiggy were out to have a good time and finding a man was never a problem for the two lifelong friends. They eyed a handsome dark-skinned man in a business suit and began flirting. Before long, the three of them had adjoined to Martha and Twiggy's room and had a hot ménage-a-trios. Twiggy and Martha used the married business man's body for their own personal delight and pleasure, taking turns on the man, each receiving multiple orgasms. Afterwards, they paid the appreciative and unbelievably lucky-feeling man and thanked him before escorting him out of their room.

The next morning, the two women set out to complete their drive to Oklahoma. Martha had on a white pair of tight fitting jeans and tan rattle-skin boots with a tan tank top and white cowgirl hat. Twiggy was dressed in a blue pair of denims with a pair of black boots complete with spurs, black tank top and black cowgirl hat. They were sexy-looking black cowgirls. They loaded their bags into the car, dropped the top and headed home.

The two women had never ventured this far north in their lives. Martha had to constantly check the map to make sure they were headed in the right direction. She and Twiggy jostled one another saying they were lost, or going the wrong way, but they were headed straight to the ranch and both women knew it. It just felt so good to the women to be free. For the first time in years, even when they were on the streets of Ghost Town, the women felt free. The sun was shining bright, the weather was warm and the scenery was beautiful. They traveled through mountains, crossed rivers and plains and rode through thick forests. The land was ever changing and both women were constantly in awe at the beauty that lay within the heart country's mid-west section.

After six hours of driving, they had finally made it to Ponca City. The two women entered town from the south east and was immediately struck with the town's beauty. It had a western feel to it; laidback and tranquil. People waved and smiled at the women as they rode through downtown headed north towards the lake area, which was near the ranch. Twiggy guided the car towards the ranch and she quickly put in Phil Collins' CD and played *Take Me Home*.

Mary had requested that they do so, as she had something special planned for Martha and Twiggy when they arrived at the ranch. They listened to the song intently and as they entered the ranch, Twiggy turned up the volume.

"Take that look of worry...mines an ordinary life...working when its daylight...and sleeping when its night...I've got no far horizons...I don't wish upon a star...they don't think that I listen...oh but I know who they are..."

The song played on as Twiggy drove slowly down the gravel road. Before long, brown, black and white objects could be seen approaching from the left and the right. Martha rose up from her seat and screamed when the objects came closer. Twiggy screamed and pointed to her right. Martha turned, and it was there that she saw her sister Mary riding a white Arabian horse. Dimples trailed her mother on a brown mustang. Martha screamed and pointed and blew kisses at Mary as she rode the horse alongside the car whilst eyeing her sister and Twiggy and yelling "Welcome! Welcome home Martha and Irene!"

"Martha! Twiggy! Welcome!" another voice yelled aloud from the rear of the car.

Martha looked behind her and saw Naomi riding up quickly from the rear catching up to Mary and Dimples. Martha and Twiggy were elated and in awe at the scene unfolding. Naomi's land went on for what seemed like miles to the two of them. Martha then looked to her left and saw her nephew Dawk riding a horse with his sisters on horseback trailing behind him, and they, too, were screaming, "Welcome home!"

Martha was overcome with emotion. The song, coupled with the scene that lay before her eyes had moved her to tears of joy. It was the most precious thing she had ever witnessed, and her sister had put all of it together specifically for her and Twiggy. Martha was on her knees in the front seat, her arms stretched out towards Mary. "You're beautiful!" she screamed to her sister, "I love you, Mary!" Martha screamed in anticipation of the death-grip hug she had in store for her sister.

The horse riders broke off before Twiggy cleared the white wooden fence that bordered the road. They pulled up to the front of the big house as the riders dismounted their horses and ran to greet the two. Martha greeted her nieces and nephews, but she was eager to get to Mary. Mary was all smiles as she ran up to her sister and everybody stepped back and clapped as they embraced. "Mary! I missed! I missed you! Ohhh God thank you! Thank you! Mary! I love you!"

"Well, hmm, hmm," Naomi said as she coughed.

Martha grabbed Naomi's hand and the three sisters embraced. Twiggy was being greeted by Naomi's eight and before long, Naomi's husband, her eight kids, the three sisters, Twiggy, Dimples, her husband Takoda and Dimples' baby boy were all entwined in one big group hug. The Holland family was finally reunited; everyone was home, so they thought.

By August of 2001, the bulk of the Holland family had been reunited in Oklahoma. They would live, for a long time, under the belief that everyone was reunited. Unbeknownst to the Holland family in Oklahoma, however, there were still family members whom they didn't know existed—Sam Holland's children.

In August of 2001, Ben Holland, Sam's son, was incarcerated in Colorado's Federal Correctional Complex. Ben's sister Samantha Holland was living in Las Vegas with her friend Trudy Tucker preparing to go join the Navy. Ben and Samantha Holland were now the only lost members of the tribe, but they, too, had an obstacle to overcome. Ben and Samantha Holland knew not of the others' existence and they did not know that there were many more Holland family members alive besides themselves. Years would pass before the full truth would be known.

It was now later in the day of Martha and Twiggy's arrival to the ranch. They had toured the houses and the land and now everyone, minus Naomi, her oldest three kids and her husband, had settled down on the patio of *Ponderosa* and began to prepare for dinner as a band began to play. Naomi looked down upon her family through a pair of binoculars from the hilltop beside the guest house as she stood in front of Ne`Ne`s grave. She was proud of her family. There were many of them —young, old, and in the middle.

"Mary hasn't a clue, y'all," Naomi said as she lowered the binoculars from her eyes and turned to her husband. "Martha and Twiggy may figure it out, Doss. You think we should let those two know upfront? Just in case something happens."

"Why, baby? I mean, we don't even do business here." Doss replied.

"I know, but you know how this business can get sometimes. If it were to hit home, they need to be made aware. You three kids be careful. We have a job coming up shortly. Just got word today. Be sure to train as much as possible before then okay?"

"Yes ma'am." Naomi's 'big three' replied in unison.

"Umm, y'all kids go and join your siblings and your aunts. Me and your father will be right behind you." Naomi stated as her three kids walked on down the hillside, hopped into a golf cart and rode back towards the big house.

Naomi was thinking hard about informing Martha and Twiggy of her outside ventures. Mary understood Naomi to be a corporate lawyer, which she was, but there was another side to her; a side that had been hidden from Mary and her youngest five children as well. Times were changing during the summer of 2001, however; and Naomi felt her sisters, at the very least, Martha and Twiggy, should be informed of her other 'business' ventures just in case things fell by the wayside; but she was conflicted about doing so.

Naomi loved her family, she loved her life, and the fear of having Mary and Martha get mad and leave is what was compelling her to inform her sisters of her outside business ventures. But on the other hand, Naomi did not want them to get upset and leave if she were to tell them the truth. "All this time Mary has never questioned me." Naomi said to her husband.

"Why would she? She loves you and believes everything you say. You know that."

"I know. And I love her too. That's why I'm having a hard time deciding. Look Doss," Naomi then said as she pointed to her left down the hillside, "the guest house is bigger than most people's homes in the Hamptons. To the east of the guest house is Ponderosa. Twice as big as the guest house. To the south the cattle, hundreds of head of cattle, they graze until they're content. The creek and the forested hillside to the west. How long before they and the youngest five of our kids start asking questions?" Naomi asked as she slid gently into her husband's arms and stared into his eyes.

"I don't know Naomi, but this here is for certain. No matter what, they not leaving your side, you can believe that."

"I hope you're right, baby. It would hurt my heart if they decided to leave."

"Well, we on one hell of run with that cash cow right about now. And it's getting more lucrative for us."

"I know. Be extra careful on this one, Doss. This is the big three's first job and we don't need anything to go wrong their first time out. You all be careful. We got everybody back, let's not lose anyone else." Naomi stated as she stared at her niece's grave.

"We not losing nobody, baby. So you gone tell your sisters or not?" Doss asked.

"Well, I won't tell them *everything*. I just can't get them involved. You're right, we do no business here. Only Lucky and his family know where we stay. Fin doesn't even know. I know we're all safe here in Oklahoma, so we'll just leave it at that for now; but I have some things I have to tell them about my life early on. Things I haven't told even told Mary since she's been here. I can tell them some things, at least up until this present day and time. Martha and Twiggy I believe, because of their history? If they do figure it out, they won't be a problem. They may even want to join in." Naomi said as she closed her eyes and rocked to and fro in her husband's arms. "We playing a dangerous game, Doss."

"Yeah, but damn, baby—"

"We're the best at what we do. Now, what's this job JunJie needs doing?" Naomi asked.

"Four take-downs and a kidnapping. It all goes down in Vegas."

"What is this kidnapping all about? That's a first for Mister Maruyama."

"Some guy named Asa Spade has a brother who betrayed him. A guy named Alvin Spencer. We have to find him, and deliver him to an address in Vegas. From there, this guy Asa Spade will handle things with his brother we handle the other half of the job. The kidnapping will be the hardest part. We have to track this guy Alvin Spencer down."

"Well, let's get it done. I'll start moving revenue around to hide the new income and we'll discuss matters after dinner."

"I'll run it by my father later on too."

"Okay, love. Let's go join the party." Naomi said as descended the hilltop, holding her husband's hand tightly.

Naomi, just like Mary and Martha, had a story behind her. And she was now ready to tell a good portion of that story. She had not a clue at the time, but her story and the events that would follow from this day forth, would unite the family fully. But the journey towards the final unification would unknowingly be wrought with serious drama, because her life, Naomi's life, was a much more complicated life and a far more dangerous one than the life the people of Ghost Town once led.

And in her and her family's line of work? There was no room for error. Naomi and Doss understood that fact...preventing those errors, however? Well, that's another story in itself...To be continued.

Made in the USA
Las Vegas, NV
16 April 2024